# EXILE

Other Fiction by A.J. Calvin

THE RELICS OF WAR
*The Moon's Eye*
*The Talisman of Delucha*
*War of the Nameless*

*The Ballad of Alchemy and Steel*


THE CAEIN LEGACY
*Exile*
*Guardian*
*Harbinger*
*Legend*


HUNTED

# EXILE

## THE CAEIN LEGACY
Book One

## A.J. CALVIN

EXILE

ISBN 978-1-7379204-7-2

Cover illustration and design by Jamie Noble

Map illustration by Dewi Hargreaves

This book is for anyone who,
even as an adult, still hasn't "found their way."
Your time will come.

# AUTHOR'S NOTE

Exile, and The Caein Legacy as a whole, was a very meaningful writing project for this author for many reasons.

Between 2010 and 2019, I was stuck in a writing drought. I started dozens of stories, none of which were finished, and most of which continue to languish in my drawer of incomplete works. It was a period of turmoil in my life between job changes, the losses of loved ones, and an enormous amount of work-related stress. I was unable to maintain the focus required to write, and I believe my mental health suffered for it.

Writing is, and has always been, my escape. Without it, I struggled.

The idea for Exile came to me more than a year before I sat down to write the first sentence. I ran it through my head countless times, always with the hope it wouldn't wind up in my drawer, yet fearful it would. I wasn't convinced I'd ever overcome the pseudo-writer's block that plagued me.

Then on May 24, 2019, I was unexpectedly at home rather than at work due to an injury, and I decided it was time. I began writing Exile on that date, which is why on the same date four years later, I'm publishing it for the first time.

Writing Exile was the therapy I'd desperately needed, though I hadn't been aware of it at the time. Through it, I not only rediscovered my creative spark, but I think I found *myself* too.

And that's why I've dedicated this book as I have. I was thirty-six when I started writing Exile, well beyond the age when most would have expected me to know what I wanted from life. I didn't before, but I do now.

Exile isn't a coming-of-age story, but it is a tale of learning about oneself, and truly accepting who you are in the process. I believe even adult readers can relate to this theme—as I said previously, I didn't truly feel like I'd found myself until I wrote this series.

The Caein Legacy hosts a wide array of characters, but I have chosen not to include a character glossary in the text of the book. The story is told solely from Andrew's perspective, and all of the other characters are seen through his eyes.

As a reader, I personally don't utilize character or place glossaries, though I know many others do. I have set up a page on my website with a list of characters (including pronunciation guides) for those interested. You can find the glossary at the following location: www.ajcalvin.net/works-in-progress/the-caein-legacy/the-caein-legacy-character-glossary/

Additionally, I would like to point out that the city named the Capitol was spelled in that manner intentionally. This is a work of *fantasy* fiction, and I do take liberties with some naming conventions. This happens to be one such occasion.

As with my other books, Exile is intended for an adult audience. While this first book isn't terribly dark, the series becomes more so as it progresses. Some themes and language may be offensive to sensitive readers.

I hope you enjoy this first installment of The Caein Legacy. There will be more books to come.

Thank you and happy reading,
A.J. Calvin

# NOVANIA AND THE SOUTHLANDS

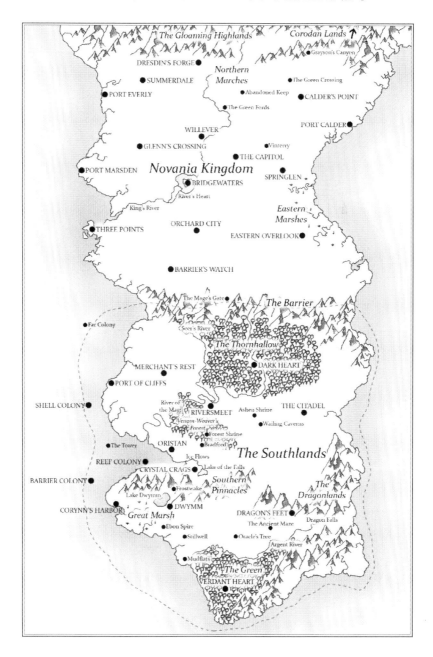

# ONE

Though I didn't know it at the time, I was about to embark on a conversation that would not only change my life forever, but would prove to be a turning point in the history of Novania Kingdom as well.

I knelt deferentially before the king, as was expected given my position. "Your Highness."

The king faced away from me. His aged countenance looked down upon the winter-bare courtyard below, its trees leafless, its paths dusted with a light blanket of snow. In spite of the chill temperature and the lowering clouds that threatened more snow, he'd insisted we meet on his private balcony. He turned slowly, then silently dismissed the guards at the door behind me with a wave of his hand.

"Good, you've come. Stand up, Andrew. Walk with me."

The balcony ran the length of the courtyard; he was often seen pacing here when he required space to think or time to himself. It was common that he held private meetings such as this one while he walked across the time-worn stone, one hand trailing along the smooth railing.

I stood and fell into step beside him. I glanced at the courtyard and noted it was empty, save for a pair of servants. They moved briskly toward the door leading to the great hall, their breath visible puffs in the frigid air.

"As you've no doubt heard, the council is pressing the matter of my succession," the king stated gravely, drawing my attention.

"Word travels quickly, sire."

In truth, I'd known within minutes of the previous day's council meeting. Most of the kingdom expected me to follow in his footsteps—I was the commander of his army, the eldest of the royal sons, respected by many—yet it was not to be. It could never be.

"I want you present at tomorrow's council, even though we both know you won't be named." He sighed heavily, his gaze fixed on a point in the distance. "I wish it were otherwise, but the laws are clear. It seems our family's dark little secret has been kept entirely too well, but it must be revealed. I have no other choice. I'm sorry, Andrew. I know this will bring shame to lovely Claire and her ambitious father. And to you."

I'd always known the throne would be passed to my half-brother, Colin. The king was not my birth father, as our family had led the kingdom's residents to believe. I was fortunate that my most notable features were nearly identical to my late mother's; even our family's closest confidantes never questioned my heritage. The king had always known the truth, but it had never stopped him from treating me as his son.

Mother had been expecting when they met, yet he was captivated by her charm, despite the gossip that would undoubtedly arise from their union. To spare her the shame of bearing a child out of wedlock, he married her two weeks after their first meeting, much to the chagrin of his own father.

The kingdom never learned the truth, but it was destined to come out at the council. I'd prepared myself for the inevitable backlash for years, but the prospect landed like a stone in my gut.

I raked a hand through my hair in agitation and bit back a curse. Colin would be elated at the news, while I'd be made a damned laughingstock.

"Before your mother passed away, she asked to speak with you privately," the king continued, seemingly oblivious to my unspoken frustration. "She also spoke with Alexander. I never asked her why, though I suspected she wanted to speak with you regarding your father. It was a private affair. I respected your mother above all others, but in the shadow of tomorrow's council, I must know. What did she tell you?"

I recalled the day a little over two years past when I'd been summoned to my mother's chambers. She was ill with pneumonia, and the castle physicians didn't believe she'd last the week. A woman who had always been so full of life, so vibrant, had been reduced to a thin husk—pale, drawn, and clearly in immense pain. She'd lain huddled in a mass of woolen blankets when I arrived. She'd appeared so small and frail, fragile beyond reckoning. I'd spent a heartbreaking few hours at her bedside while she intermittently spoke through bouts of wracking coughs.

We discussed many things, and my father was but one item on her agenda that day. She'd rarely spoken of him; she remained grief-stricken at his departure more than three decades later. Her tone had often become bitter and pained when I dared to broach the subject. That day had been no exception.

"First, she asked that I watch over Alex," I replied.

Alexander had his own dangerous secret, and she'd done her best to keep his hidden as well as she had mine. He'd been born with the Mark of the Magi. Under the laws of Novania, he should have been put to death upon its discovery. Mother should have been as well, for her role in shielding him from the law. She'd managed to hide it as he grew up and taught Alexander to do the same, but she feared his secret would be forced into the open when talk of succession began—either by the king himself, or his older brother, Colin.

"She was always partial to Alexander," the king said fondly. "He was her favorite. He's grown into a fine warrior, and it pleases me that he's chosen to join you during the summer campaigns. You've always proven yourself a worthy commander of my forces, Andrew. I have no doubt you will continue to ensure your brother's safety while on the battlefield."

I allowed him to believe mother's wishes were as simple as her desire to protect her favorite son. He could never learn of Alexander's secret. In truth, I believed many of Alexander's reputed "skills" in battle came from the inadvertent use of his innate magical abilities. He tended toward recklessness at times, and I'd been forced to intervene and save his skin on a number of occasions. I was a decade his senior, but we'd become close despite the years between us. I would have given my life for his, even without our mother's prompting.

My own renown was based less on my skill than on my unique heritage. I'm capable of rapid healing and possess greater strength than any ordinary man, thanks to my true father. It was yet another secret I was forced to keep from the king. If he were to learn my father's identity or the truth of *what* I was, I would face execution as surely as someone born with the Mark.

The king's next words drew me from my dark musings.

"I'd like you to remain commander under Colin, once he has taken the throne." The king paused mid-stride to pierce me with his gaze. "He'll need your abilities if we are to maintain peace in the Northern Marches. The Corodan have become entirely too bold of late, and no one else can claim your expertise in dealing with them."

I nodded. "They are restless, sire."

"Which is why we must speak of succession now while winter's grip holds them at bay." His eyes drifted to the courtyard. "What else did your mother speak of, Andrew? Surely Alexander was not the only topic on her mind that day."

I drew a breath, uncertain how to proceed. There were many aspects of our conversation I could never divulge, but there were certain elements I believed I could relay without risking my safety.

"She spoke of my father," I began. "She said he'd been gone from this world for many years. She wanted me to know, to prevent me from a fruitless search that would only end in frustration."

The truth was that my father's people had departed our world for another, and he'd been called away to join them. Mother suspected he never knew she'd conceived a child with him. If he had, there was a chance he may have taken her with him, and my life would have been markedly different. He'd been a powerful dragon-mage, capable of taking on the form of a human man when he wished to. Her words had become bitter when she admitted she'd been hopelessly in love with him—even on her deathbed, she mourned his loss.

The result of their union was an unusual child—my mother referred to me as a skin-changer. I was not truly human, nor truly dragon, but could assume the form of either. With this heritage came rapid healing, greater strength, keen eyesight even in darkness, and an immunity to the most frigid temperatures. As I walked the length of the balcony alongside the king, I was grateful for the last.

I'd always assumed my human form, except on a handful of occasions when I'd been alone with my mother. Faced with a death sentence if anyone learned the truth, I became adept at acting the part of an ordinary, albeit unusually tall man. I feigned wounds at the conclusion of battles, donned extra garments in the winter as though the chill permeated my skin, and took care when interacting with others to avoid revealing the depth of my physical strength.

"He is dead, then?" the king asked, drawing me from my thoughts once more. "I suspected as much, but she refused to speak of him. You look so much like your mother. It's little wonder no one has suspected you aren't my son." He sighed, a sound filled with regret. "I fear tomorrow will be a difficult day for us both, Andrew. Colin is a poor choice for king, but I am bound by the law. As my eldest son, he must be named heir."

"I understand."

"I require a promise from you, Andrew." He turned abruptly to face me. I was a head taller, and he was forced to look up to meet my eyes. "Promise me you will do everything in your power to keep Colin on the proper path once I am gone. I fear what he will become when he is granted so much power."

"I will try, sire, but as you know, Colin and I have never been on good terms. He will undermine me, as he always has, and flaunt his authority—"

"Of all my sons, you are the most even-keeled. Act as you always have, and Colin's actions will be swayed. You have made him see reason, even when I have failed to do so." His expression was unyielding. "You must intervene if he defiles the kingship."

I sighed. First mother asked me to protect Alexander, now the king asked me to watch over Colin. My half-brothers would be the death of me, whether my secret was spilled or not.

"He may not show it, but Colin respects you. He will listen when you speak. All I ask is that you intervene when necessary. Do not keep your misgivings to yourself, or the fate of our land may be sealed by the folly of one unworthy son."

He was clearly frustrated. Bound by ancient laws, he could do nothing to change them without disrupting the age-old system of succession in Novania. Attempting to do so would likely result in greater chaos than even Colin would sow, and I understood his unspoken desire to avoid the outcome. The nobility would never agree to a change, nor would the governors' council.

"I will do my best, sire," I promised.

The words were weighty as they spilled from my lips. I feared my attempts to talk sense into Colin would prove useless. The king was right to be worried for the fate of his kingdom once it passed into Colin's hands; my half-brother was stubborn, petulant, vain, and often unreasonable. Colin's foul temper had gained him an unsavory reputation amongst many of the nobles, and his petty scheming won him few friends.

"That is all I ask of you, Andrew. Do your best with the situation. Now, go. You will be summoned to the council in the morning. Prepare yourself for all it entails."

"Of course, sire."

I spent much of that afternoon mired in an internal debate. Should I inform Claire of the latest succession developments? I was uncertain if it was best to tell her ahead of the council or if I should simply wait until afterward. She'd be livid no matter which path I decided to tread, and we'd likely find ourselves in yet another pointless argument. Ours had never been a happy marriage.

In the end, I decided it was best she hear the news from me rather than through the castle's network of gossips. I genuinely believed she'd understand the situation and offer her support—I would have done the same for her. We may not have found love in our arranged pairing, but I respected her and did my best to be the husband she deserved.

I met her in the great hall that evening for supper. She chattered about her day spent in the women's quarters of the castle and complained the weather had once again been too cold to venture outside. She'd painted while her maid servants sewed a blanket with some of the other noblewomen for the chamberlain's wife, who was due to bear their fourth child any day. Claire had little interest in needlework.

The conversation should have been a welcome distraction, but the matter of the next day's council weighed heavily on my mind. I nodded when she paused and murmured brief agreements, though I had little recollection of what she'd said.

Finally, Claire narrowed her dark eyes and frowned in irritation. She pushed a strand of errant hair from her eyes and crossed her arms in a huff. "Andrew, what's wrong? You haven't been yourself this evening, and I grow weary of talking to myself."

"I'm sorry," I replied somberly. "I'll tell you once we're in private. I have some…unpleasant news."

News I didn't want the castle's ever-present gossips to overhear until the council was over and done. There were too many nobles seated at the nearby tables, too many servants eager to glean the latest tidbit of information as they went about their duties. As members of the royal household, anything we did outside our personal quarters was subject to the scrutiny of the masses, and I detested every moment of it.

She narrowed her eyes in suspicion. "Surely your father isn't sending you north again so soon? I know you spoke with him today. Leta saw you on his private balcony."

I managed a tight smile. Leta was Claire's personal maidservant, a young woman who had attended Claire since they were both children. She always seemed to be present when important matters were afoot, and I could only hope she had not overheard our conversation. Claire's innocent question was enough to assuage my doubts, but it would not be pleasant when I told her the truth.

"We didn't speak of military matters." I paused to push my empty plate to one side. "Let's go upstairs. I'll tell you my news when we won't be overheard."

Her beautiful, porcelain features were shadowed by concern, but she nodded and rose to follow me to our private chambers. I was still in awe of her, even after nearly four years of marriage. She was graceful and slender, with eyes that instantly captivated my imagination and simultaneously captured my heart. I would have done anything to see her smile; she was the most beautiful when she was happy.

But those smiles had always been few. The king had mentioned her father's ambitions, and Claire was not immune to his influence. She'd agreed to our match for a singular reason, one which I was on the brink of shattering beyond repair.

I dreaded telling her of the succession. While I didn't know how she'd react, I feared it would be explosive.

Our chambers had been readied for the night by the time we arrived. The fire was stoked and a pair of candles were lit, left on the writing table next to the door for our use. I was relieved the servants were nowhere to be seen, having fulfilled their duties and retired for the evening. My words were for Claire alone.

I closed and barred the door behind us while Claire made her way to the fire, where she perched on a cushion near the hearth. The room was pleasantly warm, despite the wind that howled beyond the outer wall. I studied her in the firelight. Her expression was drawn, her eyes distant. I didn't know if she was concerned or merely calculating.

I sighed. I could not procrastinate any longer.

I made my way across the room and sat down on a vacant cushion facing her. "Claire, you won't like what I'm about to say. The king spoke with me because he has decided to announce his successor tomorrow."

"And he wanted you to be present for the council? That is no surprise." She shrugged dismissively. "What has you so worried, Andrew? You are his eldest son. The king's eldest son will succeed him, as the laws dictate."

"Claire…" I swallowed hard and looked down at my hands. I studied the rough texture of my fingertips to avoid making eye contact. This was proving more difficult than I'd anticipated. "Claire, the king is not my father."

She was silent for several long moments before she stood abruptly and strode away. It was only then that I risked a glance in her direction. Her face was an emotionless mask, unreadable, yet hard. I tensed; I knew I'd receive no support from her.

"Please tell me you did not say what I think you said, Andrew." Her voice quavered with barely concealed emotion, but whether it was sorrow or rage, I was uncertain.

"Carlton Marsden—the king—is not my father."

Her mouth twisted into a scowl. "Why did you hide this from me?"

Her voice was a strained whisper, and I knew the emotion she'd been suppressing was anger. This was not going at all as I'd hoped— but it was going as I'd feared.

"Claire—"

"No, Andrew." She held one hand toward me, signaling with her pale, slender fingers that I should not attempt to move any closer. "For four years, I was certain that one day we would rule this land. It was only a matter of time." She shook her head and turned away once more, her jaw clenched with rage. "You knew my dream would never come to pass, didn't you? You knew, and you never had the decency to tell me!"

"I'm sorry," I managed, helpless in the face of her fury. "The king ordered that I never speak of my parentage, not even to you. Believe me, I wanted to tell you. I respect you, Claire. I wanted no secrets between us." I hung my head, defeated.

She snorted. "You are naïve if you believed I agreed to this marriage for love. I was to be queen!"

I swallowed my shock at her words. "It was never meant to be, Claire. I'm sorry."

Her confession wounded me more deeply than any weapon could have. I'd striven to make her happy, to provide the life that she deserved. Now I was faced with the realization that it had never been enough, would never be enough for Claire. I wasn't heir to the throne; I was merely a decorated soldier.

"He will name Colin, will he not?" she asked.

I looked up. She stood at the window, her back toward me as she peered into the darkness beyond.

"Yes."

"Your brother...*half*-brother is a disgrace to the Marsden name." She crossed her arms. "He is your half-brother, isn't he?"

"Yes."

"That means your mother...?"

"She was with child before she met the king," I replied hollowly.

"Hmm." Claire began to pace in front of the window. Her gaze was fixed on something beyond the shadowed panes and she did not look in my direction. "I suppose you'd like me to keep this to myself until after the council meets tomorrow?"

"If our years together have meant anything to you, please don't tell anyone."

I hated the pleading note in my tone, but I knew she was lost to me. She would never forgive me for this perceived betrayal, no matter the reason or the orders behind it. My heart ached with the knowledge that my life with her would never be the same.

"Fine. I won't tell anyone, but I'm furious, Andrew. This is an outrage. You have deceived me—*for years*. I will never forgive you for this."

"I did what the king asked of me," I replied bitterly. "If you recall, he was the one who negotiated our marriage with your father. I had no part in it, though I sorely wished it were otherwise. Perhaps this would have been averted."

"Yes, it would have." She turned to face me. Tears glimmered on her cheeks, but her voice remained strong. "We would never have been married, and I would have been wed to your brother instead!"

I was at a loss for words. Had she truly just admitted she would have married the same man that only moments before she'd claimed was a disgrace? Was she so hungry for power that our life together meant nothing?

"You would have married Colin?"

"If it meant becoming queen, yes!" she shouted. "I've been training my entire life for this, and now I learn you are useless. You are nothing but the queen's bastard son! A consolation prize to mollify my father, no doubt."

I rose from my seat but made no move toward her. "I don't know what the king's intentions were toward your father. He doesn't share those details with me. I'm going downstairs."

I strode toward the door, intent on escaping her wrath. Deep in my core, I knew we were finished.

As I reached the door, she said, "Don't come back, Andrew. Not tonight, nor tomorrow. I will petition the council for an annulment of our marriage. They can't dismiss my claim. After all, you haven't managed to sire any children."

I grimaced and strode out of the room. I slammed the door harder than I'd intended and heard the wood splinter and crack in its frame. I growled a curse; I should have kept my strength in check, but it was too late and the damage was done.

If only she'd known the truth about what I was, she'd understand why she remained childless. I would never sire children, not with Claire, nor anyone else. I'd known for years it was impossible; skin-changers—*half breeds*—were sterile, and I was no exception. She'd meant to wound me with her final words, and she'd succeeded. The reminder stung.

If she sought to end our marriage, I wouldn't stand in her way. Perhaps she'd find happiness elsewhere, though I doubted I'd fare the same. I'd hoped my actions through the years would be sufficient to overcome the devastation my news had wrought in our relationship.

I'd never been so wrong.

# TWO

I didn't sleep that night. It was impossible with the conversations of the previous evening streaming through my mind time and again.

I paced the castle's corridors, a hulking shadow filled with grief and anxiety. My final words with Claire had proven more gutting than I'd imagined, and by the time I received the king's summons the next morning, I was numb and exhausted.

A servant located me in the castle's eastern wing as I stared unseeing through a sunlit window; there was movement in the grounds below, but I was scarcely aware of it. It was cold in that wing of the castle, as it hadn't been prepared for guests in some time. The servant shivered as she delivered the summons, and I silently cursed myself for the lapse, my second in as many days. I'd left my cloak behind in my quarters—*Claire's quarters*, I grudgingly reminded myself.

I trudged behind the servant as she led me to the council chamber at the castle's heart. I took little notice of the bustle of other servants as they went about their various chores, and I ignored several nobles as they greeted me in passing. I couldn't muster the energy nor the false cheer to bid them a good morning.

As I reached the council chambers, not only was Colin waiting outside the doors, but Alexander and Thomas were present as well. The king had called all three of his sons to witness my disgrace. There was no doubt I'd leave the meeting humiliated, set to become the newest source of castle gossip for weeks. I stifled a groan and sauntered toward them.

Colin was dressed impeccably. He was garbed in a crimson tunic embroidered with gold over black trousers, and wore polished knee-high black boots. I suspected he was dressed in his finery in an attempt to hide the evidence of his vices. On closer inspection, I noted his blue eyes were bloodshot from too much drink the night before, and the shadow of a bruise marred the left side of his jaw. He was clean-shaven and his brown hair was combed and styled carefully; he looked every bit the volatile prince he was.

Colin smirked as he took in my disheveled appearance. "You look like hell, Andrew."

I shrugged in response and averted my gaze. I was in no temper to engage in verbal sparring with him.

Alexander approached me, pointedly ignoring Colin's jibe. "Andrew, what's wrong?"

Alexander and I had both inherited our mother's green eyes, blond hair, and many of her other facial characteristics as well. I was several inches taller and broader in the shoulders, but otherwise we looked much the same. Of all my half-brothers, Alexander and I were the closest; we understood one another, often without speaking aloud. His garb was simpler than Colin's, though fine enough to befit his station.

"It's Claire," I growled.

I hoped my tone was low enough that Colin would not overhear from where he lounged against the wall nearby. I didn't have the patience for my unruly half-brother's barbed tongue, and if pressed, I'd likely find myself in a cell overnight as punishment for public brawling.

Alexander nodded. Questions flitted through his eyes, but he left them unspoken. I was grateful for his discretion.

Thomas fidgeted nervously a few paces away. He was just past his twentieth name day and had never liked being placed in the spotlight, regardless of the occasion. He spent much of his time in the castle's library, assisting the clerics with their work and poring over ancient texts and histories. Thomas possessed a brilliant mind but was prone to social anxiety. As the king's youngest son, he was never expected to rule nor lead negotiations. The summons to the council had clearly made him edgy.

Like Alexander, Thomas was dressed according to his station, but had forgone the level of finery Colin sported. He'd inherited Carlton's blue eyes and brown hair, though his profile was strikingly similar to our late mother's.

We were forced to wait several minutes before the doors to the council chamber opened. One of the court heralds, garbed in crimson and black livery marked with the Marsden boar, ushered us inside. The king stood at the end of the long oaken table, flanked on either side by five of the seven governors of the realm. The governors were elected by the people of each province to represent them at court and in matters of state. The king had always valued their opinions and guidance, considering them equal to the nobility who were born into their superior roles.

To my relief, none of the nobility were present, though I was certain word would reach them within minutes of the council's conclusion. Colin wouldn't hesitate to spread word of my disgrace at the first opportunity.

We stood at the opposite end of the table from the king, with myself and Colin in the center and Alexander and Thomas on either side. Thomas continued to fidget, and I noted his father frowned in disapproval. Poor Thomas seemed unaware he caused the distraction, or perhaps he simply didn't care as his anxiety continued to mount.

"I have brought you together today to announce my successor," the king began. He locked his gaze with mine before he turned it upon the council. "As some of you have pointed out in recent weeks, I am no longer as young as I used to be, and this formality must be concluded."

His statement elicited a few brief chuckles from the governors. The king smiled, though it appeared forced. I noted the strain he was under, though he made a valiant effort to maintain his amiable façade.

"Before I announce my successor, there are a few familial matters that must be presented to the council." The king cleared his throat, clearly uncomfortable, then pressed on. "First, I present Andrew's official birth record. Please examine it carefully."

My muscles tensed of their own accord as the governors huddled around the sheet of parchment the king placed on the table between them. I knew what the record stated; I was the son of Carra Winston, and "man unknown." It was only seconds before the first governor made an exclamation of surprise and pointed animatedly at a particular line on the document.

I sighed and looked down, ashamed and humiliated. Throughout my life, I'd always hoped to be long gone from Novania before this day arrived, but duty had bound me to the king—and to my half-brothers. I wouldn't abandon my family simply to avoid the inevitable scandal that was now primed to unfold.

Colin shifted from foot to foot, his interest piqued. He remained silent but shot a smirk in my direction; he hadn't been given leave to speak, but no one could stop him from goading me with his expression. Colin could be an intolerable bastard, but he knew when to follow proper etiquette—most of the time.

"Sire, is this true?" Chadwick Norse of the Eastern Marshes asked. He appeared aghast and gaped at me and the king in turns.

"It is," the king confirmed. "Andrew is not a Marsden, and thus cannot rule."

Unable to control himself any longer, Colin laughed aloud, earning a stern glare from his father. The look served to silence him, but he continued to smirk smugly. Perhaps the lack of sleep fouled my mood, but I found his behavior more deplorable than usual. I clenched my jaw and focused on the tiled floor.

"Sire, how long have you known of Andrew's heritage?" asked Tyrus Walsh of Barrier's Watch.

"I have always known." The king cleared his throat again. "I loved Carra dearly from the moment we met. She was already with child then, but not far along. To spare her shame, we married quickly and I raised Andrew as one of my own." He paused to study each of the governors in turn. "As much as it shocks you that he cannot rule, I have asked that he continue in his role as commander of the kingdom's armies. It is a role he excels in. Are there any who disagree with this course of action?"

The governors murmured their assent, though I could feel their eyes on me. I continued to stare at the scuffed toes of my boots, willing this damned meeting to be finished so I could retreat to the barracks for some much-needed rest. I could not return to my own chambers until Claire vacated them; she'd made it clear she wanted nothing more to do with me. I was the queen's bastard son, unworthy of her company.

Tyrus voiced the next question, which only served to wound me further. "Sire, given this new information, I feel it prudent that Andrew drops the Marsden name."

My shoulders slumped in defeat as I suppressed a sigh. The petition had been inevitable, but I'd failed to see it coming. Between Claire's rejection and the loss of the surname the king had so graciously given me, I was reeling. I looked up, silently imploring him to dismiss the request, but to no avail.

"Given the laws of this realm, I suppose you are correct, Tyrus," the king conceded, his tone sorrowful. His piercing blue eyes met my own. "I'm sorry, Andrew."

I clenched my jaw and looked away. My world was shattered.

The proceedings continued, but I only half-listened to what was said. In the span of a day, my life had been ripped apart, all I knew stripped away. I was nothing. *Less* than nothing, according to Novanian law.

"The next document I present is the birth record of Colin Marsden."

I registered the words through a haze of despair.

Colin tensed in anticipation. I glanced at him briefly and wished I could wipe the knowing smirk from his face with a solid right hook. That course of action would land me *months* in the dungeon now that everyone in the room knew I was not Carlton's son. I steeled myself and looked away, resolute in my determination to keep my temper in check.

"I propose Colin Marsden be named my successor as my eldest legitimate son," the king stated. His voice was weary; the brief meeting had taken its toll. "Are there any objections to this course of action?"

There were none; the council could not dispute the ancient law that held sway over the leadership of Novania. With the formalities finally at an end, Colin rushed from my side and proudly strode up to his father. He paused to leer in my direction. In that moment, I knew the kingdom was in store for a troubled era once his father vacated the throne. I hoped we'd have many years of Carlton's rule before Colin's ascension.

As Colin began speaking animatedly to his father, I turned to take my leave of the situation. I was in the corridor before I realized that Alexander had followed me.

"Andrew," he said as he fell into step beside me, "I'm sorry it came to this." He glanced around, took note of the numerous servants nearby, then said, "Come up to my room, brother. We should talk."

Resigned, I nodded and followed him upstairs without a word.

I sat down heavily on a padded bench once inside Alexander's room, while he closed and barred the door. I stared at the patterned carpet while tendrils of despair began to wrap themselves around my heart. I'd been disgraced in front of the council, Claire was leaving me, and I believed that once the king was gone, Colin would do his best to have me exiled—or worse. I knew he would not hesitate to further my ruin. In fact, he would relish it.

"Mother told me the day before she passed about your secret," Alexander said slowly. "She said you knew of *my* secret as well, and that she'd asked you to watch over me." He paused, and a faint smile formed at the corner of his mouth. "She always worried too much about my welfare."

I peered up at him but was unable to return his smile. "She was right to worry about you, Alex. If the king knew, or if Colin finds out..."

Alexander rolled his eyes. "I know, but I have made it this far without detection. As long as I continue to—"

"Alex, you know you can't trust Colin," I cut him off. "He will inevitably do something to force your hand—and when he does, I'll be forced to act as well."

He narrowed his eyes. "What do you mean, Andrew?"

"I promised mother I'd protect you, and that's what I'll do, no matter the cost." I sighed and ran a hand through my hair. "I've already lost so damned much during the last two days. I won't lose the only brother I can rely on too."

Alexander studied my face for several moments, then nodded as though he'd learned something important. "You told Claire what the council would learn today, didn't you?"

I nodded wearily. "I hoped she'd understand. I wanted to do right by her. But that doesn't matter. She's petitioning for an annulment."

"Ah, shit, I'm sorry," Alexander shook his head. "I knew her father was ambitious, but I didn't realize she shared his lofty aspirations."

I snorted. "She is nothing if not her father's daughter. She said she'd rather have Colin."

"Andrew…"

I crossed my arms and leaned back. I needed a break from the topic of my ruination. "Do you mind if I use your bench for a nap? I can't return to my room. Claire won't allow it."

"You were pacing the corridors all night, weren't you?"

I shrugged. Alexander knew my habits well enough; when I was troubled, sleep was elusive and I had a tendency to wander.

"Get some rest, brother. I'll make sure no one disturbs you."

The room was in semi-darkness when I awoke. The dying embers of the fire from my brother's hearth produced a soft glow, but I could see well enough.

Alexander was asleep in his bed. I sat up and stretched; the bench I'd fallen asleep on was uncomfortable and had left me stiff and sore, but within a few minutes, my discomfort would dissipate thanks to my unusual physiology. I wasn't certain how long I'd been asleep, but it must have been hours.

I rose quietly and made my way to the fireplace. Frost was beginning to form on the interior of Alexander's east-facing window, and I noted the first hints of dawn were beginning to lighten the starlit sky. I'd been asleep most of the day and the entire night as well. I stoked the fire, then made my way to the window.

Alexander's room overlooked the barracks. I watched the castle's garrison stir; some dispersed for the day's watch while others returned from the night's three stories below. I would check on the soldiers later that morning, once I'd spoken to Alexander. I hoped that fulfilling my duties as commander would take my mind away from Claire and the succession.

After a time, the first rays of a pale winter sun emerged above the castle walls, painting the sky in shades of gold. The castle's residents began to bustle through the courtyard; servants scurried about on various errands, the smiths heated the forges, stable hands pitched hay and mucked stalls. It seemed life had resumed its normal rhythm, despite the previous day's revelations. No doubt they were the talk of the castle by now.

I groaned aloud and heard Alexander stir behind me.

"Andrew? How long have you been standing there?"

I shrugged but didn't turn around. "A while. I didn't want to wake you."

He snorted. "Ever the guardian." He paused amidst a rustle of blankets. "I was glad to see you rest, although I think your snoring may have awakened the dead in the crypts outside the walls."

It was Alexander's way of coping with difficult situations; he'd jest and force a smile onto the faces of those around him. Despite myself, I chuckled.

"I'll stay in the barracks tonight," I assured him. "I still have the commander's quarters there, and none of the men will complain about the noise." I turned away from the window to find Alexander had disappeared inside his spacious wardrobe.

"Not to your face, perhaps," he quipped from within. "Believe me, they'll complain to one another!"

A moment later, a pair of trousers flew from the confines of the wardrobe to land near my feet followed by a clean shirt. Alexander's face appeared in the closet doorway wearing a grin.

"You ought to change your clothes before you go wandering about the castle today. It's obvious you've slept in what you're currently wearing."

"Fine." I picked up the offered garments and began to change. The trousers were too short for me, but my boots would cover the gap. "Thank you, Alex."

He stepped into the room once more, dressed for the day. "Someone has to look after you," he replied with a shrug. "You can't always be the protector, you know."

His words forced me to recall our conversation from the previous day. "How much did mother tell you about my 'secret,' exactly?" I assumed he'd known the king wasn't my father, but I needed to know the extent of his knowledge.

"Just that my father isn't your father," he replied. A frown tugged at the corners of his mouth as he contemplated his next words. "Is there more, Andrew?"

I couldn't tell him, not yet. It would only place him in further danger should Colin ever learn of his Mark. "Yes, but that's a story for another day."

Alexander studied me for a moment, then nodded. "Fine, but I'm going to hold you to that promise, brother."

As I made my way to the barracks, it became apparent everyone in the castle knew what had been revealed during the previous day's council meeting. Conversations abruptly died as I approached, while knowing smirks were hastily concealed by many of those I passed. Growing up with the royal family had often left me the source of gossip, but until now, I'd managed to ignore the worst of it. Today I was unable to turn a blind eye; it left me depressed and irritated, primed to lash out. It took every ounce of restraint I could muster not to act on my temper's fiery whims.

The soldiers of the castle's garrison remained respectful, and if they'd received the news, they at least possessed the sense to keep it to themselves. I oversaw several training exercises that morning before I retired to the commander's quarters to speak with a pair of my lieutenants.

By midafternoon, I was beginning to feel better about the situation, but the sentiment was short-lived. I received a summons from one of the king's notaries near dusk that shattered my fragile mood.

I growled low in my throat as I read the missive, then crumpled it in my fist. I crushed it in my grip for several moments, wishing I could grind it to dust, then tossed it into the fireplace across the small room.

Claire had made good on her threats and was approved for the annulment. The notary required my signature on the document; afterwards, Claire would be free to remarry as she wished. I considered refusing, but spite wasn't in my nature, and I truly hoped she'd find happiness one day. If remarrying would grant her that, then I would sign the damned paper.

I made my way toward the castle proper and entered through a side door. I wanted to avoid the main entrance and the crowded great hall within; I'd received enough stares and untoward comments earlier in the day to last a lifetime.

The notary had asked to meet in the castle's library on the second floor. I was surprised to find Claire was present when I arrived, but I supposed it wasn't unexpected. She wanted to ensure I signed the document—and perhaps planned to rub salt in my wounds a final time.

I lingered at the threshold for a few moments and allowed my gaze to take in the massive room. It was a place I rarely frequented, though I was familiar enough with its location. Row upon row of shelves formed half-circles through the room, each crammed with an array of books and scrolls. At the library's heart was a large hearth. Several tables surrounded the hearth; Claire and the notary were hunched over a stack of documents at one of them.

The look she gave me when our eyes met could have frozen the fires within a blacksmith's forge. Had she truly only been interested in my supposed status all this time? It was plain she held no love for me now, if indeed she ever had. I tore my eyes away and focused on the notary as I approached, an elderly man whom I recognized as one of Thomas' mentors.

"Ah, Andrew, I'm glad you've come," he said with an apologetic smile. "I understand this is not an easy task, and I was just finishing up the details…"

I took the offered quill and scrawled my signature at the bottom of the page without reading the document.

"Good. Now that he's signed the annulment, we can continue with our other business," Claire stated matter-of-factly.

I scowled at her, furious she held me in such low regard after everything I'd done to secure a comfortable life for her.

"This has nothing to do with you, Andrew." She forced a smile, though her eyes were like chips of black ice. "You may go."

She'd dismissed me as if I were nothing, a mere inconvenience and a waste of her precious time. To realize she felt so little for me after almost four years of marriage was both gut-wrenching and humiliating. I shook my head and swallowed the bitter words I desperately wished to say. I turned on my heel and strode toward the library doors, seething.

"Andrew."

The voice was a bare whisper and had come from between the bookshelves. I turned to find Thomas perched on a stool with a pile of scrolls stacked before him on the worktable. I'd failed to notice him when I first entered the library, but I hadn't bothered to look amongst the shelves when I entered. He beckoned me toward him, his eyes alight with unconcealed excitement.

"I've been working in here all day," he began. "Master Shale has asked me to copy some old texts. It's nothing exciting, but I overheard everything Claire said since she came in. I think you ought to know."

I frowned and wished—not for the first time—that the day would end. "I signed her annulment paper," I growled. "What more could there be?"

"Yes, I'm sorry to hear about that. I know you always cared for her." Thomas looked down and began to fidget with the quill in his hands. "It sounded as though she has someone else lined up for marriage already. That other business she mentioned? It's a transfer of some of her father's lands for use in a dowry."

I closed my eyes and bit back the barrage of curses that threatened to spill from my lips. It wasn't Thomas' fault things had turned out as they had, and it would do me no good to lash out at him. He was simply trying to help.

"Based on our conversation two nights ago, I'm not surprised," I replied. "My deeds on the battlefield meant nothing to her. The life I built for us meant nothing. She cares only for the status she hoped I could give her, and when she learned I would not become king…" I trailed off, unable to go on without causing a scene, and I'd had my fill of the spotlight.

"Did you know mother never approved of your marriage to her?" Thomas asked. "Father was thrilled—but looking back, I think it was because he knew all of Duke Ellington's scheming would be for nothing."

I had not been aware our mother harbored any misgivings about my marriage to Claire. She'd always been distant with my wife, but I'd never considered her reasons for it.

"I'm not certain they'll come to nothing," I replied, recalling Claire's statement regarding Colin.

If she was transferring some of her father's lands to be used as a dowry, perhaps she'd already made her move with him. Knowing Colin as I did, he'd be eager to take her as his bride, if only to flaunt his newfound status—and prove he was capable of taking for himself what had once been mine. For her part, Claire would accept any offer he made in order to resume her status as Novania's future queen. And I suspected she'd do it simply to spite me.

I sighed heavily and raked a hand through my hair.

"Andrew, Alex and I will continue to support you. You're still our brother, no matter what has happened," Thomas stated earnestly.

I nodded, appreciative of his words. "Thank you, Tom. I'll be in the barracks if you have need of me." I turned to leave.

"Wait, Andrew, there's one more thing."

When I faced him once more, he offered me a tenuous smile. "Father is sending Colin to Bridgewaters at the end of the week. Our uncle, Duke Crossley, is to train him on affairs of state. And the best part was, father *forbade* Colin from taking any of his 'friends' along. You should have seen the look on his face, Andrew!"

I managed a weary smile while Thomas laughed. It was best if Colin was separated from his friends. They were the source of many of his unsavory habits; his drinking, gambling, whoring, and fighting. During his absence, I'd be given a respite from his smirking face and condescension, and perhaps Duke Crossley would instill a sense of duty in my wayward half-brother.

"It is good news," I replied half-heartedly. "Take care, Tom."

# THREE

"Cabal's Thrall is less about strategy, and more about reading your opponents." I leaned back in my chair and grinned at the trio of soldiers around the table, then allowed my gaze to settle on Jerrick Vine. "You're a loyal soldier and a good friend, but you're a terrible liar. Which is why," I said, pausing for dramatic effect as I laid my cards down for all to see, "I've won again."

A chorus of laughter accompanied my words, and I glanced out my room's only window while Jerrick collected the cards and began to shuffle. The practice yard outside was empty and snow-packed, the sky a leaden gray that threatened more snow. Mid-winter was always bitterly cold, but this year had been particularly harsh. An afternoon spent with my lieutenants near a roaring hearth as we played round after round of Cabal's Thrall for coppers was an afternoon well spent.

"Ah, so this is where you've holed up."

I ground my teeth and shot a glare toward the door and my uninvited guest. Colin leaned against the doorframe, his arms crossed while he studied my quarters with a leer. The room was furnished simply, the walls bare, save for the rack above my hearth that held my sword. It was a far cry from the plush room I'd shared with Claire in the castle, but it was mine.

I rose from my seat and gestured to the others. "Leave us."

They scurried to obey and offered salutes to Colin as they strode past. I glared at my half-brother; I'd be damned if I showed him the same courtesy.

"Why are you here, Colin?"

"Is it not enough that I grace your presence, Andrew? You ought to be flattered that I've deigned to soil my new boots with your lowborn filth."

I clenched my fists at my side hard enough my nails bit into my palms. "You're here. You've seen my quarters in the barracks. Are you satisfied?"

"Hardly." He pushed himself away from the wall and smirked. "I wouldn't have come at all if not for my father. He insisted I pay you a visit before I depart for Bridgewaters, and I bring a summons from him as well."

"Then we'd best not keep him waiting." I wrenched my crimson commander's cloak from its peg near the door and strode past him.

"I've always considered you a brute, but this proves it," Colin snarled from behind. "I'm to be king. I deserve your respect."

I scowled over my shoulder and increased my speed. "Then earn it, brother."

"You may be my mother's son, but you are not father's," he hissed. "The late queen's bastard is no brother of mine."

I growled low in my throat as I crossed the final steps between the corridor and the barracks' exit, then shoved the door open to a blast of frigid air. I pulled my cloak on for show and continued my journey, undeterred by Colin's curses and complaints about the weather. If he chose to goad me, I'd reciprocate in kind.

By the time we reached the doors to the great hall, Colin appeared miserable. He shivered beneath his finery, his nose and ears were red from the cold, and his breath issued in ragged puffs. I'd kept a swift pace, and Colin had never been one for exercise.

"My father is in the council chambers," he snarled once inside. "You're a right bastard sometimes, Andrew."

I chuckled and turned away. "According to your logic, I've always been one. Go warm up, Colin. I would hate to see your delicate hands turn black from frostbite."

His fist collided with my ribs. I steeled myself; he was trying to goad me into a fight, and given the recent downturn in my fortunes, I could not afford to engage him now. He swung again, the strike connecting solidly with my right kidney. I ground my teeth and clenched my fists, my gaze focused on a point across the room. His second punch had hurt, but I'd endured worse.

"Are you finished?" I growled as he stepped back. "You're drawing a crowd."

He barked a laugh. "For now. The king is waiting."

I shook my head and strode across the room, ignoring the stares of servants and nobility alike. By some miracle, I'd managed to hold my temper while Colin allowed his to flare.

A pair of soldiers on guard duty met me at the entrance to the council chambers, which were propped open. The king sat at the long table inside, and across from him, Alexander. To my relief, none of his advisors or governors were present. I'd suffered enough humiliation of late.

The king motioned me inside. "Close the door, Andrew. There's a matter we must discuss privately."

"Of course, sire."

"Where's Colin?" Alexander asked as the doors swung shut and I took the open seat beside him.

"Likely warming his hands and nursing his bruised ego," I replied with a shrug.

The king released a sigh. "Your brother must learn how to negotiate with people—even those he doesn't like. I've never understood why the pair of you clash as you do."

"It has only become worse since he was named your heir, sire." I dropped my gaze and noted the rumpled sheet of parchment resting on the table beneath his hands. "But I suspect Colin is not why you've summoned me."

"No, he is not." He spun the paper around to face me and pushed it across the table. "Lon Calder sent this a fortnight ago with one of his best riders. It arrived this afternoon."

I skimmed the message with a frown. The Corodan had begun to raid the villages north of Calder's Point, despite the foul weather. In my nearly two decades of experience with our insectile foes, they'd never attacked during winter. Lon Calder was that region's governor, one of the few who had been absent for my fall from grace, and now I understood why.

I looked up to meet the king's piercing gaze. "You need me to rally our troops and march north."

"Yes. Alexander has asked to accompany you, and I have decided to grant his request."

Beside me, Alexander beamed. "Thank you, father."

"I'll require perhaps two weeks to muster the necessary forces," I continued, skimming Lon's note a final time. "With our current weather, it will take three weeks to move into position. He states he's sent word to both Dukes Horace and Everly?"

"He has, and the dukes of the Northern Marches will come to his aid. They always have."

"And Duke Winston?" I asked.

The king shook his head. "It's doubtful. Your cousin is in Three Points to see his eldest married. He'll never return in time to assist."

I nodded and rose from my seat. "I'll see to the army, sire."

"I know. And I'll see to it that Colin understands the importance of your work before he leaves for Bridgewaters. I suspect he owes you an apology."

I chuckled dryly. "Colin will never apologize, sire. Don't waste your breath."

As I'd anticipated, it took more than a fortnight to rally our forces to march. We reached the city of Calder's Point after eighteen days of travel, exhausted and bitterly cold as winter continued to grip the land in her icy talons. The army made camp outside the city's walls, and we prepared to rest for two days while we resupplied. Duke Everly's men would meet us there, though there was no sign of them upon our arrival.

I ensured the camp was in hand, then bade Alexander ride with me into the city. I needed to gather recent information regarding our adversaries, and the governor of Calder's Point was a long-time friend of mine.

The city appeared emptier than usual due to the frigid weather. We passed a few brave souls bundled in several layers as they scurried through the streets while we made our way to the city center and the governor's residence. A pair of bored guardsmen lounged against the outer gate but straightened at our approach. Alexander wore the colors of the royal house, crimson and ivory trimmed in black, while I wore the simple red cloak that marked me as commander of the king's forces.

"Ah, Commander, sir," one of the guardsmen greeted us as he saluted. "And Your Highness! The governor has been awaiting your arrival since your men began to make camp."

Alexander rolled his eyes at the formality. "You may call me Alexander. The Highness is my father—and my brother. I'm here to support the commander."

"Yes, of course. Please, come in! One of the boys will care for your horses."

He ushered us inside the gate, where a stable hand was ready to take the reins as we dismounted. I patted my dapple gray's flank; Iris had proven a reliable mount on our journey north, one of the few horses that didn't balk at my presence. The stable hands at the castle had often joked that my stature set the creatures on edge, though I suspected the horses sensed the truth of my nature. Thankfully, horses were unable to share my secret, and I was grateful to the few who tolerated me.

As we approached the house, the front door burst open, and Lon Calder marched forward to greet us. He was only a few years my senior, but he did well by his people and had earned their respect. It kept him in the governorship long after many others would have been ousted. He was dressed plainly in a woolen tunic and leggings, along with a fur-lined cloak to combat the winter chill. His dark hair was thinning, and white streaked his beard.

"Welcome, Andrew! I'm glad you've stopped by—I was hoping the king had sent you to deal with our troubles. No one else can handle the Corodan as you do, my friend." He turned to Alexander and offered him the same friendly smile he'd given me. "And Alexander! It's always a pleasure to see you riding out with your brother. Come inside where it's warm, my friends."

Lon had always welcomed me in this fashion when my forces passed through his city. As we removed our cloaks inside the entrance, he shook his head.

"I heard about your troubles at the Capitol, Andrew," he said slowly. "It's a shame it came to that. A pity I was unable to make the journey myself, but things here have been a mite difficult. The bugs have been raiding farther and farther south, razing some of the smaller villages. It's out of character. It's almost as if something is driving them into a frenzy."

I chose to ignore the first part of his statement; over the weeks, I'd grown weary of hearing platitudes, and I'd never been one to seek sympathy. We followed Lon into his study, a cheery room with a large fireplace, a worktable, and a few shelves crammed with books. Detailed maps of the region hung in frames on his walls. While many of the maps on display were generations old, they remained accurate, and I'd sought his knowledge of the northern landscape on several occasions.

As we seated ourselves around the table, I asked the question that had been most prominent in my mind. "Has anything changed in the highlands? If something drives the Corodan, we must seek it and remove the threat. Cut off the source to stem the flow, so to speak."

He nodded in agreement. "It's a wise strategy, Andrew, but I don't know if anything has changed. Certainly, *something* must have, but what that is, I can't say." He sighed. "Duke Everly sent word a few days ago that he was gathering his forces to meet you here. He may have more insight."

"When we received word the Corodan had begun attacking, my father didn't want to believe the news," Alexander said. "They've never attacked in winter, but your message was certainly convincing, and Andrew didn't question it."

Lon flashed a grin. "Your brother knows I'd never request aid unless it was warranted. He's led more campaigns against the Corodan than any other." He grew thoughtful and studied me for some time before he next spoke. "I always believed it strange that the king should send his eldest to the front lines every year. You always came away in the autumn relatively unscathed, so I assumed he knew of your prowess and had come to terms with the risks involved. Now that we know the truth, your role makes sense. I wish the news had been otherwise, Andrew. No one in the north much cares for that scoundrel Colin."

"My father has already stated that he wants Andrew to remain the commander," Alexander replied.

"Alex is right. I will continue to travel north when needed, and I'll do everything in my power to protect your lands from the Corodan," I assured him. "In fact, I may make my presence permanent. There's nothing left for me in the Capitol."

Alexander scowled. "That's nonsense, and you know it, brother. Regardless, I believe Andrew will be available to lend his aid to your people, Lon."

"Did Everly give you any indication as to when he would arrive?" I asked, seeking a change of subject.

During our trek from the Capitol, the topic of my potential residence in the Northern Reaches had been broached a few times, and Alexander was staunchly against it. While I understood his reason, I'd attempted to convince him to join me. He would not, and we remained locked in a battle of wills.

"He hoped it would be today, but the roads from the east have been nearly impassable of late. He'll be fortunate to arrive by the week's end."

Lon's wife, Amelia, entered bearing a tray laden with bread and cheese, three mugs, and a kettle that steamed. "I've made tea," she said as she placed the tray on the table between us. "No doubt you can use something to warm you after so long in the cold."

I thanked her as she departed. Amelia had always been a kind soul.

"Don't mind if I do," Alexander said.

He swiped one of the cups and poured himself a mug of the steaming liquid. He held the cup between his hands for several moments before taking a sip. I tore a piece from the loaf of bread, preferring food to the drink at hand.

Once Amelia was gone, Lon sat back in his chair with an amused grin. "Some things never change." He pointed in my direction. "For example, you always think with your stomach, cold or other discomforts be damned."

I chuckled. "A man has to eat."

"Andrew doesn't care for tea anyway." Alexander took another sip from his cup. "Usually, I don't either, but it's damned cold outside."

Lon chuckled. "That I know all too well. Something stronger, perhaps?"

I grinned. I knew what came next.

He reached beneath the table and brought forth a bottle of brandy. "I keep this on hand, just in case."

He filled a cup with the clear, golden liquid and slid it across the table to me.

"Had I known this was coming, I would have waited on the tea!" Alexander exclaimed with a laugh. "Always the keeper of the best secrets, aren't you, brother?"

He'd meant the remark as a jest, but I glanced at him warily all the same. If Lon noticed my momentary concern, he didn't remark upon it. Alexander needed to be more careful; I could not always be present to protect him, though I'd promised myself I would try. It was part of the reason he was so strongly opposed to me staying in the northern lands. He'd be more secure if I remained near.

We discussed Lon's concerns for Calder's Point, though he believed his city was not in imminent danger. He had little else to share. I'd be forced to wait for Duke Everly's arrival before I could learn more.

As the day dwindled into evening, we took our leave of the governor's hospitality and made our way back to camp. Alexander was shivering within his cloak by the time we returned, and I set about stoking a fire outside our tents while one of the soldiers took Iris and Alexander's bay toward the picket lines. Alexander huddled as near to the flames as safety allowed, drawing his cloak closer about his shoulders.

"Andrew, I need to ask you something," he said after a time.

I nodded once. "You can always talk to me, Alex."

"Something Lon said earlier gave me pause. Is it true you've led more campaigns against the Corodan than anyone? I know you've been riding north almost every summer since you were a teenager. You are ten years my senior, and I can't remember a time when you weren't marching north to fight."

I shrugged. In truth, I'd never given the matter any serious thought. Alexander was right; I'd been riding north since I was fifteen, more than half my lifetime ago. The king had named me commander seven years past upon the recommendations of several of the northern governors—Lon Calder amongst them.

I'd always known that I'd never become king; instead, I'd chosen to make something of my life by becoming a soldier. The fact that I healed rapidly and possessed a greater strength than other men only served to make me a better warrior, though I'd been told on occasion I was prone to recklessness. But I knew my limits and believed I'd never been in mortal danger.

"I suppose what he said is true," I replied. "Most commanders haven't survived more than three or four campaigns. I try not to dwell on it."

"Do you think the Corodan are trying to lure you out with this winter business?" Alexander asked. "If you've survived longer than any other, don't you think they'd try something new? Perhaps they aren't being driven at all, and are simply changing tactics to throw you off."

I frowned, but his theory held merit. The Corodan were highly intelligent, though communication between our species had long been problematic. Over the years, I'd taken several Corodan prisoners with the hope of gleaning useful information or the reason behind their continued hostility. Some could speak when forced, though their use of human language was often broken and strained.

While this was only Alexander's fourth time riding north, he'd learned enough about our enemy to understand many of their capabilities. I was pleased he had not dismissed their cunning.

"It's possible," I replied. "The only way to know for certain is to confront them. I hope to detain some of them for questioning, if we're provided with the opportunity, that is."

"Andrew, if something were to happen to you…"

I looked up at him sharply. "Alex, don't."

"No, I need to say this, Andrew." He scowled at the fire for a moment, then looked up again to meet my eyes. "If something were to happen to you, I'd be forced to flee. You know that, don't you? You're the only reason I haven't traveled south already. If Colin were to find out…" He shook his head, his expression troubled. "He wouldn't hesitate to carry out the law. That's why you can't stay here, Andrew. It's why I need you near *me*."

I knew he was right. If I made my home in the north, he'd be in grave danger when he returned to the Capitol. Returning was expected of him, and royal protocol dictated that he must comply. I'd promised our mother I would protect him, and that was one promise I'd keep, the laws of Novania be damned.

"I won't leave you alone, Alex. I'll return with you when the time comes. After all, someone has to keep Colin in his place."

He managed a tired smile. "I think you'll need more than luck to pull that off, Andrew. Colin will be a terrible ruler. Everyone sees it, but the laws are clear when it comes to succession. I know you're weary of hearing it, but the kingdom truly is mourning its fate right now." He looked down and seemed to deflate. "Since mother told me the truth about your father, I've held onto the ridiculous notion that *my* father would find a way to circumvent the laws. I hoped he'd find a way to name you his heir."

I shook my head. "I don't believe he ever tried to change the laws, Alex. And even if he had, I…I wouldn't have wanted to rule. It's not who I am."

Alex studied me for a long moment, the firelight playing across his features. "I believe you, Andrew. Even so, you would have made a fine king. Think about it—every time you muster the troops, they come not because they have to, but because they *believe* in you. You're a born leader."

I grimaced. It was another matter that I'd never given much thought to; it simply came naturally.

"I do my best," I replied dismissively, hoping to put an end to the conversation.

Alexander snorted. "You're also smart enough to know when to stop if things go badly. You plan ahead. You're approachable, even to the lowest-ranking soldiers. All of those things serve to make you the best damned commander this kingdom has ever seen, and that's the reason why so many people have expressed their disappointment with the succession. *They respect you*, brother. They can't say the same for Colin."

"All of that may be true, but there is nothing I can do to change what happened."

"Perhaps not, but maybe there is something *I* can do," he replied, a fierce light in his eyes. "Colin will be Novania's ruin if he comes to power."

"Alexander, *enough*." My voice was stern, unyielding. I had to end this train of thought immediately, lest it serve to be Alexander's downfall. "There are other factors at play that you know nothing about. *I can never rule.* Drop this folly. Now."

"What other factors are there, Andrew? Everything was laid out at the council meeting. Thomas and I have been working on a plan—"

"Holy hell, Thomas, too? No, Alex! You don't understand. The two of you are going to wind up getting yourselves killed if you aren't careful." I wanted to tell him everything, but something stayed my tongue. Now was not the time.

Alexander's frown deepened, and he crossed his arms defiantly. "What don't we understand, Andrew? What more is at play?"

I clenched my jaw, incensed that he would not let the matter be. "I know who my father was," I hissed. "Because of him, I am unfit to rule—no matter what the laws might say. *Now drop this.* I've had enough."

I turned away and strode into the confines of my tent before he could pry any further. I made as though I were going to sleep, but I knew slumber would elude me for some time as our argument replayed through my mind.

Alexander said little as we went about our duties and spoke to the soldiers the next morning. He accompanied me on my rounds, but our words were sparse. He remained angry about the previous evening's outburst, and I was furious that he and Thomas had put themselves into a compromising position simply to overthrow the planned succession. If Colin were to learn of their scheming after he became king, there would be nothing they could do to save themselves. Colin was not known for his mercy, and if his attitude toward me were any indication, he'd carry out their execution with a smug grin plastered on his face.

As midday approached, Duke Everly's men began to arrive and the camp nearly doubled in size. They planned to resupply, and within another two days, we'd march north to the Green Crossing, where Duke Horace was set to join us. From there, it would be another few days before we arrived at Grayson's Canyon.

The duke met with us shortly after his arrival. He was a stern man, with iron-gray hair and piercing blue eyes, known throughout the region as a seasoned warrior. He was not a man to be crossed, nor taken lightly.

"Your Highness," he greeted Alexander first, then nodded in my direction. "Commander."

I clenched my jaw. Jonas Everly and I had never warmed to one another, but his greeting was frostier than the surrounding air. I knew the announcement of Colin as heir had forever changed the dynamic between us, and now I'd only be seen as the subordinate of my younger half-brothers. My post as commander meant nothing to the rigid nobleman.

"What news do you have for us, Jonas?" I asked, refusing to be ignored.

I received a withering glare, which I returned with a defiant one of my own. After a moment, he turned to face Alexander directly. I wanted to throttle the man.

"Duke Horace will meet us at the Green Crossing as planned," he stated. "It will take a few days to move our men into position near Grayson's Canyon, where the Corodan activity has been the strongest. I suspect—"

Alexander crossed his arms. "Give your full report to the commander, Jonas. That's an order."

The duke's eyes flashed in anger, but he obeyed. He addressed me through clenched teeth. "The Corodan activity has been strongest near Grayson's Canyon. They have razed several villages and killed many. I suggest we focus our efforts on retaking the canyon, *then* we can seek out and abolish their hive."

"Retaking the canyon could prove costly." I crossed my arms. "The Corodan would be at an advantage. We'd be forced to compress our forces into a small space, giving them the luxury of luring us into whatever traps they may have devised."

The duke's face was impassive. Clearly, he didn't want to be contradicted, particularly by a lowly commander. After all, I wasn't nobility; I was beneath him. Nevertheless, I pressed on.

"You mentioned a hive. Has it been located?"

"Not as such, but I have scouts looking into it." His reply was terse.

He would not divulge any further information—at least not to *me*, a mere commoner without a surname. Damn him.

"Even I know you have to go to the source to end the Corodan threat," Alexander stated, his tone scathing. "If this is all you have for us, I suggest you find the leader of your scouts and have *them* deliver your report."

Jonas ground his teeth. "Very well."

After the duke departed, Alexander shook his head. "Holy hell, he's a menace. I don't like him."

"Nor do I, and as you noticed, the feeling was mutual," I growled. "He's always been a difficult man to work with, but now it's worse."

"He'll defer to you as the commander. I'll see to it," Alexander promised. "Father named you to this post for a reason, and if some pompous ass of a nobleman seeks to undermine your authority simply because you have no rank, then he can take his damned soldiers and go for all I care."

"Alex, we need his forces."

"Then he'll need to learn his place, brother." Alexander smirked. "Actually, this might be fun."

"Alex…"

I feared he would alienate the duke. Everly would not hesitate to complain to the king about Alexander's behavior, and I was uncertain if I'd be able to mitigate the damage my brother would inevitably incur. Alexander threatened to walk a dangerous line.

"I promise I won't act rashly," Alexander replied.

The gleam in his eye belied his words, and I shook my head, exasperated.

"I wish I could believe you, Alex, but I can't. Please don't do anything that will cause the duke to complain to your father. That won't end well for either of us."

# FOUR

I never learned what Alexander said to Duke Everly, but our tense relationship began to improve as the days wore on. The duke begrudgingly addressed me as the final authority in the camp, and even began to relate his misgivings about the succession. It was as close to an apology as I'd ever receive from the man.

It took the army nearly eight full days to reach Green Crossing, where Duke Horace's men were already camped and awaiting our arrival. He'd always been jovial and friendly, and I considered him an ally, if not a friend. It would prove a welcome change from Everly's dour and unyielding nature.

I asked Alexander and Duke Everly to join me as I departed for Duke Horace's tent at the center of camp. I hoped he had fresh news regarding the Corodan's movements and a better plan than Jonas had suggested.

I didn't like the idea of marching into Grayson's Canyon where the chance of a successful retreat would be minimal. Jonas' scouts had confirmed the Corodan were most active there, but they'd yet to locate the leader of the hive. Our people would be at the enemy's mercy if we attempted to engage them while trapped between two sheer rockfaces. The plan was suicide, and I was desperate for a better scheme.

"Prince Alexander, this is a welcome surprise!" Jonathan Horace greeted my brother with a broad smile and shook his hand in greeting. "And Andrew, it's always a relief to see you here and prepared to deal with the bug menace. There's no one better suited for the task." He shook my hand, grinned, then merely nodded to Duke Everly. "Hello, Jonas."

Jonas grunted but made no reply, though his eyes narrowed in disdain.

"It has been nigh on six years since we last met, hasn't it, Commander?" Jonathan asked, ignoring the other duke's reaction.

I nodded. "That sounds right."

"You haven't changed a bit." He grinned. "I wish I could say the same for myself. I've put on a few unwanted pounds and had to have a new suit of armor fitted just a few months ago. Bah!"

While I knew he'd meant the remark as a compliment, his words unsettled me. I'd known the day would eventually come when I would be forced to flee or reveal myself, but I'd always hoped it was far in the future. Since my unusual ancestry provided me with the ability to heal rapidly, it also eliminated the effects of aging before they left a mark on my skin. I'd known this for several years, but had foolishly convinced myself I had time before anyone began to grow suspicious. Perhaps my time masquerading as a normal man was coming to its inevitable conclusion.

The talk returned to strategy. Jonathan didn't have any new reports, and it seemed the Corodan were trying to force us into the canyon. If we wanted to confront the hive's leader and put an end to their current threat, we'd be forced to meet them there.

"And there is no other entrance into the canyon?" I asked.

"I'm sorry, my friend," Jonathan replied, his tone filled with regret. "If we want to stop the raids, we'll be forced to meet them on their terms."

I sighed and ran a hand through my hair. I didn't like the prospect. Our soldiers would be cut down and massacred if our plans went awry, and I wasn't certain what we'd assembled was a true plan. I wasn't willing to sacrifice countless lives if there was an alternative.

A harried scout approached then, interrupting our discussion. "My lords," he said, breathless, "the Corodan have sent an emissary." The man's eyes betrayed his fear, though he didn't voice it.

"It may be a trap," Jonathan commented as we followed the scout out of the tent and into the chill evening air. Snow had begun to fall, muffling the noise from the surrounding camp.

I nodded my agreement. It was suspicious; the Corodan rarely attempted negotiations. They preferred methods of treachery and subterfuge to outright battle, though they fought openly often enough. I sensed our arrival at Green's Crossing had been anticipated by the hive, and the Corodan had been watching our moves closely while we remained unaware of their presence. The timing was too perfect to be coincidental.

We followed the scout to the camp's outskirts, where nearly a dozen armed soldiers surrounded the lone Corodan emissary, their weapons drawn. The creature stood as tall as a horse, its carapace a pale green that glistened faintly in the dying light. It tilted its triangular head to one side as we approached, a display of curiosity. Fortunately for the soldiers, it kept its razor-sharp forelegs folded against its long torso and seemed uninterested in a fight. The Corodan had always reminded me of oversized praying mantis.

A hiss issued from the Corodan's mouthparts, reminiscent of the sound produced when a snake slithered through dry grass. The soldiers closest to the creature instinctively stepped back. I frowned and pushed through them, familiar with the insect's act of intimidation.

"Why have you come?" I demanded.

Immediately the creature fell silent. It seemed to size me up with its pale, multi-faceted eyes. "You are Commander," it said in a dry, rustling voice.

"I am."

"Hive-queen seeks meeting with Commander. Hive-queen will meet at canyon-mouth after sun sets two more times. Commander must meet Hive-queen alone." It tilted its head once more, awaiting my response.

"Why does she seek a meeting? And why must I come alone?"

The Corodan released a warning rattle. "Hive-queen seeks meeting. Bids that I bring message to Commander. We do not question Hive-queen."

I suppressed a groan; I'd receive no further answers from the creature. What it stated was true. The hive obeyed their queen without question, even if she ordered them to their deaths. I suspected it had something to do with the chemical signals they employed as a form of communication, but I'd never had the opportunity to learn if it was true.

"Very well," I replied as a plan began to coalesce in my mind. "Return to your Hive-queen and tell her I'll do as she requests."

The creature hissed in pleasure. Behind me, Alexander cursed aloud. The soldiers moved aside to allow the Corodan passage. We watched it depart, then disappear into the falling snow.

"Andrew, this is madness!" Jonathan exclaimed once I turned back toward the camp. "You can't accept her terms. To face them alone is death!"

"He's right," Alexander agreed. "Damn it, Andrew. What were you thinking?"

"This is an opportunity," I replied, undeterred. "The Corodan seem overly confident, whatever their plan may be. I have no doubt that it's a trap."

"If you know it's a trap, then why agree to this, brother?" Alexander's voice was desperate, strained.

"I have an idea," I replied evasively. "Let's go back into the command tent and we can discuss it where it's warm."

"This is utter madness," Duke Horace groused after I laid out my plan. "If you're correct and they spring their trap at the first opportunity, we'll have very little time to react. I don't like it, Andrew."

I'd proposed that we march the army within archery-range of the Hive-queen's chosen location. When the time came for our meeting two days hence, I would ride out to meet her alone as she'd requested. I didn't know what the Corodan planned, but it was a risk I was willing to take if it meant an end to the decades-long hostilities that had plagued our people.

A large, open plain sat at the mouth of the canyon, and there would be no cover for the Corodan to attempt an ambush until I reached the rocky outcropping at the canyon's narrow mouth. The journey between our forces and theirs held little risk of danger. The steep hillsides on either side of the mouth were strewn with boulders, which would provide cover for a group of archers that I proposed be sent ahead during the hours prior to our meeting. The archers would cover my progress and could react swiftly once the trap was sprung. That the Corodan planned to attack me was a certainty.

If my survival was in question during the encounter, I could shift into my dragon form. The others didn't know what I was, nor could they, but I was confident I'd survive. It was an option of last resort, but one I'd utilize if it meant I'd live to see the next sunrise. If the dukes learned of my heritage—or any of the soldiers for that matter—my life would take an even darker turn, but my scheme accounted for that.

Novania's laws weren't tolerant of the dragon-kind, and Colin would uphold them simply to spite me. While I would survive the Corodan, I would not survive the kingdom's wrath if I were spotted, but the distance between the archers, the army, and the meeting place should provide sufficient cover to disguise my transformation if it came to it. I hoped it wouldn't, but it was a risk I'd take if my life was threatened.

"I can defend myself," I replied stubbornly, "and the Corodan will rue the day they attempted to outsmart me. Trust me, Jon. I'll be fine."

"I don't like it either." Alexander crossed his arms and glared defiantly.

"I believe it's the best chance we have of removing the Hive-queen's threat," Duke Everly said.

I was surprised he'd taken my side in the matter. I lifted an eyebrow in question.

"The Corodan have never been active in the winter months, and though I don't like the idea of you walking up to them alone—at a time and place *they* have designated, no less—I simply don't see a better alternative. If your plan works, the Northern Marches might find peace for a time." Jonas frowned in thought. "I know we've had our differences over the years, Andrew, but I have faith in your abilities as our commander."

Alexander's shoulders slumped in defeat. "Fine, let's do this. For the record, your plan is shit, brother."

I was certain I'd receive an earful from him later, but at present, I had an army to move.

We reached the plains south of Grayson's Canyon midmorning of the planned date. I ordered the soldiers to make camp a mile from the canyon's mouth, then asked them to get some rest. The trek from the

Green Crossing was grueling at the best of times, but the weather had been uncooperative, forcing us to march through driving snow and biting winds. Some of the soldiers grumbled, but word had leaked about my plan, and most endured without complaint simply out of respect and loyalty to me. It was heartening to find I'd retained their support, despite the succession.

As the day bled into afternoon, Alexander dispatched the bowmen to a location near the canyon's mouth. They'd remain hidden from the enemy's sight but provide crucial surveillance. He insisted he'd accompany one of the groups. Though I understood his desire, I asked him to remain behind. He was a prince, and I couldn't guarantee his safety as I went through with my scheme.

"No, Andrew!" He was vehement in his reply. "If you're going through with this idiotic plan, then I'll stay close to render help should the need arise. I am not going to let you get yourself killed, brother! Your plan is reckless at best, madness at worst. What will I tell my father when I return, should you die today?"

I sighed and ran one hand through my hair in frustration. "Fine, go, then. Be safe, Alex."

He nodded once and turned to leave. "You as well, brother."

I waited until the sun was low in the western sky, then mounted Iris and rode to the camp's perimeter. Dukes Everly and Horace were forming the soldiers into ranks; they'd march behind me at a distance, far enough back that the Corodan would not see them as an immediate threat, but near enough they could charge the enemy should the need arise. I hoped to deal with the Corodan swiftly, eliminating the need for backup, but the army's presence was reassuring.

There was no sign of the Corodan as I crossed the snow-covered grass. I had no doubt I'd find myself in danger before long, however; it was too still, too silent. The world held its breath, for even the bitter wind dwindled to little more than a hushed whisper. I could not see the bowmen or Alexander amongst the rocks as I neared the chosen location; they had camouflaged themselves well.

It was not until I began to pass into the canyon's mouth, where its steep, rocky sides jutted skyward from the landscape, that the Corodan made their first move. Three appeared from behind a boulder and came to stand directly in my path. The Corodan in the center of the trio was easily twice the size of the others, and I assumed she must be the hive's leader.

"Commander," she hissed. "Come closer. We must talk."

I urged Iris forward warily. The horse took not more than five steps before we were inexplicably falling. I landed hard on my side and rolled away from the horse as she screamed in agony. No doubt she'd broken at least one leg in the fall, but I was forced to ignore her as I took stock of my new surroundings.

I'd fallen into a large pit. The Corodan must have devised a covering of dried grasses to disguise its presence; I hadn't noted a change in the ground as I'd nudged Iris forward. The sides of the pit were sheer and at least a dozen feet high; there would be no climbing up without aid. Nearly two dozen Corodan filled the pit. They began to make an eerie rattling noise as I regained my footing. I drew my sword as the large female appeared over the rim above.

"We learned from you, Commander," she hissed. "Remove the leader, and the rest fall into chaos."

She leaped down to join the others of her kind, as did her two guards. The other Corodan moved aside to allow her space to maneuver.

"You must die."

In that instant, I knew if I were to survive the encounter, I had but one option remaining. I dropped my sword, and as the Corodan began to surge forward, I shifted for the first time in nearly twenty years.

The change occurred in an eyeblink. My body swelled and elongated, sprouted a pair of enormous leathery wings, and a long, powerful tail. I now looked down upon the Corodan, my body protected beneath a thick layer of glossy, black scales. Those nearest skittered backward, crashing into one another as panic took root. I released a powerful roar and lunged toward them, tearing with my claws and lashing with my tail.

The Hive-queen continued to urge the others to fight, even as I cut them down and rent them asunder as I'd witnessed them do to so many of my people over the years. In that moment, I wanted nothing more than revenge—revenge for all of my fallen comrades, revenge for the innocent people they'd terrorized, revenge for the damage they'd inflicted year after year on my homeland.

A pair of Corodan slipped beneath my right foreleg and sliced at my belly while I was engaged with another. The Corodans' razor-sharp forelegs were unable to penetrate my scaly hide—a fortunate discovery on my part. I would marvel at my newfound knowledge later, but at present, I had insects to dispatch. I swatted them forcefully away, and both careened into the pit's steep wall. The sound of chitin cracking on impact accompanied their collision, and they crumpled, their forms unmoving.

Within moments, only the largest female remained. I stared her down, daring her to speak. Instead, she charged toward me with a loud hiss. I roared again and tore her in two. Ichor splashed across my face as I grimaced.

"Andrew!" I heard a shout from above. The voice was some distance away, but I recognized Alexander's tone.

I shifted to my human form and belatedly realized my armor had been destroyed during the transformation. Bits of steel lay strewn amongst the carnage I'd wrought; it had exploded outward with tremendous force. I scanned the pit and located my red cloak, miraculously intact, and threw it around my shoulders just in time to hide my nakedness from Alexander. I noted with dismay that during the course of the fight, Iris had been killed. I didn't know if she'd been cut down by the Corodan, or if I had inadvertently slain the poor beast in my desperate rage.

I groaned, weary and uncertain how to field the inevitable questions my brother would ask.

"Andrew!"

Alexander was panting for air as his face appeared above the rim of the pit. Steam rose from his breath, and mud stained his armor. His expression shifted from sheer panic to confused awe as he surveyed the destruction I'd left in my wake. Insectile limbs were scattered in a wide arc around my person, and the floor of the pit was slick with yellowish ichor. As his eyes met mine, he broke into a relieved grin.

"You're alive! Holy hell, when we saw you fall and disappear, I thought surely…" He shook his head, then turned around. "He's alive!" he shouted to others behind him.

I located my sword and drew the cloak tightly around myself. I turned back to Alexander and noted that several of the bowmen had arrived as well.

"Go fetch some rope," Alexander ordered a teenaged soldier. "And tell them Andrew is alive."

He nodded and turned to leave, his eyes wide.

"Wait," I called to him. "Bring me a change of clothes too."

Alexander frowned at me. "And a pair of boots," he added before the boy departed. "What happened to your armor, Andrew?"

I didn't know how to explain my sudden nakedness or how I'd managed to slay two dozen Corodan without receiving so much as a scratch. I hesitated as I searched for a plausible explanation, but I could think of nothing.

"The bugs like to toy with their victims," one of the bowmen stated matter-of-factly. "I've seen them cut the armor off a man without harming him, just to have a bit of fun before they kill him."

"Looks like they picked the wrong man to toy with," a woman agreed with a chuckle. "You damn well showed them, Commander!"

I was relieved they'd devised their own theory about what occurred and I wouldn't be forced to explain myself. I simply nodded, though I could see Alexander didn't believe the story. I owed him the truth, but that must wait for a time when we were alone.

It was fully dark before soldiers arrived from the camp with the requested items. While those above worked to construct a rudimentary ladder by torchlight, I donned the fresh clothing and boots. When the rope ladder was flung down, I began to climb without hesitation, grateful to be moving away from the chitinous wreckage, the remains of the thwarted Corodan ambush... And poor Iris' mangled form.

I replayed the brief battle in my mind. The power I experienced while in my dragon form terrified me. I'd never felt safe enough to experiment with it, though for much of my life, I'd yearned to do so. Perhaps one day, when I finally traveled south beyond the Mage's Gate, I'd learn more.

As we made our way back to camp, Alexander drew me aside and waited as the rest of the army moved forward. He didn't speak until he felt certain we were beyond hearing range.

"Andrew, I don't know how you survived. I thought you were gone as soon as the ground fell away beneath you." He looked away and released a heavy sigh. "I don't believe those bugs were 'toying' with you, but let the others think what they want."

I didn't know what to say. I wanted to tell him the truth, to finally share my story with someone, but in the end, I said nothing. Thirty-six years of hiding was a difficult habit to break.

He sighed again, frustrated. "Andrew, you know my secret. Are you the same?"

I shook my head. "No. I am…different."

My father had borne the Mark, but I wasn't cursed with the additional danger of bearing one myself. Life as a skin-changer was its own burden.

"But there is something," he pressed, never one to leave well enough alone.

I glanced toward the retreating backs of the soldiers ahead of us, then peered beyond the reach of Alexander's torchlight, making certain there was no one near enough to overhear our conversation.

I met his gaze, unblinking. "I'm not exactly what I appear to be. I never have been." When he didn't respond and merely continued to hold my gaze, I said, "Do you recall the stories our governess used to tell us when we were small?"

"Fairy stories, mostly," Alexander replied with a shrug.

I shook my head. "Not all of them were fairy stories, brother."

He frowned. "So, tell me. I'm growing impatient with you dancing around the subject like this. It's not like you."

I clenched my jaw and wished that it were easier to divulge the truth. The secret I'd borne for decades had only been known to our mother. When I was small, she'd protected me fiercely, aware the consequences would be dire should anyone learn the truth and alert the king. She'd protected Alexander in much the same way. To her, all life was sacred, rules be damned.

"Alex, do you remember when she spoke of the dragons?"

"Of course, those tales were always my favorite!" He grinned. "But those tales were true. Everyone knows the dragons existed, and the last of them only left about thirty-five years ago…" A slow realization dawned on him, and he stared at me with wide eyes. "Andrew, you can't mean…?"

The dragons had left our world only a few months before my birth, and I was certain he understood.

"I'm not fully human," I replied slowly. "I've never told a soul. Mother knew, of course."

"Wait a minute, Andrew. Are you saying you're half human? And half dragon?"

"A skin-changer," I confirmed. "Alex, you can't tell anyone." My voice became pleading, though I knew he would never betray my trust.

He shook his head, stunned and awestruck for a moment before breaking into a laugh. "That explains the noise. Just after you fell, there was a terrible sound—a *roar*. Then it happened again as I was nearing the pit. I've near heard anything like it. I believed the Corodan had built a new weapon, and I'd find you dead. But it was *you*." He laughed again. "Holy hell, that explains what happened to your gear. You didn't have time to remove it before you changed. And it explains why you were so damned stubborn about agreeing to their terms. You knew you'd come out unscathed."

"No, I didn't. I've never tested what I'm truly capable of. I learned today that dragonhide is incredibly tough, and the Corodans' blades were unable to penetrate it. But I didn't know that before."

"I understand now why mother asked you to look after me," Alexander flashed a grin. "You and I have more in common than I realized, brother."

# FIVE

Duke Everly's scouts returned the next morning with word there was no further Corodan activity in the area. Relieved, I informed the dukes and their soldiers they were free to return home. Alexander and I would depart for the Capitol with our own forces after stopping in Calder's Point for a final resupply.

The remainder of the day, and part of the next, was spent with soldiers breaking camp and moving on, eager to return to the warmth of their hearths. The weather had relented somewhat; it no longer snowed, but the bitter cold persisted. I wouldn't force our people to remain when it seemed the threat to our lands had been eliminated.

During the afternoon of the second day, a scout strode toward me, bearing news. "Sir, there's another Corodan emissary." Her face was drawn with worry. "Judging by its size, it must be one of the females."

I frowned. It was unusual for a female to venture anywhere without a contingent of subordinates, and the timing indicated the Corodan were aware we'd begun to depart. Duke Everly had disembarked only hours before.

"Is she alone?" I asked.

"Yes, sir. She's traveling from the north and bears a white banner. I'm not certain if they understand our signal for surrender, but it's similar. I don't trust her, given what occurred in the canyon."

I followed the scout to the northern edge of camp. A number of soldiers had stopped mid-task to stand ready as the Corodan approached. It was a female; there was no doubt given her size. She lumbered toward us unaccompanied, bearing an unadorned white banner, our universal signal of peaceful intent. I hoped it was so. I couldn't risk shifting into my dragon form with so many witnesses present.

Duke Horace and Alexander joined me a few moments later. Alexander held up one hand to shade his eyes from the sun's glare as it reflected against the snow. "What do you suppose this is about, Andrew?"

I shook my head. "I don't know. They've never acted in this manner before."

The Corodan paused as she came within bowshot of the camp and scanned the faces of our soldiers with her multi-faceted eyes. Weapons were drawn in anticipation of an attack, but I motioned for the soldiers to back down. I moved past those in the front and crossed half the distance toward her.

"Why have you come?" I called.

"I come not to fight," she rasped. "Peace. Peace."

I eyed her warily, then nodded. "Very well. We will speak."

She approached skittishly, wary of the other soldiers. "You are the commander?"

"Yes."

"You slew Krizzt-keh, Hive-queen," she stated. "A blessing."

I blinked in surprise. The other Corodan had disagreed with their former queen? Before I could form a response, she continued.

"Krizzt-keh became powerful more than thirty cycles ago. Krizzt-keh wanted war with humans. Many disagreed. Krizzt-keh sent signal, compelled us. We obeyed. We fought. We could not defy."

"I believe I understand," I replied evenly as she confirmed some of my longstanding suspicions regarding Corodan communication. "The Hive-queen I faced yesterday was Krizzt-keh?"

"Yes. Her signal faded. Gone forever. I come for peace."

"She forced your people to fight even though you didn't wish to?"

"Yes." The Corodan's voice dropped in volume, and she appeared remorseful. It was a behavior I'd never encountered from one of their kind. "Corodan wish peace. I am sent by Kash-kah, new Hive-queen. No more war. Peace. *Peace.*"

"How do we know you lot will keep your word?" Jonathan demanded as he strode forward to stand at my side. "After all that has happened, how can we trust your people to keep their word?"

"When Krizzt-keh fell, she sent final signal. We all felt. *Danger. Power. Death.* She feared the commander."

I tensed, terrified of what the creature might reveal. We didn't fully understand the Corodan system of communication; whether they transmitted mere emotions, or if they were capable of something more complex was a mystery. Was it possible the former Hive-queen knew what I was? Her final words were innocuous and vague, much to my benefit, but I could not be certain if the Corodan knew the truth of what had transpired—the truth about *me*.

"Kash-kah does not want war. Kash-kah wants peace. I am sent as messenger. Corodan want peace, now that Krizzt-keh is gone. Kash-kah compels. Peace."

"What do you make of it, Commander?" the duke asked, mystified.

"I believe she's genuine." I crossed my arms and studied the emissary. "Tell your new Hive-queen this: We will not pursue your people so long as you remain in the Highlands. The plains, here, are our lands. If the Corodan cross into our borders, we will defend ourselves."

She tilted her head to one side as though listening to something only she could hear. She remained in that position for several moments before she abruptly straightened. "Kash-kah accepts your terms. Kash-kah is pleased. Peace comes. I leave now."

As I turned to face the others, Jonathan was beaming. "Andrew, this is remarkable. Peace with the Corodan! Who would have believed it?"

It took the better part of three weeks to make the trek back to the Capitol. As we traveled south, snow gave way to rain, and the roads became muddy and treacherous, though the air was decidedly warmer. I was uncertain which weather condition had been worse on the soldiers and morale, but at least now, they had the prospect of home to look forward to.

Alexander sent word ahead of the agreement I'd unwittingly wrangled with the Corodan and the tenuous terms of peace that had been laid out. I anticipated a warm welcome upon our return, perhaps festivities to celebrate the end of our decades-long war. While it would be a fine way to celebrate our victory, I planned to make myself scarce. Festivities meant Colin would be present, and I hoped to avoid him.

As we neared the Capitol, one of the king's guardsmen met us on the road a few miles away. "Sir, the king has planned a grand feast to mark your heroic return. He has gathered the people of the city to watch as you and the army travel to the castle."

I groaned while Alexander laughed. "It sounds like father," he said, his cheer unblemished by my lackluster response.

Trumpeters were stationed atop the city walls. They began playing with fervor as we passed through the gates of the lower city, and more joined in the chorus from rooftops as we proceeded toward the upper city. The street was lined on both sides by townsfolk, many of whom waved banners and cheered despite the relentless rain. It took twice as long as would have been typical to reach the castle grounds due to the throngs, but the mood was festive and buoyant. Some of the bystanders darted into the street to embrace loved ones amongst the ranks, further slowing our progress, but I didn't mind.

The longer it took for us to reach the castle, the longer it would be before I was confronted with Colin's smirking countenance.

Beyond the gates of the upper city, the crowd remained just as dense as it had been below. There were more nobles in the upper city, come to see us home with their household staff in attendance. Many of the highborn onlookers waved to us from windows and balconies rather than be seen rain-drenched in the streets below.

The king himself met us in the castle's courtyard, flanked by Colin and Thomas. The king was in a convivial mood and Thomas was likewise thrilled to see us, but Colin scowled. I wondered what had transpired to cause his dour mood. Perhaps it was merely that I'd returned home successful, and he was forced to acknowledge my presence on orders of his father.

"Hail, Commander! And Prince Alexander! I welcome you home joyously. News of your brave deeds has preceded you." The king beamed at us. "A feast is being prepared to celebrate the peace you have wrought with our long-standing foes. We shall dine as the sun sets! For now, rest and be at ease."

"Thank you, sire," I said as I knelt before him. His speech was a mere formality, but I was obligated to continue in the same manner with so many eyes upon us.

"Father, the commander deserves all credit for what occurred in the north. I was merely a bystander," Alexander stated. He, too, had fallen into the formalities of court speech.

"Very good," the king replied. "I shall see you both at the feast tonight."

Dismissed, I rose to my feet. Colin had disappeared inside the castle, but Thomas bounded down the steps to greet us as the soldiers dispersed.

"When we received the message from Duke Horace, I could scarcely believe it!" Thomas was breathless in his excitement. "You've defeated the Hive-queen single-handedly, and you've negotiated with an emissary to achieve peace with the Corodan's new leader. The duke claimed the Hive-queen had a sizeable escort, and your combat prowess was unrivaled. Andrew, it's incredible!"

"Jon has a tendency to embellish his tales," I replied, uncomfortable with the attention.

I proceeded to tell him of the encounter with the second Corodan emissary. I didn't know if they'd keep their part of the bargain, but I was hopeful. It was more progress than we'd made in decades.

"We have fought for years with the Corodan," Thomas persisted, "and now we have peace. It's amazing. Everyone here thinks so."

I frowned. "Colin didn't seem overly pleased."

"Oh, he's angry about his betrothed refusing to join him to greet you," Thomas replied off-handedly, then his eyes widened and he froze. Clearly, he'd said something he believed he should not have.

"Tom, when did Colin announce his engagement?" Alexander asked. "We've been gone for two months. He wasn't involved with anyone—officially—when we left."

Thomas' face was as red as my commander's cloak. "I'm sorry, everyone here knows. It happened a few days after you left. I shouldn't have said anything…"

"Tom," I said evenly, "we need to know."

He fidgeted nervously, but forced himself to look at me with his wide blue eyes. "Andrew, it's…Claire Ellington."

I clenched my jaw, incensed, but I was unsurprised by the news. It was little wonder Claire had refused to greet us; she likely wanted nothing to do with me, even though I'd returned home from the Northern Marches a hero. It was easier to avoid me than apologize for her past behavior. It continued to irk me that she'd retaken her father's name after our marriage was nullified, even if it was permissible by law, given that I'd never been a Marsden. Her utter lack of regard for me—and all I'd done for her over the years—was infuriating.

"I'll be in the barracks until feast time should either of you need me," I growled.

Faced with the prospect of Colin and Claire together, I needed time alone. The castle gossips were no doubt poised to pounce on any encounter I might have with my former wife, eager to savor the renewed taste of my misfortune. The nobility rarely left the castle proper, and the barracks were seen as beneath their purview. It was my haven, the only place I could seek solace from the bored and spiteful amongst them.

I sought my quarters. My saddlebags had been delivered while I'd spoken with Thomas, and a stack of papers sat unread on my writing table. I noted they were invoices from the chamberlain and blacksmiths, tasks I could complete another time. I glanced toward the single window and found the practice yard empty due to the festivities of the day. My mind drifted as I stared through the rain-streaked panes.

I don't know how long I stood there, unraveling the tangle of my thoughts, but I was roused by a knock. I hoped it would be one of the soldiers or perhaps Alexander. To my dismay, it was Colin. He wore a smirk, while his blue eyes glittered maliciously.

"Hello, Andrew."

I ground my teeth together. Protocol dictated that I address him as nobility and the future king, though I sorely wanted to ignore it. "Sire."

He arched an eyebrow, amused, and pushed his way inside the room. "I see you've learned some manners since our last conversation. You know, father told me you could have your old room in the castle returned to you if you wished it."

"This suits me."

He laughed. "I suppose it would, given your station."

I clenched my jaw and resisted the urge to throw a punch at him. "Why are you here?"

"Well, it has been almost two months since you left with the army. Good job on that bit of business up north. Who knew you were such a skilled negotiator?" His tone was carefully modulated to exude boredom, yet it was filled with subtle venom. "But back to the matter at hand. I'm sure you've heard of my betrothal by now?"

I swallowed and looked down at my hands. My jaw was clenched so tightly it had begun to ache. "I have. I would offer you my congratulations, but I'm sure you understand why I will not."

The smirk returned to Colin's face. "Claire deserves better than a no-name military grunt." He examined his fingernails as if the conversation no longer deserved his attention. "She allowed me to see the annulment papers, Andrew. She thinks you're sterile."

I closed my eyes in an attempt to steady myself. It was my final effort to engage him without violence. "She can think whatever she wants. She's your problem now."

This new, vindictive side of Claire had only surfaced when I'd come to her with the truth of my parentage. Or perhaps it had always been there, and I'd been blind to it out of misguided devotion to her. Regardless of its source, it soured my temper.

"Oh, but she's used goods," Colin replied off-handedly. "At least her dowry is worth something."

Rage nearly blinded me. "Get out, Colin."

He moved toward the door, stunned by my reaction, but it seemed he realized he'd gone too far. "Gladly. If I stay any longer, the reek of the commonfolk will soil my clothes."

I sat down heavily on the bed after his departure and waited for my anger to subside. I'd nearly come to terms with Claire's betrayal, but I would never abide hearing a man speak so rudely of a woman, no matter who she might be. As deeply as Claire had wounded me with her actions, she deserved better than a petty schemer like Colin.

After my encounter with Colin, I desperately needed some air.

I took up my sword and made my way to the practice yard, despite the rain. It was better to vent my frustrations on a straw-filled training dummy than on one of the soldiers. Angry as I was, I failed to rein in my strength as I'd become accustomed to doing over the years. On my second swing, I drove my sword clean through the straw sack and into the thick post it was attached to. The blade wasn't designed to withstand the force. It splintered on impact, while the post snapped in two. I cursed aloud, drawing the attention of one of the soldiers as she strode by.

Ignoring her stare, I gathered the broken shards of steel and trudged in the direction of the blacksmith's forge. I left the mangled dummy, the broken post, and a cascade of straw in my wake. I'd meant to visit him another day, but my temper had forced a change in plans. I'd need a replacement sword, and I needed to speak with him regarding the armor I'd ruined during my fight with the Hive-queen.

The forge was staffed by a half dozen brawny men and women of various ages, but Desmond Gill was their leader. I'd always been on friendly terms with him, and that hadn't changed since Colin had been named heir to the throne. If anything, the fact that I'd never been nobility seemed to have solidified his opinion of me.

As I approached the forge, I noted that only he and a young man, likely an apprentice, were at work. No doubt he'd given the others leave to enjoy the festivities.

"Commander! It's always good to see you return." Desmond greeted me with a vigorous handshake. "I heard you killed that Hive-queen alone. You've always been quite the swordsman." It was then that he noticed what I carried in my free hand. "Ah, I see why you've come."

He collected the shards with a sad shake of his head. "I don't think I can repair this blade, Andrew. I can salvage the hilt, perhaps, but it would be best to forge the blade anew."

I nodded, resigned; I'd expected this outcome. "I also need a new set of armor."

His eyebrows shot up in surprise. "Your armor was crafted by my predecessor. It's a beautiful piece of work. What happened to it? No, don't tell me. It's probably best I don't know."

Desmond was a firm believer that blacksmithing was one of the highest artforms. Each item he crafted was exquisitely made, durable, and in the case of weapons, lethal. I could think of no one better to head the king's forges.

"Will you need measurements?" I asked.

He shook his head. "That won't be necessary. I have everything on file. Did you know the king finally gave in last year and allowed me access to one of his scribes once a week? They've been cataloging the garrison's specifications. Now everyone who comes to me for new armor only has to ask—I have all of their information at hand!"

I smiled in response. Simply hearing him talk about his work was soothing. Desmond didn't pass judgment on others for their misfortunes and refused to participate in castle gossip on principle. I wished more of the castle's residents would follow his example, but few bothered to converse with the genial smith unless they were a member of the garrison.

"The sword can be readied by the end of the week," he continued. "I'll craft it myself. As you know, blades are my specialty." He glanced at the young man working not far away. "The armor will take more time, but Liam shows great promise. Perhaps an order for the commander is the spark he needs to realize his true potential."

"With peace on the horizon, I hope I won't have need of the armor anytime soon. Take all the time you need." I shook his hand again, then bid him farewell.

My mood much improved, I returned to my quarters in the barracks. I needed to bathe before the feast and don a fresh set of clothes.

An hour later, I made my way toward the great hall. The sun had begun its final descent toward the western horizon as I reached the doors. A pair of guardsmen stood on either side of the entrance, dressed in ceremonial finery trimmed in ivory, crimson, and gold. One held a pair of colorful banners aloft. The doors were thrown wide, and the drone of conversation greeted me from within. Most of the tables were filled, with the exception of the king's table at the far end of the room. The hearths on each side blazed merrily, providing warmth and a welcoming ambiance.

The chamberlain bustled up to me as I entered, then frowned. "Andrew, I'm glad you've finally arrived. The king asked that you dine at the head table tonight. I have set aside a place for you on the end."

He gestured to the left-hand side of the table. There was an open seat between a woman whom I recognized vaguely, and Duke

Crossley's eldest son, Emile. Only the center of the table was empty; the king and his immediate family would enter last, according to royal protocol.

I nodded. "Thank you."

I took up my assigned seat as a pang of sadness twisted my gut. For most of my life, I'd been seated with the king and my half-brothers, but no longer. So much had changed, and little of it for the better.

"You're the commander, are you not?" the woman beside me asked.

I turned toward her. She had fair skin, red-gold hair framing a delicate face, and appeared to be of an age with me. She was familiar, yet I could not place how I knew her.

"Yes," I replied. "And you are?"

She laughed. "I see you don't remember me. Lord Sandson was my late husband."

I nodded, recalling her name, and swallowed my embarrassment at the lapse. Lord Sandson had been aged, and many of the court ladies pitied Vera when her father agreed to the marriage. I'd stopped by Sandson's estate during my travels with the army to resupply on occasion. I remembered hearing of his passing, perhaps five or six months prior. Her connection to Sandson was not the source of my chagrin, however; Vera was the king's niece, and I'd interacted with her numerous times since we were children. I should have recognized her immediately.

"Lady Vera, yes, I remember you now."

She smiled knowingly. "Don't fret. Given all that has happened recently, I don't blame you for having a faulty memory."

As I was about to reply, a pair of trumpeters began to play a brassy fanfare behind us. We rose to greet the royal family as they entered, along with everyone else gathered in the vast hall. I watched as the king, followed by my three half-brothers and Claire, made their way down the steps behind the table and came to stand behind their allotted seats. Thomas fidgeted and glanced across the packed hall nervously. Beside him, Alexander appeared weary. On the other side of the king, Colin stood with Claire on his arm. She gazed forward with an icy demeanor while Colin openly leered at me. I forced myself to look away and stared at the polished wooden table top.

The king spoke briefly before announcing that the feast should be served. I was so focused on ignoring Colin that I missed the entirety of his brief speech.

"It's in poor taste that he flaunts her about so," Vera said quietly as we resumed our seats. "It's obvious he only acts as he does to anger you."

I shrugged. "I'm doing my best to ignore him."

"Sound judgment," she agreed as the first course, an onion soup, was served. "You should not allow him to ruin your evening. After all, the king said this feast is being held in your honor, and Prince Alexander's, of course. We wouldn't be enjoying peacetime without your brave deeds."

"I suppose so, but I tire of all the pomp and fanfare. I wish this was over." Colin had soured my mood, and her attempts at small talk did little to improve it.

"Oh, come now," she countered with a laugh. "Your men are surely happy to be home after weeks spent marching through the snow. Let them enjoy themselves. You're entirely too serious, Andrew. May I call you that?"

I managed a smile. "Yes. That is my name, after all."

"You know, I was first introduced to you when we were both children. My mother brought me to court here in the Capitol." She took a sip of soup before continuing. "It was mid-summer. You'd go to the practice yard every morning to hone your skills. I used to watch you from the balcony of our quarters."

I looked up at her sharply, uncertain of where her story was headed.

"I told my mother that I fancied you, and she slapped me for it." A shadow passed over her face at the memory. "She believed we were cousins, Andrew. It would have been forbidden."

I frowned at my nearly empty bowl. "I suppose I ought to apologize for what happened to you. We aren't cousins."

"All of that is in the past." She waved one delicate hand dismissively and smiled. "It doesn't matter. I'm the second daughter of the king's youngest brother. It was never my station to choose the man I married. Father saw to that."

The second course was served then, a meat pie with a flaky crust and thick gravy. Servants scurried between us to remove the dirtied dishes and refill flagons of wine.

"Don't misunderstand me," she continued, "Lord Sandson was kind. He even left me his estate when he died. Vinterry has a wonderful vineyard." Her tone was wistful and tinged with sadness.

"I'm glad to hear he was kind," I replied. "When the match was made, it caused quite the stir. I recall my mother was particularly incensed."

She arched an eyebrow. "Her Ladyship cared about me?"

I smiled; I had little but fond memories of my mother. "She cared about everyone. She would have reversed the betrothal if she'd held the power, but the laws wouldn't allow it."

"It's nice to know that someone was concerned for my welfare."

I studied her for a time, taking in her lightly freckled countenance, the soft curve of her lips as she smiled, the way the firelight danced within her blue eyes and caused them to sparkle. Vera Sandson was a beautiful woman.

"It was not a bad marriage," she went on. "Yes, he was thrice my age, but as I said, he was kind. I was left with enough gold after his passing that I'll never be forced to remarry unless I choose to."

I realized I'd relaxed significantly simply through the act of talking with her. She had an easy manner, and she didn't seem to be making an attempt to pry into my affairs. Had I been seated alongside any other lady of the court, they would have been hanging on my every word simply for the sake of gossip. Vera was genuine, and I found I enjoyed her company. Her demeanor was a refreshing change from that of most noblewomen.

"Tell me of your vineyard," I said.

"There isn't much to tell at present," she replied and graced me with another smile. "In a month, the vines will start to green and leaf out. By the end of summer, they'll produce the most wonderful red grapes, perfect for making good, strong wine." She paused to scan my face, gauging my reaction. "Perhaps if your duties allow it, you can visit my estate one day."

The prospect of a visit held a certain appeal, and we were both unattached. I couldn't deny I liked being around her, and with each moment I spent at her side, my attraction grew.

"Perhaps I will."

Her smile illuminated her face. "I look forward to it."

We engaged in small talk for the duration of the next two courses. For the first time in weeks, my thoughts were not dogged by my misfortunes or Claire, and many of my worries began to fade. Perhaps it was time to finally move on and forget the woman I'd spent four years trying—and failing—to please. Vera was markedly different, and I craved a change for the better.

As the final course was served, Colin rose from his seat. He swayed slightly, and his face was flushed; he'd clearly had his fill of wine. Alexander frowned while the king narrowed his eyes in disapproval, but he did nothing to stop Colin from speaking.

"I have an announcement!" he shouted above the din of the crowd, then waited impatiently as the drone of voices vanished into nothingness.

"The Lady Claire and I have set our wedding date," he continued. "We shall be wed on mid-summer's eve." He turned his bleary gaze in my direction. "Ours will be a truly *royal* wedding. Commoners will not be allowed."

I clenched my jaw as he returned to his seat, my hands balled into fists. Colin was making a point to humiliate me at every turn. I wanted to believe it was due to the alcohol he'd consumed, but I knew my half-brother's temperament. Colin antagonized me simply because he could do so without repercussion, and there was very little I could do to counteract him.

Claire stood to address the hall. "What my betrothed means is the ceremony will be closed to all but nobility." Her icy stare arced briefly in my direction. "There will be a grand parade throughout the whole of the Capitol, however, and anyone may attend that affair."

I was on my feet in an instant. The room had become stifling, and I would abide no more of Colin's taunts nor Claire's pointed insults. I had to take my leave of the feast before my temper flared beyond my control.

I strode toward the nearest exit, a side door that led to the winter-barren courtyard beyond. The air was cool, and the beginnings of frost sparkled on the ground in the pale moonlight. I stood still and breathed deeply in an attempt to calm my rage. It had been one matter when Colin openly snubbed me, but when Claire joined him, it was more than I could bear. In spite of everything she'd done, I still cared for her. I cursed myself for a fool and gazed up at the night sky, seeking answers from the silent stars above.

I was startled by a light touch on my arm. I looked down to find Vera standing at my side.

"That was appalling," she whispered. "Andrew, I fear for the future of our kingdom with that pair coming into power."

"As do I." I sighed and returned my gaze skyward. The moon was at three-quarters; its pale glow radiated outward to form a shimmering halo in the chill air.

Vera took my hand in hers; her touch was soft and cool. "You are not alone, Andrew."

I looked at her once more and managed a tired smile. "Thank you." In that moment, I knew that even if nothing else developed between us, Vera Sandson could be counted amongst my dwindling number of true friends. "May I escort you to your quarters?"

She smiled. "Yes. That would be nice."

She took my arm as we reentered the castle. We walked a circuitous route to avoid the great hall and its guests, though we encountered a few who watched us pass with unconcealed curiosity. Her room was located on the second floor directly above the kitchens, and we took our time reaching the destination. We said little, but simply being near her was enough to grant me a sense of peace. It was a sensation I was unfamiliar with, but I found it soothing.

"How long do you plan to stay in the castle?" I asked as we neared her door.

"Until the end of the month," she replied. "Perhaps a bit longer if traveling conditions are unfavorable." She held my gaze as another smile crept across her lips. "I hope to see you again, Andrew."

I returned her smile, marveling at the way her eyes sparkled in the dim torch-light of the corridor. "I'd like that."

"Good." Impulsively, she stood on her tip-toes and brushed my cheek with her lips. "I look forward to our next meeting. Good night, Commander."

I stared after her, dumbstruck, as she disappeared into her room. Given all that had transpired with Claire and her vicious rumors, I'd believed I would be deemed undesirable by any woman who crossed my path. I possessed no lands, no title, and could never provide her with an heir; I no longer even held a surname.

Yet Vera was clearly interested. My pulse had thrummed and quickened at her brief kiss, and I knew I must see her again. Only during the early days of our betrothal had Claire managed to have the same effect on me. Her personality had rapidly dissolved my attraction—but Vera was different.

I lingered in the corridor for some time while I sorted through my thoughts, then returned to the ground floor. I made my way to my quarters in the barracks while bypassing the great hall once again. My evening with Vera had calmed my ire enough that I believed I'd sleep peacefully.

Alexander awaited me when I arrived. He'd built a fire in the hearth and lounged against the wall next to it, relishing the warmth.

"Where have you been?" he demanded. "I thought I'd find you skulking here when I left the feast, but I've been waiting a while."

"I see that." I kicked off my boots and sat on the edge of my bed facing him. "I was speaking with Lady Vera."

He smirked. "I thought you might like one another. I asked my father to have her seated near you. She's kind and thoughtful—and she's always held an interest in you, if the rumors are true."

I grunted in mock annoyance, but didn't deny he'd been right. "I didn't need a matchmaker, brother. But, thank you."

He laughed. "The mighty Andrew doesn't always see what's best for himself. I have to look out for you too." He sighed then and appeared pensive. "I wanted to speak with you because some other events occurred after your departure from the feast. You ought to know what happened."

"If it's about Claire and Colin, I'm not sure I want to hear it." I'd suffered enough humiliation at their hands for one day.

"Oh, no, you'll want to hear this, Andrew. Father was furious at what they said about their wedding and publicly shamed them. He told Colin he was an unworthy sod, and it was a shame the laws had forced his hand. He said Colin was an unworthy heir! I thought Colin was going to spew his wine half way across the room."

I arched an eyebrow. The king must have been furious if he'd confronted Colin in a public setting. It was a rare occurrence to witness Carlton lose his temper, even in private.

Alexander continued, warming to his tale. "Then he turned to Claire. He told her that even though you were not his son, you were still of noble birth on your mother's side, and therefore the laws allowed you to attend the ceremony if you wished it. He told her to drop her ridiculous notions of vengeance and behave like a proper lady. I thought she was going to choke on her berry tart." He laughed gleefully. "She wronged you, brother, and everyone sees that. She hasn't tried to hide the fact that she sought Colin's hand simply for the prestige and title."

"I hope Colin will leave me be from now on," I replied more acidly than I'd intended. "I've no intention of attending his wedding, invitation or no."

Alexander frowned. "You may have no choice in the matter, Andrew. Father practically ordered that he invite you." He paused to scratch the back of his neck. "Colin was none too happy about it, either. I didn't hear what Colin said in response, but it could not have been good. Father was enraged, and he left the banquet. He's never done that before."

It was troubling that Colin had gone so far as to cause the king to leave his own feast prematurely. Colin had always been a self-centered ass, but his behavior this evening had been intolerable. I wondered how much of Claire's icy demeanor was simply the result of her proximity to my half-brother, rather than from the animosity she bore for me.

"Do you suppose his newly-acquired power has gone to his head, or is it something else?" I mused.

Alexander shrugged. "I miss the days when he thought you were the next king, Andrew. You could put him in his place without repercussion."

I looked down at the smooth stone floor. "Perhaps that's the only reason the king drew out our charade for so long. Colin was more likely to behave." I leaned back with a sigh. "Have you spoken to Thomas about your needless plans?"

Alexander nodded. "I told him it was useless to continue down that path. I didn't tell him why, only that you had information on your real father that made any claim you had invalid. Now he seems to think mother was in a dalliance with an outlaw or pirate before she met father…"

I chuckled. It was so like Thomas to allow his imagination to wander. "I suppose that's the best I can hope for. He can't learn the truth."

"Agreed." Alexander's tone was uncharacteristically serious. "We're in this together, brother, like it or not."

# SIX

It was nearly two days before I found time to see Vera again, but she'd been a constant in my thoughts. Claire had never managed to preoccupy me so thoroughly, even in the early months of our marriage when things between us had been better. Perhaps it was the mere fact that Vera seemed to care for me as a person rather than as a means to an end. Regardless, she'd captured my attention.

I met Vera in the rose garden behind the castle. The plots were bare, though I spied the red-purple nubs that would soon become leaves along the carefully pruned stems, the first indication spring was drawing near. The gardens were peaceful and rarely visited by the nobility during the winter months; they were a respite.

The snow had begun to melt, and the afternoon sun was warm enough that Vera opted not to wear her fur-lined winter cloak. She wore a woolen dress of dark blue, and her hair was pinned up in one of the current favored fashions. She smiled warmly at my approach.

I offered her my arm, which she readily accepted. We began to walk along the crushed gravel path that wound through the garden. It would be awash in color within a few short months, but at present was little more than greening stems poking up from the mud. I was content in a way that I had not experienced in many years.

"I wish I could have come sooner," I lamented. "The king gave me a list of tasks to fulfill, and I've been unable to take my leave of the barracks until now."

"I would have waited longer if you'd asked." She smiled wistfully. "Perhaps I'm being foolish, but I often dreamed of you, Andrew. I thought we could never be together, based on your station, and then father married me off like some prize. If he and my mother were still alive, they would likely have forced me into another marriage by now. Since they are gone and I am a widow, it has given me time to consider what I truly want from life."

"And what do you want, my lady?" I asked.

"If I remarry, it will be for love," she replied softly. "I'm not certain I know what it feels like, but it should prove interesting to learn."

My desire was strong, and patience wasn't something I excelled in, but I would not rush her decision. We were relative strangers, learning to navigate our attraction, but I would give her the time and space to make up her mind. At present, I was content to stroll through the winter-bare garden and learn more of her thoughts and desires.

"I'm still trying to understand how I was placed at the head table for the feast," she mused. "I'm the king's niece and the widow of a minor lord. I thought it strange."

I chuckled. "That was Alexander's doing."

She arched an eyebrow. "I didn't realize he'd taken notice of me."

"He seemed to think that seating us together would make for interesting dinner conversation. I also believe it was an attempt on his part to distract me from Claire," I added with a shrug.

"Your brother fancies himself a matchmaker, hmm?" she asked playfully. "I suppose he hasn't done a bad job so far."

I looked down at her, amused. "It doesn't bother you?"

She laughed. "Of course not. I see no harm in what he did, and if nothing else, I've found friendship where I had none before." She paused to study a patch of roses that would bloom crimson come high summer. "Being the topic of court gossip tends to dissolve friendships. After my marriage to Lord Sandson, it was all anyone wished to speak with me about. I grew weary of it and stopped making the journey here."

"What brought you to the Capitol this time?"

"As a Marsden by birth, it was expected that I travel here to give Colin my congratulations once the betrothal was announced," she replied with a frown. "Storms began a few days after my arrival and have made traveling too dangerous, so I decided to stay until the Spring Festival. The Capitol is lovely during that time, and it has been many years since I was last present to witness it."

The Spring Festival was in a little over three weeks. The king had already commissioned hundreds of vendors and traveling performers for the event, and the entire city would be festooned in spring blooms: tulips, daffodils, crocus, and lilies. The annual event lasted several days and often heralded the onset of warmer weather.

She looked up at me with her clear, blue eyes. The afternoon sun shone in her auburn hair, bringing out its reddish tones. I smiled, unable to stop myself; she was beautiful.

"Andrew, I'd like to ask you something."

"Of course."

"You shouldn't commit so readily without having heard what it is," she teased.

I grinned. "Very well, then. What is it you need, my lady?"

She rolled her eyes at my mock formality. "I was hoping to arrange a modest escort when I return to Vinterry. I thought perhaps you could spare a few of your men?"

The flicker of an idea came to me then, and I nodded. "Perhaps I can arrange to escort you myself."

She lifted her eyebrows in mild surprise but continued to smile. "That is a very generous offer. I hope it won't be too much of a bother."

If she only knew the depth of my attraction, she would have understood that I'd have done anything she asked of me. I was convinced I'd never harbored feelings of this magnitude for Claire. My sudden awareness of it only heightened my interest in Vera all the more.

"I don't think you could ever be a bother, Vera."

She met my gaze and held it for several moments without speaking. Her eyes were the same rich color as the cloudless sky. I could have gazed into them for an eternity.

"Perhaps I misspoke earlier when I mentioned love." She smiled, eyes sparkling. "I think I'm beginning to understand."

I reached up to touch the side of her face. Her skin was cool, but she blushed prettily at the contact. I wanted desperately to kiss her, but the timing wasn't right. Amongst nobility, there were rules for courtship—none of which I was currently following—and I feared to push her too far too soon.

She placed her hand atop mine and leaned into my palm. "This is nice."

I smiled and reluctantly pulled my hand away. "If we continue to see one another like this, there will be more court scandal, you know."

She nodded. "I've considered that. And frankly, I don't care."

I grinned. "May I see you again tomorrow?"

"Yes. And the day after as well."

During the next two weeks, I set my plans for Vera's escort in motion. I spoke to several of my lieutenants; there was one I had in mind for the job, but I didn't tell them of my scheme. I couldn't risk an uproar amongst the castle garrison until after I'd spoken with the king.

I requested a private audience and was granted one during my second week of plotting. I knew he'd be disappointed with my request, but I also believed he'd understand my reasons for making it.

"Andrew, welcome," he said as I was ushered into his private study. "I've heard most of the tasks I set before you have been completed. Are you here looking for more work?"

I knelt in deference to him, but he bade me stand up again.

"No, sire, I've come on other business."

He looked at me sharply, his gaze unreadable. This was going to be more difficult than I'd anticipated.

"I would like to name Jerrick Vine as commander of the forces, and I request to formally resign from my post." I met his gaze unflinchingly and noted the sudden flash of disappointment in his eyes.

After a long moment, he sighed heavily and nodded. "Tell me of this Jerrick Vine. What makes him the best choice for commander?"

I launched into a lengthy description of Jerrick's years of service, his deeds on the battlefield, his knack for strategy. I was certain the army would be in good hands.

"And why do you seek to step down?" He was always one to save the most critical questions for the end of a conversation.

"With the Corodan threat eliminated, I see no good reason to continue. I'd also like the freedom to travel—"

"We both know this has more to do with Colin than you are letting on. I don't fault you for your desire to leave the Capitol. As long as I reign, you will always be welcome here, no matter what Colin may say or do. Do you understand?"

I nodded. "I plan to leave after the Spring Festival."

He nodded again, unable to conceal the sadness in his eyes. "We will speak again before then. You may not be my son, but I've always loved you as one of my own. Don't allow Colin's actions to distance you from your family. And you *are* family, if not by blood."

"Thank you, sire."

I looked away, unaccustomed to the well of emotion swirling within. He'd always been good to me, and he'd been the best mentor and role-model any boy could have hoped for.

"You're a good man, Andrew. You will do well, no matter what you choose to do with your life."

I nodded and swallowed the complicated emotions that had threatened to overwhelm me. "I will never be able to repay you for your kindness over the years. I thank you, sire. For everything."

As I took my leave, I anticipated our final farewell would prove difficult. He wasn't wrong when he referred to Colin as the primary reason behind my departure. Damn Colin and his condescending ways.

I returned to the barracks, stopped in my quarters to retrieve an item, then sought Jerrick. Upon delivering my news, he was at once both elated and shocked. I'd never seen him at a loss for words, but today he struggled to find his voice. I watched as a range of emotions played over his gruff features and offered him an understanding smile.

"Jerrick, I've chosen you, and the king was impressed with your skills. You'll do well." I reached into a pocket and withdrew the deck of cards we'd often used to play Cabal's Thrall. "It's the commander's deck," I said, and pressed it into his hands. "It belongs to you now."

He stared at the cards for a moment, then shook his head. "But, sir, where are you going?"

I shrugged. "Away from the Capitol. I haven't decided on a final destination, but this place has become stifling. I think it's best that I leave."

It was true; my final destination had not been set. I intended to escort Vera as promised and looked forward to more time spent at her side. Being near Vera was akin to standing in the sunlight after a lifetime mired in darkness; after only a fortnight, I was well and truly smitten.

I hoped our relationship would continue to progress favorably, but nothing was certain. Perhaps by the time the festival arrived, I'd have a better understanding of my future.

Jerrick nodded thoughtfully. "Your brother isn't making it easy on you, I've heard. Might be best to head away for a time. I thank you for the honor, sir. I didn't know you'd planned to name me as your successor."

I clapped him roughly on the shoulder. "I thought it would be best to keep it a surprise."

I left to gather my scant belongings from the commander's quarters and move them into one of the standard rooms. Jerrick would need the extra space they afforded, whereas I no longer did. As I entered, I spied a note from Desmond on the table. My new armor was awaiting me at the forges. I smiled and tucked the note in my pocket before I began the task of moving my things.

Perhaps an hour later, there was a light tap on the door. I turned to find Vera in a gown of pale gold, a white cloak thrown over her shoulders. She smiled, though I could see a dozen questions in her eyes. I welcomed her inside, where she perched carefully on a wooden chair.

"Andrew, I heard you've stepped down from your post. From the looks of it, the rumor is true."

I nodded. "I spoke with the king, and I've named a replacement."

Concern etched her features. "I don't understand."

I stopped packing my wardrobe and knelt before her, then took her hands in mine as I gazed into her eyes. "Vera, I'm not leaving until the festival is over. I still intend to escort you home as promised, but I won't return here. This place holds too many foul memories, and I've grown weary of Colin's jibes."

She nodded uncertainly. "Where do you plan to go?"

I shook my head. "I…don't know."

"Hmm." She appeared thoughtful and turned her head to stare out the window. I would miss the view of the practice yard; my new room did not have the luxury of a window.

I stood and released her hands while she turned to face me, her eyes narrowed in thought.

"Meet me in the rose garden when you're finished," she said. "I'd like to walk, as we have so often done. It helps me think more clearly." She offered me a smile then. "I also enjoy your companionship."

I grinned. "I'm nearly finished. These are the last of my personal effects."

"Then I shall wait for you," she replied. "We can walk to the garden together from here."

I nodded and gathered the last of my items. She followed me as I headed to my new space at the end of the corridor. The room was half the size of the commander's quarters, with only enough space for a bed and a single chair. It sported a small hearth, but without windows, the room was dim. I dropped the last of my items unceremoniously on the bed, then turned to Vera. I offered her my arm as we prepared to leave.

She smiled and accepted, then we made our way outside. We'd be forced to walk through most of the castle's outdoor commons to reach the rose garden; it would be impossible not to draw someone's notice at this hour of the day. During our previous excursions, we'd traveled to the garden separately. We walked from the barracks, past the smithy, and were passing the stables before she broke our amicable silence.

"I've been thinking, Andrew."

"And what has been on your mind, my lady?" I asked.

She blushed prettily. "You."

"What would you like to know?"

"Hmm, what wouldn't I like to know is the better question." She laughed lightly. "I believed I'd solved the puzzle that is Andrew, but the news about you leaving the commander's post came as a surprise. You never struck me as impulsive, so I believe you've planned this for some time."

"Not truly," I replied. "I made the decision only recently."

She arched an eyebrow. "Perhaps I was wrong about you."

I shook my head. "Most of the time, I plan things well ahead of time. This decision... Perhaps it was rash, but I need to leave. It's past time."

We walked in silence for several minutes and finally entered the rose garden.

"You know, I need someone to help with the vineyards at home," she said slowly. "Someone hard-working and strong."

My heart leapt at the implication. "Vera—"

She turned to face me and pressed one finger to my lips. "Hush, Andrew, I'm not finished." She grinned bashfully. "There is an important condition that comes with this offer. I know we are still learning about one another, but I believe this is the right path. The offer is only valid for a man who is my husband."

I blinked, thunderstruck. I'd hoped she felt as I did, desperately needed her to, and now that she'd spoken the words aloud, I was momentarily stunned. I recovered as quickly as I could manage and drew her into my embrace. I found her lips with my own, no longer concerned if anyone might see us or what they might say. Perhaps my fortunes were finally changing for the better. I lost myself in her arms for a moment, and when we parted, I was breathless.

"Vera," I said, beaming, "allow me to make a few arrangements. I'd hoped—dreamed—that this moment would come. I want to do this right. For you."

Her smile was dazzling. "I feared if I was too forward, it would drive you away. It seems you've been holding back."

"I wanted to be certain," I replied uneasily. "I have nothing to offer you but myself. I have no lands, no title—"

"Andrew, none of that matters," she said with a laugh. "I simply want what I've always wanted—*you*."

I kissed her again. I wished the moment would never end.

It took several days, but I called in my remaining favors with the various craftsmen around the castle. I commissioned a pair of gold rings to be fashioned and spoke to the tailor regarding a proper gown for Vera. She was delighted at the prospect of sewing something for a noble lady other than Claire or her retinue. Finally, I spoke to the chaplain and one of the notaries.

The king offered us the use of the castle's solarium for the ceremony once I informed him of our intentions. It was a regal space with an abundance of natural light, yet a room not often frequented in the castle. It wouldn't draw unwanted attention—or the ire of Colin, who would likely see it as an insult that I planned to remarry before he wedded Claire.

I was simply grateful to have a space inside the castle proper, to be acknowledged for the years of service I'd given the king. And Vera was radiant with each new preparation she made.

I asked that a feast not be prepared in our honor, considering how badly the last one had gone. Reluctantly, the king agreed. We planned to hold the ceremony during the afternoon on the first day of the Spring Festival.

For her part, Vera worked diligently with the castle chamberlain to secure flowers for the solarium. She painstakingly penned official invitations to those we wished to have in attendance and distributed them in person once they were complete.

While we busied ourselves with preparations, the castle gossips wasted no time in spreading word of our upcoming nuptials—and our scandalously short engagement. Whispers abounded when I passed through the castle on business, but I paid them no heed. For the first time in my adult life, I was truly happy. I was at peace.

I saw little of Colin and nothing of Claire. We sent the pair an invitation, much to my chagrin, but if we did not, there would be hell to pay. I feared one or both of them would attend simply to cause another scene, but Vera assured me it was unlikely. I hoped she was right; she deserved better than my half-brother's petty insults and Claire's withering glares.

By the time everything was in place, there were only four days remaining before the Spring Festival was set to begin.

Those four days could not pass quickly enough.

# SEVEN

Vera and I walked through the rose garden. It had become our habit, our respite from the bustle of the castle and preparations for our wedding. It was afternoon on the third day prior to our scheduled ceremony.

The garden was beginning to show signs of life after the long winter; the canes had become a vibrant red-green, while the first leaves had unfurled to take in sunlight. We spoke of the wedding and our future at Vinterry. The day was warm, and I was content.

We'd been strolling for only a few minutes when we were interrupted by the sound of rapid footsteps crunching on the gravel path behind us. I turned to see who approached, and was dismayed to see Claire.

She was dressed in more finery than she'd ever donned during our marriage. She wore a satin gown of crimson and fine white lace, a white cloak, and a ruby necklace. Her dark hair was pulled back from her face but hung long in the back, where it fell in loose curls to her waist. Her expression was unreadable, though her dark eyes glittered with intent. I hadn't spoken to her directly since I'd signed the annulment months ago.

She stopped a dozen steps away and studied us thoughtfully. "Colin has forbidden me from attending your wedding," she stated woodenly. "I know I've behaved terribly, Andrew, but I wanted to offer my congratulations. There was a time when I believed I loved you. But *we* were not meant to be."

"Claire…" I began uncertainly, concerned by her words.

Colin had *forbidden* her to attend? I'd been expecting her to decline the invitation out of spite, but her words gave me pause.

"There is nothing you can do to assist me, Andrew." She offered me a faltering smile, and I realized she was on the brink of tears. "Colin will not attend your ceremony. He seeks to further your humiliation as much as he is able before you leave the Capitol." She swallowed and drew a shuddering breath. "I spoke with the king. You'll have armed guards at your ceremony. I fear Colin has something dire planned."

"What do you mean?" Vera asked, one delicate hand rising toward her throat.

Claire shook her head as the first of her tears burst forth. "He ordered me not to speak with you, but... I can't sit idly by and allow him to go through with his schemes!" A heart-wrenching sob escaped her, and she covered her face with her hands.

Vera strode to her side and consoled her softly. I stood rooted to the spot, uncertain what I should do and stunned by Claire's revelation.

"I've told you what I know," Claire sniffed after a minute. "Please, be careful. Both of you." She turned on her heel and fled back the way she'd come.

Vera stared after her, then returned to my side. She took my hands in hers. "Andrew, why is Colin so set on your destruction?"

I shook my head, baffled. We'd always had our differences, but his recent animosity was beyond reason.

"I don't know."

She sighed. "It makes me uneasy. It will be a blessing when we finally depart."

That evening, we took our supper in the great hall at one of the side tables. The hall was bursting with activity in preparation for the festival; bouquets adorned the walls, doors, and nearly every open surface within, while chains of white daisies hung from the chandeliers.

But the festive mood was dampened by the guards seated on either side of us. They'd met us before we left the rose garden and had refused to leave, despite my protests. The king had sent them in the wake of Claire's visit.

They were watchful, their eyes restlessly scanning the great hall for any sign of trouble. It was difficult to have a meaningful conversation with them nearby, and their presence only increased my tension. Undeterred by our escort, Colin had the audacity to stroll toward our table with a smirk.

He leered down at me. "I won't be attending your wedding, Andrew."

"I'm not surprised." I turned back to my food, hoping he'd grow bored and leave.

"I've told Claire she is not to send you an invitation to our wedding, either. I don't care what father said."

I looked up, nonplussed. His malicious sneer was maddening, but I would not rise up in anger. The intent of his visit was plain; he was trying to provoke me into an act I'd regret.

"I wasn't planning to attend."

He clenched his jaw as the conversation took a turn he'd failed to anticipate. "This isn't over, Andrew."

I met his gaze and kept my features neutral, though I sorely wished to end the confrontation with my fists. I held my temper, and after a moment, he snorted in disgust and stormed away. I shook my head and turned back to Vera. She was visibly outraged.

"He was trying to prod my temper," I told her with a shrug. "Contrary to the rumors you might hear around the barracks, I *can* keep it in check when I need to."

"I'm grateful. I wanted to slap that awful look off his face," she replied. "I know why you kept your composure, and I thank you. It wouldn't do to have you locked in the dungeons so close to our wedding date."

I grinned. She'd learned how easily Colin provoked me, but I'd vowed to do better. I reached across the table and covered one of her hands with my own.

"I won't do anything to ruin our day. You have my word."

She smiled. "You'd best keep that promise, Andrew. I look forward to returning home—*with you*. I need a break from this swirling cesspool of scandal."

"As do I, Vera."

At that moment, Alexander arrived, grinning from ear to ear. "Andrew, may I have a word?"

I excused myself from the table and followed him a short distance away. "What is it, Alex?"

"I just passed Colin in the corridor. He was in a foul mood." Alexander bounced on his toes, unable to hide his elation at whatever had just transpired. "Father stopped him and told him to keep away from you and Vera. He said he knew what Colin is planning."

"And what *is* Colin planning? He was just here." I relayed our brief conversation.

Alexander laughed. "Apparently, Colin's great scheme was simply to rile you up enough that you'd threaten him or strike him. I don't know. You saw through him, and he was none too happy about it."

"There are still two days until the wedding," I reminded him. "Colin has time—"

Alexander laughed aloud. "No! Father told him that if he could not follow orders, then he'll be confined to his chambers. Colin told him the guards would let him out if he asked, and Father said, 'The guards are under *my* command, in case you have forgotten.' Then he asked the nearest three to escort Colin to his room and keep him there." Alexander laughed again.

I was cautiously optimistic but wasn't certain I'd be free of Colin's harassment so easily. Colin's behavior was disconcerting, and Vera clearly feared him.

"Do you think he'll remain there, Alex? Claire warned us that he was scheming, and she was thoroughly upset."

Alexander arched an eyebrow. "I'm surprised she spoke with you at all. She's been keeping to her rooms and will scarcely see anyone. I've heard Colin has been to see her a few times, but it sounds as though their meetings have been...tense."

Despite Claire's recent behavior, I continued to worry for her well-being. It was clear she wasn't happy with her decision to pursue Colin, and I hoped she'd find a remedy to her situation before it deteriorated any further. Though I had no proof Colin would become violent toward her, there were numerous rumors that indicated he was certainly capable of it. He'd hit me often enough when he lost his temper, and prior to the succession announcement, I'd been free to retaliate in kind. Colin knew he was outmatched if he drew me into a fight, but now he was protected as heir to Carlton's throne.

"I still wonder what this is about," I mused, casting a worried glance about the hall.

Alexander shrugged. "Likely, Colin was drunk and misunderstood some bit of conversation he overheard and it threw him into an unfounded rage. You know how he is."

I frowned. Alexander's explanation was plausible, but unlikely. I believed something deeper was driving Colin's actions.

"Don't be so dour, Andrew," Alexander said with a laugh. "You're getting married in a few days. Enjoy yourself! I'm certain father has Colin in hand now."

"I hope so."

Alexander rolled his eyes, exasperated. "Go to your bride, brother. And don't worry—Tom and I have already decided we'll keep an eye on Colin for you. He won't do anything to ruin your wedding day."

I nodded, grateful that my two youngest brothers remained allies. Colin's actions troubled me, but there was nothing I could do about them at present. Alexander was right; I should focus my attention on Vera and the upcoming ceremony.

Vera gave me a questioning look as I rejoined her at the table.

"Alex seems to believe Colin won't cause us any further problems," I told her.

"Your brother looked positively giddy," she replied.

I relayed Alexander's story and admitted I still harbored misgivings about Colin's recent actions. Our guards seemed keen to listen in, eager to pass on the details to others around the castle at the first opportunity. I was beyond ready to leave the gossip and intrigue that plagued the royal court behind.

"Your brother is right," she said gently. "Don't allow Colin to ruin this moment for us by worrying about what he may or may not do. Let's proceed as we've planned, and in a few days, we'll depart for Vinterry."

The next morning, I packed a pair of sturdy trunks with the personal effects I intended to take with me when Vera and I left the Capitol. One trunk held my clothing, while the other held the new set of armor I'd commissioned from Desmond and the array of medals I'd earned during my service to the king, the mementos of my past life as a soldier.

I left my new sword atop one of the trunks where it would be accessible. While the roads were typically safe between the Capitol and the eastern cities, there were periodic reports of bandits harassing travelers in the region. We'd be traveling east, and I planned to keep it on my person as a deterrent to any would-be thieves.

I finished packing and exited the barracks not long before noon. Outside, the castle's commons were in chaos. I dismissed the uproar as continued preparations for the Spring Festival, but as I strode toward the great hall, I realized something was amiss. A crowd was gathered near the stables, where people milled and shouted in apparent confusion. I pushed my way through the throng of servants, determined to locate the source of the trouble.

A woman lay on the ground, unmoving. The crowd encircled her, though it seemed no one had offered assistance. Dark hair fell over her face, concealing her identity, and she wore a simple shift, as though she'd not yet had the opportunity to dress for the day. I shoved my way through the onlookers, irritated that no one had attempted to help.

I knelt at her side and moved her gently. The hair fell away from her face, revealing Claire's battered features. Her skin was purple with bruises, while blood trickled from her nose and a split on her lower lip. Gasps of shock rang through the audience. I was furious the servants had wasted time staring when they should have been acting.

I pointed at the nearest man. "Go to the physician, and tell him what happened here. I'll carry her there." I pointed at another. "You, inform the king. If he's busy, speak with Prince Alexander or Prince Thomas."

Claire was breathing, though shallowly, and remained unconscious. I lifted her gingerly; she was feather-light and appeared more fragile than I remembered.

"Did anyone see what happened?" I demanded.

Most of the servants shook their heads and began to disperse, but one of the stable hands came forward as I began to make my way to the doors of the great hall. "She wasn't here until but a few moments ago, sir," he said. "I heard a noise outside and went to see what the commotion was. I didn't know it was Lady Claire, else I would have done something sooner!" The man's face was ashen and drawn with worry.

"It shouldn't have mattered *who* she was," I growled. "She was clearly in need of help, and you stood about gaping. Someone should have assisted her."

I ground my teeth, biting back several choice words. He could not be blamed for the behavior of the entire throng, but I'd instill a sense of guilt for his own role in the affair.

"I…I'm sorry, sir."

"Tell Lady Vera that I'm at the physician's suite. Ask her to meet me there."

As I neared the physician's suite on the ground floor of the castle, Claire stirred in my arms. Her right eye fluttered open; the left was swollen shut due to her injuries.

"Andrew?" she breathed, her voice weak.

"I'm taking you to the physician," I assured her. "You're hurt."

"Andrew, I'm so sorry. For everything."

"Hush, Claire, it's going to be alright."

Tears began to leak from her eyes, and she turned her face away, ashamed. "I should have stayed with you…"

My heart lurched in my chest. I knew I would never receive a full apology from Claire—her pride would never allow it—but to know she regretted her previous actions meant much. In that moment, I was certain I knew what had transpired.

"Did Colin do this?"

A sob escaped her throat, and she nodded.

I closed my eyes and swallowed hard. I'd once cared for her deeply, and to see her in this state was gut-wrenching. I could not help but feel at least partially responsible. After all, Colin had unleashed his rage on her after she'd spoken to me. I cradled her in my arms and hoped she'd recover.

The physician's door was propped open. He stood within, his aged hands clasped before him. I increased my pace and placed Claire carefully on the examination table he'd hastily prepared. Within moments, the king and Thomas arrived. Trailing in their wake was Vera and her guard escort.

"She's awake," I said to the others. I moved away from the table to give the physician space to work. "None of the servants saw what happened."

"I must ask you to go into the corridor," the physician interrupted. "I cannot protect her dignity with spectators."

I nodded, and we regrouped in the hall. Thomas closed the doors behind us.

"She said Colin was responsible." I paced while clenching and unclenching my fists. "You can't allow this to go unpunished, sire."

The king turned to one of the guards. "Check on my wayward son, please. I want to know if he's within his chambers as I've ordered. If he is not, return to me immediately."

As the guard left to carry out his orders, Alexander sprinted toward us from the opposite end of the corridor. "What happened?"

I allowed the king to fill him in on the details and moved toward the windows that lined one side of the long hall. I stared outside, unseeing in my rage and frustration. I knew I could not intervene, though I sorely wished I could do something. Colin didn't deserve his position as heir, he didn't deserve Claire. He was a menace and a damned disgrace.

I turned as Vera placed one hand gently on my arm, breaking me from my dark reverie.

"Andrew, don't blame yourself. This was not your fault."

I nodded. I knew she was right, yet I struggled to relinquish the guilt that gnawed at my gut.

The door to the physician's suite opened, and one of his assistants stepped into the corridor. He spoke in hushed tones with the king, then nodded in my direction. The king turned and beckoned me to join them. With a reluctant glance at Vera, I moved across the hall.

"Andrew, she's asked to speak with you privately." The king's tone was solemn. "She has confirmed what you told us earlier. Colin was the perpetrator of this crime." He paused as anger flashed through his eyes. "He will answer for this."

"Thank you, sire."

I followed the assistant into the suite. The curtains had been drawn over the large windows, and the room was lit by flickering candlelight. Claire had been moved to a cushioned bench near one of the windows, and a thick quilt was draped over her petite form. The blood from her wounds had been washed away, but her face remained swollen and bruised.

I knelt beside her to look her in the eye as we spoke. "They said you asked for me."

She managed a faltering smile, a single tear tracing its way down the side of her face. "Andrew, I... I'm sorry for everything I've put you through. It was my fault..."

"No, Claire. You can't blame yourself for what Colin has done."

"You don't understand." Her voice was strained. "At first, it *was* my fault. I was so angry at your lies, your betrayal. I wanted revenge, but it was foolish. I see that now." She looked down as more tears spilled from her swollen eyes. "I manipulated Colin into helping me humiliate you time and again. But then... It awakened something inside him. When I told him I was done with the game, he laughed at me. He told me it was over only when he said it was."

"Claire..." I didn't know what to say. Many of my suspicions had just been confirmed.

"After I spoke to you yesterday, I made up my mind to confront him. That was foolish too." She paused to dab at her eyes with the corner of the quilt. "He knows how to provoke an argument—and not only with you. We shouted at one another, and then I told him something I should have kept to myself." She looked up at me then. "I told him that leaving you was the greatest mistake I'd ever made and he would never be your equal. That's when... That's when he started to hit me." She dissolved into sobs.

I gathered her into my arms. She needed to be comforted, and there was no one else present to do so. I knew Vera would understand.

"Claire," I said thickly, "I forgive you."

I could not continue to condemn her for what she'd done. She'd paid dearly for seeking her petty revenge.

"You see?" she said through her tears. "You always do the right thing, the noble thing. You're a good man. I wish I'd seen it sooner." She sniffed and pushed me away. "I told your fa—the king that I cannot marry Colin. Our engagement is over." She swallowed hard. "I wish you and Vera the best. She is a lucky woman."

"You are welcome to attend our ceremony, Claire."

She shook her head emphatically. "Looking like this?" She waved a hand before her face. "No, I will not, but thank you." She drew a shaky breath. "I'll write a letter to my father and tell him all that has transpired. Once I've recovered, I will return home."

I nodded. "Take care of yourself, Claire."

I left her huddled near the window and made my way to the corridor outside. Alexander and Thomas had remained with Vera, but the king was gone, and the remaining guards with him. I raised an eyebrow in question.

Thomas spoke first. "Father went to confront Colin. He was in his room, as he was supposed to be." He sighed. "I can't believe he'd do this!"

"Claire has broken off their engagement."

I spoke of her intent to return home but left much of our conversation unsaid. I would share the full account with Vera later, but my two half-brothers didn't need to be privy to the more personal details.

"Tom, why don't you fetch the guards to watch over Claire now that Andrew has returned?" Alexander asked. "You promised father you would."

"Right. I did," Thomas replied with a brief nod. He scurried away on his errand.

"The castle garrison is busy protecting everyone from Colin," Alexander grumbled. "I hope father can set him straight."

I nodded my agreement, and Vera took my arm, twining her fingers through mine. "As do I," she replied firmly. "All I ask is that he leave us be for two more days. Then we'll be done with this place."

Alexander met my gaze, a frown twisting his lips. "I wish you weren't leaving, Andrew." He sighed and looked at the floor between his boots. "I don't want to stay here alone."

I understood the meaning behind his words and wished there was something more I could do for him. "I won't be more than two days' ride east, Alex. Call on me if you need anything. You know I'll come."

"Of course, you and Thomas are welcome to visit any time you like," Vera added with a smile.

Alexander nodded, his expression relieved, but uncertainty lingered in his green eyes. "Andrew, I'd like to speak to you later. In private. If you have time, that is."

"Of course. Come by my quarters in the barracks, and we'll talk as long as you like."

"Thank you, brother. I'll come by tonight," he replied before taking his leave.

We remained outside the physician's suite until the guards Thomas had summoned arrived. Vera expressed her desire for a walk in the garden; I knew she wanted to discuss what had transpired while I spoke with Claire. Another of the castle's guards trailed behind us, though at a respectful distance. He would not overhear our conversation.

Vera remained patient, waiting for me to speak first. We walked in silence for some time while I sorted through my thoughts enough to share what Claire had revealed. Vera appeared lost in thought after I finished my tale and didn't speak for several minutes.

"She's right, you know," she said finally, a faint smile playing upon her lips. "You *are* a good man. I'm fortunate to be with you." Her grip tightened on mine. "I pity her for what has happened. As vile as she acted, no one deserves to be hurt like that. You showed great kindness when you forgave her, Andrew. I'm not certain I could have done the same."

I looked at her sharply, surprised by her response.

"Not everyone is so noble," she replied softly. "It's part of what made me fall in love with you. You always strive to do the right thing."

I shrugged, uncomfortable with the praise as I continued to struggle with my lingering guilt.

"You *are* a good man, Andrew," she said again. "You'd make a wonderful father."

The statement caught me off guard, and I stopped in my tracks. I would have to divulge that portion of my secret, no matter how painful it might be.

"Andrew?" she asked, concerned.

I shook my head and began to walk again, clearing my throat. "Vera, there is something I need to tell you. I hope it won't change things between us." I glanced behind us, noting the guard was still well out of earshot.

She frowned, her eyes brimming with unanswered questions.

"Vera, I…can't. I'm not able to…"

I felt my skin grow hot with embarrassment, and I looked away. As my bride, she deserved to know, but it was proving more difficult to tell her than I'd anticipated. I didn't want to disappoint her further.

I swallowed hard, then forced myself to look directly into those sapphire blue eyes of hers. "Vera, I'll never be a father. It's not possible."

She blinked a few times, then nodded slowly. "I understand. We can always adopt, you know. There are many in the orphanages who could use a good home."

My relief was palpable. She still wanted me, despite my innate shortcomings. "Vera, you're not upset?"

She shrugged, then smiled. "No. I love you, Andrew, and this doesn't change how I feel. But I am thankful you've told me."

I drew her into my embrace and kissed her fiercely. "You are incredible. Amazing. Wonderful." I kissed her again.

She giggled as we parted. "I think you've embarrassed our guard."

I glanced over my shoulder to find he'd conspicuously turned away.

I chuckled. "In two days, we'll be on our own. No more guards to follow us about and ruin the moment."

"You know," she said, "I believed that bit of gossip was just a malicious rumor spread by Claire."

I closed my eyes, ashamed, and shook my head. "No, it's the unfortunate truth. It pains me that she spread the rumor, but I'm not surprised she did. I wish it were otherwise. When I was younger, I used to dream of having a family of my own."

"As I said, we can always adopt." She beamed. "You can still have a family if that's what you desire. As for me, I'm happy either way. *You* are what is important."

I grinned. She was truly amazing; there was no other woman in the world that I wanted to spend my life with. I'd fallen in love with her because she was beautiful and kind, but the more I learned about her, the more I couldn't imagine a single day without her at my side. It was a feeling I'd never experienced before, and I didn't want it to end.

"I love you, Vera."

Her smile outshone the afternoon sun. "I love you too."

That evening, Alexander visited me in my quarters as he'd promised. I stoked the fire and placed the single chair the room afforded near the hearth prior to his arrival. Though the days were beginning to grow warmer, the air temperature remained cold after sunset. I sensed we would be speaking for a lengthy period of time, and I wanted to ensure he was comfortable.

He took the chair as I'd anticipated, while I closed the door to my chamber behind him. His face was pale and lined with worry.

"Andrew, have you heard what transpired between father and Colin?"

I had. As soon as Vera and I returned to the castle from our stroll, we'd been waylaid by Thomas, who had been bursting to share the news. The king had placed Colin on house arrest until Claire was well enough to travel home to her father's estate. Guards had been posted outside of his room and below each of his windows.

It seemed he'd gone out through the windows when he assaulted Claire, then returned in the same manner, undetected. I was stunned no one had witnessed his escape. Thomas had also mentioned that once Claire was safely away from the Capitol, Colin would appear before the governor's council to answer for his crime.

"I have, Alex."

"What you probably didn't hear was how Colin reacted." He slumped forward in the chair and raked both hands through his hair. "He threatened father. He vowed that as soon as he was free, everyone who has conspired against him will pay dearly. I hope his words were only spoken out of anger, but Colin's temper has been volatile. I told father to take his threat seriously."

I nodded as the first pangs of true worry began to twist my gut. Colin was certainly capable of carrying out his threats, and I understood Alexander's concern. Though the council might proclaim Colin guilty of his crime, there was little they could do to punish him. He was the king's heir, and as such, was exempt from many of the laws that governed the rest of the kingdom.

"If I can do anything to help, all you need do is say the word," I offered.

He smiled and gazed into the fire. "I knew you would say that. Thank you, brother, but no—you're to be married in two days, and you need to focus on your bride. She thinks the world of you, you know."

I grinned. My spirits lifted at the mention of Vera.

"We spoke while you were with Claire," Alexander continued. "I don't think I could have arranged a better match for you if I'd tried. I hope you've forgiven me for seating her beside you at the feast." His eyes gleamed with mischief.

I laughed. "How could I be upset with you? You set in motion a wondrous thing. I once believed I knew what love was, but I was sorely mistaken. Vera is…" I trailed off, trying to find the correct words to describe what I felt, but could think of nothing sufficient. I sighed happily and settled on, "She's wonderful."

"Have you told her…?"

I shook my head. "How can I, Alex? If my secret becomes common knowledge, I'll be a marked man. If she knew, it would only put her in danger. I can't live with that."

He nodded solemnly. "I'm the only one who knows, then."

"Yes. I'd like to keep it that way."

"I understand." He sighed heavily, and I knew there was something more weighing on his mind. "Father is pushing me to marry," he blurted, then immediately averted his gaze.

I understood the implications of his words. "What will you do?"

He shrugged. "I don't know yet. Unlike you, I can't masquerade as a normal person. I have no way to hide what I am. As soon as I take my shirt off, it'll be obvious. I can't get married, Andrew, but I also can't tell father why. He doesn't know—and I must keep it that way." He rose and began to pace before the hearth. He stopped mid-stride to focus his gaze upon me. "I'm terrified, Andrew. I don't know what to do."

"What did you tell father the last time he started pushing you?" I asked.

He frowned. "I told him Colin hadn't settled down yet, so why should I? I don't think that will work a second time."

I shook my head. "No, I don't think it will, either."

"Andrew, I'm desperate. Without a campaign to prepare for this summer—because so far the Corodan have kept their word—I don't

have any reason to leave the Capitol and avoid father's questions. I…"
He raked one hand through his short hair and growled in frustration.

I'd rarely witnessed my brother so agitated. The only excuse I could think of was to ask that he travel with us when we left, on the premise that an extra swordsman would be welcome as we traveled east through the outlaw-infested plains.

"Alex, sit down. I have an idea."

I related to him what I'd come up with, and he shook his head, amused. "Father knows what kind of swordsman you are, Andrew. I doubt he'd believe that you require another to assist you. Besides, you and Lady Vera deserve some privacy after your wedding. Thank you for the offer, but I'll figure this out. It's past time I learned to stand on my own."

I was relieved he was no longer in a panic over the prospect of marriage, but my concern didn't subside. I vowed I'd find a way to get him safely beyond the Mage's Gate one day.

"Don't forget, Vera invited you for a visit. Perhaps if you give us a few weeks, you can make the trip yourself on some other pretense." I wouldn't relent until I was certain Alexander was in better spirits.

He brightened at my words. "She did. Perhaps I can convince Tom to come along too. It would do him good to get out of the library for a time."

# EIGHT

"Holy hell, I've never been this nervous." I raked a trembling hand through my hair only to receive an irritated grimace from Alexander in return.

He rose from his seat and strode to where I stood before the tall mirror, then swiped the comb from the nearby table and thrust it in my hand.

"That's the third time you've mussed your hair in as many minutes," he said with a chuckle.

"I wasn't this edgy before my first wedding."

"You didn't love Claire. Your nerves this time are a good sign, brother." He sighed and shook his head in mock disapproval. "Let me fix your buttons. They're crooked."

I turned to face him while I ran the comb through my hair—again. My hair was perpetually of a length that required little maintenance yet was impossible to style. It never grew, and I'd never questioned it until I'd met Claire. During our first year together, she'd begged me to stop cutting it, as longer locks had been the current fashion at court. I'd manufactured the excuse that long hair was impractical for a soldier, but the truth was, my hair was unchanging, a byproduct of my unique physiology.

Alexander worked the buttons on my dark jacket, then stood back with an approving grin. "That's better."

I turned to examine his handiwork in the mirror. It *did* look better.

I wore a white button-down shirt beneath the dark jacket. My trousers matched the jacket; the garments were plain, but cut of fine cloth and adorned with silver buttons. Polished, knee-length black boots completed my attire.

Alexander was dressed in identical garb. Our reflection proved we were brothers; we shared our late mother's nose, blond hair, and green eyes. Though I was a head taller and broader of shoulders, we could have been mistaken for twins.

A twinge of unease writhed in my gut. We appeared to be the same age, though I was a decade older. As elated as I was with the prospect of marriage and a life with Vera, I feared it would be fleeting. I didn't age, and people would undoubtedly begin asking unwanted questions within a few years. Comments had already been leveled in regards to my similarity with Alexander.

An abrupt knock sounded on the door, drawing our attention.

"You look great, brother," Alexander said with a grin. "I assume that's Tom outside. It must be time."

I nodded and followed him to the door, where Thomas greeted us with a shy smile. He was attempting to grow a beard, which he'd trimmed short; the facial hair served to make him appear older than his twenty years, but it suited him. He was dressed in a similar fashion to us, though he'd chosen shades of brown rather than black.

"Andrew, you're late," Thomas complained. "People are being seated!"

"I tried my best to get this lout ready on time," Alexander replied with a smirk. "And he did his best to undo all of my efforts!"

I chuckled and motioned for Thomas to lead the way to the solarium. I hoped all of Vera's painstaking work over the past days remained intact. Despite the guards we'd been assigned and Colin's house-arrest, I still feared he would find a means to escape and wreak havoc on our wedding day.

I surveyed the room as we entered, relieved to find all had remained as I'd left it. It had been transformed from an airy, stone room into a vibrant indoor garden. Flowers lined the walls and filled every conceivable shelf and table. Small bouquets were tied to the back of each guest's chair, and a larger arrangement was placed in the front of the room where Vera would stand. The heady scent of lilies permeated the air while rain lashed the window panes.

The abundance of flowers brightened what would have been an otherwise dreary day. A handful of people were seated, but the room was largely empty. I frowned at Thomas, who shrugged uncomfortably.

"The chaplain sent me to, ah, 'collect' you." He looked down and began to fidget.

Alexander flashed a grin. "We're excited for you, Andrew. You and Vera deserve the best."

"Indeed," Thomas agreed, a proud smile on his lips.

I took my place next to the chaplain and greeted the other guests as they trickled inside while my brothers seated themselves in the front row. Many of those we'd invited were from the castle's garrison—men I'd spent many years with and had come to consider friends. Some arrived with their wives; others came alone. Desmond the blacksmith appeared, wearing his finest attire; I almost didn't recognize him without his battered leather apron and stained tunic. Several of the lords and ladies of the court had also been invited, and they arrived in their usual finery to seat themselves near the front of the room.

It was a vastly different mix of people than had attended my first wedding. Claire had insisted every noble in the kingdom be invited, and our ceremony had taken place in the great hall downstairs. I preferred this smaller, more intimate affair, and I hoped Vera would find it to her liking.

Soon, every seat was filled. The king arrived last and was seated in the front row next to Alexander and Thomas. Colin was nowhere to be seen, and I began to relax. Claire was also absent, but I didn't begrudge her; she required further time to heal. I hoped she'd find true happiness one day, but until she stopped chasing dreams of power and prestige, it was unlikely.

I strode to the front of the room with the chaplain, nervously awaiting the entrance of my bride. I was forced to clasp my hands lest I fall into Thomas' habit. Anxiety of this magnitude was not something I was accustomed to, and I hoped I wouldn't make a fool of myself once the ceremony began.

When the doors opened several minutes later to reveal Vera standing in the corridor, the guests turned in unison and rose from their seats. The gown I'd commissioned from the tailor was beautiful;

comprised of pearlescent white satin with lace trim, it fit her slender figure perfectly. The gown trailed behind her, but she walked forward without the assistance of a maidservant. She clasped a bouquet of pink tulips and golden daffodils in her hands. Her auburn hair was pulled away from her face but left loose in the back, and she'd taken time to curl its loose ends.

Her smile was radiant as her eyes met mine. I stared at her, captivated.

She handed her bouquet to the chamberlain as she reached my position, and I took her hands in my own. The chaplain began to speak, though I scarcely heard his words for some time, lost as I was in the depths of her blue eyes. It wasn't until the chaplain asked for the rings and Alexander rose to deliver them that I became aware of all that had transpired while I'd been transfixed. Damn, she was beautiful.

"These are the physical embodiment of a lifelong promise," the chaplain stated as he handed us the rings. "With this exchange, two souls become one."

I held Vera's delicate ring while she held mine. My hands continued to shake as I slid the slim golden band onto her finger. Her hands were steady and sure as she reciprocated the action. If she was nervous, she hid it well.

The chaplain smiled. "I pronounce you husband and wife. Congratulations."

A notary came forward bearing our marriage document and placed it on the table behind the chaplain, where a quill and ink awaited. I hesitated as I took up the quill and reminded myself I no longer bore the Marsden name. I signed as "Andrew" alone.

Vera squeezed my hand in reassurance before she took the quill from my hand. She'd understood my hesitation but did not remark upon it. We'd spoken of how we planned to handle this part the day before; she would keep the Sandson name since I no longer had a surname to offer. It was an unusual process for the record-keepers, but we had little choice.

"Andrew and Vera," the chaplain said in a kindly tone, "under the laws of this great kingdom, you are now wed."

That was my cue. I grinned, then gathered Vera into my arms for a kiss. Our guests clapped and cheered, and I was certain I heard

Alexander whistle raucously. I stepped back and smiled, happier than I'd been in years, and offered her my arm. We exited the solarium to further applause and made our way downstairs to Vera's quarters on the second floor. A pair of guards stood vigil in the corridor outside and offered their congratulations as we entered the room. I beamed and nodded my thanks.

For the first time in several days, we were alone. After the bustle of preparing for the ceremony and the constant fear that Colin would do something to disrupt it, the solitude was welcome.

"I took the liberty of having your trunks moved here this morning." Vera gestured to where they rested alongside another half-dozen that belonged to her. "I hope you don't mind."

"Not at all. It will save me a trip to the barracks before we leave tomorrow."

She smiled, then stood on tip-toe to plant a kiss on my lips. "I've been waiting for this," she whispered, leaning into me. "Help me get out of this dress, Andrew."

I kissed her fiercely in return. "Gladly."

She giggled as she spun around. She pulled her hair over one shoulder to reveal a myriad of tiny buttons that cascaded in a single line from the nape of her neck to the small of her back. I fumbled with the first few as I struggled to make my large, rough hands work them properly.

"Your tailor had a fondness for buttons."

She laughed. "You selected her. But now you understand why I needed a maidservant's assistance this morning."

"I do." I kissed the side of her neck, momentarily distracted from my task.

"Andrew, there is something I should tell you." Her voice wavered with sudden uncertainty.

"Of course."

"Lord Sandson and I…We were never intimate. Not like this. I suspect he was simply too old." She paused to peer over her shoulder. "I could have requested an annulment, but he was kind to me. I couldn't do it."

"Are you saying this will be your first time with a man?" I asked, finally at the half-way mark with the interminable buttons.

"Yes."

I leaned forward and kissed her softly below her ear lobe. "I'll be gentle. I promise."

I awoke the next morning with a grin. I'd slept better than I had in months.

Vera was curled beside me, soundly asleep. She'd pulled most of the blankets over herself during the night, but I didn't mind. I didn't need them for warmth, and she was adorable, wrapped in them as she was. I studied her in the daylight spilling from behind the heavy curtain covering the room's single window. I knew we should rise and start our departure soon, but I didn't want to wake her yet. She appeared peaceful. I was loath to disturb her.

I lay beside her, replaying the previous day's events in my mind. We'd made love twice before dressing in standard attire and making our way to the great hall for supper. Upon our return, we'd made love again. I'd fallen asleep for a time afterwards, but had awakened in the darkest hours of the night to find her gazing at me fondly. We'd spoken for a time, then she'd snuggled closer, only to fall asleep in my arms minutes later. Watching her now, I wished we had time for another round of passion before we departed, but it was not to be.

I'd been awake for perhaps a quarter-hour when there was a loud knock on our door, followed by Alexander's unmistakable laughter. I sighed and stood slowly, locating the pair of trousers I'd discarded the previous evening where they lay in a heap at the foot of the bed. I pulled them on while Vera stirred.

"Andrew, what is it?"

"Alex." I gestured to the door and offered her an apologetic grin. She smiled sleepily and lay back down.

I opened the door to find both Alexander and Thomas in the corridor beyond. Thomas was speaking with the guards, while Alexander stood smirking at me as I stood in the doorway. I was shirtless and barefoot, which caused him to flash a mischievous grin at Thomas.

"Ah, sorry, Andrew, we thought you'd have been awake by now," Thomas apologized as he turned to face Alexander. "Alex, we should go."

94

"No, the two of you are here and have sufficiently interrupted my morning," I replied with a laugh. "We'd best get this over with."

Alexander burst out laughing and motioned for Thomas to speak. Thomas rolled his eyes and shook his head in disbelief.

"We just wanted to see you before you and Lady Vera departed," Thomas replied. He began to fidget and averted his gaze.

His laughter under control once more, Alexander said, "He forgot to mention the part about us placing bets on what state you'd be in this morning." He grinned wickedly. "I won."

Thomas cast a look of annoyance in Alexander's direction, clearly finding his brother's conduct inappropriate. Alexander pointedly ignored the look and pressed on.

"We wanted to say goodbye before you went on your way. We'll miss you." He paused, then in a lower tone, said, "Some of us more than others."

"You can let them in, Andrew," Vera called from within.

I glanced over my shoulder to find she had dressed and was perched on the edge of the bed, combing her hair. I moved aside to allow my brothers entrance, then went about the task of locating the rest of my clothing.

Alexander whispered something to Vera that I couldn't hear, and she giggled with a glance in my direction. I rolled my eyes; it was typical of Alexander to spin tales about me while I was standing in the same room. Having located my shirt, I pulled it hastily over my head.

"I know you're spreading rumors, Alex," I growled.

"Of course I am. What sort of brother would I be if I didn't warn your new bride about some of your habits?"

His words elicited another peal of laughter from Vera. I was half afraid to learn what he'd told her.

"It's nothing to worry about, Andrew," Vera replied with a smile. "I informed Alex that I was well aware of your snoring."

I groaned and turned away to locate my boots while Alexander laughed again. "You're too serious," he chided. "I'm just trying to lighten the mood. Your leaving isn't easy for us, you know."

"No, it isn't," Thomas agreed. "Father has extra guards posted around Colin's quarters this morning. He feared Colin might attempt something before your departure."

I pulled on my boots, then went to the trunk that held my armor. I needed my sword at hand should anything go awry, but I didn't believe I'd need the armor. I trusted the king to keep his eldest in line.

Behind me, Alexander whistled. "New armor, I see. Desmond outdid himself, I'd say."

"It's a fine set," I agreed, admiring the smith's work for a few moments before I closed the lid. Wearing a full set of armor was cumbersome and tended to restrict movement; I preferred to travel without it, but it would work splendidly on the battlefield.

"Has Andrew spoken to you about us visiting this summer?" Thomas asked Vera. His voice had gone up in pitch slightly; he was either nervous or excited.

She shook her head as I turned around to face them. "When have I had time, Tom?" I asked. "We were a bit preoccupied yesterday."

Alexander snorted, thoroughly amused. "I'll say."

"Alex!" Thomas and I both scolded him at the same time, which threw him into another peal of laughter.

To my relief, Vera was smiling, amused in her own right. "Perhaps one day you'll understand, dear Alexander." She patted him gently on the shoulder. "A lady has needs, you know."

Alexander blinked as his face turned a shade beyond mere crimson. It was now my turn to laugh; rarely was someone able to embarrass my brother so thoroughly.

"Well, ah, about this summer?" Thomas stammered, his face nearly as red as Alexander's.

"These two good-for-nothings want to pay us a visit in a couple of months," I informed Vera.

"That would be lovely!" she exclaimed. "High summer is my favorite season. The vineyard will be green and the grapes will be beginning to grow in size. And the gardener has an amazing array of roses, which should be in bloom by then. He uses the roses as indicators for the soil—if something is amiss, the flowers will be affected first, and it gives us time to remedy the problem before it affects the vines." She smiled. "Yes, you must come. I insist."

"Then it's settled," Alexander said, his face still a tinge more red than usual. "Tom and I will visit you at high summer."

"Thank you both," Thomas replied, offering a shy smile to Vera. "I'd also heard your manor has a library—"

"No, Tom!" Alexander cut him off. "This was supposed to be a visit to get you *away* from the library, remember?"

Thomas shrugged. "I like books."

"There is a small library," Vera confirmed, "though it's rarely used since Lord Sandson passed. Most of the works he kept are historical. You'd be welcome to peruse them while you're there."

Thomas flashed a triumphant grin in Alexander's direction. "Thank you," he said to Vera. "Alex, we should go."

Alexander nodded. I trailed them to the door, where Alexander turned toward me one last time. "I'm going to hold you to your word, Andrew. If I need help, you're the first person I will send a message to. Promise me you'll come."

I nodded. "I'll be there. You have my word."

He nodded and drew me into a rough embrace. "I'll miss having you here, brother. Take care of yourself, and take care of *her*. She's good for you."

"Goodbye, Andrew," Thomas added. His eyes were shiny with unshed tears. He swiftly turned away.

"Take care of yourselves," I replied, my voice gruff from an upwelling of emotion. "We'll see you in a few months."

As they made their way down the corridor, I turned away from the door. Goodbyes with my brothers had always been difficult, but this time was even more so. I'd always intended to return when I left on campaign, and never gave a second thought about my own welfare; I'd assumed I would return to see my brothers again.

This time, I had no intention of returning to the Capitol. Guilt plagued me. I'd always been there to protect them from Colin, and now I was walking away, leaving them to fend for themselves. I knew Thomas would be fine, but I worried for Alexander.

Vera drew her arms around me gently and rested her head against my shoulder. "We'll see them again soon," she whispered. "I know you worry about Colin, but there is nothing more we can do. The king will take care of it. You'll see."

I marveled at how easily she picked up on my thoughts after only a few short weeks together. I nodded and kissed the top of her head. "We should be going."

# NINE

The trek between the Capitol and Vera's estate to the east was uneventful, with no sign of bandits. As we neared her estate, the landscape began to transition from flat grassland to rolling hills and forested expanses. The trees were just beginning to unfurl their leaves after the long freeze of winter, and birds chirped and flitted between the trees. Tiny purple wildflowers poked through the grasses as they reached toward the elusive sunlight. It was a part of Novania that I'd rarely traveled, and never in spring. It was picturesque, despite the damp weather.

A smaller dirt trek broke away from the main road as we reached the beginnings of a true forest. Vera directed our guard escort to follow the path, as it would lead us to Vinterry. The road wound through the trees for a few miles before it opened into a sprawling meadow. A manor house encircled by a low, white-washed stone wall sat in its heart. A gurgling stream ran through the meadow and ended in a small pond nestled amongst the trees on the eastern side of the wall. Behind the manor house, several hills had been cleared of trees, where row upon row of gnarled grapevines grew on wooden trellises. I understood Vera's love of the estate; Vinterry was idyllic, peaceful and serene.

"Welcome to Vinterry, Andrew." She leaned into me and tilted her face up with a smile.

She'd asked that we ride together on the big chestnut gelding we'd borrowed from the castle stables. Ben had been the only horse who hadn't balked at my approach, and he'd proven a gentle giant. I suspected Vera's insistence was due in part to Ben's size, but she also hoped to make a statement to her staff upon our arrival. I was comforted by her presence and didn't object.

"I wish I'd visited more often," I told her. "It's soothing."

She smiled and released a contented sigh. "I believe so too. It's even more beautiful in the sunlight. It's a pity the weather is unpleasant."

"There will be plenty of sunny days ahead," I replied.

"I'm happy to be home again, and even more so that I'm with you."

She sat up abruptly as the path wound through the gate in the stone wall. She directed me to the stable on our right, where a pair of stable hands greeted us. The elder of the two offered his hand to assist Vera.

"You must be Andrew," he said as I dismounted and handed him the reins.

"I am."

"It is a real pleasure to meet you, sir." He grinned. "I've heard of your exploits in the north. You'll have to indulge an old man with some of your tales later. I was a soldier in my youth."

"Andrew, this is Giles, and the youngster is his grandson, Gregor," Vera chimed in. "I'm certain they'll love hearing of your battles."

Once the horse was settled, Vera led me into the house and out of the drizzle. I followed as she gave me a tour of the house and introduced me to the remainder of her staff. Each was friendly and welcomed me, despite my history of scandal. It was a refreshing change from the intrigue and treachery that so often plagued the Capitol and the royal court.

By the time the introductions were finished, night had fallen. Vera led me to the dining room, where Cassandra, her amiable cook, had prepared a meal.

"I usually invite the household to join me for supper," Vera said. "I know it's uncommon amongst the nobility in the Capitol to do so, but I care about these people. They've worked hard for their positions here, and I reward them with my hospitality—and friendship—as I can."

"Then let them join us. I've no qualms about their presence, and I'd like to learn more than their names."

She smiled. "Tomorrow. I wanted tonight to be special. It's your first night here." She sighed and looked down. "I suppose I'm trying to make a good first impression."

I studied her for a long moment, surprised she was concerned about pleasing me. "Vera, I love you. Marrying you was the best thing I've ever done in life. You don't need to worry over what I think."

She reached across the table and took my hand. "Thank you. We'll dine with the staff tomorrow."

I settled into life at Vinterry swiftly. It was calm, and everything about the estate moved at a much slower pace than what I'd been accustomed to; it was a welcome change. I spent time with the vintner, Hiram, learning the process of wine-making and the importance of careful cultivation of the vines. Giles and his grandson often sought me out in the evenings after we'd supped, eager to hear tales from my time as commander. On occasion, Giles even challenged me to games of Cabal's Thrall. Vera was ever-present, and her smile brightened each day.

By mid-summer, I'd spent enough time outdoors amongst the grape vines that my skin had tanned considerably. We received word that my brothers had arranged to visit as promised, which sent the estate into a flurry of activity. The staff was both thrilled and terrified that two members of the royal family were traveling to the secluded estate, but I assured them that Alexander and Thomas would not be an imposition. I was met with skeptical looks; they were princes, after all.

The night before they were scheduled to arrive, Vera drew me aside after the evening meal. The night was warm, the wind was calm, and crickets chirped in the vineyards. I suggested we walk amongst the vines and beneath the stars. She readily agreed.

We strolled through the vineyard for some time before she spoke. I sensed something troubled her, but she struggled to broach the subject. I'd learned over time it was best to remain at her side and wait patiently; she would speak only when she was fully prepared to do so.

"Andrew, I'm uncertain how to begin. I know it's a sensitive subject." She turned away to study the line of trees beyond the vineyard. "Before we married, you said you could not father any children. Perhaps it's my inexperience speaking, but you seem to manage things quite well in the bedroom."

I chewed on my lower lip as the first pinpricks of fear ran the length of my spine. I wanted to tell her the truth, but I feared her reaction. Would she accept what I was? Would she scream and run away? Would she flee to the Capitol and inform the king? I swallowed hard, thinking furiously as I attempted to manufacture a plausible story that did not involve my ancestry. She knew enough about my past that I wasn't certain I could fabricate a believable tale.

"Vera, I—"

"I'm not complaining, Andrew," she said evenly. "I simply don't understand how both conditions can be true."

I grimaced. I hated lying to her, but what other choice did I have? The truth would place her in danger—or me, if she reacted adversely to the news.

"I was injured long ago. Colin and I were fighting, and he kicked me—hard." I looked at the ground, unable to meet her gaze. "The physician was called, and he determined there was internal damage. He said it would be a miracle if I ever fathered a child, and based on my time with Claire, I'm fairly certain he was right."

Once I'd started, the words flowed smoothly, almost as though I spoke the truth, but guilt twisted my gut, and I continued to look away. She deserved to know, but would taking that risk prove worthwhile? Holy hell, I didn't know what to do.

She narrowed her eyes while her nostrils flared in anger. "I know when you're lying to me. Whatever happened to you, you can tell me. *Trust me*, Andrew. Damn you and your insufferable pride."

I closed my eyes for a moment as I gathered my thoughts. I didn't want to keep secrets from her, but would she still love me if she knew what I was? And if I told her the truth, what would be the outcome? There were only two scenarios I could foresee; she would accept me as I was and life would go on, or she would run away, screaming in terror, then notify the king or his authorities. If the second occurred, I'd be hunted relentlessly and ultimately killed, while she would fare no better, and the promises I'd made to Alexander would be forfeit. Novania permitted sport hunting of the dragon-kind and sanctioned execution for those deemed sympathetic.

Even if she accepted me, the knowledge she'd bear would place her at risk. Did I dare share my secret with the woman I loved?

When I opened my eyes, her gaze was locked on mine. Her eyes glittered in the moonlight, genuinely concerned, yet furious. She deserved to know.

I drew a deep breath and decided to take the greatest risk of my life.

"Vera, you're right, and I'm sorry." I clenched my jaw and raked a hand through my hair. "The truth places us both at risk, and I can't bear to see you hurt. Not on my account."

"Whatever it is, it won't change how I feel about you. You ought to know that by now." She moved closer and took my hands in her own. "We're married, Andrew. Please don't shut me out."

I nodded, then glanced around the vineyard. We were on the farthest hilltop, the house a good distance away, but it was too exposed. There was nothing to block the view from the manor house to our present location, and I could not allow anyone else to witness what I planned to do. The trees of the forest weren't far, and their cover was the best I had available.

"I think it will be easier to show you, but I can't do it here." I gestured toward the trees.

"Andrew, this makes even less sense than before," she protested as she followed me toward the forest.

My heart was pounding as I led her a short distance into the trees. It had been difficult to tell Alexander, but that circumstance had been markedly different. Alexander had a secret of his own to keep, and I knew he would never betray me. I wanted to trust Vera, but I was terrified of her reaction. I didn't want to lose her, not so soon after I'd finally found a place at her side.

I turned to face her once I deemed we were no longer visible from the manor. "Vera, I'm not exactly what I appear to be."

She frowned while her eyebrows knitted together in confusion. "I don't understand."

I pulled off my shirt. "Please, give me a moment. I'll show you what I mean."

I continued to remove my clothing. If I did not, I'd have further explanations to manufacture when we returned to the house—*if* we both returned. And I rather liked the shirt I'd been wearing.

I stepped away from her to ensure there was sufficient space between us. She stared at me as though I'd fallen inexplicably into madness, and perhaps I had. She moved to take a step forward, and I held up one hand to stop her.

"Vera, don't come any closer. It won't be safe."

"Andrew…?"

"Know that whatever happens after this moment, I love you more than anything in the world," I whispered fiercely. "Please, understand… This will put us both at risk."

Her lower lip trembled in the near-darkness, and her eyes were shiny with unshed tears. "Andrew, please, you're frightening me."

"I will *never* hurt you, Vera. Please don't be afraid."

I shifted. My body swelled and elongated to many times its previous size. I stretched my wings expansively before I folded them along my now-scaly back. I was petrified of her reaction and kept my gaze fixed on the canopy of leaves above.

"Andrew?" her voice no longer quavered; her tone was one of awe.

My heart thundered, and given its present size, I was certain she could hear it in the stillness of the evening. She hadn't fled or screamed in terror. I drew a deep breath and swiveled my head to look at her.

She'd moved forward and stood only a few steps away, her eyes wide with wonder. "A skin-changer," she breathed. She reached toward me, then withdrew her hand. "Andrew, if I had not witnessed you change, I would never have believed it possible. You're…magnificent." She took another step closer. "May I touch you?"

I nodded and lowered my head so that it was within her reach. Tentatively, she placed one hand on the end of my snout. I could feel the warmth of her palm through the thick scales and was pleasantly surprised. I'd never made physical contact with anyone while in my dragon form. I closed my eyes and relished the contact, profoundly relieved that she had not run away, terrified by my transformation.

A low rumble came from somewhere in the depths of my chest. The sound was involuntary, and it startled us both. Her eyes widened and I peered down at myself in wonder.

After a few seconds, Vera laughed. "Andrew, are you purring?"

The sound was akin to that of a cat, but on a much grander scale. I hadn't been aware I was capable of the reaction, and I certainly *was* purring.

When I nodded again, she shed the last of her fears and placed one hand on either side of my enormous, scaly face. The involuntary rumble intensified in both strength and volume, and I grinned. She gazed into my eyes as a small smile formed on her lips.

"Your eyes are the same color," she said after a moment. "That mossy green suits you in both forms."

I nuzzled her playfully, eliciting another laugh.

"What is it like to fly?" she asked after a moment.

I'd never attempted flight, though I assumed I could fly if I tried. If I stretched my wings, my wingspan was longer than the manor house was wide, which would allow me to become airborne with ease. Since I'd spent the majority of my life hiding my true nature, I didn't know what I was truly capable of.

I tried to respond, but my words were garbled. My jaws were longer, my tongue thicker, and my teeth were the size of daggers. The combination made speech difficult. I tried again but only succeeded and uttering more of the strange, muddled syllables. I shook my head, frustrated.

"Andrew?"

I sighed and shifted back to my human form. "I couldn't get my mouth to work properly," I told her as my face flushed. "I tried to tell you I've never flown before, but it came out as the rubbish you just heard."

She collected my discarded clothing and handed it to me.

"Does it hurt when you change?"

I shook my head as I pulled on my trousers. "No, but the sensation is difficult to put into words. When I become a dragon, there is a sensation of raw power. It's exhilarating. When I return to this form, I feel like I've lost a part of myself, and I am…lessened. But neither cause me pain."

Once I was dressed again, we began to stroll back toward the manor house. She took my arm in hers and seemed satisfied with the outcome of our conversation.

"This explains so many things about you, Andrew."

I arched an eyebrow in question.

"Well, it adequately explains why you can't have children," she replied. "It also explains why you're never cold and why you're so incredibly strong. It's all a part of what you are." She leaned into me and smiled. "My library has a collection of books on your people's history, you know. I've read some of them. Lord Sandson was particularly interested in dragons and why they decided to leave our world. It seems they left at least one of their own behind."

I nodded. "Mother told me she doubted my father knew she was with child. He left when the other dragons did, shortly before she realized she was carrying me. He was a powerful mage and could change his form, which is how I came about. She'd been terrified that I'd emerge in my dragon form, but fortunately, I was born human." I shrugged. "I still marvel that she managed to hide what I am from the king. She was fiercely protective of me until I was old enough to understand that I must not change on a whim. I learned to control the urge to shift and went about life as a relatively normal boy."

"With practice, would you be capable of speech?" she asked, genuinely curious.

I nodded. "I believe so. I've only changed forms a handful of times, and I'm still learning what I'm capable of."

"Does anyone else know?"

"Alex."

She chuckled. "Yes, of course Alex would know. The two of you were nearly inseparable before I came along."

"He'll keep my secret," I assured her. "You can trust him implicitly."

"But Thomas doesn't know?"

I shook my head. "Tom is a good man, but he's very strict when it comes to the law. If he were to learn, he'd feel obligated to report me. I'd be forced to flee south or risk being hunted like an animal. For the first time in many years, I'm happy. It would be a shame if I was forced to leave this behind."

She squeezed my hand. "It gladdens my heart to know you're happy, Andrew."

I smiled at her words, supremely content. Had I been in my dragon form, I would have begun purring again. I replayed the scene in the forest and noted it was this exact emotion I'd experienced when the sensation first began. The reaction had been involuntary, but I'd relished it.

As we neared the back entrance to the house, she spun in front of me to block my path. "Thank you for being honest with me, Andrew. I understand why it was so difficult." She stretched onto her toes and kissed me. "I will happily keep your secret, so long as you promise that one day, you'll take me flying."

I laughed and drew her into my arms. "Vera, you're amazing. And I promise that if it's safe to do so, we will fly together."

# TEN

"Oh, hell, what am I to do?" Cassandra peered through the window while her hands twisted the hem of her apron. "We've just finished lunch, and the princes are at the stable!"

I bolted from my seat and joined her at the window. My brothers had dismounted and were speaking with Giles while two soldiers in royal livery led their horses away.

I glanced over my shoulder to grin at Vera, unable to hide my excitement. "Alex and Tom are here!"

Vera rose gracefully and took my arm. "I'm certain they'll understand, Cassandra," she said to the cook. "They may be royalty, but they're reasonable. We'll have an early supper in their honor."

Cassandra nodded absently but still appeared stricken. "Of course."

We made our way outside to greet my brothers. Thomas, always the formal one, shook my hand, then bowed to Vera. Alexander ignored protocol and drew me into a rough embrace, then clapped me on the shoulder with a grin.

"This place is fantastic!" he exclaimed. "It's no wonder you were so eager to come here."

"How was your journey?" I asked.

"Ah, not too bad, in truth," he replied. "We had to scare off some bandits the first night out, but it was nothing we couldn't handle."

Thomas shook his head. "Alex makes it sound as if it was nothing. Those men were brutes, and it's a lucky thing I insisted we take the guards along."

I raised an eyebrow. "Alex?"

He scratched at the nape of his neck. "I thought we'd be fine, just the two of us, but Tom's right. The guards were a big help that night... I'm as good with a sword as you are, Andrew, but I was deluding myself. We would have been outnumbered."

"Are you hurt?" Vera asked, concerned.

Alexander laughed. "No. We drove them off, as I said. I would have been in sorry shape if we'd traveled alone, though. One of the bandits was positively massive!"

"Let's go inside where it's cooler," Vera said. "Cassandra will begin preparing supper, and while she cooks, you can catch up on recent events."

I led them to the modest parlor where we took seats facing one another.

"You seem to be doing well, Andrew," Thomas observed after a moment. "You're happy and hale. Vinterry has been good for you."

"Tom's right," Alexander agreed. "Perhaps moving away from the Capitol was the best thing you could have done for yourself. Colin's been a terror since he was released. He's been going out of his way to antagonize father."

"I haven't received any news from the Capitol since we departed," I said. "If Colin has been let off house-arrest, that means Claire made it to her father's estate safely?"

"Yes...and no," Alexander replied as a troubled frown creased his face.

"Claire went home as she intended and arrived safely," Thomas explained, "but as soon as father let Colin off house-arrest, he left in pursuit of her. He apologized to her father profusely, and Duke Ellington relented. He signed Claire's marriage documents for her, and she's back in the Capitol with Colin. She's hardly spoken a word to anyone since her return, though I don't believe Colin has hurt her again."

I was outraged. "That's unacceptable! Does the duke even know what Colin did to her?"

"Oh, the duke knows," Alexander replied, "and he doesn't care. In his eyes, the glory of his daughter being wed to the kingdom's heir outweighs any risk to her personal safety."

"Father has spoken with Claire on the matter, and it seems she is resigned to her fate," Thomas added. "Her father is as unrelenting as they come."

I could attest to that. Duke Ellington would stop at nothing until he achieved his goals, and his primary ambition had been to see Claire on the throne. I'd never liked the man. When he'd believed I was heir, he'd spared no expense as he'd tried to impress me time and again. I'd despised the false congeniality he'd shrouded himself in and maintained my distance when able. No doubt he had nothing pleasant to say about me now that Colin had been named in my stead.

"There's more," Thomas said, breaking through my reverie.

I looked at him sharply. Behind him, Vera appeared in the doorway. I motioned for her to join us, and she took a seat next to me.

"Andrew, I'm sorry…" Thomas looked down and began to fidget.

Alexander sighed in exasperation. "Two days before we left, Claire announced she was with child."

I understood the implications. Now that she was expecting, she could not seek an annulment should Colin harm her again. It was infuriating.

"I believed those nasty rumors she spread about you were only vindictive nonsense," Thomas said apologetically.

I rolled my eyes and bit back a reply as Vera placed a hand on my arm. Her light touch calmed me. It wasn't Thomas' fault that Claire was pregnant by Colin and had ultimately proved that not only was I a bastard, but a sterile one at that.

"Before you start down that path, I knew before we married what to expect," she told Thomas sternly. "It didn't change how I felt about him, and it doesn't matter to me if I never bear children. He's a good man, and that should be enough for the rest of you."

Thomas nodded and managed a nervous smile. Alexander caught my eye, one eyebrow arched in question. I nodded subtly, indicating that we should talk later when Thomas was busy elsewhere.

"What other news do you bring?" I asked, seeking a change of subject.

"The Corodan are keeping their end of the bargain," Alexander replied. "The reports from the north claim all is well. Father is especially pleased. Your chosen replacement is set to be married soon but has also resigned, and it caused a bit of an uproar. No one wants the commander post if it means they have to work with Colin."

Thomas snickered. "He's made many enemies. It's going to become troublesome for him one day."

We spent the remainder of the afternoon chatting about Vinterry. Thomas was fascinated by the wine-making process, and Vera promised she would introduce him to the vintner in the morning. He also requested to see the library after we'd supped, eager to get his hands on some new reading material. Alexander scoffed at the request. He'd done what he could to tear our youngest brother away from his studies with their journey, but Thomas' appetite for knowledge was insatiable.

When Cassandra announced the evening meal was ready, Vera led us into the large dining room where most of the staff had gathered. Further introductions were made as we sat down to enjoy the spread; venison chops, new potatoes, and fresh vegetables from Vinterry's garden were paired with some of Hiram's finest wine. Cassandra had outdone herself—the meal was exquisite.

"You know," Alexander said after sampling a few forkfuls, "you could run the kitchen back home if you wanted to. This is fantastic."

Cassandra blushed at the compliment. "I thank you, my lord, but I prefer living here."

Alexander laughed. "I certainly understand the appeal. And call me Alex. I'm here as Andrew's brother. I don't require special treatment."

"That applies to me as well," Thomas added. "Tom is fine."

After the meal was finished and Cassandra began clearing the dishes away, Vera asked Giles to escort Thomas to the library. As the rest of the staff dispersed for the evening, I asked both Vera and Alexander to accompany me outside. The sun was setting; the swatch of sky visible above the trees was awash in orange and crimson amidst a chorus of crickets.

"Alex, I wanted to talk with you about what was said earlier."

"I'd ask 'which part,' but I think I already know." He grinned. "You told her, didn't you?"

"I...Yes." I glanced at Vera, who smiled.

"It wasn't so much telling as it was showing," she replied.

"Wait! She's *seen* you? Even I haven't had that opportunity." Alexander pouted as though he were a child, and I laughed.

"Alex, it was the only way," I said. "I fought with myself for months about whether or not to say anything. It was one of the most terrifying decisions I've ever made." I glanced at Vera and smiled fondly. "It went in my favor, however. She didn't run away screaming as I'd feared she would."

"Actually," Vera cut in, "I think we could use your help. Andrew needs to learn more about his abilities, and while you're here, perhaps you can assist."

Alexander brightened. "Yes, anything. But where would we go? I assume your staff doesn't know?"

"They don't, and it's best we keep it that way." She gestured to the nearby forest. "There are no other settlements in this region unless you're willing to travel more than a day. Vinterry is secluded, which is ideal for what I have in mind. I suggest you head north into the forest—it's farthest from the road, and there is nothing there that will draw my staff's attention. Go under the guise of a hunting expedition. No one will question you."

Her plan had merit, and it was obvious she'd put considerable thought into her request. "Thank you," I said.

"After everything you've done for me, it's the least I can do in return. Alex will finally see your other form and can learn more about it." Vera shifted her attention to Alexander. "He needs to work on speech, foremost. Nodding is all well and good, but it's limited in its capacity to convey what must be said."

Alexander tilted his head to one side, thoughtful. "Speech is that different for you?" he asked. "I've heard you roar, and believe me, that bellow could wake the dead."

I was growing uncomfortable under their combined scrutiny and shook my head. "A dragon's jaws are much different than a man's. I tried to speak, but nothing intelligent came out of my mouth. I can speak, but I need practice."

Alexander nodded. "So, we're 'hunting' tomorrow, then? Shall we plan to bring something back for supper? If we have all day, I'm sure there will be time."

Vera smiled. "If you bring game back, Cassandra will make something of it. If not, we have plenty of chickens for slaughter."

"Please make sure Tom takes a break to eat something during the day," I said. "When he becomes absorbed in his reading, he's been known to go whole days without food. It isn't good for him."

"I'll keep an eye on him," she promised. "I think I'm beginning to believe what Alex said before we married. You worry about everyone entirely too much and often forget to take care of yourself."

We left the estate just after dawn the next morning. Thomas was relieved we were going off on our own; he was eager to spend more time in the library and didn't wish to be disturbed by Alexander's teasing. As Vera had anticipated, no one questioned our plans.

We traveled north as sunlight began to stream through the trees. The day was warm despite the early hour, and by noon it would be sweltering. As part of our ruse, we each carried a bow and a quiver of arrows, though I doubted they'd be used.

I didn't speak. My silent anxiety began to grate on Alexander's nerves after a short time, and he shot me several irritated glances before he gave in to his need for conversation. He'd never handled silence well.

"Andrew, you're too quiet."

I nodded. "I'm sorry, Alex. I'm—"

"You're *worrying*." He frowned, though a hint of amusement danced in his eyes. "I know you. You're brooding because you aren't certain of the outcome. I agree with Vera. You need to learn what you're capable of. I *know* your secret, brother. Nothing will change between us." He paused to scratch at the base of his neck. "I don't trust Colin, and I'm afraid of what will happen when he comes into power. Andrew, I'll need your help—and not your usual brand, either. You need to do this. If not for yourself, then do it for me."

I held his gaze for several moments. It was out of character for Alexander to ask for help, and he was clearly terrified of the possibilities should his Mark be discovered. I couldn't blame him. Colin would ensure he suffered.

I nodded. "You're right. I wasn't considering your part in this. I'm sorry, brother."

Our path led through the forest for some distance, and our conversation once again faltered as we finished the remainder of our trek. We stopped when we reached a small clearing with a pond at its heart. The space was large enough to accommodate my other form, yet distant enough from the estate that we wouldn't be overheard or inadvertently seen. I surveyed the space, filing the pond into memory as a potential fishing hole, and decided it would suffice.

"This seems adequate," Alexander said, as though reading my thoughts.

I nodded and drew a breath. "Are you ready?"

He laughed. "I've been waiting for this since the day you shared your secret. Hurry up, brother."

I chuckled. "Fine."

I undressed and tossed the garments at my brother, then stepped away from him, giving myself space. I shifted. The familiar sense of expansion washed over me, followed by the heady effect of the power I possessed as a dragon. I stretched my wings, recalling the promise I'd made to Vera. I would fulfill it one day. Now that it had been planted in my mind, the notion of flight was tantalizing.

Alexander's eyes widened at my sudden transformation, and his face paled. He gaped and backed away instinctively.

I grimaced and hung my head, frustrated that he seemed to fear me despite a lifetime spent in one another's company. I didn't know how to assure him I posed no danger. My previous attempts at speech had been a horrific failure.

"Holy hell, Andrew."

I peered at him sheepishly.

Alexander shook his head, bewildered. When he spoke, his voice trembled. "The stories we were told describe dragons as large, but…you're *enormous*. I hope you don't take offense, but you're a bit terrifying right now."

I was covered in black scales, and I understood the basic form my body had taken, but I only knew what I could see. I swiveled my neck to look into the pond and blinked several times in surprise. I'd seen drawings of dragons in books, and while my form was true to the artists' renderings, it was a shock to look at myself through a dragon's eyes.

Vera was right; my eyes were the same shade of green, but the pupils were now slit vertically and were unmistakably reptilian. A ridge of stiff, black spines ran from the top of my head down the length of my spine to the end of my tail. Experimentally, I stretched my wings and noted they were webbed; the undersides were a dusky shade of purple and lacked scales. I turned away after several moments to face Alexander.

He seemed so small, but it was only a matter of changed perspective. Our gazes locked, and I wished I could say something to allay his fears.

He studied me for a moment, then strode forward. "You said you have difficulty speaking. I think I can see why…" He examined me for several more seconds, then nodded. "The shape of your jaw is different. Open your mouth. I want to look inside."

I eyed him skeptically, and he burst out laughing. "That expression! That is such a *you* expression, Andrew."

I rolled my eyes, then lowered my head to his level and opened my jaws. I wasn't certain what he'd learn, but we'd come for this purpose. I'd humor his curiosity.

"Holy hell," he repeated, awe-struck. "Your teeth could be used as short swords, or at the very least, kitchen knives. I think that's part of your problem."

He'd moved his head, and I could no longer see him beneath the elongated shape of my snout. I was forced to wait for him to finish his inspection and step away before I could close my jaws.

"Do you remember when we were small, and the governess had to go through speech exercises with Tom? Well, I was small. You would have been a teenager."

I nodded. Thomas had been slow to start speaking as a child, and it had taken intensive instruction with the governess before he could properly converse. Since I'd been much older, I'd never been present for his lessons, busy with the castle garrison and campaigns as I'd been.

"She taught him to think the words through first, then speak slowly, with precision. Until you become used to speaking, I think you'll need to do the same."

I nodded again.

"Let's begin. Remember, think of the words, *then* speak them." He paused and frowned thoughtfully. "What was it like to change and fight the Corodan?"

I drew a breath and tried to launch into the story, ignoring his instructions. I succeeded only in making a series of unintelligible sounds and a number of hisses. Frustrated, I growled low in my throat and looked away.

"Andrew, you have to take it slow. I know that isn't your style, but it's the only way this will work."

Alexander placed his hand against one of my forelegs in an attempt to comfort me, but I wasn't certain if this exercise was worthwhile. It should not have been so damned hard.

"Try again, brother. Think about your words, then speak *slowly*."

I heaved a sigh and glowered at him. This required a level of patience that I simply did not possess. Alexander was doing his best to encourage me, and I didn't want to disappoint him, so I grudgingly tried again. I concentrated on my words and the form my mouth must take to pronounce each syllable.

"Alexsss…"

I was startled by the meager success. My voice was far deeper than I was accustomed to, but I supposed that should have been no surprise, given my present size.

He laughed. "That was good! Keep going."

"I fell…down. Corachhh—" I shook my head in irritation. "Hive…queen met…me…I drew…sssword."

"Go on."

"If…I…did not…ssshift…ssshe would…kill…me…Ssshe wasss…not…allao. Allao… Alloo…"

I lost my temper and roared at the sky, furious that I could not complete the simple task of forming a sentence. Ashamed at my sudden outburst, I turned away.

Alexander strode around my enormous body to stand in front of me. "Andrew, I understand this is difficult. We have to keep trying, but you *can* do this. I understood most of that—until you lost the battle with your temper." He smirked. "By the way, that roar of yours is one of the most terrifying things I've ever heard."

I glared at him sullenly. We'd only been working on this for a few minutes, and already I'd had my fill.

"Give it one more try, Andrew," he said. "If it still doesn't work, we'll do something else. Deal?"

When I nodded, he said, "You said if you didn't shift, the hive queen would have killed you. And that she was not…something."

"Ssshe wasss…not…al…one. Al…one." I nodded. "Alone."

"Good. See? You can to this, brother. How many were there?"

I allowed the memory to replay in my mind. There had been dozens of Corodan waiting in the pit, prepared to attack me at the hive-queen's command.

"Many… Dozensss."

"Dozens?" When I nodded, he asked, "Then what happened?"

We conversed in that stilted, aggravating manner for some time. Alexander continued to pose questions while I fumbled for a response. After an hour, I needed a respite. I was making little progress, and the "s" sounds were proving to be a distraction each time I pronounced them. Beyond that, it was growing hot and I was developing a headache.

"Alexsss…I need…ressst."

He nodded, understanding. "What else can you do, brother? Show me something."

I paused for a moment, considering what I was capable of. Beyond destroying something with brute strength, I was uncertain. The prospect of smashing something was appealing, however; I was weary and resented my lack of progress.

I lumbered toward one side of the clearing and selected the largest tree within my reach. It was a tall oak with a broad trunk, a tree that had likely stood there for a century or more. I glanced at Alexander, who had remained behind. He watched my movements with mild curiosity.

I lifted my right foreleg experimentally and flexed the clawed hand. Alexander had asked for a demonstration, and I'd give him one. I smashed my fist into the tree with as much force as I could muster. The trunk shattered with a satisfying crack, then rocked precariously to one side. I caught it with my other hand before it crashed to the ground and laid the broken tree carefully onto its side.

I turned to face Alexander with a grin plastered on my face. His expression was one of horrified awe before he burst out laughing.

"Damn, Andrew, that was something!" He laughed again. "It's funny. Every time you make one of those expressions, I can see *you* in there. I mean, it *is* you, but you're different now. I didn't expect to recognize your facial expressions beneath those scales."

He strode across the clearing to stand at my side while inspecting the damage I'd inflicted upon the tree. He shook his head in amusement. "One strike and that tree came down like it was made of sand. I suppose I did ask you to show me something, didn't I?"

"Yesss."

"And knowing you as I do, you feel much better after expending your pent-up fury on a poor, inanimate object."

"Yesss."

He grinned and glanced skyward. "If we leave now, it'll be noon before we reach the estate," he said. "I think we've made progress today, don't you?"

I growled. I didn't share his optimism.

He rolled his eyes. "I can understand some of what you're trying to say. It's better than the rubbish you were spewing when we first began."

I gazed at him levelly, mildly annoyed, and hoped my current stature would intimidate him into an agreement. I refused to acknowledge he was right.

When he smirked and said nothing, I knew my ploy had failed. After a moment, I shifted back to my human form and ran a hand through my hair with a weary sigh. While I dressed, Alexander continued to study the fallen oak.

As we began our trek back to the estate, he said, "I much prefer you in this form, brother. The dragon is a mighty powerful beast, but I'll admit, you're intimidating. And holy hell, that roar..." He shuddered dramatically.

I snorted. "If the need for a dragon arises, intimidation might be warranted."

"I understand why the Corodan emissary feared you. *Danger. Power. Death.* You'd told me by then what you were, but after seeing it, I think those words aptly describe my own feelings."

"Alex, I'd never hurt you." I was mortified that he would even consider the possibility.

"I know, Andrew, I know. It was…an instinctive reaction. I knew it was you, but…" He sighed and trailed off, uncertain how to describe his experience.

I frowned and crossed my arms. "I could not have been that terrifying. You stuck your head in my mouth just to get a better look at my teeth."

"That was after my initial shock." His voice was quiet, contemplative. "How did Vera react?"

I smiled and recalled how I'd felt when she placed her hands on my face; the strange, yet wonderful sensation that she'd called a purr. "She was in awe but seemed unafraid."

"If it's alright by you, I'd like to speak with her later. We ought to compare our experiences, and perhaps then I can help you more effectively."

"She may have some insight about the speech trouble as well." I shrugged. "There is nothing more frustrating than knowing what I want to say, yet being unable to properly communicate it."

"I think that poor oak tree can attest to your frustrations, brother," Alexander teased. "I hope Cassandra has lunch ready when we return. I'm famished."

# ELEVEN

I peered toward the manor house as we approached from another of our "hunts," troubled by the commotion in the yard. It was past noon, I was weary and hungry, Alexander was in a foul temper, and our collective patience was spent. I'd made little progress over the past week and grown more frustrated with each outing. The strain was taking its toll on both of us, but Alexander had borne the brunt of my building rage.

Neither of us was in a mindset to deal with the uproar, but it seemed we'd been spotted. I ground my teeth and forced a smile as Gregor ran toward us. The boy skidded to a halt once he was near, then beamed, oblivious to the tension between us.

"Alex, sir! There's a man at the stable!" He was breathless from the run and from the excitement at having been sent on what he deemed an important errand.

"We'll be there in a moment," Alexander replied.

Gregor took that as his cue to dash back the way he'd come.

Alexander chuckled. "I don't know if I ever possessed as much energy as he has."

I snorted. "You had thrice that and some to spare."

"I wish I had it now. Your temper is wearisome, brother." A tight smile crossed his lips. "I hope you know I've only been trying to help."

I winced, but nodded. "I do. I'm sorry I've taken my frustrations out on you."

He smirked, the mischief rekindled in his gaze. "As Vera said last evening, there's no one better suited to tame the beast."

I swatted at him, but he danced away with a laugh. The sound died abruptly when the rider came into view. He was standing beside his horse, hands on his knees, exhausted. The poor creature was lathered and blowing, a clear sign the man had come in haste. He was dressed in the colors of the royal court, and I recognized him as one of the garrison's scouts.

"My lord." He knelt in deference at our approach. "I bring urgent news from the Capitol."

He withdrew a scroll from his tunic. Its ends were sealed in red wax and bore the royal boar insignia.

Alexander snatched the scroll with a groan. He broke the wax seals and unfurled the parchment with an irritated frown. I stood at a distance to allow him a moment of privacy, but I recognized the sprawling and near-illegible script that belonged to Colin. From my position, I couldn't make out the words, but I knew any message from Colin was sure to bear foul tidings.

Alexander's face fell and became ashen. He looked up at me, his expression stricken, and thrust the message into my hands. "Read it," he croaked. "I can't..."

*Dearest brothers,*

*It is with a heavy heart that I ask you to return prematurely from your holiday. Our father, the king, passed away in the night. I require your assistance. Come home quickly, and ensure that Andrew does not accompany you. He is no longer family, and is not welcome to join in our private affairs.*

Colin had mustered the audacity to sign the scroll as "Novania's new monarch." I was more incensed by the assumption of his father's title than I was by his blatant refusal to include me in what should have been a family affair. By law, he could not call himself king without a proper coronation ceremony. It was an affront to Carlton's memory.

Finished reading, I looked up to find Alexander struggling to maintain his composure. I took him by the arm and led him into the house, where I bade him sit in the parlor. He stared at the floor, his expression haunted.

"I'll fetch Tom," I stated thickly.

I placed the scroll on the small table beside his chair. He managed a nod as tears began to leak from his eyes.

Thomas was in the library, perched on a padded bench alongside an open window, a thick volume spread across his lap. He'd been so engrossed in his reading, he'd failed to hear my approach.

I stood beside him for a moment, then cleared my throat. "Tom." He looked up, startled. "Andrew? I'm sorry, I didn't hear—"

"Tom, we need you in the parlor. It's important."

He frowned, his expression pinched with concern as he laid the book aside. By the time we returned to the parlor, Vera had arrived and was attempting to console Alexander. Overwhelmed with grief, he held his head in his hands and sobbed, while she offered what comfort she could. Witnessing his grief stoked my own, and I felt the first sting of tears threaten.

I gestured to the parchment for Thomas' benefit. He plucked it from the table and began to read.

Thomas stumbled; I took his arm and guided him to one of the empty chairs. He looked up, his eyes shiny with emotion. "Andrew, this letter was not addressed to you, and... Colin has made it clear he doesn't consider you family any longer. That aside, I wish you would accompany us to the Capitol."

"Tom, he's the crown prince. I can't defy his orders."

I swallowed hard as my grief swelled. Carlton Marsden had always been kind to me, had raised me as one of his own. To think him dead was unfathomable. To be denied the opportunity to pay my last respects to the man who raised me was the greatest insult Colin could have contrived. I was certain Colin knew it too, the bastard.

Thomas nodded and wiped at his eyes. "I know, Andrew. Father was in good health when we left. It wasn't even a fortnight..."

"I'll tell you this, Tom," Alexander cut in fiercely. "Colin had a hand in his death. Mark my words."

"Alex, you don't know that," I replied. "Colin will ascend the throne in a few weeks. Be careful of your words, brother. He won't accept grief as an excuse for your accusations."

Alexander scowled. "I hear you, brother. Will you inform the messenger that we'll depart in the morning?"

My brothers left with the dawn. I maintained a stoic façade, but was devastated that I'd been forbidden to join them. The king had been the father I'd never truly had. As soon as my half-brothers were out of sight, I retired to our bedroom, unwilling to face the remainder of the day. I needed time alone, to grieve out of sight from the piteous glances of Vinterry's staff.

Vera instinctively understood my needs and left me to my grief for much of the day. She ventured upstairs with a tray from Cassandra as afternoon began to wane into evening. I was seated in the chair beside the window, though the heavy curtains were drawn, casting the room in shadows to mirror my dark mood. I'd wept once alone, but by the time Vera arrived, my tears were spent. I was numb, left hollow and empty by the king's death and Colin's snub.

She placed the tray on the bedside table and knelt beside me. "Is there anything I can do?"

I shook my head but made no reply. A tight knot had formed in my throat and I was uncertain if I could voice a response.

"Very well," she whispered, concern in her tone. She leaned over and kissed me lightly on the cheek. "If you need anything, let me know. I'm here for you."

I nodded as she took her leave. I was grateful for her support, though it would be some time before I could properly thank her. I remained in the chair for another span of time, recalling memories from my younger years when both the king and my mother had still been alive. Those had been happier times.

When I finally crossed the room to the tray of food Vera had left behind, I realized I was ravenous. I tore into it and devoured every morsel, though it had grown cold while I wallowed in misery. Feeling marginally better, I decided to return the tray to the kitchen. The staff that I encountered gave their condolences and were quietly respectful. They understood what I'd endured over the past months, and the loss of the king was yet another painful blow. I was grateful for their empathy.

Cassandra was in the midst of preparing the evening meal when I entered her domain. She glanced up sharply, then her features softened. "Will you be joining us this evening, or shall I prepare another tray for you? It's all the same to me." She offered me a smile.

"I'll join the household," I replied. "Have you seen Vera?"

She nodded. "She's in the library. It seems that bookish brother of yours found something interesting before he was called away."

"Thank you."

The library's curtains were tied open to allow the fading light to spill across the room. Vera was seated on a cushion near the cold hearth, poring over the same thick volume that I'd spied in Thomas' hands the day before. She looked up as I entered and offered me a tentative smile laced with concern.

"Andrew, is there anything I can do?"

I nodded and seated myself beside her. "I grew tired of being alone with only my thoughts for company."

"I understand." She gestured to the book she held in her hands. "I think you will find some of this interesting. Thomas came across it a few days ago and mentioned it contains valuable history. It seems there is no copy of it in the Capitol."

"What does it speak of?" I needed something to occupy my mind apart from the tragedy of Carlton's passing and Colin's insult.

She arched one eyebrow knowingly. "Dragons."

"Ah." I nodded, but couldn't muster a smile. "Tom's always been fascinated by the stories, but sometimes I don't think he believes them. I wish his temperament was different—he'd be a great help. As it is, I can't risk telling him."

She took my hand in her own. "I know, but I think you ought to take a look at this book. If even half of this is true, you come from a very fascinating lineage."

"I'm not truly in the mood for reading," I admitted. "I came here to be with you."

She smiled. "I know books don't interest you, Andrew. Perhaps I can share some of what I've read?"

I nodded.

She squeezed my hand gently, then leafed back a few pages. "This section talks about why the dragons left our world. The writer claims to have spoken with the some of the last *emissaries*, as he calls them, before they departed."

"Why did they leave?" I asked.

The stories I'd been told by the governess as a child featured the exploits of the dragons, their powerful mages and unrivaled warriors, and their society prior to the Mage Wars nearly a thousand years ago. I had little knowledge of the more recent history of my father's people.

She frowned. "The dragons believed it was their birthright to roam the skies, but when King Philip Marsden came to power, he banished the dragons from Novania. He enacted a law that stated dragons could be hunted for sport if they crossed the kingdom's borders. The dragons were an incredibly intelligent species. It sickens me to think someone would allow that to occur."

"Philip Marsden was Colin's great-grandfather," I replied. "Colin has always taken a keen interest in his reign, though I don't believe he was-well liked by the people."

My mind traveled a dark path with Vera's summary. I was certain Colin was aware of the law, and he'd waste no time enforcing it should my secret be revealed. An image of Colin on horseback, a wicked spear in his hand as he chased me through the plains, played through my mind. I grimaced and shook my head in a futile attempt to dislodge the unwanted vision.

"The dragons left Novania during Philip's reign," Vera continued. "Most traveled south, beyond the Mage's Gate, but it seems a few scattered groups went north beyond the Gloaming Highlands. Andrew, didn't your mother grow up in the north?"

I nodded. "She did."

"Then it would make sense if your father was from one of those northern clans," she mused. "Although, if he was a mage and could pass himself off as human, he could have come from the south." Returning to the book, she said, "At the end of Philip's reign, the dragons began to form a plan to leave this world entirely. They wished to live without persecution and believed there were no more viable options here. It took many years before they carried out their plan... There is a long passage about gathering resources and artifacts, and consulting someone known as 'the Oracle.' It goes on to say that in the year King Carlton was crowned, the dragons were poised to make good on their plan. Their greatest mages performed a ritual to open a gateway to another world. The entire species departed to pursue their destiny elsewhere."

"And Carlton is—*was* Colin's father. He was crowned only a few months after he met my mother. She was pregnant by then... She'd told him her former lover was killed by brigands as he defended her honor, but we know the truth." I raked a hand through my hair and sighed. "He was a good man and a good father. I will sorely miss him."

"We all will, Andrew," she said softly. "You more so than most. I truly believe Colin will be the ruin of this land."

I nodded. "I hope Alex will be careful. He has a habit of saying things that land him in trouble, and given Colin's recent behavior, he won't stand for it."

"I've never understood why Colin goes out of his way to humiliate you as he does."

I shrugged. "Colin assumed I would be named heir to the throne. I never corrected him, though I knew the truth—and that turned out to be a mistake. Colin has always been vain and jealous. When he was named heir, he began to publicly embarrass me. I believe it's his way of flexing his newfound power after living so many years in my perceived shadow." I paused to stare out the window as I gathered my thoughts. "Looking back, it shouldn't have been a surprise. It hurts like hell knowing I'm unable to pay my last respects to the king. He may not have been my father, but he acted the part."

The strangling knot reformed in my throat, and I hung my head. Vera drew her arms around me, and I leaned into her embrace. I was vulnerable and needed her in a way I'd never believed possible—I'd always been the protector, the guardian to those I loved, but now, I felt fragile, weakened by grief. She was a comfort as I grappled with the onslaught of emotions, my tether in the maelstrom my life had become. I slid one arm around her slim waist and held her close, drawing solace from her presence.

"We'll get through this, Andrew," she promised. "I will be here for you every step of the way."

I received a letter from Thomas two weeks later.

I'd begun to move on with life. I busied myself with preparations for Vinterry's grape harvest. It would start with the onset of autumn, only a few short weeks away. My days were filled with moving casks and repairing barrels, hauling crates of bottles from the storage building, and assisting in the myriad of other tasks Hiram needed done prior to the harvest. The work took my mind away from the recent tragedy.

In the evenings, Vera and I supped with the staff, then retired to the library where she continued to read the thick volume Thomas had discovered. I'd begun to regain my sense of self, though I knew the pain of loss would never completely fade.

The messenger arrived as evening fell. Giles led her inside as we gathered for supper in Vinterry's spacious dining room.

"News from the Capitol, my lady."

The woman behind Giles paled as her eyes met mine. I didn't recognize her, but it was clear she knew me. She bowed stiffly and presented a folded letter to Vera.

"A message from Prince Thomas, my lady," she said, then flicked another nervous glance in my direction.

"Thank you," Vera said with a smile. "Would you care to join us for supper? No doubt you've had a long ride."

"I thank you, but no. I must be on my way swiftly." She bowed again, then allowed Giles to lead her outside.

Vera gripped my hand beneath the table. "We'll read your brother's message once we've finished supper," she whispered. "It's strange Thomas addressed it to me."

I grimaced. "Thomas is nothing if not clever. I suspect he is circumventing another of Colin's damned mandates."

We dined, then took the message to the library where we could read its contents in privacy. Once there, Vera broke the wax seals and opened the parchment. She handed it to me without reading it.

"The letter is addressed to you, Andrew. You were right."

I managed a smile, pleased by Thomas' ingenuity. His handwriting was neat and precise, the lines of script evenly spaced. He'd crammed as much onto the single sheet as would fit, but the words were legible.

*Andrew,*

*Things in the Capitol have become tense. When we arrived, Colin had already spoken to the council of governors and scheduled his coronation ceremony. It is set for the date immediately after the required mourning period for our father.*

*Father's body is lying in state, but Colin has refused to allow access to the commonfolk. It is a severe breach of protocol, and many residents are angry and on edge. I fear Colin's actions will incite an insurrection, but Alex believes the tensions will abate given time. I hope he's right. I'm not cut out to defend the castle from an attack.*

*Father is scheduled to be buried tomorrow, but it will be done before you receive this letter. I'm sorry you were unable to say goodbye properly. Father would have wanted you here, but Colin has been very insistent that you not be involved.*

*Alexander has inquired into what happened to Father with the aid of Dukes Horace and Crossley, but Colin has refused to say anything more than father passed in his sleep. He was hale when we left the Capitol to visit you, and I find the circumstances suspicious. Alex may have been right when he said Colin was involved.*

*Claire refuses to leave her rooms. I believe she lives in terror of Colin, but she has nowhere to go. Her father has seen to that, and with ours now dead, she has no escape. I've tried to pay her a few visits, but she has declined. I fear for her safety.*

*Duke Ellington has come to the Capitol, and it seems he is in Colin's favor. They have spoken frequently in private, and I find it concerning. I believe they are plotting something more, but I have no proof. Another man seeks audiences with Colin nearly every day, though I am unfamiliar with him. His name is Robert Claybourne, a minor lord. If rumor is true, he is mean-spirited and crude. There is talk he may be granted your old commander's post.*

*I fear I have little in the way of good news, other than the Corodan have continued to keep their word. I hope this letter finds you well, Andrew. Give Vera my regards.*

*I advise you to destroy this letter after reading it, in case Colin decides to pay you a visit. He cannot be trusted, and my words may incriminate us all.*

*—Tom*

I read the letter a second time, memorizing every detail. His account of the events in the Capitol were concerning, but there was nothing I could do at present. I sighed and handed the missive to Vera.

She nodded, worry creasing her brow as she read the message. When she'd finished, she set it aside. "What will you do?"

I shrugged. "What can I do? Unless Alex or Tom are in danger, I think it best that I remain here. Vinterry is a more welcoming place than the Capitol, and I happen to like its seclusion—and its mistress."

She smiled at my words. "I'm pleased you like it here, Andrew. Now, let's go back to the others. Cassandra made raspberry tarts for dessert, and I'd hate to miss that. There's nothing we can do at present."

I retrieved the letter as we exited the library. When we reached the dining room, I slipped it into the hearth and watched it burn while the tarts were retrieved from the kitchen.

# TWELVE

"I don't understand the last passage we read," Vera said as she pored over the tome regarding dragons once more. "It doesn't seem possible. No creature can heal so rapidly. The book made it sound as though it was nearly instantaneous!"

I clenched my jaw, weary and aggravated. I'd attempted to explain what I knew as fact, yet she refused to believe me. I was spared what would have been an unfortunate retort by the rap of knuckles on the library's open door.

I looked up to find Giles bearing a carefully folded letter sealed in red wax and bearing Thomas' concise script on the outside. "A letter from the Capitol," he said with a grin.

I rose to retrieve the message and muttered a thank you. It had been months since Thomas' last letter; winter had settled over Vinterry, and rather than a stroll through the vineyards to occupy our post-supper hours, Vera and I had begun to frequent the library. She was determined to learn as much about dragons—and skin-changers— as she was able.

"It's from Tom," I said as I resumed my seat next to her.

"I hope it holds better news than the last message we received from the Capitol." Vera snuggled closer, seeking my warmth in addition to that of the hearth at our backs.

I nodded as I broke the wax seals with my thumb. The last missive had been an official decree by Novania's new king and my vindictive half-brother. Colin had announced the birth of his first child, a daughter they'd named Verena. Every noble of rank was required to attend her name day ceremonies in the Capitol—with the exception of the widow Sandson and her commoner husband. It had been yet another snub, but to my relief, Vera appeared unperturbed.

Thomas' letter was a welcome sight after Colin's royal missive.

*Andrew,*

*I must keep this letter brief, as Colin has forbidden communication with you. You've been placed on his list of potential state enemies and are currently under investigation by the governor's council. I advise you to remain at Vinterry and don't try to intervene. Vera's name is not on his list, which is why I've addressed the outer letter to her.*

*But I digress. I write to you regarding Claire. Colin was furious when their child was born a girl. He is desperate for a "proper heir" and blames Claire for his supposed misfortune. I have tried to explain she does not have control over the child's gender, but he cannot be reasoned with. I haven't seen her in a fortnight, and when I last did, she sported bruises. He has become violent again, and she is trapped.*

*You cannot intervene, but I believe you should know. Claire suffers greatly for her role in Colin's affairs. I will do what I can to extricate her from the situation if she'll allow it.*

*Please do not visit the Capitol. Colin will react abhorrently, and I fear what will occur if you do. I will write again when I'm able.*

*—Tom*

I growled a string of curses and crumpled the letter in my fist. "Damn Colin. Damn him!"

Vera placed a hand on my forearm. "Tom is right. It isn't safe for you in the Capitol. Let your brother assist Claire as he can."

"I knew she was in danger the moment we learned her father married her off to Colin against her wishes." I turned to toss the letter into the hearth. "He's a menace to her, to this kingdom, to *everyone*. Damn him."

She shifted the book in her lap and pointed to the passage we'd been discussing prior to Giles' arrival. "Perhaps we return to our previous conversation? There is nothing we can do to help Claire— not without placing you in danger, and I won't stand for that."

I heaved a sigh. "Fine. You didn't believe me when I said the book speaks true in regards to my healing ability. I'll show you."

I rose and picked up the iron poker resting beside the hearth. It had a sharp point and would be sufficient for the task. In my present mood, I was walking the dangerous line between recklessness and fury-induced impatience. A demonstration was in order, and a few minutes of pain would serve to clear my head.

I braced myself, then jammed the sooty tool through the palm of my left hand. Vera gasped in shock and clambered from her seat, her eyes wide with horror.

"Andrew, what have you done?"

With a grunt, I yanked the poker from my hand, then held my palm toward her as blood streamed down my arm. I dropped the poker and allowed it to clatter across the floor. She gazed, transfixed, as the wound began to close on its own. Within a quarter-hour, my hand showed no sign of the injury beyond the streaks of drying blood on my skin. She gaped, stunned into silence by my act, while I frowned impassively.

She'd believed me when I said my scales were nearly impenetrable, and she'd never questioned my strength or my immunity to the cold. But rapid healing had been incomprehensible. I shouldn't have been forced to prove it to her, but she'd left me no choice.

I cleaned the blood from my arm with the end of my shirt while she continued to stare in silence. I replaced the poker and sat down facing her.

Finally, she said, "I'm sorry. I should have listened to you. The book only describes how *dragons* heal, and you're a bit different. But you know more about yourself than a book could ever hope to."

"While I'm not exactly a dragon, I have many of the same attributes," I growled. "I've known since I was a child how rapidly I can heal... But there is a downside to this ability, I've learned."

She gave me a strange look, and I knew I'd have to explain my remark.

"Vera, as a skin-changer, I don't age. Sure, I did as I grew up, but once I reached maturity, I stopped. I will always look exactly as I do now... No matter how old I truly am." I gestured to my face. "I haven't aged a day in over ten years."

"That doesn't seem so bad," she replied.

I shook my head in frustration. She didn't understand what I was trying to convey. One day, she'd appear much older than I would, even though we were roughly the same age. I hoped she wouldn't grow to resent me for it.

"I thought you should hear it from me before you found out for yourself reading that damned book." I paused to study her for a moment. "I love you, Vera."

Her confused frowned deepened, but she said, "I love you too."

"I hope you'll always say that."

As I gazed at her, I couldn't muster a smile. She narrowed her eyes, then gasped as she finally understood.

"Oh, Andrew," she said, exasperated, "I think I know what you're concerned about. I will *always* love you, no matter what you look like and no matter what happens with your brothers."

A few nights later, as we sat beside the hearth in the library while snow fell heavily outside, Vera discovered a passage that spoke of the dragons' exodus. It didn't merely explain the reason why they'd departed—it went into detail regarding some of what it had taken to achieve the feat.

Her voice conveyed her wonder as she read the text aloud. I gazed out the window, watching fat flakes spiral toward the frozen ground as I listened.

There were three dragon-mages of great power tasked to open the gateway with the assistance of ancient artifacts they'd gathered over centuries. The Mark of the Magi was rare even amongst the dragon-kind, though with their exceptional longevity, there were many more dragon-magi than there were magi of other races.

Caelmarion Zorai, an elder amongst the dragon-kind, and two of his proteges, Zayneldarion Caein and Miranetha Fohn had carried out the task. Prior to performing the ritual, both Caelmarion and Zayneldarion had traveled through the forsaken lands of Novania in search of the last artifact they required. The two were considered emissaries—dragon-mages with the ability to appear in human form. Having secured the artifact, they traveled south to the lands beyond the Mage's Gate.

The book went into detail about their travels through Novania, but became sparse once the pair journeyed beyond the kingdom's border. Both dragon-magi had stayed in the northern city of Dresdin's Forge for a period of several months, posing as human merchants while they conducted their search. They'd used the names Cael Masterson and Zayne Blackwell.

I stopped Vera as she spoke the names, but stared into the fire for several moments as my thoughts whirled. Dresdin's Forge was the city where my mother had grown up. I was certain one of the two dragon-magi must have been my father.

"Andrew, what is it?" she asked after a period of strained silence.

As I told her what I'd just pieced together, she smiled and threw her arms around me.

"This is wonderful news! Perhaps now you know what to seek when looking for information about your father. If they were in Dresdin's Forge, there must be some record of them there."

"If my mother were still living, it would be simple," I lamented. "She'd been involved with him for a while before his departure, but I never bothered to ask for his name, and she never gave it."

Mother had been deeply hurt when my father left her, even though she'd understood his need to depart. She'd rarely spoken of him, and I'd never pressed her. I'd hated seeing her in so much pain.

"I'm confident he was one of the two named," Vera stated. "The timing is right, and they were in the same city as your mother." She paused, then peered up at me. "How did your mother meet the late king?"

"He was touring the kingdom as crown prince and happened to stop in Dresdin's Forge," I explained. "The entourage had not provisioned sufficiently between Calder's Point and Port Everly, and was forced to make an unplanned stop half way in between. That was Dresdin's Forge. My mother was the only daughter of Duke Winston, and naturally she was introduced when the new king arrived at her father's manor. According to her, they fell in love on sight. According to the king, it took a few days of coaxing before she warmed up to him. Either way, they were married before he departed Dresdin's Forge. He knew she was with child before they said their vows, but she wasn't showing yet. It was fortunate I inherited so many of my mother's features—at least in this form. No one ever questioned them."

"Your mother obviously knew your father was a dragon."

I nodded. "He told her before he left. She admitted once that she'd feared I'd be discovered, particularly when I was very young. Without mother's protection, it's likely I would have been killed as a child."

"I'm fortunate your mother cared for you so," Vera replied, snuggling into my arms. "I can't imagine what life would be like without you in it now that you're here."

I smiled down at the top of her head and kissed her hair. "And what else does this passage say?"

"After they found the artifact, the two dragons returned south to perform the ritual to open the gateway," she replied. "There are no details concerning the ritual itself, and it simply goes on to say that the dragons left as planned." She looked up from the book with a sigh. "I wish there was more. You deserve to know the truth."

"I've learned a great deal since coming to Vinterry," I said. "Much more than I could have discovered in the Capitol. The king didn't allow many books on the subject of dragons."

"I think I understand Thomas' interest in *this* library, then." She smiled up at me. "Alex spent some time in here too, you know. He came early in the morning, before daylight, and looked at several obscure texts over there." She flicked her fingers in the general direction of the shelves lining the southern wall of the room. "I don't think he knows I learned he was coming here, but the staff keeps me informed of everything. He made certain to leave before Thomas came in. Why is that?"

Cold dread knotted my gut. I suspected I knew the topic of Alexander's research, but it wasn't something I could share with Vera. Instead, I shrugged and said, "Alex probably didn't want to tarnish his reputation by being seen in the library with Tom. What books are on that shelf?"

"More historical texts," she replied. "Nothing very interesting, I'm afraid."

I made a mental note to take a closer look at the titles in that section, certain there was something about the Mage Wars or magi located therein. Alexander would not have been secretive unless he sought knowledge of his Mage's Mark.

It was uneasy knowing he hadn't confided in me about his visits to the library, and I hoped he wasn't planning something rash. Colin wouldn't suffer his insubordination, let alone a demonstration of whatever power Alexander might be capable of. And if my brothers were right, Colin was not above plotting murder as a means of revenge against a fellow royal.

The next morning, I rose early and returned to the library to scour the titles Alexander had been perusing. The library had grown cold during the night and was dim in the pre-dawn light, but I didn't start a fire in the hearth. I didn't require its warmth nor its light to read by, and I didn't want to draw the attention of the staff.

A glance outside the darkened windows told me we were in for another day of falling snow. I sighed, restless and eager for a sign of spring.

I scanned the titles on the shelf Vera had indicated the night before. Most were historical texts recounting various wars and the reigns of Novania's most prominent kings. I was about to move on and dismiss Alexander's odd behavior when I spied a slim tome titled "The Southern Gateway." I pulled the book from the shelf and opened it gingerly; the pages were brittle and yellowed with age.

Across the first two pages, the author revealed the text told the history of the Mage Wars and the creation of the great southern Barrier. There was only one means of passing through the Barrier, a passage that later became known as the Mage's Gate. I'd never been through the southern expanse of the kingdom during my travels, though I'd been told of the strange, shimmering Barrier that ran the length of Novania's border with the Southlands. The book described the Barrier as a vast structure crafted of magic. It was said to be impenetrable and rose from the ground far into the sky, effectively blocking any means of passage by air.

The Mage's Gate was located due south of the Capitol, but would require several days of hard riding to reach from there. Many of the lands south of the Capitol were occupied by farms, and there were few large towns along the route. The author stated the road became increasingly difficult to navigate as one traveled into the less populated lands, and claimed the Mage's Gate was located within a valley resting between two mountain peaks.

I flipped through several pages before locating an exquisitely-drawn map. The southern Barrier was marked in fading, reddish ink, and a dark triangle had been drawn at the location of the Mage's Gate.

The top corner of the page was folded conspicuously. I imagined Alexander studying the page carefully, memorizing its every detail in the gray, pre-dawn light of summer.

A pained sigh escaped my lips. He wasn't planning to provoke Colin as I'd feared. No, he was seeking a means of escape from our brother's rule.

With a heavy heart, I replaced the tome on the shelf and exited the library to begin my tasks for the day, Alexander's plight foremost in my mind.

# THIRTEEN

Winter grudgingly gave way to spring, and as the warmer weather began to take hold, the lands surrounding Vinterry greened and bloomed into life. Gregor expressed an interest in learning the art of the sword during the long winter, and I began to teach him daily. We spent an hour each afternoon behind the stables, wooden practice blades in hand. He was a quick study and rapidly improved. His grandfather would often watch us from a distance, a proud smile lighting up his aged face as the boy thrust and parried.

It was on one such afternoon as I was finishing Gregor's lesson, that Giles called out to me. "A rider approaches from the main road."

"We'll finish this later," I said to Gregor with an apologetic grin.

"Of course, sir. Maybe it's news from the Capitol?"

I chuckled as he took my wooden blade and darted toward the shed where it was stowed between sessions. Vera rose from her seat beneath the nearby elm tree and took my arm.

"Let's see to our visitor," she said.

I nodded and led the way toward the stables. The rider wasn't far, but he pushed his mount to an excessive speed as he neared Vinterry.

As the man approached, it became apparent he'd been riding hard for hours. His horse was winded, and flecks of foam were visible around the exhausted beast's mouth. My eyes widened in recognition as the man rode closer; it was Thomas.

I broke away from Vera and ran toward him. I knew something was terribly wrong—Thomas would not have ridden alone unless given no other choice.

"Tom!" I called as he reined in his mount.

He stumbled as he dismounted and doubled over to clutch his left side. His tunic was discolored; the dark brown wool appeared almost black beneath his hand. Where his fingers touched the fabric, they came away stained with blood.

"Tom, you're hurt. What happened?"

I put my arm around his shoulders and guided him toward the house. Vera called for Cassandra and directed the staff to make a space for Thomas, while Giles and Gregor tended to his lathered horse. Thomas leaned heavily against my arm as we made slow progress toward the others.

"Colin," he said with a grimace. "I only just made it out of the Capitol before he closed the gates. Alex…needs your help."

"Did Colin do this?" I asked with a gesture toward his injured side. I helped him onto the steps leading up to the house, where he sat down heavily.

He shook his head. "No, bandits. I don't think it's deep, but it hurts like hell."

Cassandra appeared with a clean cloth and a tub of warm water and soap, intent upon cleaning Thomas' wound. I moved aside as she carefully peeled away his tunic to look at the damage beneath. Thomas made a face as she began to scrub it clean.

"Andrew, Colin's mad. He's locked Claire in one of the towers citing a crime of 'defiance.' No one has seen her for several weeks, and I fear for her welfare. But that's not the reason I've come." Thomas grimaced as Cassandra continued her ministrations.

"It's not deep," she said softly. "You're lucky. It will heal in time, but you must rest."

Thomas shook his head. "I don't think I can. There's no time." He managed a weak smile for her benefit, then returned his attention to me. "Colin reinstated the Mark inspections from long ago. He executed several townspeople last week in a very public affair. Alexander demanded he stop, that it was baseless tyranny. The people have done nothing wrong."

Icy dread gripped my heart as I realized where his story would lead. "Tom…"

He held up one hand, seeking patience. "Colin was enraged that Alexander would attempt to stand in his way. He accused Alex of trying to usurp the throne—which is nonsense! Alex doesn't want to rule." He groaned as Cassandra began to wrap a bandage around his wound. "Colin ordered the castle guards take Alexander to the dungeons, where he forced Alex to stand for inspection as well. Colin summoned me there too."

I ran a hand through my hair as the beginnings of panic set in. "Shit. Colin knows."

Thomas looked at me sharply, his blue eyes piercing. "You know about Alex, then?" The question was pointed, his tone filled with unmasked frustration.

I nodded and stared at the ground, my throat suddenly parched. I swallowed. "Mother told me before she passed away. She asked me to look after him…"

"Colin ordered the guards to strip Alex of his clothing," Thomas continued, his tone somber. "The townspeople that Colin executed— their Marks were small, insignificant things. Alex's is… It covers his entire torso, Andrew. It's a wonder nobody noticed it sooner." He shook his head. "Colin forced me to undergo an inspection after Alex, but I'm… I'm normal."

"Is Alex…?"

I feared to continue as I envisioned the worst. I'd failed Alexander. I'd promised to protect him, that I'd be there for him should anything happen, and I hadn't followed through. I'd been selfish, seeking solace away from Colin's barbed tongue and heated glares, and had abandoned my brother to his fate. I was little better than the damned tyrant who leered from Carlton's vacant throne.

"He's in the dungeon at present," Thomas replied. "I spoke to him before I fled, and he asked me to come here. He had the preposterous notion that you might somehow rescue him. He said, 'Andrew is the only person who can save me.' I don't know why he believes it, unless you also harbor some terrible secret?"

I grunted and glanced up as Vera appeared from within the house. "I'm not Marked if that's what you're asking."

"Then I fear he is lost to us." Thomas hung his head.

"How much time does he have?"

A plan was beginning to form in my mind; if I could somehow intervene, I might be able to save Alexander. I couldn't breach the castle's dungeons without causing unnecessary bloodshed, but perhaps there was another way.

"Colin scheduled Alex's execution for the end of this week. That would give you three days." He frowned and shook his head adamantly. "Andrew, there is nothing you can do. He'll be guarded day and night. Colin was going to make Alex's execution into a...carnival of sorts." He grimaced. "He plans to hold it in the jousting arena. He hired musicians and entertainment—"

"I won't give up on him, Tom!" I cut him off sharply. "Alex doesn't deserve this, and you know it. It's why you're here."

The jousting arena was located outside the main walls surrounding the Capitol. If I could disguise myself, I could pass as a guard and sneak inside unnoticed. I'd attempt to talk sense into Colin first, but if that didn't work, perhaps I could provide him with the "entertainment" he craved. I would travel to the Capitol and do my damnedest to save my brother. I owed him that much.

"Andrew, it's suicide. I can't lose you too!" Thomas' voice cracked. He turned away to hide the sudden onslaught of tears.

Cassandra had finished tending his wound and rose to her feet, clearly uncomfortable with the conversation. After a nod from Vera, she scurried inside.

"Tom," I said evenly, "I have to try. Regardless of the outcome, I have to try."

He shook his head stubbornly. "Andrew, if you insist on this folly, I'm coming with you."

"Tom, you're hurt—"

"—and *you're* following a path to madness," he cut me off sharply. "Alexander is my brother too, and I want to help him however I can. I came here because he asked it of me, and I'll return to the Capitol with you to see this through. No matter what's in store for us, I *will* be there."

I glanced at Vera. She nodded in understanding.

"We'll leave as soon as I can gather provisions," I promised him. "While I do that, you should rest. You need it."

He shrugged noncommittally, but reclined against the steps and closed his eyes. I accompanied Vera into the house and filled her in on the portion of our conversation that she'd missed. I retrieved my sword and sword belt from the trunk in our bedroom, then went to the kitchen for provisions.

"I can't believe Colin would restore the old laws," she said, stricken. "No one deserves to die over a matter of their birth that clearly hasn't harmed anyone. And Alex! He's right, Andrew. If anyone can save him, it's you."

She filled a satchel with bread, cheese, and a handful of strawberries that had been picked earlier in the day.

"Vera, I'll come back when this is over," I said. I hoped we wouldn't be forced apart long.

Her expression was fierce, determined, and unwavering in her support. "I know you will. Save your brother. I'll be waiting for you—no matter how long it may take."

I gathered her into my arms and kissed her passionately. She'd become much more than merely my wife; she was my anchor in rough seas and my light in the depths of night. I marveled that she had chosen me to spend her life with and counted myself among the most fortunate of men. My love for her would endure for eternity. When I stepped away, she was breathless.

"I love you, Vera. I'll return soon."

She nodded and pushed the food-laden satchel into my hands. "I will hold you to that promise, Andrew. Now, go. You don't have much time."

Within an hour, we said our goodbyes. It was the first time I'd departed Vinterry since I'd arrived with Vera over a year ago. I could not shake the feeling that it would be the last time I would lay eyes on the beautiful estate before tragedy struck, but I pushed those morbid thoughts aside. I would save Alexander or die in the attempt. Though Vera didn't voice her concerns, I believe she understood my reckless resolve.

Giles had prepared a fresh mount for Thomas while he'd rested. "Silver's the swiftest horse we have. She'll see you safely to the Capitol, my lord." He turned to me with sadness in his eyes. "Ben's ready for you, Andrew. I wish you luck. Alex is a good lad."

Vera and several of the other servants came outside to see us off. Gregor bounded ahead of them, his wooden practice sword in hand. "I'll defend Vinterry while you're gone," he promised solemnly.

I knelt before him with a shake of my head. "You've had less than a month of true practice, Greg. If the king's men arrive, you're better off hiding. *Please*," I added with emphasis. Gregor was only a boy. I hoped he wouldn't try anything foolish if Colin sent soldiers to Vinterry.

I rose and embraced Vera a final time. "I will return. Stay safe."

"Don't worry about me," she whispered as she blinked away tears. "Go to Alex. He needs you."

We pressed the horses as fast as we dared. The trees and grasses along the roadway sped by in a blur of green, and we spoke little. Each second spent traveling was less time we'd have to formulate a plan to save Alexander. Thomas refused to allow exhaustion to overtake him and kept pace with me until well into the night. It was nearing midnight when I called a halt to our desperate flight, my concern for him overriding my desperation for a time. Thomas swayed in his saddle, though from his injury or lack of sleep, I wasn't certain.

"Tom, we need to rest, at least for a while. The horses could use a break too."

To my surprise, he nodded and dismounted without argument. I led the horses a short distance from the road and kept watch while Thomas slept. It was only moments before he began to snore softly. I sat down a few feet away and listened to the sounds of the night. The constant chirp of crickets filled the air, accompanied by the occasional hoot from hunting owls as they flew above in search of prey.

I'd kept my vigil for a few hours when I noticed the night creatures had abruptly fallen silent. I moved noiselessly toward Thomas and woke him with a gentle shake. I gestured that he should remain silent, then went to the horses' location and took up their reins. I led them further away from the road and into a small stand of trees.

"Andrew, what's going on?" Tom whispered once we'd arrived in our new hiding place.

"I'm not sure. It's unnaturally quiet. Perhaps it's bandits, or perhaps a large predator is nearby. Either way—"

I stopped mid-sentence as the sound of horses drifted to us from the direction of the road. The cadence of their hooves and the jingle of tack was unmistakable. It was accompanied by clipped voices as they carried over the still night air.

"—not certain how much farther we have to go. I don't think it's much more."

"And what if he's not there?" A second voice asked.

"We have our orders. We'll search the area."

"I don't like this one bit, sir—"

The voices faded along with the sound of the horses. They'd been traveling swiftly, and there had been more than the two speakers we'd overheard.

"Andrew, I think those men were from the castle garrison," Thomas whispered. "We shouldn't linger."

"Do you think Colin sent them to prevent me from leaving Vinterry?" I asked as I swung into my saddle.

"I have no doubt of that, Andrew." He grunted in pain as he mounted his horse. "Damn."

"Tom?"

"I'm fine. Let's go."

We'd been fortunate the soldiers had failed to notice us as they passed. I worried for Vera and her staff—I didn't know what Colin's orders were, but they could be nothing good. I hoped for her sake they'd leave without incident once they learned I was gone.

Once I rescued Alexander, I would return to Vinterry and ensure she was safe. Colin couldn't be trusted, but I hoped the soldiers under his command would retain their consciences despite their king's temperament. And Vera was a resourceful woman—she'd find a way to keep herself and the staff safe in my absence.

We rode for the remainder of the night and until almost noon the next day, stopping once to allow the horses to rest and eat. Thomas insisted that I sleep, but I couldn't do so. I had to ensure we arrived in time to save Alexander, and if that meant pushing through despite my exhaustion, then so be it. I'd survived longer periods without sleep during my campaigns against the Corodan and knew I could travel for many hours more.

The Capitol was within sight by late afternoon. We remained at a distance and took time to observe the movements of the guards and vendors surrounding the tourney field. We tethered the horses within a stand of trees, then cautiously drew closer to the festivities. As Thomas had indicated, Colin was making something of a carnival out of our brother's pending execution. Revelers and musicians performed near the arena, while small crowds of onlookers traversed the area, gawking at the colorful displays. The sight caused my blood to boil. I swore profusely.

"We need to get inside the arena," Thomas said after we'd spent some time surveilling from afar. "Perhaps tonight, after the festivities have ceased."

I nodded, though I had no further plan of action. Infiltrating the arena would be one matter, but saving Alexander would be another entirely. I must be inside in order to intervene, but in the past, spectators were rarely allowed entrance to the field. I clung to the hope I'd manage to secure a guard's attire—I could see no other way of gaining entrance without a bloody fight.

"Is the old barracks at the far end of the arena still in service?" I asked after a time.

"Yes. What are you thinking, Andrew?"

"I need to acquire a guard's uniform. I must be near Alex when he's brought out, but I can't risk being recognized. If Colin wants a spectacle, I'll give him one."

"Andrew..." Thomas sighed and scratched at his beard. "I meant what I said before we left your estate. I can't lose both of you. Please tell me you have a plan."

I shrugged. "I have a plan."

I didn't want to tell Thomas any more than was necessary. I hadn't completely formulated my plot to rescue Alexander.

He grunted in frustration. "Andrew, tell me. Alex doesn't deserve to die, and even though I have long stood by the laws of this kingdom, I believe what Colin is doing is wrong. I need to know the details if I'm to be of help."

I chewed my lower lip in thought while I attempted to force my nebulous plan to coalesce into something more than it was. Colin was nothing if not predictable when it came to fanfare and vanity; perhaps

I could use that to my advantage. Once inside the tourney field, I'd wait for my opportunity, and then…

I didn't know. Beyond the necessary location, I could only promise I'd do whatever was necessary to rescue Alexander. I didn't want to cause needless bloodshed, but if words failed to sway Colin, I would use force if necessary. And if I were outnumbered, I would shift; my dragon form could withstand a greater assault, and I'd have the advantage of surprise. I was uncertain if I ought to inform Thomas of my ability, though I was beginning to believe he'd understand. He'd insinuated he knew I harbored a secret, and he'd still insisted he'd help.

I shared my vague scheme while Thomas stared at me as though I'd grown a second head.

"Andrew, that's madness. We both know Colin will never back down, and he'll have dozens of guards present. You'll be outmatched! Colin won't allow you to leave the arena alive if you confront him."

I frowned, braced myself, and decided I must tell him. He'd accepted Alexander's Mark after all, and his journey to Vinterry was proof enough of his loyalty. He wouldn't betray me if he truly wanted to save Alexander.

"Tom, I spoke the truth when I said I wasn't Marked, but I do have an ability that Colin won't be expecting. It will see us both through this—you have my word."

Thomas crossed his arms, winced at his injured side, then fixed me with a stern glare reminiscent of his late father's. "I'll need more than vague assurances, brother."

I met his glare unflinchingly. "I'm a skin-changer, Tom."

He narrowed his eyes while he considered my words. "Andrew, do you mean…?" He frowned and shook his head in disbelief. "No, that's impossible. Our records state the dragons are gone. There are no more in this world."

I kept my features neutral. "Think about the timing, Tom. How old am I?"

"I suppose the timing fits. Hmm." He lifted one hand to stroke his beard. "Wait a moment. I read an old book at your estate last year. It mentioned a pair of dragon-magi in Dresdin's Forge—that's where mother was from!"

"It is. And one of those two magi was my father, though I'm not certain which. Mother never told me his name." I looked at him evenly. "If things go badly, I *can* protect Alex, but you need to keep yourself safe."

He nodded, all traces of his previous skepticism gone. "I will, Andrew. But first, let's get you into a guard's uniform. I can help you break into the barracks."

The revelers disappeared into their brightly colored tents as night fell, and fewer guards seemed to be on patrol. We waited another hour, until only a pair of guards remained, neither overly vigilant in their duties. They paused periodically in their rounds to chat with one another and laugh raucously.

During one of their pauses, we made our move. We raced through the shadows of Colin's impromptu carnival to the barracks' door, then glanced behind us to ensure we hadn't been spotted. The guards continued to converse some distance away, oblivious to our intrusion.

I frowned in disapproval; there were no guards posted at the barracks' entrance. If I'd still been in command, the post would not have been vacant. Perhaps Colin had not yet found a replacement for Jerrick Vine, or perhaps the newest commander was more lenient with the garrison's duties. Despite my displeasure at the change, it was fortunate for our errand.

Thomas pushed the door inward, but we waited several moments before entering. The interior of the barracks was dimly lit; a single torch burned in a wall sconce some distance along the main corridor. There was no indication anyone was within.

I glanced at the patrol and noted they had moved farther away. "Let's go," I whispered.

We stepped inside and began to inch along the corridor. Thomas rapped his knuckles on the first closed door we came across, then glanced at me to ensure I was prepared for whoever might be inside. I nodded once in affirmation as a sleepy "Hullo?" resounded from within. Thomas pushed the door open while I remained along the wall, out of sight.

"My lord! This—this is unexpected!" The man was clearly shocked to see my brother. "His Majesty said you were away on business and to report to him at once if we noticed your return."

"His Majesty doesn't wish to be disturbed." Thomas' tone was authoritative in a way I'd seldom heard from him. He was playing his part well.

"But my lord, I have orders—"

I was done skulking in the shadowed corridor. I charged into the room, pushing past Thomas, and came to stand in front of the man. I noted the red cloak draped over the room's single chair—this sniveling swine was Colin's new commander. I stared daggers at him, daring him to speak.

His eyes widened at my intrusion. "Andrew? Shit! The king said you were to be detained and—!"

I balled my hands into fists. In rapid succession, I struck him in the gut with my left, then along the jaw with my right. I pulled my punches; I didn't want to cause any lasting injury, but I struck hard enough that my first punch winded him, and the second knocked him out cold. I glanced at Thomas warily before helping myself to the man's armor and uniform, which were piled on one side of his narrow bed.

Thomas' eyebrows were raised. "Damn, Andrew. I've heard stories about your fights, but I've never had the opportunity to see you in action. Claybourne had little chance."

"Exactly." I strapped on the breastplate and leg plates with a grimace. The man was a head shorter than I was, thinner, and not as broad in the shoulders. The armor didn't fit well, but it would suffice.

Thomas glanced nervously into the corridor. "How long until he wakes?"

I strapped on the bracers and kicked off my boots. "Not long, perhaps a few minutes." I pulled on the man's armored boots, which were snug and uncomfortable. "I can hit him again if it'll make you feel better."

Thomas' eyes widened, and he shook his head. "No, I don't think it's necessary. Claybourne is vile, but we can't risk injuring him."

I cracked a sly smile. "Very well." I pulled Claybourne's garrison tunic over the armor, followed by his gauntlets, then picked up the helmet. It sported a visor that could be raised and lowered as needed. "I'm done here."

We left the way we'd come and had no further encounters with the castle's garrison. I pulled the helmet on as we reached the door but left the visor up. With it down, my vision would be restricted, and I needed to see our surroundings properly. The boots caused my feet to ache, the armor dug into my shoulder blades, and the gauntlets were too tight on my hands. I'd be in for a rough night, but freeing Alexander was worth it.

We avoided the patrolling guards while we moved through the shadows between the barracks and the arena. Coarse laughter floated to us on the still night air as the guards made their rounds. I was thankful for Colin's lackadaisical approach to his security.

We made our way into the arena and took the downward-sloping path that led to the tourney field. The wooden stands surrounding the field were empty, though come morning, they would begin to fill with the permitted spectators, slavering to witness a prince's untimely demise.

The image twisted my stomach into a vicious knot. I had but one opportunity to save my brother, and I could afford no mistakes.

I surveyed the field as we approached. A thick wooden post had been driven into the center of the tourney field, a position visible to every spectator that might fill the stands. Several lengths of rope were coiled on the ground nearby, visible in the pale illumination of the half-moon. I suppressed a groan as I realized Colin intended to march Alexander to the center of the field, then tie him to the post in order to maximize his brother's humiliation prior to the climax of his macabre festival.

I located an area near the base of the stands where I could sit down while I waited for morning. I could see both entrances opening onto the field but was partially obscured from sight by a pair of royal banners. While I possessed garrison armor and could pass as a soldier, I couldn't risk anyone inspecting me too closely. To be recognized prematurely would put an unfortunate end to my schemes.

Thomas sat beside me, his face drawn with worry. "Andrew, I still can't believe Colin is going through with this. How can he be so callous as to destroy his own family? First father, and now Alex." He slumped in his seat, forlorn.

"Did you find proof he had a hand in the king's death?" I asked.

"Yes, and no," he replied. "We found a flask in Colin's quarters with the apothecary's label still attached. It was an extract made from yew berries. The symptoms father had mimicked what I know of those berries' effects when consumed. Colin claimed the flask had been planted in his quarters by someone who hoped to undermine him. The governors are terrified of him and won't put their word against his, and most of the nobles won't either. I *know* he killed father, but I can do nothing about it." He sighed. "A few days after we uncovered the flask, Colin began his 'inspections.' When Alex demanded he stop, Colin seized his opportunity. I've often wondered if Colin knew Alex's secret and was simply waiting for a chance to expose him."

"I don't think so, Tom," I replied. "Unless Alex told Colin, I don't see how he could have known. It was simply the worst damned luck."

"I wish you would have confided in me sooner. I would never betray you, but I understand why you didn't. Novania has never been safe for you." He paused and gazed across the darkened tourney field. "Where will you go when this is over and done?"

I shrugged; I didn't want to think about it. Not yet. "I'll return to Vinterry first. Not to stay—that wouldn't be safe for us or Vera—but she deserves a proper farewell. And then… I don't know. Perhaps we'll travel south."

"Through the Mage's Gate." Thomas nodded and averted his gaze. "It's your only option, isn't it?"

"It may be."

I didn't want to acknowledge that this was likely our last goodbye. Thomas wasn't prepared to leave Novania, even if it meant he was forced to live in the foul shadow of our brother. Novania was no longer safe for Alexander, and if my secret were revealed, it wouldn't be safe for me either.

There truly was no other option but to travel south, leaving all that I'd ever known behind. If it meant Alexander would live—and perhaps even harness his innate abilities—then it would be worth the struggle.

"Tom," I said slowly, "I don't know what tomorrow will bring."

I wanted to tell him that I hoped we'd reunite with him one day when circumstances were better. I wanted to thank him for bringing Alexander's message to me, for doing his part to save our brother. I wanted to say so many things, but I was terrible with goodbyes. To his credit, Thomas seemed to understand my inner turmoil, even though I was unable to express it in words.

He nodded, his gaze fixed on the far side of the tourney field. "I understand. Colin will hunt you relentlessly when you thwart his plans. I may not be the warrior you are, but I can make my own way in this world. I'll wait and hope that one day we'll see one another again. Tell Alex I said that. I doubt I'll have the chance."

# FOURTEEN

I positioned myself at the eastern entrance to the tourney field as the sun rose, red and bloated as it peered above the horizon. The thin clouds that streaked across the sky were painted in lurid shades of orange, crimson, and pink. A thick mat of dew coated the grass and had settled on the wooden stands at the perimeter of the arena. Thomas took his leave, and I hoped for his sake that both Alexander and I would live to see the day's end.

People began to file into the arena as soon as the sun crested the horizon, though the atmosphere was subdued. Vendors and performers called out to passers-by to inspect their wares or to watch their various exploits from beyond the spectator area. Several different bands of musicians played in competition with one another, producing a cacophony that assaulted the senses. The scent of bacon and baking sweet breads wafted from somewhere outside. I stood sentinel at my self-appointed post, garbed in the commander's stolen armor as I awaited my opportunity—and prayed desperately that it would come.

By mid-morning, the stands were filled almost to bursting. The crowd seemed both curious and horrified, but their conversations were hushed, providing a soft susurration in the background. My thoughts flitted between a dozen possible scenarios, and I grew restless. Another pair of guards appeared and stationed themselves at the opposite entrance from my post. I forced myself to remain still, and waited while I observed them. They lounged against the sides of the entrance in a clear display of boredom.

Not long after, four more guards emerged from the entrance where I stood vigilantly. In their midst was Alexander, his wrists bound in front of him and his legs shackled. He was shirtless and his back was marred with large welts, while his arms were covered in dark bruises. Some of the welts had split, and dried blood was smeared across his flesh. He hung his head in defeat and stumbled forward at the guards' prodding.

He was marched to the center of the field, where the guards untied his wrists momentarily, only to bind them behind his back and around the pole. The Mark that covered most of his torso was starkly visible as it arced from his left shoulder toward his right ribs, then back toward his left hip. The crowd jeered and screamed profanities, their previously subdued nature riled into a frenzy by Alexander's presence.

It was the first time I'd seen the Mage's Mark. The flesh around the edge was raised and pale, reminiscent of scar tissue. The skin that spanned the width of the mark was recessed from the edges and was a mottled gray-white, in stark contrast to Alexander's much pinker complexion.

I followed the quartet of guards as they moved across the field, leaving the visor of my stolen helmet down. The guard responsible for securing Alexander's wrists stepped back, seemingly satisfied with his work, as another began to remove the shackles from his ankles. They didn't seem to think he'd be running anywhere.

"You, there," one of the guards said to me, "double-check his wrists, will you? Bandon is terrible with knots."

I nodded while my heart leapt at the unexpected opportunity. I stepped behind Alexander as the others began to disperse while pretending to secure the ropes that bound him.

"Alex," I whispered. "It's me. Don't say anything. I don't have much time."

I loosened the ropes, but kept the knots for show. "Nod once if you think you can slip out of those when the time is right."

He nodded once, and his fingers grasped mine for the briefest of seconds.

"I won't let him kill you, brother," I promised. "Wait for my signal."

I stepped away and nodded to the guard who had ordered me to secure the knots, then made my way back toward the sidelines. I'd wait until Colin made his move, then counter him as necessary. Colin had not yet arrived, which provided me with more time to consider my course of action.

I scanned the myriad faces in the crowd as they continued to spew insults toward Alexander. I would receive little assistance from them, nor would I garner sympathy. The people scented blood, and the prospect of spilling *royal* blood was a rare and exotic phenomenon. I grimaced within my stolen helm and turned to study the guards. More had entered the field to position themselves at intervals along the length of the stands, while a full dozen stood at the base of the dais where Colin would undoubtedly stand as he attempted to orchestrate his brother's murder.

My gaze shifted to Alexander. He stood erect, his jaw clenched in defiance. The crowd continued to launch insults from the stands, but he appeared to ignore them. My brief words had renewed his confidence and reinvigorated his will to live.

It wasn't long before trumpeters heralded the entrance of the king. Colin ascended the dais, regal in a black tunic emblazoned with silver embroidery and paired with a cloak of deepest crimson. Claire stood at his side in matching attire. I noted with a heavy heart that one side of her face was purple with fading bruises. Their infant was cradled in her arms, her face contorted as she wailed. Claire stared toward the unruly crowd in the stands with a glazed expression, heedless of the child's distress. She was broken, a mere shell of the woman I'd once known.

Colin stretched his arms wide as he addressed his raucous audience. He waited until the crowd noise lessened to a hushed roar before he began to speak.

"I have gathered you here today to witness the death of a blood-born traitor. Under the ancient laws of this land, those born with the Mage's Mark are considered an abomination, the greatest threat to our kingdom's security. The laws are clear. Those born with the Mark must be executed!"

Gasps warred for prominence over the cheers erupting from the stands. I glowered at Colin. I'd be forced to intervene soon.

"Here today, I have my own brother, Alexander Marsden. He bears the Mark, and has for the entirety of his life. A traitor from the start, he must be dealt with swiftly. Our lands cannot bear the taint of the magi! Novania is a land of proud men and women. Our people will not bow to those with his brand of unnatural power. As our laws demand, those who bear the Mark must die!"

Colin had worked himself into a frenzy, and the crowd was drinking in his every word as they roared with anticipation. Claire stared blankly toward the horizon, seemingly oblivious to what occurred around her. The child in her arms let out a terrified screech, but she made no move to quiet it. I pitied them both while my animosity toward Colin intensified. Alexander wasn't the only victim of his despicable schemes; he was simply the most noteworthy.

"The time has come for this blood-born traitor to be dealt with!" Colin shouted.

He waved his arms to encourage the crowd into an even greater uproar. Howls and jeers followed his statement as the crowd hungered for the spectacle set to unfold.

Colin gestured toward the entrance opposite my location, where a hulking man dressed in black and wearing an executioner's mask strode into the sunlight. He carried a heavy two-handed axe, its blade curved into a wicked half-moon. The executioner began to advance across the tourney field toward Alexander. I could wait no longer.

I stepped forward and ripped the stolen helmet from my head, then strode across the field toward Alexander. "Colin, enough! This is madness. You must stop this farce!"

Colin's face twisted as though he'd taken a bite of something sour. "Andrew." His tone was like acid. "I should have known you would find your way here."

I glanced toward the executioner, who stopped his advance, uncertain how to proceed. His hesitation bought me further time.

"I'll not allow you to kill your own brother! Alex has harmed no one!"

"You would defy your king, Andrew?" He sneered.

"If it means saving Alexander from the rantings of a tyrant, then yes, I damn well would."

Colin examined his fingernails, exuding haughty boredom. "Petty insults don't become you, Andrew. I wonder— how did you avoid the men I sent to detain you? I gave them very explicit instructions not to allow you into the Capitol, even if it meant taking your head."

I glared at him. The soldiers that had passed us on the road had been on Colin's errand as we'd suspected. A pang of worry ricocheted through my core as I considered what may have occurred at Vinterry, but I shoved it aside. I must focus on freeing Alexander.

"I didn't encounter any of your men," I replied. "Even if I had, they would not have stopped me from coming."

"Overconfident and arrogant, as always," Colin sneered. "It will be your downfall, Andrew." He glanced at the executioner, then gestured to the guards stationed along the sidelines. "Kill them both."

Rage consumed me. "You will live to regret this, Colin!" I shouted as the men began to advance.

Colin laughed mirthlessly from his stage.

I was outnumbered. There were fifteen guards and the executioner moving toward me. I had only seconds to determine my next course of action. Words had failed to sway Colin's inane judgment, and my sword wouldn't do—not against so many. I glanced at Alexander, and he nodded once. He understood what I'd planned.

I shifted. The stolen armor rent and splintered as my body expanded. I released a powerful roar and glared in Colin's direction. His face grew ashen, his eyes wide with fear. Under any other circumstance, I would have taken a moment to revel in his reaction, but there were soldiers hell-bent on our destruction that must be dealt with first. I would not fail Alexander a second time.

I batted several guards aside. For the first time in my life, I utilized the full magnitude of my strength, unconcerned with the damage I wrought. I struck again with a powerful lash from my tail. The blow connected with a pair of guards that thought to flank me, and they were sent careening into the stands. I fixed my gaze upon the executioner, who had once again halted his progress toward Alexander. The man's eyes were wide with terror behind his mask and the unmistakable tang of urine hit my nostrils. He fell backward under my furious gaze and began to scuttle away, dragging his axe behind him.

Colin shouted for more guards, his voice teetering on the brink of hysteria. The crowd erupted into screams. People fled the stands, trampling others in their desperation to be away from the spectacle that was unfolding on the field. More of the castle's garrison poured into the arena, but it was clear most were unwilling to do battle with a dragon. I roared again as a few brave archers loosed a volley of arrows. Those that hit their mark bounced off my hide, ineffective.

I glanced at Alexander. He'd freed his arms and was sprinting across the field toward me. I lowered myself to the ground and allowed him to clamber onto my back before I rose once more.

I swiveled my head to take in the approaching soldiers, uncertain of how to proceed. Flying was the fastest and most secure option, but I had yet to attempt flight and didn't know if I'd manage to clear the stands. My other option was to run headlong through the crowd and hope my size and strength would be sufficient to see us safely away. I roared again, frustrated.

Some of the guards had regained their courage and began advancing toward us once more. I lashed my tail at them in warning, but they backed away only briefly. We were running out of time.

"Andrew, you have to fly!" Alexander shouted, his tone desperate.

I knew he was right. I craned my neck to peer at him; he was perched between two of the stiff spines that ran the length of my back, directly between my shoulder blades. "Hold on," I said, and hoped with all I was worth that I'd succeed in becoming airborne.

I'd watched birds often enough with Vera as we walked through the forest to know they often beat their wings many times after alighting from a branch. Once the wind bolstered their wings, they could lessen their wingbeats and remain aloft. Birds were orders of magnitude smaller and infinitely lighter than I was, but my wings were enormous when fully extended. I hoped it would be enough.

I stretched my wings and knocked aside some of the nearer guards in the process. I leapt powerfully into the air and beat my wings frantically, uncertain if I would manage to gain sufficient altitude. My immediate sense was one of falling, but my wings caught the air and we sailed over the stands. Another volley of arrows followed my progress, but none reached our position in the sky.

I beat my wings a few more times and rose higher. The wind rushed past in a cool current, bearing the scent of spring greenery.

The relief I felt was palpable. Suddenly giddy, a bubble of laughter welled up from my chest and burst forth. Alexander was safe, we were both alive, and Colin had been given the spectacle he'd craved, if not the desired outcome.

Once in the sky, it required little effort to remain aloft. My wings acted like sails and kept me airborne so long as they were outstretched. I flapped my wings occasionally to adjust our altitude, but nothing more—I could have glided for hours if I wished to. It was a simple act and felt strangely natural.

I would have enjoyed it if not for the dire situation we'd escaped from moments before.

After a few minutes, I looked down at the land rushing beneath us and attempted to gather my bearings. Once oriented, I banked east toward Vinterry.

"Andrew!" Alexander shouted to be heard over the wind. "I... Thank you!"

I felt one of his hands drop from the hard spine he'd been grasping, and he placed it firmly against the scales of my back. He patted the spot twice, then resumed his hold on the spine.

"Where are we going?"

"Vinterry. Then sssouth."

"I hope Tom was there!" Alexander laughed. "He has always wanted to see a dragon."

"I told him lassst night," I said over my shoulder. "He needed to know."

"Well, there is no keeping your secret any longer, brother!" he cried. "Colin invited half the nobles in the kingdom to attend his festivities today. Word will spread."

Alexander shifted his position. I craned my neck again to see him better. He'd moved slightly to the side and leaned forward, one arm tucked beneath him, while the other grasped the spine for balance.

"Alexsss?"

"It's cold up here, and I don't have a shirt!" He shouted. "You're warm, though. I'm trying not to freeze, brother."

I chuckled. After everything he'd been through, he was still the same younger brother that I'd grown up with. In that moment, I was content; I'd rescued him from Colin's insanity, and I would continue to protect him until we reached the Mage's Gate. Neither of us was welcome in Novania any longer, and Colin would undoubtedly send men to follow us. Thankfully, I could travel much faster through the air than on horseback. The Capitol had already dwindled to a mere speck behind us, and there was no sign of pursuit—yet.

"Did you know you'd be able to fly?"

"No."

Alexander whistled. "This is your first time, then? I suppose you would have risked being noticed if you'd tried sooner, but I could get used to sitting up here!"

"I thought you were cold."

"I am, but the view is incredible!" He laughed again and slapped one hand against my back. "This is amazing, brother!"

I marveled at how quickly he'd allowed his cares to slip away. Only minutes ago, he was on public display and moments from execution. Now he laughed, carefree, and paused to enjoy the view of the landscape as we sped through the sky. Alexander was nothing if not resilient.

I grinned. Despite the odds we'd faced, I'd freed him from Colin's grasp.

# FIFTEEN

Smoke billowed on the eastern horizon. What at first appeared to be a smudge against the darkening sky coalesced into a discernable pattern; a thick plume spiraled into the warm spring air, bloated with ash.

Dread coursed through my veins. As we neared Vinterry, I recalled Colin's acerbic words. He'd sent men to detain me, under orders to kill if I resisted. But I was well on my way to the Capitol by the time they'd passed us on the road. Had they lashed out at Vera in my absence?

Holy hell, I hoped she was safe. I didn't want to imagine my future without her. She was my salvation.

A trip that would have taken the better part of a day had taken us only a few hours by air, but as panic gripped my heart, I pushed my wings to carry us faster. The quantity of smoke visible could not have been produced by a mere cookfire. Each stroke of my wings was more powerful than the last.

I glanced at Alexander, perched between the spines of my back. "Sssomething isss wrong. Hold on!"

He grasped the nearest spine with both hands in response. I arrowed toward the source of the smoke, more certain it was Vinterry with each second that passed. As we surged forward, Alexander released a whoop of surprise, and his grip intensified.

"Smoke!" Alexander shouted above the roar of the wind, a note of fear in his voice. I'd forgotten my eyesight was far superior to his.

The plume grew from a tendril to a towering pillar, the harbinger of devastation. My heart sank as I recognized the meadow from above, the dirt track that led south toward the main road and the rolling hills that marked the vineyard. I pushed myself even harder as I clung to the hope that we wouldn't arrive too late. Fear clutched me in its icy grip as I worried for Vera's safety and that of her staff.

Colin's words returned to me yet again, and I strained against the wind. I was near the limit of endurance, my wings and shoulders ached and protested, but I would not relent.

*"I gave them very explicit instructions not to allow you into the Capitol, even if it meant taking your head,"* Colin had said.

I roared in frustration as terror fueled my flight. If Colin had ordered his men to kill me, would the same apply to those I'd left behind? Colin was without conscience, and he wouldn't care how many innocents suffered so long as he achieved his own narcissistic goals. I hoped I was wrong and I'd return to find Vera smiling, Cassandra ready to greet us with a tray of freshly-baked pies, and little Gregor eager to hear of my latest exploits.

As we came upon the glade, my hopes were dashed. The manor house and the stables had been set ablaze, reduced to cinders, leaving only the charred remains of the stone foundations behind. Acrid smoke continued to issue from the wreckage. Fire had spread into the vineyards and toward the encroaching forest beyond. Some of the vines had been over a century old, but now they were nothing more than ash. I circled the meadow twice but spied no signs of life amongst the ruins below. Vinterry had been razed, its residents gone.

I attempted to land lightly for Alexander's sake, but I misjudged the distance and hit the ground with more force than I'd anticipated. The jarring impact coursed through my legs, and I shook my head in momentary frustration. There was no time to critique my landing; I needed to locate Vera.

Alexander slid along my side as soon I touched down. He ran toward the ruin that had once been Vera's home, calling out to her, Giles, Cassandra, or Hiram. A breath of wind pulsed through the air, the only reply to his frantic cries.

I scanned the area, searching for an indication of their whereabouts. I hoped they'd managed to escape and were hiding somewhere in the forest. There was no sign of Colin's soldiers.

While Alexander searched near the smoldering buildings, I made my way toward the vineyards beyond. We'd yet to uncover any bodies, and a wild hope surged within. Perhaps they'd made it to safety, but I wouldn't leave until I was certain.

"Andrew!" Alexander called from behind the ruins of the stable.

I turned away from the vineyard and charged toward him. His eyes met mine, and I knew he'd found something I didn't wish to see. I skidded to a halt as I caught sight of what lay behind the remnants of the building while my breath hitched in my throat.

Alexander knelt beside a pair of bodies, anguish in his gaze. The stout form of Cassandra lay face down in the dirt, a pair of arrow shafts protruding from between her shoulder blades. Giles lay a few paces away, his torso a mass of bloody gashes. He clutched a woodcutter's axe in his gnarled fingers, but he'd been outnumbered or outmatched in the fight. I judged both had been deceased for several hours due to the stiffness in their limbs and the number of flies that had congregated. There was no sign of Vera, Gregor, or Hiram.

"Colin has gone too damned far!" Alexander bellowed as he rose to his feet. He clenched his fists and gazed skyward before releasing an agonized howl.

There was no denying that Colin must be stopped. How many innocents would fall to his reckless scheme for power? How many lives would be snuffed out, their families sundered, while he pursued this madness? I wished we were in a better position to do something about the tyrant our brother had become, but at present, my only concern was Vera's safety. Colin must wait.

"We have to find Vera," I said gruffly.

I returned to the vineyards. The forest would have provided the best refuge for those attempting to escape, and I continued to cling to the hope Vera was safe. The trees were thickest north of the estate, and I believed she would have taken her staff there. Perhaps she'd led the others to the pond Alexander and I had discovered the previous summer; it provided fresh water and was distant enough that they may have eluded the soldiers. I desperately hoped I'd find her there, shaken, but unharmed.

As I began moving toward the line of trees to the north, a glimmer of metal caught my eye between the charred rows of grapevines. The fire had burned itself out in that portion of the vineyard, leaving a swath of blackened husks in its wake. I turned to see what had drawn my attention. A knife lay on the ground, and inches away from it, I spotted a hand. Though I couldn't make out the rest of the body from my position, I would have recognized those slender, delicate fingers anywhere.

My heart clenched and stuttered as I stumbled forward, drawn toward the unmoving form. I shifted without realizing I'd done so and staggered through the row of grapevines. A few wayward branches struck and scratched my naked form as I ran, half-blind with unshed tears.

I knew what I'd find at the end of the row, yet I was unable to stop my forward progress. I didn't want to look upon the horror I'd uncover, but was helpless against my desire to uncover the crimes the soldiers had committed in Colin's name. As I reached the location of the knife, my eyes were greeted with a macabre sight. My legs crumpled beneath me as grief's talons ripped through my heart.

Vera lay face-up, her hand outstretched toward the knife that had failed to defend her. Her eyes were glassy and unseeing. Several arrow shafts protruded from her abdomen, and a ragged gash rent her pale throat. The dress she wore had been a shade of light green, but it was now darkened by blood and soot.

I pulled her cold form against my chest as a keening wail erupted from the depths of my being. I'd failed to protect her, the woman I loved above all others. My grief consumed me; I wept openly, heedless of Alexander, the time, or whether Colin's soldiers planned to return. She'd been my rock, my greatest supporter, and my truest friend.

I don't know how long I knelt in the ashes of Vinterry, cradling her lifeless form while I cursed myself for leaving her unprotected. I should have been there when Colin's men arrived. I could have saved her... Yet if I'd done so, Alexander would be dead. Colin was a heartless bastard, and he'd made a true enemy of me that day. I would see to it that he paid for his crimes.

It was fully dark before I realized Alexander was kneeling beside me. He'd said nothing, and I'd been unaware of his presence. He drew my attention when he spoke, his voice rough with emotion.

"Andrew, I'm so damned sorry. This is my fault. If it hadn't been for me, you would have been here to protect her." His voice cracked and he looked away, too ashamed to face me.

In my grief, I wanted to lash out at him, to agree with his assessment, but I swallowed the harsh words. The rational part of my mind scolded me for even considering it; there had been no indication that Colin would resort to these barbaric measures. It wasn't Alexander's fault, and I knew I must tell him that. I opened my mouth to speak, but the knot in my throat wouldn't allow for anything more than a strangled croak.

When Alexander turned his gaze toward mine, I simply shook my head. I hoped he understood. I didn't blame him for what had transpired. His botched execution, Vinterry's destruction, Vera's murder… Alexander was not at fault. Colin was the perpetrator, and I'd do my damnedest to ensure he faced justice one day.

"Colin must pay for this," he whispered fiercely. "Vera was innocent."

I nodded and stared at the lifeless form clutched in my arms. Even in death, she remained beautiful. With her demise, a part of myself had been severed, leaving a raw, gaping wound that I didn't believe would ever fully heal. Since Colin had been named heir to the throne, I'd lost everything—my title, my name, my first wife, and now, my first love. There was nothing left for me in Novania but heartbreak and pain.

I'd been so consumed by grief that Alexander was forced to say my name twice before it registered. I looked at him sharply, then heard the sound of distant hoofbeats. They came from the direction of the main road and were rapidly drawing nearer. As I'd anticipated, we'd been followed from the Capitol.

"Andrew, they're coming back. We have to go!"

Reluctantly, I released Vera. She deserved a proper burial, but we'd run out of time. I couldn't tell how many horsemen approached, and though I could have used a good fight to vent my building rage, I wouldn't risk Alexander's safety a second time. Too much blood had been spilled for one day.

I stood and stumbled a short distance away before shifting once more. With my larger size, I could see over the wreckage that had been the manor house. Near the southern border of the meadow, horses approached at a gallop, the unmistakable crimson and ivory livery of the castle garrison emblazoned across the chests of the riders. I harbored no doubts Colin had ordered them to kill us both.

I roared to express my anguish. I didn't want to leave Vera or her staff in this manner, but Colin left me no choice. I hoped her spirit—wherever it might be—would forgive me.

"Andrew?" Alexander asked warily.

I released a heavy sigh and bent low to allow him to climb upon my back. In my torment, I wanted to charge toward the riders, to destroy the lot of them for having committed atrocities in the name of their delusional king. The king, my damned half-brother.

My muscles tensed as the notion flitted through my mind. When Alexander's hand patted my shoulder to indicate he was ready, I realized the folly of the action. I'd lost my world to save my brother. I would not risk losing *him* in a reckless bid for revenge—Alexander was all I had left.

I abandoned my foolhardy impulse and leapt into the night sky.

We flew for several hours through the darkness. I traveled in a southwesterly direction, guided by little more than instinct and my vague recollection of the map depicting the Mage's Gate Alexander had uncovered in the library. Vinterry's library, which lay behind us in a smoldering ruin. I swallowed a fresh wave of grief and pressed on.

The air was cool. I lost myself in the sensation of the wind coursing over and around my body while my wings sliced through the air. We didn't speak; I wasn't in the right temperament for conversation, and Alexander battled both guilt and exhaustion. After a time, he fell asleep while I flew, a black-scaled shadow against the night sky. I glanced over my shoulder periodically to ensure he remained secure.

It was well after midnight before I decided to land. Fatigue had finally broken through my heartache, and my eyelids grew heavy.

"Alexsss," I said over my shoulder, "I need ressst."

He startled at my words. They were the first I'd spoken since I'd discovered Vera's lifeless form sprawled on the ground in the vineyard she'd loved. I was uncertain if I would ever recover; Vera had been everything, and now I'd been condemned to live without her. She'd done nothing to incur Colin's wrath other than wed me, but perhaps that was justification enough for my malicious half-brother.

We'd flown into a region of grassland, and there was very little in the way of cover. I had not spied any roads for some time. I hoped we were far enough away from the more traveled areas that we wouldn't draw notice. I landed—a bit more gracefully than I'd done at the conclusion of our first flight—and Alexander slid down my side. He landed deftly on his feet, as though he'd been performing the act for years.

He shivered after the prolonged flight. He remained shirtless from Colin's demonstration earlier in the day, and anything he might have used to cover himself at Vinterry had been destroyed. We'd fled without supplies, he was without half his clothing, and I had none. We must obtain some basic necessities in the morning, but at present, we both required sleep.

Alexander seated himself a few feet away and gazed across the darkened plains. "Andrew, I'm truly sorry for all of this. I would never have asked Tom to bring you my message if I'd known what Colin would do…"

"Don't blame yourssself, brother," I replied. "You aren't at fault, and we are in thisss together."

He swallowed, then looked up at me as tears spilled from his eyes. "I knew you would come, Andrew. You've always been my protector… But I can't help but feel responsible for what happened. I liked Vera. She was so damned good for you." His voice cracked, and he looked away. He drew his knees into his chest and hugged himself while he continued to shiver.

On an impulse, I gently moved my tail to encircle him. I hoped to provide him with some measure of warmth, and I had nothing else to offer. It wouldn't be safe to start a fire, even if we carried flint and tinder. He glanced at me quizzically but said nothing.

"You're cold."

He barked a laugh that dissolved into a sob. "You see, Andrew? Always the protector."

Alexander wept, but after a few minutes, he'd fallen asleep once more. I settled into a more comfortable position and allowed myself to rest. I craved a dreamless sleep but doubted I'd be granted a peaceful respite as the scenes of Vinterry's destruction replayed through my mind.

It was mid-morning when I awoke. I hadn't intended to sleep late and was startled to find the sun had climbed high into the sky. Alexander was awake and had acquired a shirt, some bread, and a handful of strawberries, which he munched as he studied me. The sight of food caused my stomach to rumble. I hadn't eaten anything since the evening Thomas and I had reached the Capitol.

Alexander smirked. "There's a farmstead to the east. I borrowed a shirt from one house—it was left overnight on the line—and I acquired the bread from another. I found the berries on my way back here."

I hung my head in despair. We'd been reduced to stealing; it was a bitter realization that further wounded my pride. Without clothing, I'd be unable to shift if anyone was nearby, and I wondered what it would take to feed a hungry dragon. My stomach rumbled again, and I knew I'd need to figure it out sooner rather than later.

Alexander raised an eyebrow. "Why don't you change? I'll share this with you," he said, indicating the stolen bread.

I shook my head. "I have no clothing."

He rolled his eyes. "Andrew, in case you haven't noticed, we're in the middle of the plains. I doubt anyone will come *here* looking for us. And in your dragon from, you're the largest thing out here. How do you think I found my way back so easily?"

I conceded that he had a valid point. I scanned the area and noted the outline of distant houses. If the residents hadn't noticed my presence, it was a small miracle. "Fine."

I shifted, self-conscious and awkward without clothing, but the allure of food was strong and I pushed my discomfort aside. Alexander tore the loaf of bread in half and handed a chunk to me along with some strawberries. I was ravenous and could have eaten thrice the amount, but it would have to suffice.

After a few minutes in which we both ate, Alexander said, "I know you headed south last night, but I'm not sure where we are. I'd like to get our bearings before we travel much farther. I found a map in Vera's library last summer that showed the location of the Mage's Gate."

I nodded. "She mentioned you'd been in the library several times. I found the book with the map."

I popped the last of the strawberries in my mouth. I felt better after our scant meal, though thoughts of Vera sent a spear of anguish through my heart. It wasn't fair that she'd been killed when Colin only sought my blood. I sighed and ran one hand through my hair.

"Andrew… I'm sorry." Alexander looked away, his expression wracked with guilt.

"It wasn't your fault. I've never lost someone I cared so deeply about before… And I *loved* her. I thought I knew what love was before we met, but I was wrong. *So damned wrong.* If Colin intended to wound me, that was, without a doubt, the greatest injury he could have hoped to inflict. He'll pay for it one day." I grimaced and looked up from the ground to meet my brother's eyes. "But first, we need to find the Mage's Gate. If the stories are true, we'll find sanctuary there. And perhaps be granted the time and opportunity to formulate a plan."

Alexander nodded in agreement. "And maybe I can learn about my own abilities." His face reddened slightly in embarrassment. "I never imagined I'd say something like that. I never truly believed I'd be going south…"

"We're in this together, Alex. Colin has already taken so much from me—I will *not* lose you to him as well."

I didn't tell him that he and Thomas were all I had left in the world. Everything else was gone, burned away with the ashes of Vinterry. I had nothing left to live for but the two half-brothers who stood beside me and one another.

He nodded. "Thank you, Andrew. I hope Tom can keep himself out of harm's way while we prepare."

"Tom's more resourceful than we give him credit for," I replied as I recalled our last conversation. "I think he'll do well enough for a time."

# SIXTEEN

I was sunburnt and intensely uncomfortable, despite my body's rapid ability to heal. I would not spend another day exposed to the elements until I obtained a proper set of clothing, no matter how much Alexander protested. I didn't seem to suffer burns in my dragon form.

As soon as the night grew sufficiently dark, I shifted and sighed with relief.

Alexander snickered. "You've been sunburnt before, Andrew."

I glowered at him. "Not in sssome areasss, but I will heal before the night isss over."

He had the decency to blush beneath his own burnt cheeks. "I hadn't considered that. I'm sorry." He paused to study the landscape around our location, then shook his head. "I still haven't determined where we are, but if you flew due south last night, perhaps we head slightly west? There should be a road between the Capitol and the Mage's Gate, if the map was correct."

I nodded and lowered myself to the ground, allowing him to climb up to his favored perch between my wings. I leapt into the sky and marveled at the relative ease with which I gained altitude. Each flight became easier than the last.

I scanned the landscape below for signs of pursuit as I searched for the road. I didn't know how far we'd traveled, but since we had not yet encountered any of Colin's lackeys, I assumed we'd outpaced them. If we were fortunate, they'd lost our trail entirely. I desperately clung to that glimmer of hope.

The southern road became visible perhaps two hours later. It was in disrepair and little wider than a wagon track, but it was the landmark we needed. I spied it long before Alexander did; there was little moonlight to guide us, but my vision was unaffected by the darkness.

There was no movement on the road, nor any structures to be seen between the horizons. I breathed easier, certain we weren't hunted at present. I wouldn't relax until we passed through the Mage's Gate, but I welcomed the respite, however brief it proved to be.

I banked due south as we neared the road but remained some distance from it, fearful we'd attract notice from any travelers who might appear. I kept it in my field of vision and began to utilize it as a guide for our journey.

The landscape transitioned from grassland to rolling hills dotted with stands of trees. We encountered few buildings and only a single town as we continued south, and by the time we paused to rest as dawn lightened the eastern sky, it had been many hours since we'd glimpsed a settlement. Even farmsteads had become sparse. The relative emptiness of the land mirrored the hollowness in my soul as I continued to dwell upon the events at Vinterry.

Damn Colin. He'd destroyed everything.

I located a copse of broad-leafed trees large enough to conceal my enormous form and touched down nearby. The landing was smoother than my previous attempts, yet far from ideal. I grimaced as Alexander slid to the ground.

"I need to learn to do that better," I said apologetically.

"This was your third flight, brother. As with speech, it requires practice." He laughed and clapped a hand against my foreleg. "Be patient, Andrew."

I rolled my eyes. I had little time for patience.

Once we were safely ensconced within the copse of trees, I lay down, exhausted. Alexander cast a worried glance in my direction, but I ignored his unspoken concerns—I simply needed to rest. The prolonged flights and lack of food were taking their toll. I'd pushed myself harder than I should have, but the urgency of our situation had propelled me onward. I wouldn't allow Alexander to suffer the same fate as Vera. My failure to protect her would haunt me for eternity.

It was only a few minutes before I fell into a deep and dreamless sleep. It was the reprieve I'd desperately needed.

I awoke sometime after noon. Sunlight streamed between the tree branches to create a dappled effect on the ground. The day was warm, the wind calm. Bees buzzed nearby, their drone accompanied by the chirp of an insistent cricket, and the scent of spring's greenery wafted through the air. Alexander was asleep, curled on his side in a mound of grass not far away.

I felt better since I'd slept, but I knew I'd need to eat soon. As if it had been awaiting the thought, my stomach rumbled loudly enough it roused my brother from his slumber.

He sat up and looked around as he rubbed the sleep from his eyes. "Andrew? I heard…something."

I grimaced and looked away, embarrassed. "It wasss nothing."

He arched one eyebrow as my stomach gave another loud rumble, then burst into a fit of laughter. "We need to find you a proper breakfast, but I don't recall seeing any settlements nearby."

"If there are no people near, I can hunt."

I'd considered the option previously but was hesitant to act on it. I wasn't certain what it would take to alleviate my hunger while I maintained my dragon form, and though the human half of me was revolted by the idea of consuming raw meat, the dragon half had begun to salivate at the prospect. My stomach twisted into a knot of indecision, disgust, and concern over how Alexander might react.

"If you're determined to stay in this form, then by all means, hunt," Alexander replied. "I imagine you need more food than your normal intake. I'll wait for you here."

I shook my head as a pang of worry sliced through my chest. "We ssshould ssstay together."

I feared if I left him, I'd return to find him dead while Colin's men awaited me, prepared for an ambush. I knew the scenario was unlikely, but given what had occurred at Vinterry, I was loath to part from him. I could not protect him if I wasn't nearby.

He crossed his arms with a frown but nodded. "Fine. Let's find you a meal, brother."

We flew south, keeping the dark ribbon of the road on our right. In the daylight, it was apparent the road was in a state of disrepair; numerous ruts marred the path, and the center was choked with weeds.

I couldn't imagine anyone successfully driving a wagon along it without frequently stopping for repairs.

We had not been airborne long when I spied a herd of grazing antelope in the grassy plains to the east. I shoved my revulsion aside and peered over my shoulder.

"I sssee a herd. I'll dive into them and hope I take them by sssurprise."

He renewed his grip on my spines in anticipation. It was a maneuver I'd never tried before, but I'd watched hawks perform similar feats and was confident I could emulate them. My wings lacked feathers, but their mechanism seemed much the same.

I folded my wings along my body and arrowed toward my quarry on the ground. The wind rushed past and became a deafening roar in my ears as the ground drew rapidly nearer. The antelope didn't notice my approach until I was upon them; they attempted to scatter in several directions, but the one I'd targeted wasn't swift enough to escape. I caught it in my claws as I spread my wings to arrest our fall. By the time I'd landed, the terrified creature was dead.

I reacted instinctively and tore into the antelope's flesh before Alexander had even made his way to the ground. I was ravenous and desperate to sate my raging appetite. Within minutes, there was little left of the antelope but pale bones and spilled blood.

It was only then that my rational mind intervened. I recoiled at the sight and backpedaled, ashamed I'd surrendered to my basest impulses. I hung my head and eyed Alexander sheepishly.

He stood some distance away with his arms crossed, observing me with an expression of amusement mixed with mild disgust.

I turned away, unable to meet his gaze any longer. I'd succumbed to my primal urges, and he'd borne witness to my terrible transformation. Perhaps the ancient kings of Novania had reason to fear the dragon-kind; in my desperation, I'd become a monster.

His footsteps heralded his approach, but I didn't turn to look at him.

"Andrew?" he asked, concern in his tone.

I didn't know what to say and made no reply.

"Andrew, look at me."

I swiveled my head to face Alexander.

He smirked at me in the maddening way he so often did, at once mischievous and smug. "Are you feeling better?"

I nodded. "I'm sssorry."

He rolled his eyes skyward and snorted a laugh. "Andrew, I understand better than you realize. We haven't eaten much since we left the Capitol, and you've been flying like mad. Holy hell, I knew you were hungry when your stomach was loud enough to wake me. I'm just glad you went after the antelope rather than me." He cracked a grin. "I'd give you indigestion on purpose, brother."

I chuckled and managed to relax. "I wasss hungry, and I didn't think. I... I reacted."

"That was one hell of a ride, though," he said, mercifully changing the subject. "For a few seconds, I wasn't sure you'd pull up in time, and we'd crash headlong into the ground. But the speed! That was incredible."

He turned to face south once more and said, "You also landed near our destination. Look."

He gestured toward the mountain range we'd spied on the map, marking the border between Novania and the Southlands. The peaks rose above the grassy plains, though from our present distance, we still had many miles of travel before we'd reach their rocky slopes.

There was a strange greenish shimmer in the air, rising from the mountains far into the sky. As I studied the anomaly, orange and gold bands of light danced across its surface, accompanied by ripples of blue and gray. It was translucent; the peaks beyond were clearly visible, but I had the distinct sense it was impenetrable.

"It's the Barrier," Alexander said, breathless. "If we continue along the southern road, we should come to the Mage's Gate. It should be located at the entrance to a canyon or a chasm—I could never determine which." He sighed and appeared troubled, but I understood what plagued his mind.

"Do you believe Colin knew we would travel here?" I asked.

If Colin had sent his men in the direction of our initial travel—east—then we should encounter no resistance at the Mage's Gate. If he'd anticipated our actions, however, he would have sent men south in an attempt to intercept us. How long would it take horsemen from the Captiol to reach our location? I was no longer certain if it had been two days or three since I'd freed Alexander; time had blurred and melded into a confused tangle of worry, tension, hunger, and overwhelming grief.

Alexander shook his head. "I don't know, Andrew. He's been unpredictable since our father's death, and he seeks the advice of Duke Ellington and that Claybourne man. It's just as likely he sent his men north or west as it is south or east. He may have dispersed his forces and sent them in each direction." He frowned, then suddenly brightened. "On the other hand, I think we've outpaced any horsemen he might have dispatched in this direction. Judging by the state of the road, they'd be hard-pressed to match even half your speed."

I shrugged. "We'll know sssoon."

I didn't share Alexander's confidence that we'd flown far enough to outpace Colin's soldiers. While we'd traveled a significant distance, we'd also rested several times, squandering hours in our effort to conceal my enormous, scaly form. I turned toward the decrepit roadway, unconvinced of our apparent good fortune. I scanned its length for some time, skeptical after all we'd endured that Colin would not thwart us again before we reached the Mage's Gate.

"Andrew, I..." Alexander stopped short and looked down as though embarrassed.

I shot him a quizzical look and wondered what he'd been about to say.

He sighed, then pressed on. "I want to reach the Mage's Gate as soon as we're able. I know that it's daylight, but there's nothing here— and we can see the Barrier. It can't be much further, and I'd... I'd feel safer on the other side."

I nodded in agreement, and allowed him to climb on my back. I hoped that whatever lay in store for us beyond the Mage's Gate was more favorable; I detested that we'd been reduced to stealing from farmers in order to survive. And I'd allowed my primal instincts to override my rational mind as I grappled with hunger. The burn of shame heated my face as we took to the sky once more, and the cool air cascading along my body did nothing to alleviate it.

I banked and flew directly above the road. There was no sign of movement, but the stillness unnerved me. Colin would have done everything in his power to intercept us; the spectacle we'd put on at the Capitol would have undoubtedly sent him into an unmitigated rage. I hoped Claire had not suffered due to our actions, but I didn't believe there had been another way to rescue Alexander.

The Barrier rose skyward above the mountains and stretched in both directions as far as I could see. The greenish hue of its shimmer intensified as the sun began to set. As we drew nearer, it became more difficult to discern the landscape beyond its unnatural border. Other bands of subtle color danced across the surface in a dizzying display, and a scent akin to ozone permeated the air.

The road ended abruptly a quarter-mile from the Barrier. A grassy field lay between the end of the road and two enormous black boulders. I could no longer make out what lay beyond the Barrier; the shimmer had grown brighter as we neared and outshone the landscape beyond its protective shield. Between the boulders was an empty, black void, at odds with the colorful display surrounding it.

I landed in the grass and Alexander slid to the ground. He strode forward, his jaw set and his eyes narrowed with determination.

I followed reluctantly in his wake. The Barrier and the black space within it made me uneasy; I was unfamiliar with magic and didn't know what to expect. I almost wished there had been soldiers awaiting us— at least then, I'd have known how to handle myself. I was wholly unprepared for what Alexander must do and hoped he'd uncovered some knowledge from Vera's library on how to proceed.

"Andrew," Alexander said reverently after a time, "this must be the Mage's Gate." He pointed at the blank space in the Barrier. "The description I read of the surroundings was a precise match to this location. The book described the 'gate' as a solid block, devoid of light or color."

"How do we enter?" I asked, glancing over my shoulder to ensure we were still alone. The prickling sensation that came with being watched intensified as we drew nearer to the gate, but it was impossible to see through the magical construct.

Alexander frowned. "I don't know. I'd hoped it would be obvious, or there would be someone here to act as a guide." His shoulders slumped in defeat. "I'm sorry, Andrew. I wish I knew more."

A strange humming filled the air as we spoke, emanating from the far side of the black space. I moved in front of Alexander, uncertain of what was in store for us. I would shield him from danger if I was able; I'd survive a direct attack more readily than he would.

After a moment, a vertical white line appeared at the center of the black space, and the black panels—for that was what they were—swung inward. A bald man of indeterminate age stood within the opening. He wore an unadorned woolen tunic and leather breeches, and clutched a gnarled walking stick in his right hand. He gazed at me, awestruck yet unafraid.

"It has long been my duty to guard the gateway," he stated in a firm, clear voice. "It has been many years since one of your kind has sought entrance. How is it that you remain in our world, Lord Dragon?"

I blinked, baffled and confused by the honorific.

Alexander stepped around me with a smirk, amused by my reaction. "Andrew is a skin-changer," he explained. "He's my half-brother. We traveled here to seek asylum—"

"Ah, yes. The Oracle has foreseen that many will arrive at the Mage's Gate in the future. Times have become difficult for those with the Mark." He eyed Alexander thoughtfully. "People such as yourself, it seems. Please, follow me."

Alexander gaped at me, startled that this man knew he was Marked. I nodded in encouragement and followed him through the space he'd created in the barrier. On either side of the gate were steep mountains, their flanks comprised of exposed, reddish stones. A few resilient pines had found footholds between boulders, but most of the mountainside was steep and sheer. Directly south of the Mage's Gate was the mouth of a canyon. The trickle of water sounded from somewhere ahead.

"My name is Gwerin. Give me a moment to close the gate, then we'll talk," the man said once we were through.

He began to move his hands in an intricate pattern while a sharp odor reminiscent of vinegar permeated the air. The gate began to close as he worked, and the black space moved into its previous position. The Barrier was once more impenetrable.

I sneezed profusely; the odor irritated my nostrils. Once Gwerin finished his task, the smell disappeared, leaving behind only the strong scent of ozone that I attributed to the Barrier.

Gwerin laughed heartily. "Ah, yes, skin-changers are said to react adversely when certain magics are performed. It's the hallmark of a being borne of magic, you see." He paused, sizing us up, then nodded as though satisfied with what he saw. "You never answered my question, friend. How is it you remain in our world? Your kind left years ago."

I told him what I knew of my parentage and that I suspected one of the dragon-magi who had traveled to Dresdin's Forge was my father. I explained how my mother had married Carlton Marsden, Alexander's father. Alexander described what had happened since his father's death, his suspicions regarding Colin's role in it, and what had transpired that forced us to flee. Gwerin didn't speak until we'd finished our tale.

Gwerin reached forward and touched my foreleg. "I'm sorry you lost your wife, Andrew. I cannot imagine your present sorrow." He shook his head, outraged. "And your own brother is the cause of your strife!"

"Gwerin, you wouldn't have a spare set of clothing somewhere, would you?" Alexander asked. "I believe Andrew will be more comfortable speaking if he shifts."

I nodded my agreement, and Gwerin laughed. "Yes, yes. Follow me. My cabin is not far from here."

Gwerin led us into the canyon. A small river ran along one side of the sheer cliffs to disappear beneath the mountains on the eastern side. A dark opening in the rockface led into a subterranean cavern at the same location the water exited. The western side of the canyon was lined with a variety of trees, some broad-leafed and others evergreen, and a few sported flowers. Gwerin's cabin was nestled just inside the canyon, along its curving wall. Lights twinkled through the windows, a sign of welcome as darkness fell.

Alexander followed him inside while I awaited them. A few moments later, he returned with a bundle of clothing.

"Gwerin's wife has prepared supper," he informed me with a smirk, "though I wasn't sure you'd be hungry so soon after your recent feast."

I shifted and took the proffered clothing as my face reddened. "I'm not—yet."

The clothing was snug but not uncomfortable. It would serve until I was able to procure something better tailored for my height and build. Satisfied, I offered my brother a tentative grin.

The inside of the cabin was airy and open. A sitting area, kitchen, and dining space were arranged in the front room, and a bookcase lined one wall. A round oaken table occupied the center of the space with several sturdy chairs arranged around its circumference, and a vase of wildflowers was displayed at its heart.

Gwerin introduced me to his wife, Arabelle, who was ladling stew into several bowls. I declined the offer of food, but accepted a mug of ale.

After a few moments, Arabelle looked up from her bowl and her gaze met my own. "What is it like, being a skin-changer?" she asked, curious.

Since I'd spent most of my life hiding what I was, I'd never considered how others might perceive me. I was uncertain how to answer her question, but decided I ought to make an attempt to describe my experience. She and Gwerin had already done much to help us, and it was the least I could do in return.

"I'm still learning," I replied with a shrug. "For most of my life, I passed myself off as a normal man. I've always known I could change forms, but I was wary of the danger that would come with it."

"You will not be persecuted here," Gwerin stated firmly. "The Southlands are home to many like myself and your brother. We bear the Mark of the Magi. Your father's people also lived here before their great exodus. You'll be safe."

I nodded thoughtfully and wondered what Colin would do if he discovered our location. "How do the Barrier and the Mage's Gate work?"

"Long ago, when the Novanian kings first began to persecute our kind, many of us fled to this land," Gwerin explained. "Some of the most powerful magi—human, dragon, and Merael—gathered in this canyon to perform one of the greatest rituals in history. The Barrier is constructed of pure, magical energy, and it surrounds the entirety of the Southlands. If you were to travel far enough east or west, you'd find the Barrier extends beyond the coastline and travels along its length, encircling our refuge far to the south." He paused to look at me pointedly. "As a skin-changer, you most likely could scent the Barrier well before you came upon it."

I nodded, recalling the ozone-like odor in the air as we'd flown.

He smiled. "I thought so. You'll always be more attuned to constructs of magic than others, even though you don't bear the Mark. It's simply a part of what you are." He paused to take a bite of stew before continuing. "The Barrier is energized by sunlight. It was built to withstand the ravages of time and does not require continuous maintenance or upkeep. It has been in place for well over a thousand years and provides us with sanctuary from the madmen in the north. The gate was devised as the only means of entry and exit. Every generation, there is at least one mage charged with guarding the gateway. Of course, we must possess the proper attunement to be selected for the duty. Arabelle and I have been guarding the gateway for seven years."

"What do you mean by 'proper attunement?'" Alexander asked.

"Ah, yes, you would be interested in that," Gwerin replied. "You see, each person born with the Mark is expected to travel to the Citadel at some point in their lifetime—if they wish to uncover their ability, that is. The Oracle resides there and holds audience with each would-be mage when they seek her out. She has the ability to see glimpses of the future, but she is also adept at reading one's innate abilities. She'll perform a reading and determine yours. For example, mine is of wind and air. My attunement made me a candidate for guarding the Mage's Gate. Other magi can perform elemental magics using fire or water, and some are healers. Others possess more mundane abilities, such as sending messages or opening locks. The Oracle will sense your attunement when you meet with her."

"Then that's where we'll go next," Alexander said. "I'd like to visit the Oracle and learn what I'm capable of."

Gwerin nodded in encouragement. "I'll give you directions in the morning. It's a long trek to the Citadel from here, though you might make it in three days if your brother flies."

I shrugged, open to either possibility. It was relaxing to have a normal conversation, to know we weren't hunted, and to sit inside, warm and secure in our surroundings. All were things I'd taken for granted. I appreciated them more now than I'd ever done before.

Alexander grinned at my reaction. "We'll work something out tomorrow, but I suspect Andrew enjoys his time in the air."

# SEVENTEEN

I spent the night next to the hearth in Gwerin and Arabelle's cabin. The wooden planks of the floor were uncomfortable, but I was exhausted after our long flight and fell asleep almost immediately. Alexander was given the guest bed, tucked away in the tiny room behind the kitchen. I awoke with the dawn, refreshed and rested. Arabelle was awake and kneading dough in the kitchen as I sat up and ran my hands through my hair.

"Good morning," she said pleasantly.

I stretched and made my way toward the table where she worked. "I wanted to thank you, Arabelle. For the food and your hospitality. We had nowhere to go."

She smiled. "When I married Gwerin, I expected to receive unannounced guests every now and again. Refugees like yourselves, fleeing from the northern kingdom. I suppose it's fortunate we have not had any guests until now, but after what you told us last night, I believe you are but the first of many." She paused in her work to give me a quizzical stare. "Is it true that the new king is your brother?"

I nodded. "He's gone mad with power. As we grew up, his father never divulged the fact that I wasn't his son and most assumed I'd take the throne. Colin has always been a thorn in my side, but he was never openly malicious. It wasn't until the king named him heir that he began to change for the worse. I don't understand his decision to execute Alex—he's done nothing wrong, harmed no one! And after what I did to save Alex, I'm certain I've made his list of those marked for death as well."

"It's a shame that blood ties mean nothing to him," Arabelle replied vehemently. "I had a brother and a sister, you know. They both died in their youth from the black pox. I would give anything to have them back in my life, while your own brother would toss you aside. His actions are infuriating. He'll come to regret them one day. A man like that will never find love, nor will he find peace."

I looked up as Alexander entered the room. I noted the dark circles beneath his eyes had receded during the night, and his eyes shone brighter than they had in several days.

"Good morning," Arabelle greeted him without turning away from her work. He strode across the room to stand at my side.

"I slept better than I have in weeks!" he exclaimed. "Thank you for allowing us to stay here, Arabelle."

She smiled, placed a cloth over the mound of dough, and dusted her floured hands on her apron. "It's part of our duty as gatekeepers," she replied. "Gwerin should be rising soon. He is always a later sleeper than I am. In the meantime, make yourselves comfortable. I'll prepare breakfast."

It wasn't long before Gwerin joined us at the table. While Arabelle busied herself in the kitchen, we spoke of our plans.

"Do you still wish to visit the Oracle?" he asked. When Alexander nodded, he said, "Good, I was hoping you'd say that. I can sense your power. Your Mark must be extraordinary."

Alexander shrugged uneasily. "I don't know. It's always been something to keep hidden. Otherwise, I risked death. Do Marks vary much between people?"

"Oh, yes," Gwerin replied adamantly. "The size of the Mark indicates the person's innate power. Larger Marks mean greater magical aptitude. The coloration of a Mark may also indicate something of the person's attunement, as well."

I watched Alexander carefully during the exchange and noted he appeared decidedly uncomfortable. His Mark was unusually large, if Thomas' description of the other unfortunate souls Colin had executed were accurate. Though I knew little of magi and Marks, the coloration of Alexander's had puzzled me. Gray mottled with white, it appeared unnatural against his skin. I pondered the implications and wondered what my brother was capable of.

Alexander chewed on his lower lip in thought. "May I see yours?" He asked Gwerin.

Gwerin smiled. "Of course."

He rolled up his left sleeve to reveal the familiar crescent shape on his bicep. The skin within the raised portion of the flesh possessed a blueish hue.

"Does the location of the Mark mean anything?" Alexander asked. "The others... The others that my brother killed, their Marks were located in the same area. But mine..."

Gwerin lifted an eyebrow, clearly interested. "The location sometimes has meaning, but for others, the placement is simply due to size. May I see it, Alex?"

Alexander chewed on his lip some more, then glanced at me warily. I shrugged; the choice was his. He scowled, but whether in irritation at me or his own misgivings, I was uncertain.

Finally, he said, "Very well."

Gwerin nodded. "It's natural that you're mistrustful, given your upbringing. You don't have to show me."

"No, I will," Alexander replied. "I'm not certain why I hesitated. Colin put me on public display as it was." He unbuttoned his shirt and pulled it back to reveal the Mark that arced across his torso.

Gwerin's eyes widened in surprise as he bent closer to examine the Mark. "I don't believe I've ever encountered a Mark of this size. It's said the dragons' Marks were large, but you don't share Andrew's lineage. And the coloration... I've never seen mottling of that sort, nor a Mark bearing two distinct colors." He looked up from his examination to meet Alexander's gaze. "You're unique amongst us, my friend. I'd be very interested to learn what the Oracle tells you."

"Perhaps you should travel with them," Arabelle suggested as she carried a platter of eggs and a plate of bacon to the table. "I can manage the gateway while you're away. Besides," she said with a pointed look at her husband, "it would do you some good to travel on occasion."

Gwerin considered the prospect briefly, then nodded. "Very well. As long as you don't mind?"

"Not at all," Alexander replied. "It would be nice to have someone along who knows the lands and how to reach our destination."

"Excellent," Gwerin replied with a grin. "After breakfast, I'll gather what we need for the journey. We can set off well before noon."

We would fly to the Citadel. Gwerin estimated it would take approximately three days if we weren't delayed by weather, and he packed several maps amongst his belongings. I learned he'd made the journey from his cabin to the Citadel only a few times, each at the behest of the Oracle. Gwerin assured us he could guide us to each resting place he'd chosen from the air, and I grudgingly agreed to his plan.

I didn't mind acting the ferry for my brother, but Gwerin was a relative stranger. In the face of Alexander's elation at our journey, however, I shoved my misgivings aside.

When we were nearly ready to depart, I followed Alexander outside while Gwerin said goodbye to his wife. I removed my borrowed clothing, which Alexander stowed in the pack he'd been given, and shifted into my dragon form. Gwerin exited the cabin a few moments later and strode up to us, wearing a pleased grin.

As Alexander clambered onto my back and found his purchase, Gwerin gestured briefly with his hands and began floating up from the ground. He moved himself slowly through the air until he'd located a position behind Alexander in which to hold himself during our flight. My nostrils twitched as he performed his magic and the tang of vinegar wafted through the air. I snorted but managed to avoid a bout of sneezing.

Alexander patted my shoulder twice, a signal they were ready to depart. I leapt into the air and reveled in the cool breeze that enveloped us. Gwerin directed me to follow the course of the canyon until it opened into a vast forest, which he called the Thornhallow. We would stop for the night near its center, where the settlement of Dark Heart was located.

"The Thornhallow is the home of the northern Merael," Gwerin shouted over the wind. "Have you met any of their kind before?"

"No," I heard Alexander reply.

"They are forest-dwelling people, not so different from humans, but unique in their own right. Few bear the Mark, but some can speak with animals and others with the trees and plants." Gwerin paused in his tale, and I felt one of his hands release its hold on my spine. "The Merael have long been allies of the dragon-kind, but they are said to be wary of skin-changers."

I grunted. "Why?" I asked over my shoulder.

"Superstition, from what I understand. It may be prudent to remain in your current form until we depart Dark Heart," Gwerin called. "I can't guarantee your reception will be favorable if they know you're a skin-changer."

I frowned at the prospect of remaining in this form another night. I would be required to eat in order to maintain our flight the next day, and my appetite was extensive. I hoped it would not be a burden on our unsuspecting hosts to provide enough to sate my hunger.

"I don't want to burden them," I replied with a scowl. "I'll be hungry at the end of the day."

Alexander laughed. "He's right. Andrew requires a considerable amount of food as a dragon."

"As I said, the Merael were allies of the dragons," Gwerin stated. "If they don't know the truth, they'll treat you graciously. Don't worry, my friend."

By mid-afternoon, we'd been flying over the vast expanse of trees for some time. The dense canopy stretched to the horizon line in every direction, relatively unbroken as far as my eyes could see. The trees were large, broad-leafed varieties, and the interwoven branches formed a nearly impenetrable mat beneath us. I hoped Gwerin could guide us to our destination accurately. I could see no markers that would indicate our location in relation to the ground, and I doubted my ability to navigate beneath the canopy without risking the safety of my passengers.

"There, to the southwest," Gwerin shouted. I imagined he pointed toward whatever he'd seen, though I didn't turn to look at him. "Do you see the cluster of trees, taller than the rest? There should be an open space surrounding them. That's Dark Heart."

I turned in the direction he'd indicated and noted a cluster of trees that towered above the canopy. I banked slightly to adjust our direction, and within a short time, the clearing Gwerin had mentioned became visible. I noted with a smile there would be sufficient space for me to touch down. It was a relief to know I wouldn't be forced to attempt the landing within a confined space.

As we approached, I slowed to better survey the area. Thatch-roofed homes dotted the clearing below. They were spread far enough apart that I should not have difficulty maneuvering between them. I settled to the ground as gently as I could, and was pleased to note it had been my best attempt yet.

Alexander slid down my side as was his custom, while Gwerin used the vinegar-scented magic to glide through the air to the ground. When I looked away from them, I was startled to see we'd drawn a small crowd of onlookers whom I assumed were the Merael.

They were smaller in stature than the average human. Their skin was green of varying shades; some the dark green of leaves, others the brighter green of grass, while some were more olive-toned. Each sported lustrous black hair and dark eyes, ranging from sapphire blue to muddy brown to deepest black. The men and women were easily discernable from one another, and there was a mix of both in the crowd.

I folded my wings carefully and remained still, uncertain of what to do next. After a few moments, a pair of elderly Merael made their way through the curious throng and approached Gwerin. They remained some distance away, perhaps out of uncertainty, or perhaps outright fear.

"Gwerin, my friend," one of the Merael greeted him with a smile. They embraced as though long acquainted. "Please, tell us why you've come." He glanced nervously in my direction and added, "And how you came to be traveling with a dragon."

Gwerin introduced Alexander and stated that he was taking my brother to the Citadel to meet with the Oracle. He told the Merael that I'd been traveling with Alexander before passing through the Mage's Gate—which was true—but he didn't elaborate further on our relationship. At the mention of the Oracle, however, the elderly Merael beamed with joy.

"Do you know, my niece also needs to visit the Oracle?" he asked. "Emmarie has the gift. She's a Wild-kin. Perhaps she can travel with you?"

I suppressed a groan, irritated with the notion of yet another unfamiliar passenger on my back.

The crowd began to disperse as they realized the visitors were known to the elders of the forest. The friendly elder with whom Gwerin was speaking was introduced as Tylmar, and the other, who was more reserved, was Veldyn. Tylmar asked one of the others to send word to his niece, then continued to chat amicably with Gwerin.

I was out of place and largely ignored in the conversation. I supposed that was to be expected; Gwerin knew the Merael, and they seemed to understand Alexander's journey well enough. I was something of an oddity, a lone dragon who'd failed to flee with his kin. Given Gwerin's earlier warnings, I knew it was best simply to play my part and move on when the time came.

Tylmar's niece joined us after a time. She was in her late teenage years, perhaps twenty at most. She was introduced to Gwerin and Alexander, but quickly grew bored with their conversation. She turned away and gazed at me with her nearly-black eyes. I studied her as she approached; she was thin and pretty, dressed in leathers, her long, dark hair loose as it fell to her waist.

She peered up at me, unafraid. "I know who you are," she said in a hushed whisper, then glanced behind her to ensure none of the others had followed. "I know my uncle told Gwerin of my planned visit to the Oracle, but did he also tell you of my talent?"

I nodded. "A Wild-kin."

"And do you know what that means?"

I shook my head.

"I can communicate with the creatures of the forest. They bring me tidings and news from beyond the Thornhallow. Your arrival at the Mage's Gate was a topic of intense conversation." She flashed a grin. "I have not told my uncle, nor anyone else, what you truly are. They would send you away to wait outside Dark Heart while the others conduct their business. I don't believe it's warranted—the sparrows claim you're a good sort, and I trust them. My people cling to some unfortunate and outdated customs," she finished with an air of exasperation.

I'd been unaware that our arrival had been noticed by anyone other than Gwerin and Arabelle, but I'd not counted on wild animals bearing the news. "What did you hear about our arrival?"

"The first message stated there was a dragon in the Southlands, which I believed was strange," she replied. "The dragons have been gone for decades. But that news came from a raccoon, and they tend to embellish their tales. Then I received *another* message from a much more reliable sparrow. *She* said it was a mage and a skin-changer, not a full-blooded dragon." She crossed her arms. "Alexander is a mage, yes?"

I nodded. "He will be when trained."

She glanced toward the others to reassure herself they remained engrossed in their own conversation. "That means *you* are the skin-changer. I thought it was odd, but it seemed more likely than a *dragon*. And the sparrow overheard much of the tale you told Gwerin. I didn't want to believe it until you arrived here." She smirked knowingly. "I learn much more about what goes on than the elders realize. I think it's why they're sending me to the Citadel. They want to keep me from mischief."

"Will you be traveling with usss, then?" I asked her.

She shrugged. "Perhaps. I would like to, but it will ultimately depend on my uncle's decision. As an elder, he dictates what I must do, whether I agree with him or not. I've never been outside the Thornhallow, but I would love to see more of the world."

I sensed Emmarie tended toward impatience and impulsiveness. I didn't know what awaited us during our travels, but I hoped she would not cause trouble. Her youth gave her confidence, and it might become problematic if she refused to listen. I hoped our journey would be free of peril, but Alexander and I knew nothing of the Southlands. I wasn't certain of anything.

"If I travel with you, will you fly?" she asked.

"Perhapsss," I replied. "Gwerin knowsss the land. I don't."

She narrowed her eyes briefly. "You're uncomfortable. You prefer your human form to this."

She was more perceptive than I'd given her credit for. I nodded.

"Once we're away, I'll speak with Gwerin. You shouldn't be forced into this form if it is not your preference." She folded her arms across her narrow chest. "My people make the journey to the Citadel frequently. It's long, but there is little danger. The only advantage flight brings us is speed." She appeared thoughtful, then asked, "Why do you prefer your other form?"

"I am unfamiliar with thisss one," I replied.

She nodded. "I believe I understand. Perhaps the Oracle can help you, as well as Alexander. She does many things beyond assessing the magi's abilities." She looked down and a shadow seemed to cross her face. "I'm sorry you were left behind when the rest of your kin fled. It can't be easy knowing you're the last."

I blinked, surprised at her sudden empathy. In truth, I'd never given my situation much thought. It simply was. I was about to reply when she was called away by her uncle.

She turned to go, then spun to face me once more. "I think we'll have time to speak later. I like you, Lord Dragon." Her tone may have been mocking, but I wasn't certain. She smirked as she strode away.

I was baffled by her behavior, and it must have shown. As soon as she joined Gwerin and the others, Alexander walked toward me.

"Why so puzzled, brother?" he asked.

"Emmarie isss an interessting one," I replied thoughtfully.

He lifted an eyebrow in question. "I hope that won't be a problem. Gwerin has already agreed that she will accompany us to the Citadel."

# EIGHTEEN

We left Dark Heart the next morning with the dawn. There was still little in the way of sunlight beneath the canopy of leaves, but once we burst into the open sky, I noted the day would be clear. Gwerin directed our path toward the southern end of the forest, but it was after midday before we finally passed the last of the trees.

The land beyond the Thornhallow was comprised of rolling hills and stony outcroppings. A variety of field grass blanketed the land, broken by occasional clusters of bushes, but there were few trees. From our vantage point, herds of antelope and deer could be seen, but there were few signs of people beyond the single road that wound through the hills southeast of the forest.

We decided to land a short time after noon. I looked forward to the break and a meal.

As soon as we were on the ground, Emmarie made it clear to Gwerin she was privy to my true nature.

"Gwerin, you ought to let him change." When Gwerin's eyes widened, she smirked knowingly. "I knew you were traveling with a skin-changer before you ever departed your cabin. I didn't tell my uncle—or anyone else, for that matter." She turned to face me, hands on her slim hips. "Go ahead and shift. I know you're uncomfortable."

I glanced toward Alexander, who was rummaging in his pack. A moment later, he produced my borrowed clothing, and I nodded to Emmarie in thanks before shifting.

The relief that washed over me as I took my human form must have been evident in my expression. As Alexander handed me the clothing and I began to dress, he said, "Why didn't you say something, brother?"

"I believed I'd grow used to it, given time." I paused as I scrambled to adequately describe how I felt. "There isn't pain, Alex. I'm so damned *large,* and I'm still learning my own capabilities. It's…awkward. In any case, I'd much rather eat as a man than as a dragon. My appetite is more manageable."

He chuckled. "I won't disagree with you on that account. You ate enough for ten last night."

The previous evening, I'd been led to a clearing on the outskirts of Dark Heart, where the Merael had roasted two whole pigs. They'd indicated both had been reserved for me. While I'd been grateful for the meal, it was a source of embarrassment knowing the sheer quantity of food I was required to consume. I'd waited until the others departed before I'd begun to eat, uncomfortable with an audience. A dragon's jaws did not allow me the delicacy required for a social setting.

I looked past Alexander and met Gwerin's eyes. "If it's alright with you, I'd like to remain this way for a time."

Emmarie came to stand next to Alexander once I was fully clothed again and looked at me with an expression of intense curiosity. "You're tall for a human. You also look very much like your brother. Is that by choice?"

I looked at her, confused. "What do you mean?"

"You're a skin-changer. Can't you choose your appearance when you shift?"

I shook my head. "It doesn't work that way, Emmarie. When I'm human, I look like this. When I'm a dragon, I appear as you saw."

She rolled her eyes. "Have you *tried* to change your appearance?"

Again, I shook my head. "Why would I?"

She shrugged. "Reasons."

Gwerin began to distribute some apples he'd acquired while in Dark Heart and small chunks of hard, yellow cheese. While we ate, I considered Emmarie's suggestion. I knew instinctively that I could not change my appearance on a whim. It simply wasn't how the shifting process worked, and I wasn't a mage as my father had been. I didn't have the means nor the ability to *choose* my appearance in either form. Both were set and unchanging.

"If we continue from here on foot, it will take us an additional three days to reach the Citadel," Gwerin said around a mouthful of apple. "That would be four days from now. If we fly there, we'll reach before noon tomorrow."

I nodded. Perhaps if we reached the Citadel sooner, I'd have more opportunity to spend time as a human. One more day spent flying through the skies as a dragon would not be terrible, and I enjoyed flying, after all.

"I can fly," I replied with a shrug.

I heard a shrill cry from overhead and looked up to see a hawk circling in the air above. Emmarie rose, gazing intently into the sky, then produced a sound that was eerily similar to the hawk's cry. The bird banked to its right before diving toward us. Emmarie stretched out one arm, unafraid, and the hawk landed lightly on the offered perch. The hawk's feathers were a lustrous brown-red, its eyes a brilliant yellow. It peered at each of us in turn, then seemed to dismiss us. It turned its full attention on Emmarie, and they began to communicate in a series of whistles, chirps, and cries.

It was then that I understood what Tylmar meant when he'd said she could speak with animals. After a minute, the hawk leapt into the air to resume its hunt.

"She came from the north," Emmarie informed us. "There are three more humans at the Mage's Gate, and Arabelle has allowed them through. She—the hawk—went beyond the Barrier to survey the lands near the gate. She said there will be others. They are fleeing for their lives."

I ground my teeth together in a burst of rage. "Damn Colin. He's going to destroy that kingdom!"

Emmarie nodded. "I know your story from the sparrow, as I told you yesterday. Colin is the king, yes?"

When I nodded, Alexander said, "He is. And I regret that he is also our brother."

"You must meet with the Oracle as soon as you can," Gwerin replied. "I sense something much worse than fleeing refugees will befall us, and the two of you will likely be the key to whatever lies ahead. Blood ties cannot be ignored."

Emmarie scowled at him in annoyance. "Gwerin may be correct. The Oracle will be interested in you, but your journey seems even more important now." She turned to look directly at me. "I know you've already agreed to fly us the rest of the way to the Citadel, but I wonder: How fast can you travel?"

I shrugged. I didn't have an answer to her question, and I was puzzled by their sudden urgency. Did the fact that more people had fled from Novania through the Mage's Gate indicate something more had occurred beyond Colin's continued tyranny? Alexander and I had been the first of what I assumed would be many, though I wasn't certain how common the Mark was amongst Novanians.

Gwerin's eyes shone with intensity. "We should leave, and soon, Andrew. I fear the implications of this news."

I nodded, taking his hint, and began to peel off my clothing once more. I handed it to Alexander, but before I moved away, he said in a low whisper, "Fly as you did near Vinterry. You've never been so swift since. I think there's more going on than we've been led to believe."

I agreed; Gwerin hadn't told us everything—but would the Oracle?

I moved away to shift while I considered the situation. Flying would give me an opportunity to think, and perhaps come up with a plan. The others frequently spoke amongst one another, but it was often difficult for them to make themselves heard to me over the roar of the wind. Even though there were aspects of my dragon form I was still adjusting to, I'd discovered flight was soothing, and the apparent solitude allowed me to think more clearly. Once the others resumed their previous perches, I leapt into the air and followed the road as it wound south and east.

I pushed myself faster until I sped swiftly over the landscape, and the world below transformed into a green-brown blur. To the west, dark clouds were beginning to build, threatening evening storms. Gradually, the landscape began to change; rolling and rocky hills gave way to vast plains. Stands of trees dotted the landscape, their leaves dark green with a purplish sheen, their smooth bark a stark white. A short distance to the east, the glimmering silver ribbon of a river appeared, shining in the golden afternoon sunlight.

While we flew, my thoughts whirled around all that had happened in the past week. It had begun with Thomas' arrival at Vinterry, our wild flight to the Capitol, and the terrible spectacle Colin had devised to celebrate Alexander's execution. I'd foiled his plan and saved Alexander just five days past. It seemed a lifetime ago.

I hoped Thomas fared well and wished there was some way to send him a message. I knew he'd eventually learn of what had transpired at Vinterry and what we'd discovered upon our return. My heart ached anew as I thought of Vera, her life cut brutally short in Colin's mad scheme to secure his power. Vera had been innocent, caught in the crossfire of our feud despite my best efforts to remain beneath Colin's notice. She'd deserved so much better than what life had provided.

The painful memories drove me onward. A part of me hoped the grief would melt away and disappear if I simply kept moving, but it stubbornly remained.

My thoughts drifted. I'd done as Colin asked and remained at Vinterry when news of the former king's death had reached us, believing my compliance with his senseless demands would provide Vera with some measure of safety. Vinterry had been relatively isolated, and again, I'd been lulled into a false sense of security. If Thomas had not arrived when he did, there was no doubt the soldiers we'd passed would have attempted to detain me from racing to Alexander's aid. On the other hand, if Thomas had not come, Vera would still be alive, but I would have lost Alexander. I don't know if I would have coped with that outcome any differently. Perhaps I would have fared even worse.

Rain began to fall, but I was oblivious to the storm. I continued for some time before I realized the weather had turned, lost within my thoughts as I'd been. But when I heard the distant rumble of thunder, I knew instinctively it wouldn't be safe to remain aloft. While I'd learned I was capable of enduring many physical injuries, I doubted I'd survive a lightning strike.

I landed swiftly and hoped the others weren't upset with my delay. They were sodden and miserable, but kept their complaints to a minimum. The rain fell steadily, and soon they were drenched. It formed beads and ran off my scales; I seemed to be the only one unaffected by the change in the weather. I decided to remain in my dragon form until the storm passed.

Experimentally, I stretched one of my wings and held it above the others. I hoped to shield them from the rain.

Alexander looked up sharply, then broke into a laugh. "Yes, keep that up, brother! We might be able to make a fire now."

I smiled, pleased to contribute something helpful on what would otherwise become a gloomy and uncomfortable evening. Perhaps it would be sufficient repayment for my previous lapse.

Gwerin performed some magic that caused the air beneath my wing to stir, and within moments the space began to dry. I sneezed as he worked, the vinegar scent irritating my nostrils despite the rain. Neither Emmarie nor Alexander noticed the smell.

After a few minutes, Alexander was convinced he could make a fire. It didn't take long before a nice blaze took hold, and the others huddled around it to warm their hands. I continued to hold my wing above them, providing what shelter I could.

"We should arrive at the Citadel before midday tomorrow, so long as the weather lets up," Gwerin stated.

"How long wasss it raining before we landed?" I asked.

"Not long," Gwerin assured me.

Alexander rolled his eyes. "Long enough for us to get soaked, but as quick as that storm rolled in, there wasn't much you could have done, Andrew." He drew his cloak tighter about his shoulders and leaned toward the fire. "Stop fretting over things you have no control over."

"That isss not what I wasss referring to," I growled, frustrated by his sour attitude.

Alexander levelled his gaze at me, his expression unreadable.

"I wasss thinking of Vera," I confessed. "I wasssn't aware of the rain. Not until I heard the thunder."

His expression softened, and he nodded. "It's been one hellacious week, hasn't it, brother?" He sighed heavily and dropped his gaze to stare into the flames. "I hope Tom's safe. He risked so much for me…"

"I want to sssend him a messsage, but I don't know how," I replied.

"There is a way," Gwerin said slowly, and we both turned toward him attentively. "When we arrive at the Citadel, I will look into it. I cannot make any promises right now, but if a certain mage is in the city, he can help. His talent allows him to send letters over vast distances."

"We should try it," Alexander stated firmly, and I raised my head to meet his gaze. He looked directly at me and must have understood something of my thoughts. "Tom might not have believed in magical occurrences before, but I can assure you, he'll be less likely to discount them now."

I narrowed my eyes. "What happened, Alexsss? Tom gave me a rundown of what Colin did, but—"

"Colin wouldn't allow Tom to visit me after I was taken to the dungeons," he said, his voice flat with anger. "I was livid. Not only due to the humiliation Colin planned for me, but I wasn't allowed visitors either. No one else could help me. I raged at the guards outside of my cell, and then suddenly I felt *something*. I struck the bars, and they gave way... I thought at first they'd been weakened over time, but that wasn't the case." He looked down, a small, bitter smile playing on his lips. "If I'd anticipated the bars breaking as they did, I could have escaped and saved us both much sorrow. But I was stunned, and the guards subdued me before I realized my opportunity. I was placed in another cell, one with solid walls and no light."

"Alexsss—" I began, shocked at what had occurred.

We'd scarcely had time to speak of those events; we'd been too busy simply trying to survive. Had the bars given way because he'd somehow managed to tap into his power? And how did Thomas fit into his story?

He held up one hand, indicating that he would answer my unspoken questions. "Tom heard I'd been moved and assumed Colin had broken his word. He forced Colin to promise I would be treated with respect, and a lightless cell was not appropriate. Tom was angrier than I'd ever seen him—honestly, I didn't think he had it in him. He stormed into the dungeons and demanded the guards allow him entrance. It was the middle of the night, and the guards on that shift were terrified of him." Alexander snickered. "I heard him railing at them well before he arrived at my cell. We both knew we had little time, so I told him the only thing I knew that might save me. I asked that he ride to Vinterry and tell you what happened."

Alexander hung his head and looked at the ground. Tears shone in his eyes, and when next he spoke, his voice was thick with emotion. "Andrew, I will spend every damned day regretting that request. I was so relieved when I learned you were in the arena, and again when we escaped, but—" His voice broke, and he looked away. "The price was too high. Vera didn't deserve to die."

I closed my eyes briefly. "No ssshe did not," I agreed, "but neither did you. I left her, thinking Vinterry would be sssafe. I came to your aid, believing Colin would not threaten her. Vera wasss nothing to him. I failed to protect her." I ground my teeth together as rage flowed through me. "The real villain isss not you, nor isss it me. Colin did thisss."

"He's right, Alex," Emmarie said softly. "You can't blame yourself for your brother's crime. My people believe that for each wrong committed by a person, their punishment will be fourfold. He will pay severely for what he has done, one day."

Alexander clenched his jaw. "I wish he could pay now. Vera was not the first he's killed."

"You mentioned there were others with the Mark," Gwerin added.

Alexander nodded. "That wasn't all. He killed our father too." He peered at me then. "I found proof, Andrew. I was going to confront him…"

"What did you find?"

"Claire wasn't Colin's only conquest," he replied with a frown. "He had at least two mistresses, one of which possessed a vengeful streak. She gave me the key to Colin's private chambers. I found several poisons. I also found correspondence between Colin and Duke Ellington. Colin received a hefty sum from the duke after our father's death, along with a note expressing the duke's thanks for services rendered. As you know, the duke and father never got along." He groaned and scratched his neck. "As I say it now, it sounds too circumstantial, but I *know* he had something to do with it!"

"If I may interrupt?" Gwerin asked. When Alexander nodded, he pressed on. "You said you 'felt something' when you struck the bars of your first cell. Can you explain what you meant?"

"I don't know," Alexander said, chewing his lower lip in thought. "It was almost…a vibration, or resonance. It passed through me. I was so consumed with rage, I dismissed it as a manifestation of my fury, but when the bars gave way..." He trailed off and shook his head in disbelief.

Gwerin studied him carefully. "While it is rare for someone without proper training to tap into their innate power, it is not unheard of, particularly when the mage in question bears a powerful Mark. Based on your description, I believe your abilities may be tied to your physical strength. The Oracle can tell you for certain. I don't believe you're an elemental, as I am. That much is clear."

Alexander glanced at me, fear evident in his eyes. Whatever power he possessed had brought us to this place, and it was obvious he was terrified of his future capabilities. Knowing him as I did, he'd never admit it, nor could he hide it from his expression.

"Alexsss," I said, "whatever happensss, I'll be with you." He needed a reminder that he was not alone.

He nodded, seemingly grateful. "Thank you, brother."

The rain continued through much of the night. While the others slept, I kept watch—and held my wing above them to keep them dry. When the weather finally relented, it was only a couple hours before dawn. I lay down to sleep while I could, then folded my wings to allow them a respite. They'd grown stiff during my vigil and ached fiercely.

I gazed at the others for some time as I willed myself into slumber. Alexander slept fitfully; I knew he worried over the outcome of our upcoming meeting with the mysterious Oracle, but I would keep my promise to him. I'd be there for him, no matter what trials awaited. After all, Colin had taken nearly everything else; my brothers were all I had left, and I'd do my damnedest to ensure their safety.

I hoped Thomas was faring well. Gwerin's belief there was a mage who could help was reassuring, but it wasn't a guarantee. Tom needed to know that Alexander and I were safe, but I also craved news from home. It had only been a few days since the spectacle at the Capitol, but those days had stretched and expanded until they felt as long as decades.

When I finally drifted to sleep, the eastern sky was beginning to lighten with the first glimmer of the dawn. It seemed I'd only closed my eyes a moment when I was awakened by Alexander. He peered into my face from only a few inches away. I startled, blinking in the bright rays of the early morning sun. It was perhaps an hour past dawn.

Alexander laughed. "I didn't mean to startle you, brother. I tried calling to you, but you were out cold." In a quieter tone, he said, "Gwerin is ready to depart. He's eager to learn what the Oracle has to say, but I'm… I'm not certain I want to know."

I held his gaze. "Alexsss, I will keep my word, no matter what the Oracle tellsss you."

He nodded. "I know, but I'm afraid. What if I'm dangerous like the old stories claim? What then?"

"Then we'll manage it," I stated. "You and me."

He nodded again but didn't appear convinced. I understood what he was going through, even if he did not; managing a strange power with no guidance wasn't an easy task. I believed Alexander would receive advice, and perhaps even mentoring, once we reached the Citadel. It was more than I could claim for myself.

I convinced Gwerin to postpone our departure until after I'd eaten. I left the others to hunt; I didn't want Gwerin or Emmarie to witness the carnage I'd wreak. I located a herd of antelope a short distance away. After sating my hunger, I returned to the others. I hadn't been gone long, but Gwerin was impatient and eager to be off. I found his enthusiasm grating. Perhaps it was simply my conversation with Alexander that had left me in a dour mood, but I glowered at the mage as he and the others found their perches along my spine.

We flew along the road for an hour before the Citadel came into view. A single, massive tower constructed of white stone thrust skyward above the forest that sprawled along its base. The tower was wide at the bottom, tapering as it rose, then flared out again near its apex. Arching windows ringed the top, surrounded by an open-air balcony. The roof overhung the balcony and was supported by graceful white columns. I'd never encountered construction of its nature and wondered if it had been built with magic. Conventional techniques could not have wrought something so graceful and beautiful, yet durable enough to withstand both weather and time.

A city ringed the tower's base, though many of the buildings were obscured by the forest. The city appeared as large as Novania's Capitol, but lacked its walls.

Gwerin directed me to land upon the tower's balcony. As we passed above the city, I heard merchants calling their wares, the hammer of a blacksmith, snippets of conversation, the neighing of horses. The Citadel was undoubtedly the heart of civilization in the Southlands.

As I approached the balcony, I noted that while the city below was populated and bustling, the tower itself was silent, seemingly devoid of life. I landed carefully; the gap between the balcony's railing and the roof's overhang was only just large enough to accommodate my bulk, and my passengers were forced to duck low.

As the others dismounted and began to look around, a woman appeared in a nearby doorway. She was tall with a willowy frame, her long hair was loose and startlingly white, though her face betrayed no sign of advanced age. She wore a loose, flowing robe of pale gray that billowed as she walked. Her eyes were a striking shade of violet, unlike any I'd encountered before.

She walked forward purposefully until she stood only a few steps away. "Zayneldarion," she addressed me, "I told you years ago that I'd foreseen your return, and my visions are rarely incorrect."

# NINETEEN

I gaped at the white-haired woman in confusion. The name she'd spoken—Zayneldarion—was familiar, but I was unable to place how I knew it. I shook my head.

"You are missstaken," I replied.

She frowned and stepped forward, then swiftly reached out with one graceful hand to place it along the side of my snout. A strange tingling sensation accompanied the contact, and I almost pulled away from her touch in surprise. A faint citrus aroma enveloped her, though if it was from perfume or her variety of magic, I wasn't sure. She kept her hand firmly in place and closed her eyes in concentration.

I glanced toward the others, uncertain who she was or what she was doing. Alexander shrugged; he appeared as confused as I was, while Gwerin nodded in encouragement. Emmarie appeared disinterested; she stared across the balcony with her arms crossed.

After several moments, the woman dropped her hand, and the tingling sensation vanished. I wanted desperately to scratch the location where she'd touched me, but I refrained. My scales itched from the contact.

"I understand," she said slowly. "Please forgive my earlier assumption. I was mistaken, as you've stated. You are an exact image of him, and I've always believed he would one day find the means to shed his curse." She shook her head. "It is not to be, as he told me many times." She drew a breath and steeled herself. "Change into your other form, Andrew, and we shall talk. I'll await you inside."

Gwerin and Emmarie followed the woman through the door while Alexander remained outside with me. I gaped after her, stunned. She'd known what I was without inquiry, and whatever she'd done when she touched me had provided her with information she couldn't have known otherwise. She knew my name without a formal introduction.

As soon as I was human again, I surrendered to the urge to scratch the side of my face. Given what I'd learned from Gwerin, she'd used a form of magic, and I'd reacted to it.

"What just happened?" Alexander asked as I began to dress. "Is she the Oracle?"

I shrugged and pulled on my trousers. "She must be, but I don't know what happened any more than you do. I hope she plans to explain herself." I scratched the underside of my jaw.

"Well, it seems Gwerin has found the excitement he was looking for," Alexander grumbled. "That man was about to drive me mad!"

I laughed as I tugged on my boots. "He means well, Alex."

Alexander rolled his eyes and frowned. "I doubt he believed the Oracle would speak with you first, though. I wonder who she thought you were? That name…Zay…Zan… Whatever it was, it's strange."

I shrugged indifferently, but I harbored my suspicions. I knew my human appearance had much in common with my late mother, so it was not a stretch to think my dragon appearance would appear like my father's. In that moment, I recalled where I'd heard the name Zayneldarion. Vera and I had been in the library, perusing the book Thomas had located, and she'd located a passage regarding the dragon-magi in Dresdin's Forge. Zayneldarion had been one of those magi.

I swallowed hard and stared at the arched opening leading into the tower for several long moments, stunned. The woman had known my father. I was certain of it.

"Andrew?" Alexander's tone was laced with concern.

I shook my head in an attempt to clear my thoughts. "I'm fine," I replied, then beckoned to him. "Let's find out what she has to say."

The interior of the tower was a vast, circular room ringed by arches, most of which were open to the outside air. The floor was decorated with a tiled mosaic depicting a crescent and a trio of stars. At the center of the room, a narrow spiral staircase led upwards, while on the eastern side, a broader staircase led to the lower levels. I was grateful we'd flown to the balcony; the trek to this level from the ground floor would have been exhausting.

The woman who had met us outside stood near the central staircase with Gwerin and Emmarie. As we entered, she motioned for us to join them while her unsettling violet eyes studied us closely. When we stopped alongside the others, she nodded as if she'd come to an important decision.

"You are brothers." It wasn't a question, but I nodded in confirmation. "Do you know what occurred when I touched you, Andrew?"

I shook my head. "No, but my skin itches." I resisted the urge to scratch my face again, though I sorely wanted to.

She smiled faintly. "I suppose it would. Skin-changers have always been sensitive to magic. I was reading you—or rather, your memories. I had to be certain what you told me was true and that you were not Zayneldarion Caein, as I'd believed." She paused and arched an eyebrow. "You are not him, but there is no doubt you are his son."

"You knew my father?" I pressed. I wanted—*needed*—to learn more.

She nodded morosely. "Zayneldarion was one of the greatest dragon-magi, though he was young for his kind. He'd been named emissary to the Citadel by his mentor, Caelmarion Zorai, and he often came here on business, representing his people. *Your* people, Andrew. He possessed a powerful Mark. Very few dragons harbored the ability to change their appearance on a whim as he did, and it made him a valuable asset. Times were troubled, though no less than they are now."

She paused to assess me further. "You look like him. I'd always believed my vision had foreseen his return, but it wasn't Zayneldarion I glimpsed. It was you. It's rare that I'm wrong when interpreting what I've seen, but your coming is perhaps even more of a portent than his would have been."

"A portent?" Gwerin asked, unable to conceal his sudden interest.

She glanced at him briefly and nodded. "I don't know for certain. I must speak with you more, Andrew, and your brother as well."

She turned toward the downward staircase, where a pair of women had appeared. Both were garbed in soft blue tunics and matching leggings. The crescent and star emblem was emblazoned across their garments.

The Oracle turned her gaze to meet Gwerin's. "Please, allow my assistants to show you out, Gwerin. Emmarie, you as well. I will summon you at a later date. I believe we will have much to discuss, but now is not the time."

Gwerin and Emmarie followed the women downstairs and vanished from our sight. Alexander and I were left alone with the strange, white-haired woman and her unsettling magical talent.

"I wished for privacy before we discussed your presence here further," she said after a lengthy silence. "We'll speak upstairs in my private quarters where we will not be overheard."

Alexander and I exchanged glances before we followed her up the tight spiral of steps. I had a dozen questions and more, and I was certain Alexander felt the same.

She paused midway up to ensure we followed. I suppressed a sigh and continued on. Her mysterious demeanor left me uneasy, and my skin continued to itch from our previous contact. I hoped she didn't plan to pry into my memories a second time.

The room at the top of the staircase was decorated in various shades of blue. The rugs on the floor were a shade akin to the midnight sky; the filmy curtains tied back from the arching windows were a paler shade; the cushions strewn about the floor were the color of a robin's egg. The Oracle strode to the center of the room, chose a cushion for herself, and sat gracefully. She spread her hands to either side in a gesture of welcome.

"Please, make yourselves comfortable," she said. "I believe this will take some time."

I glanced at Alexander as my uncertainty deepened. To his credit, Alexander remained stoic and betrayed nothing of his thoughts in his expression. I sat down cross-legged and steeled myself for the Oracle's next revelation. Alexander remained standing, his feet spaced wide, his arms crossed.

"I sent Gwerin away because while he means well, his duties lie elsewhere," the Oracle began. "I selected him to guard the Mage's Gate, not due to his magical ability, but because he is an excellent judge of character. There will be those who attempt to enter our lands in disguise as they follow the orders of the Novanian king—your brother."

She studied us each in turn, gauging our reactions. I clenched my jaw as my anxiety continued to grow. She knew of us, our situation, from glimpsing my memories. The notion set me on edge.

"I spoke of portents," she continued after a time. "There was a vision granted to one of my predecessors that has not yet come to pass. It's unusual for an Oracle's vision to go unfulfilled for so long, and has become something of a legend in the Southlands. I would like to tell you what I know of it." She paused to study her hands, turning them first one way, then another.

"What did this vision foretell?" Alexander asked, putting voice to his curiosity.

She raised her eyes to meet his. "The vision involved a pair of strangers. They came to our land, seeking asylum. Both required guidance and both possessed vast potential and unusual power. The vision indicated one of this pair was the last of his kin, though if the Oracle who beheld the vision knew what his kin was, that bit of information is lost to the ages. The vision stated the pair's arrival would herald the onset of war. Strife would come to our lands in their wake, pursuing them as they attempted to flee. It didn't state *what* they fled from. Our interpretation has been that this pair—and the powers they hold—would be the keys to ending the war that followed. They alone would conquer the armies sent to destroy them—but only after much trial and sacrifice."

Her strange, violet eyes shifted between us as she spoke. Her gaze was steady, her voice matter-of-fact. She paused to study us carefully as we absorbed her words.

I considered the story. A pair of strangers with unusual power could describe the two of us, but her description of the situation was vague and could have applied to anyone. That one of the strangers was the last of his kin unsettled me—I believed she had spoken of me. I was the last of my kind, the dragon-kind.

I swallowed hard and looked away, uncomfortable with the mysticism and magic she employed. If social niceties had allowed, I would have bolted for the stairs at the first opportunity.

"When I touched you, Andrew, I glimpsed your life's history," she continued after a time.

Prickles of unease ran along my spine with her words. I suppressed a shudder of revulsion and couldn't shake the sensation that my mind had been violated by the strange woman who now sat before me. She'd acted without my consent, and while I had nothing in my past I was truly ashamed of, I wished she would have asked.

"The legend is vague, as many visions are, but I sense you are connected to it. You're the last of your kin, and a skin-changer's power was incredibly rare, even when the dragons remained." She shifted her gaze to Alexander. "The vision was clear that it was a *pair* of strangers, which means if Andrew is the first, then you are the second, Alexander."

Alexander shifted uncomfortably under her scrutiny. "It's true that we sought asylum," he replied. "Do you truly believe Colin will send his army after us?"

I scowled at the carpeted floor. I knew the answer to his question and knew he wouldn't like it.

"Yes," I growled. "I made a fool of him when I rescued you and gave him more of a spectacle than he'd bargained for. He won't forgive me."

"Gwerin insisted that you come to me for guidance," the Oracle cut in before Alexander could reply. "He was right in doing so, though he should not have abandoned his post. I'll ensure he departs for his cabin tomorrow." She paused to rise gracefully from her seat. "Alexander, please come here. I must perform a reading of you, as is befitting a would-be mage."

Alexander stood rigidly for several moments, his jaw clenched and his eyes wide.

"Alex, remember what we discussed," I whispered. "I'll be here."

He nodded, drew a breath, and steeled himself, then stepped toward the Oracle, who took his hands in her own. She closed her eyes, and I detected the faint citrus aroma once more. She released her grip after a few seconds, then nodded, seemingly satisfied.

"I need to see your Mark for myself," she stated. "The power you possess is…strange to me. I cannot read you as easily as I can most others."

Alexander scratched at the nape of his neck and glanced at me uncertainly. I shrugged, indicating the choice was his alone. He closed his eyes briefly. When he opened them, he pulled his shirt over his head and tossed it to the floor near his feet.

The Oracle gazed at his bare torso for some time, her expression unreadable. Finally, she stretched one slender hand forward and placed it upon the Mark my brother bore. Alexander gasped and his eyes widened as she made contact. I sprang to my feet, prepared to do whatever was necessary to ensure his safety, but my concern was unfounded. She withdrew her hand before I could close the distance between us, a knowing smile playing upon her lips.

"Your power is tied to your physical strength, Alexander," she said. "It's an unusual gift. It seems your specialty will be in combat. A mage-warrior. It has been many years since a mage with your potential has come to the Citadel, and longer still since a mage-warrior graced our ranks. With the power your Mark exudes, you will become a formidable opponent to any who dare challenge you—but you are untrained and untested."

Her gaze shifted to me. "Your brother looks up to you, and you have long protected him. The journey he must undergo will take months. It will be arduous, and the Southlands pose a unique set of dangers apart from those the Novanian king will present. Alexander will require a guardian."

"I've given him my word," I replied without hesitation. "I plan to be there for him."

"I know. I've glimpsed your memories, after all." She smirked. "There are few as well-suited to this task as you are, Andrew. Mages are rarely so fortunate to travel with a guardian of your caliber. Your battle prowess will be a boon to his journey." She turned back to Alexander. "You must undertake a pilgrimage in order to understand your innate ability. As I stated, it will be dangerous and it will take time. Even if the Southlands are threatened by the war the vision foretold, you must reach the conclusion of your pilgrimage. It is of the utmost importance that you complete your training, else you risk madness and death. Once you start along this path, you cannot stop until you have mastered your power. Such is the way of magic."

Alexander nodded stiffly. "I understand."

"Do you?" she asked cryptically. "I wonder." She turned toward me. "As your brother's guardian, not only are you responsible for his safety, but you must also ensure he does not abandon his task. The war that follows in your footsteps must be ignored until he is finished with his pilgrimage. Give me your word that you will not allow him to waver from this path."

She asked me to not only keep Alexander out of harm's way, but to avoid being drawn into Colin's battle. The atrocities that Colin had committed caused my blood to boil each time I was forced to recall them. I sought revenge for Vera and for the former king, for Vinterry's staff, for Alexander… The Oracle demanded that I abandon my rage and go against my very nature by ignoring the call of battle. I was uncertain I'd be up to the task.

"I must have your word, Andrew, or I will not guide your brother any further. Without guidance, he will eventually succumb to his power. He has harnessed it unwittingly on at least one occasion. Without proper training, his power will consume him, to his detriment."

Her words sparked a fury within me. Who was she to threaten my brother when we'd come to her for help? She'd gleaned more of my nature than I'd realized and sought to use my loyalty to Alexander as leverage. I ground my teeth in anger.

"I promise," I snarled, then whirled away. I strode to the nearest window and glared through the gauzy curtain, my arms crossed as I seethed. I wanted nothing more to do with the Oracle if she was determined to manipulate us.

She sighed, but I refused to turn and acknowledge her.

"He has inherited his father's temper, I see," she told Alexander.

Despite myself, I was drawn into the conversation. I wanted to know all I could of the father I'd never met.

"Zayneldarion had a similar reaction during his first encounter with me. It is not my intention to anger those who seek my wisdom, but sometimes it's inevitable."

"You forced his hand," Alexander snapped.

"Your brother is a man of his word," she replied. "He will not break his oath now that it has been made. I did what was necessary to ensure your survival, Alexander."

Alexander snorted in annoyance. "What is this pilgrimage? Why must I do it? What does it have to do with my training as a mage? If you've read our damned memories as you've claimed, you know we're not familiar with the process."

"All fair questions," she replied evenly. "When a mage comes to me seeking an assessment of their ability, there is one of two outcomes. In the first, they are assigned a mentor—someone with a similar ability who can teach them what they need to know. The second outcome is more unusual, but is necessary for many. It is to embark on the pilgrimage. The would-be mage will visit each of twelve ancient shrines, and in so doing, will learn to control their power. Those who must undertake the pilgrimage have rarer gifts and often cannot be taught by another—or in cases such as yours, there are no others alive to teach them."

I turned during her explanation and listened intently. "What is needed for this pilgrimage?" I asked.

"I will assign a guide to accompany you," she replied. "It will be another mage, one who knows the land and how to reach each destination. Alexander, you already have your guardian, but for others who come to me, I must choose one for them. You will require provisions and the supplies needed for a prolonged journey. I will ask one of my assistants to help you procure them, but I must think upon who shall guide you. Many are qualified, yet few enjoy undertaking a pilgrimage not their own."

She paused to study us in turn. "In the meantime, I have more to speak of with you, Alexander. Andrew, please see my assistant downstairs. She will take you into the city, where you may send a message to Thomas."

When I blinked in surprise, she smiled in amusement. "I read many things when I made contact," she replied.

I glanced at Alexander, who nodded. He seemed to accept the situation and had relaxed considerably since our arrival. I was no longer concerned about leaving him alone with the Oracle, though I remained unconvinced of her motives. I assumed she wanted to discuss his ability and his upcoming journey; it was unlikely he'd come to harm.

I descended the spiral staircase and was met by one of the blue-garbed women. She had straight dark hair and hazel eyes, an olive complexion, and an ageless countenance akin to the Oracle's. When I explained the Oracle's instructions, she smiled.

"I know a mage who can send a message," she replied. "His name is Bryson Feige, and he specializes in sending letters. Is there anything else you require? The Oracle may need a few hours alone with your brother."

I blinked, uncertain why the Oracle would need Alexander alone for a prolonged period of time. "Hours? She didn't mention that."

The woman shrugged. "She has a reason for her actions. I've been employed in the tower for nearly a decade, and when she seeks a private audience alone with a man, I've learned it's best not to inquire." She paused to look me over. "Perhaps we can locate some better-fitting clothing? It looks as though you borrowed those, and they are too small for your frame."

I felt my face flush and managed a nod. I wanted to ask her what she'd meant regarding Alexander and the Oracle, but sensed she would continue to dance around the subject. Instead, I focused on her final statement.

"They were borrowed, yes."

"I thought so." She smiled. "You will no doubt want something sturdy enough for traveling. Or do you prefer armor?"

I had not considered my own needs for some time; I'd been more concerned with delivering Alexander to safety.

"I don't know," I replied. "I'm not sure what we'll face on this pilgrimage. Do you have any suggestions?"

She looked at me searchingly for a time. "Did the Oracle name you his guardian, then?" When I nodded, she said, "Armor would be best then. Some of the lands are dangerous, I've heard, but you have the look of a warrior. Is that why you were chosen?"

I smiled faintly, amused. "In part. Alexander is my brother... Well, half-brother, truly. The primary reason she chose me is due to my own ability. I'm..." I paused; it was strange to admit my heritage freely without fear of repercussions. "I'm a skin-changer."

Her eyes widened in surprise, then she grinned, her face alight with excitement. "It was *you* we saw fly into the tower earlier! News of your arrival spread through the tower and the city—no one has seen a dragon in almost forty years! It was the first time I've ever laid eyes on one." She paused to regain her composure. "I believe there is one more place we should visit while we're in the city. Truthfully, it's outside the city, but it isn't far. I'll take you to the Stone Grove."

# TWENTY

During our long trek down the tower staircase, I learned the woman's name was Lileen. She was a daughter of the Oracle, as were several others who worked within the tower. Lileen was thirty-two, one of the youngest of the Oracle's female children. When I asked about their father, she smiled, amused.

"Fathers," she corrected me. "We each have a different sire. The Oracle chooses a man every so often to father her next child in the hope it will be granted her magical gift. So far, none of us possess her talent, though most of us are Marked. We have our own, more limited, abilities. The girl born with her gift will become the next Oracle. Not all of my siblings work in the tower, but many do. It's a position of honor."

I nodded, though the concept was baffling. "Do you have brothers, or are all of the Oracle's children girls?"

She laughed. "I suppose that's a fair question since you didn't grow up in the Southlands. Only a girl-child can become an Oracle. I'm not certain why that is, but there has never been a male Oracle in our history. I have several half-brothers. One is a blacksmith in the city below, another bears a Mark, but we seldom see him." She shrugged. "I don't know where he travels, but he conducts business for our mother."

We walked the rest of the way in relative silence until we reached the ground level. The sounds of the city enveloped us as we exited the tower, and Lileen led me through the winding streets with ease. We traveled through a market sector and past several taverns before we arrived in a quieter area comprised of individual homes. She located the house she sought and bade me follow her as she called upon its owner.

A young man answered the door and smiled nervously as he noted his visitors, though he welcomed us inside readily enough. Lileen introduced him as Bryson Feige, the messenger-mage.

"You have something you'd like composed, then?" he asked once the introductions were complete. "I've had a busy afternoon, to be sure! People wanted to send word to distant kin that the dragons had returned—although I only happened to see one."

I nodded but didn't care to rehash my story a second time. I needed to send word to Thomas, and the city's fixation with the dragons' purported return could wait. This man didn't need to know the details of our journey, and I assumed he would learn the truth soon enough from others around the Citadel.

"First, I'll need to know where your message needs to be sent—or to whom, if you don't have a location," Bryson continued as he led us to a table near a hearth. "Then, I'll need to know what you'd like relayed, or you can write the missive yourself if you know how. Depending on the distance, it may take time to locate the recipient."

"I need to send word to my half-brother, Thomas Marsden." When he nodded, I said, "Tom's somewhere in Novania. I hope that won't be a problem."

Bryson looked at me sharply. "Novania? What's he doing there? It's dangerous that way—especially for folks like myself."

I sighed. "I'm aware of those dangers. I grew up in Novania."

His eyes widened, then he nodded. "I see. I can send him a message, but I may need your assistance with some of what I must do. He's your half-brother, you said?"

"Yes, but I have three half-brothers. Will that make a difference?"

He frowned. "Not truly, since I know his name." He paused, then gestured to a nearby table cluttered with sheets of paper and pots of ink. "Can you write, or would you like me to pen the message for you?"

"I'll write it myself," I said, then asked, "Can he respond to us?"

Bryson nodded. "I can arrange it so he can write a brief message in return, though I will need to explain that to him in your message."

I nodded. "Please do."

"Very well. Leave me a bit of space at the end of your note."

I sighed as a wave of despair settled over me. I didn't relish what I'd be forced to write. I settled into the indicated chair and pulled a clean sheet of paper toward me. It was fine quality, as was the ink. Thomas would have been envious had he been present.

I scribbled a brief message, sharing that we were safe but that Vera was not. I wrote only that Vinterry had been razed and Colin was responsible; I knew Thomas would intuit what I'd left unsaid. I asked him for news, then sat back to grimace at my handiwork. My handwriting would never be as neat as Thomas'.

I passed the sheet to Bryson, who scanned it with a troubled frown. "I'll just add my instructions to the end," he said.

I waited as he finished, then turned the sheet toward me. "If you're satisfied, I'll send this now."

When I nodded in approval, he oriented the sheet on the tabletop and held his hands above it. The odor of a strong onion permeated the room, and within seconds, I began to sneeze repeatedly. I hurriedly excused myself and jogged outside, unable to bear the scent of Bryson's magic. I heard Lileen speaking to Bryson as I made my escape, and moments later, she emerged from his home.

"Andrew, are you well?" she asked.

I offered her a sheepish smile. "Every time I'm near someone performing magic, it affects me. Each magic I've encountered has a different scent. His happened to be strong enough it caused me to sneeze. Gwerin said it was a typical reaction."

"I didn't realize," she replied, her dark eyes wide with fascination. "I'll tell Bryson you're well."

She disappeared within the dwelling once more, but I remained in the sparse yard. I watched the passers-by on the street as they went about their errands or spoke among friends. The populace of the Citadel seemed no different than that of the Capitol, though there didn't seem to be any nobility. It was several minutes before Lileen returned.

"He sent your message, Andrew. He's finished with the magic, though I don't know how long its residue will remain. If your brother responds, he'll receive a reply soon."

I nodded, willing to risk another bout of sneezing if it meant I might hear something from Thomas. When we entered the house, the onion smell was gone. I apologized to Bryson, who laughed and waved it off.

"Lileen told me what happened. All those notes I sent earlier—it was you that everyone saw fly across the sky to the tower." He smiled. "While they may have been wrong about there being *dragons*, it was quite a sight, to be sure. For many, it was the only glimpse we've been privileged to."

"I'm not exactly a dragon, though," I reminded him. "Most of the time, I'm just a man."

He was about to respond when something caught his eye. He turned to the writing table with a grin. The parchment we'd written on earlier materialized above its surface and hovered in place, as though waiting for someone to pluck it from the air. I recognized Thomas' precise handwriting immediately and reached for it.

*Andrew,*

*I'm pleased to hear you have made it safely beyond the Mage's Gate, though my heart breaks at the news of Vera. I am so very sorry for what Colin has done.*

*I have gone to stay with our uncle, Duke Crossley, in Bridgewaters. The Capitol is no longer safe for me, and I fear Colin seeks retribution for my act of defiance in going to Vinterry. It had to be done for Alexander's sake, and I would do it again.*

*You put on quite the show at the tourney field, Andrew! I will never forget the day, nor the look on Colin's face when you changed form. Half the kingdom's nobles were in attendance as well. Some were horrified, but others remained silent when questioned about the event. You have allies here, though we are scattered at present.*

*I do not know how the mechanism of this letter works, but I would very much like to hear from you again. Stay safe, Andrew. I believe the day is coming when we shall need your aid. Colin must be dealt with.*

*Regards, Tom*

I shook my head in disbelief. Thomas was in hiding, plotting against Colin. He hadn't known what transpired at Vinterry, but at least he was safe at present. Duke Crossley was a good man and had been loyal to the late king; he held little love for Colin, and I believed that given enough time and reason, Crossley would make a stand against Novania's new ruler. I was confident Thomas would be protected so long as he remained with the duke. I would tell Alexander what I'd learned once we returned to the tower.

"I know it's none of my business," Bryson said slowly, "but this message from your brother sounds serious. Who is Colin?"

I raked one hand through my hair, then gave him a brief description of the recent events in Novania. When I spoke of Colin's plot to execute Alexander, Bryson and Lileen were both aghast.

"Your own brother did this, and now the two of you have fled here?" Lileen was outraged. "Does family mean nothing to him?"

I shrugged. "Apparently not." I turned to Bryson. "Thank you for contacting Tom. I'm relieved he's well."

Bryson beamed. "Come back anytime. I'm happy to help."

I followed Lileen outside and into the city; the sun was beginning to near the western horizon, and the buildings cast long shadows across the cobbled streets.

"We have an hour until sundown," she informed me. "It will take us half that time to reach the Stone Grove, but I believe you ought to visit it. You will understand when we arrive."

I nodded, though I wondered what could be so important she was convinced I must see it. I followed her through several residential streets, and soon, we reached the outskirts of the city. Lacking a wall, the city simply tapered off into the forested wilderness. Once beyond the bustle of the streets, the forest seemed profoundly still. It was peaceful beneath the leafy boughs; the only sounds were our footsteps, the chirping of crickets, and the occasional trilling calls of birds.

Lileen led me along a winding path that threaded through the trees. It was well-worn and clear of obstacles. The trees grew densely together, and in the limited space between the trunks, a riot of gnarled undergrowth carpeted the ground. If the path had not been clear, it would have taken a substantial effort to traverse the forest.

The path crested a small hill, and Lileen paused at the top of the rise. She peered at me, her eyes alight with intensity.

"At the base of this hill, the forest opens into a small clearing. We call it the Stone Grove," she said. "It's the place the dragons came to perform their final ritual, where they opened the gateway to their new home world. But powerful magic often exacts a steep price." She looked down, choosing her words carefully. "From our brief conversations, I've gathered you know little of your father. He was a great mage amongst his people, one of three tasked with performing the ritual to open the gateway. He and the two others remain in this grove still."

I narrowed my eyes, confused, though a sudden, wild hope filled me. "What do you mean, he's still here? I was taught the dragons all left—"

She nodded. "They did. What I meant was the three mages could not join their people. The price of the magic they summoned was too high."

"You mean they sacrificed themselves," I stated, stunned at the realization.

"Yes, but they are not deceased. We call it the Stone Grove because of what remains there. It will make more sense once you see it for yourself, Andrew." She began to descend the hill, and I raced to follow her.

As we entered the grove, it was immediately apparent that a great catastrophe had befallen the place. Many of the trees were petrified, and near the center of the clearing, the ground had been blasted by a cataclysmic force, scarred irreparably. There was no plant growth within the blast zone, as though the very earth had been rendered barren. But what drew my gaze was not the trees, nor the damaged earth. Near the grove's heart, standing in a circle around the blast's circumference, were three dragons.

My heart leapt at the sight, and I took several steps forward before I realized there was no movement among them. They remained fixed in place, rigid and unblinking.

"What happened?" I asked in a strangled whisper.

"When the gateway magic was summoned, the three mages paid a terrible price," Lileen replied somberly. "They were petrified, turned to stone, just as many of the trees were."

I stumbled into the grove and stood between two of the stone dragons. The one to my left was smaller than the others and had finer features; to my eye, it was female. The dragon to my right was large and bore several scars along his flank. He had a broad snout and a bulky frame. The last dragon, which stood across from me in the circle, was instantly recognizable; I'd seen his face the day I peered into the pool and looked at my own reflection. The dragon across the circle was none other than Zayneldarion, my father.

I took another few steps forward, my gaze riveted on his frozen features. I wondered what he would think of me, the son he'd never known.

"I can help you, Andrew," Lileen stated after a while. "My ability allows me to communicate with many people. I've come here in the past and spoken with the dragon-mages. I can act as a conduit if you'd like to speak with him."

I nodded without taking my eyes from my father's countenance. I wanted to speak with him. I needed to know so many things about what I was, what I was capable of. Finally, I tore my gaze away and turned to Lileen.

"Should I change first?" I asked, uncertain what I should do. If the dragons were aware, could hear and speak, perhaps it would take less explaining or convincing if I were to shift beneath their stony gazes.

She appeared thoughtful for a moment, then nodded. "I think it would save us some time."

I turned away from Lileen to peel off my clothing and boots. I tossed them to one side of the clearing where they would not be in my way. I looked up at Zayneldarion's face and shifted; once in my dragon form, I stood tall enough to look him directly in the eye. His features had not moved, but I wanted to believe he recognized me.

Lileen strode up to the stone dragon and placed one of her hands firmly on his foreleg. She closed her eyes, and a small smile formed upon her lips. "He knows you," she whispered, her voice reverent. She stretched her other hand toward me, and when she made contact, I suddenly heard his voice in my head as a faint tingle emanated from her hand.

"My son." The voice was deep, warm, charged with feeling.

"I wish I could have come sooner," I told him. I didn't have to vocalize to communicate through Lileen's magical link. "I've hoped for this moment my entire life. I've always been alone."

"When you entered the grove, I knew, even before you shifted forms. You look so very much like Carra. She didn't tell me she was with child." His voice was filled with sorrow. "I would have taken her with me. I would have ensured she had a place in the new world. You would have grown up with others like yourself. I have failed you both."

I shook my head. "No. She protected me when I was small and allowed me to survive the laws of Novania. I believe that I'm here for a reason, and that reason is to protect my half-brother while he goes through his pilgrimage. I don't believe you failed at all."

"What name did she give you, my son?"

"Andrew."

"Andrew Caein. A good name." I could hear a smile in his tone, and it filled me with pride. He'd given his surname willingly, without question. "Is your mother well? I've often thought of her as I stand trapped in this unmoving shell."

I looked down. Of course, he could not have known her fate. "She passed away several years ago from an illness that none could cure. I'm sorry."

He sighed, a sound filled with grief and pain. "I loved her, though I don't know if she understood that." He fell silent, and I didn't speak, at a loss for words. Finally, he said, "Your half-brother is a mage, then?"

I nodded. "Yes. The Oracle named me his guardian, though it's a role I've held for many years. Alexander and I have always been close, and after the recent events that led us here, I intend to do whatever I can to protect him. I have little else left."

"Your words are laced with grief. Tell me what has transpired."

I found myself retelling our story, but this time, I started at the beginning and spoke willingly. I told him of my life in the Capitol, raised by the king and my mother, while the rest of the kingdom remained unaware of my true origins. I spoke of my time as a soldier and later as the commander of the king's forces. I expressed my desire to learn more about myself, but admitted it had never been safe for me to do so until after I'd moved to Vinterry. I told him of my battles with the Corodan, and of the final showdown I'd had with the hive-queen; how I'd been forced to shift in order to defend myself and had slaughtered the Corodan who sought to ambush me. I spoke of Colin and Claire, of Alexander, Thomas, and finally, Vera, the woman who would always hold my heart. I explained what I'd learned while at Vinterry and why I'd been drawn away, how I'd saved Alexander from execution, only to return to find my wife savagely murdered by Colin's men. I told him of our flight south and the strange meeting with the Oracle.

When I finished, it was well past sundown and the grove had fallen into darkness. Faint stars twinkled overhead in the inky expanse of the night sky.

"I'm sorry you were forced to hide what you were, Andrew," he said after a time. "More than that, I'm sorry I could not be there for you, to watch you grow into the fine being you are now. I'm honored to call you my son. I hope you will return here from time to time. I want to know all I can of your life."

I smiled, grateful, hopeful, proud. I'd finally reached my father, and he accepted me as I was. What was more, he was proud of me. I was at a loss for words.

"It grows late. You should return to the Citadel."

I nodded, though I was reluctant to leave. "Father, I... Thank you."

"Go now, Andrew Caein. We will speak again. Thank you for coming here. Knowing that you live makes this curse more bearable."

Lileen said little as we walked through the darkened forest and into the lantern-lit streets of the Citadel. She appeared exhausted, and I wondered what the cost had been for her to maintain the lengthy conversation I'd had with my father. She didn't complain, though she swayed on her feet on occasion.

While we traveled, I replayed the conversation in my mind. I would return to the Stone Grove as often as I could; I wanted to learn as much from him as I was able. I didn't know if his life could be restored or if he and the others were cursed to remain encased in stone for eternity, but at least I'd been granted the opportunity to speak with him. It was more than I'd ever hoped for, and I would always be grateful to Lileen for facilitating our first contact.

When we arrived at the tower, we were met by another blue-garbed woman in the foyer. She was very petite; at first glance, I believed she was a child. She had short, dark hair framing an ageless face, her skin was dark brown, and her eyes were nearly black in color.

"Lil, you need to rest," she stated matter-of-factly. "I'll see to our visitor."

Lileen nodded and disappeared up the long staircase. The other woman sized me up for a moment before she turned to lead me up the stairs in Lileen's wake.

"My name is Canna. The Oracle asked me to prepare one of the guest chambers. There is also a meal awaiting you."

"Thank you," I replied. I wanted to speak with Alexander first; the meal could wait. "Can you take me to my brother?"

She arched an eyebrow, and a knowing smirk appeared on her thin face. "Your brother will be occupied for much of the night, I believe. You may speak with him in the morning."

I frowned. "What do you mean? I have news for him."

She sighed patiently. "Did Lileen not tell you why you were sent from the Oracle's chambers earlier?"

I shook my head. "The Oracle wanted to speak with Alexander privately, but that's all I know."

Canna continued to smirk. "Every so often—usually once every few years—the Oracle chooses a man to spend the night with. She waits until the time is right, when she knows she'll conceive. She has yet to produce an heir, and her time is drawing to an end. She has chosen your brother for this purpose."

I gaped at her for several seconds, then shook my head, speechless. Lileen had mentioned the process but had not indicated Alexander was chosen. I wondered how he'd fare—for the entirety of his adult life, he'd remained celibate out of necessity. Now that we were safely away from Novania, his concerns regarding his Mark were baseless. To be chosen by the Oracle seemed a profound occurrence, and I was uncertain what it might mean for him.

Canna laughed lightly. "I believe she made the decision as soon as you arrived. Your brother's Mark is powerful, and it draws her, calls to her in a way that is difficult to explain. Some of the others mentioned they could sense his Mark from afar—that is a rare thing."

She paused to look down at her hands. "I hope your brother will sire the next Oracle. There have been few men selected over the past several years, and the Oracle is aged, though she doesn't look it. She fears she will die before she births an heir. Our society cannot function without an Oracle to act as our guide, and she has become desperate. Since the time of the Mage Wars, it has always been this way."

"But why Alex?" I pressed.

She shrugged. "Why does anyone choose a mate? If your brother is half as good-looking as you are, I can't say I blame her for the decision."

My face flushed, and I looked away. "If what you say is true, I won't see Alex until morning."

She laughed and led me along a landing toward a series of doors. She pointed toward the nearest one. "This is your room. I bid you a good night."

# TWENTY-ONE

The room I'd been given for the night was small, yet comfortable. It was furnished with a bed and a small wardrobe, though I had no belongings to place inside beyond the borrowed clothes I'd arrived with. I made a mental note to obtain at least one other set, preferably some that fit my frame better, before we set out on Alexander's pilgrimage. The room featured a small, arched window that looked out over the city and the forest below. I slept soundly, at peace for the first time in many months.

The next morning, I was awakened by another of the Oracle's assistants. She bore a tray of fruit and light pastries and informed me that I would be summoned to the mosaic room soon. I was eager to tell Alexander all that I'd learned, but I doubted I would see him until I was called to speak with the Oracle again. He was likely still with her if what Canna had said was true.

I'd just finished eating when Canna arrived. She indicated the Oracle was prepared to see me. "Your brother is already upstairs," she added with a knowing smirk.

"I assume she'll be sending us on our way, then?" I asked.

Canna hesitated a moment, then shook her head. "I'm not certain. You'll leave soon, but not today. She has called Lileen as well. Your departure may be delayed a few days, based upon what I sensed of her temper. She has…*seen* something."

"You mean a vision?" I asked, mildly annoyed. I was growing weary of the vague responses the Oracle and her assistants continued to supply.

She shrugged and appeared troubled. "I'm not certain. She wouldn't say."

She increased her pace, and we ascended the remainder of the stairs without further conversation. When we reached the open floor with the crescent and stars mosaic, the Oracle was standing at the base of the central spiral staircase awaiting us, her face serene. Alexander stood off to one side, scowling. He gazed through one of the arches leading to the balcony, his arms crossed and his jaw clenched.

Clearly, his time with the Oracle had left him in a foul mood.

"Canna, you may go," the Oracle said swiftly as we approached.

I raised an eyebrow, surprised by her abrupt demeanor. Canna bowed once and made her exit, leaving me alone with the enigmatic Oracle and a surly Alexander.

"We have a few minutes before Lileen will arrive," the Oracle stated. "There is a matter which concerns you both—and she must not overhear my words." She looked to where Alexander stood, his back to us. "Alexander, please come here."

He continued to scowl, and for a moment I believed he planned to ignore her request. After a few seconds, he released a heavy sigh and turned to stride across the large room. He came to stand beside me while staring daggers at the Oracle.

"I was granted a vision with the dawn," she continued, unperturbed by my brother's temper. "There was a vast battlefield, with many wounded. Fires raged, and a terrible storm rumbled through the sky. There was…*so much death*."

Her voice was pained, and she closed her eyes with a grimace. In that moment, she appeared ancient, no longer ageless, a woman who had watched countless lifetimes pass. Abruptly, she looked up, and her violet eyes focused on mine. I stared at her unflinchingly. I wanted to know what more she had to say.

"Above the battlefield soared a black dragon. There is no one else it could have been but you, Andrew." She turned her gaze to Alexander. "And I saw you, as well. Standing in the midst of the destruction, bodies piled around you, while you brandished an ancient sword. A cursed blade, if I'm not mistaken." She drew a breath but seemed to deflate, as though it had sapped all of her energy to relay what she'd seen.

"My visions do not always come to pass as I see them. Sometimes they are merely symbolic. I believe this was one such instance. What it means is this: You will both go to war, and you will cause much death and suffering. The power that you each wield can be catastrophic if you choose it to be." She studied Alexander for a time. "The sword you held—I believe it exists, and I believe you will find it during your pilgrimage. It holds substantial power but is immeasurably dangerous. Be wary, Alexander."

He frowned and crossed his arms again. "I should have been more wary of coming *here*," he snarled.

I narrowed my eyes, certain something had transpired between them that went beyond Canna's implied liaison. While I didn't like to be left out of a conversation as it occurred in front of me, I also didn't believe it was my place to pry into what seemed a private affair.

The Oracle gazed at him evenly, her expression devoid of emotion. "It is the way of things, Alexander, no matter how much you dislike the outcome."

At that moment, Lileen entered, her hazel eyes wide. "I'm sorry if I interrupted," she said with a bow.

"Don't apologize, Lileen. You were expected," the Oracle replied with a wave of her hand. "I ask that you take Andrew and Alexander into the city today. They require supplies, clothing, armor. You have leave to use whatever you need from the coffers to cover the expense." She paused to study her daughter for a moment, then nodded once. "And return to the Stone Grove as well, if you have time. I sense Zayneldarion will be grateful." Without another word, she turned to ascend the steps to her private quarters, leaving us to our assigned errands.

Alexander glanced at Lileen. "Might we have a few minutes to speak privately before we leave to do her bidding?" he asked, his tone bitter.

Lileen nodded and disappeared down the stairwell.

"Alex, what happened?" I asked as soon as she was gone.

He groaned and averted his gaze, then scratched at the back of his neck while his face flushed with embarrassment. "After you left yesterday, everything was going well. She said she had chosen me. I didn't understand what she meant at first, but I learned soon enough."

He grinned sheepishly, then shook his head. "I'd never been with a woman before. It was…incredible. And then this morning, she told me the rest of the story." He clenched his jaw as his nostrils flared. "She chose me to sire a child. That part, I was fine with. I've always wanted to be a father."

"Then what's wrong?" I pressed.

He narrowed his eyes. "Children of the Oracle are forbidden contact with their fathers until they've come of age. I'm not allowed to be a part of the child's life! *My child* won't know me because of some damned ancient and superstitious tradition. What's more, she intentionally withheld that from me, knowing I would never agree to bed her if I'd known the truth." He made a sound of disgust.

I didn't know what to say; I understood his anger, but I was also envious. He could have children, whereas I never would. Finally, I settled on telling him the one thing I knew to be true.

"Alex, there will be other women. You'll have a proper family one day. I'm sure of it."

"I know, Andrew. I'm upset that I allowed her to manipulate me. I wasn't thinking clearly."

I decided it was past time to change the subject. "I sent a message to Tom yesterday and received a response."

His face lit up. "Tom's well then?"

I nodded. "He's doing what he can." I filled him in on the remainder of Thomas' reply while he listened raptly.

When I was finished, Alexander frowned. "Perhaps what she saw this morning will prove more accurate than we realize. War *is* coming, Andrew. Perhaps not to the Southlands, but certainly to Novania."

I feared he was right. "There wasn't much more that Tom could share, but I'm glad he's safe for now."

Alexander chewed his lower lip. "Andrew, before she left, the Oracle said something about a stone grove and your father's name…? What was that about?"

"Zayneldarion," I replied. "I spoke with him last night…"

I told him of Lileen's unusual ability and how she'd facilitated a conversation between us, even though the three dragons in the Stone Grove had been petrified by the very magic they'd harnessed to save the rest of their kind. I summarized what was said, then described in detail how honored I'd been by his reaction to me.

"He called me Andrew Caein," I said, still in awe of the encounter. "Caein is his family name—and mine."

Alexander smiled. "After all that Colin put you through, it's good to see you've been granted this much. It gives me hope, as strange as that may sound."

"I wish Vera had been there," I lamented. "She always said it didn't matter if I had no surname to share, but it always bothered me that I lacked even that. She deserved better. And now that I have my true father's name, she's gone."

I looked away as I battled another wave of grief; I missed her presence and her kind words, her smile, her delicate touch. I knew the pain of losing her would fade over time, but it would never disappear. I didn't believe I would ever truly love another—not as I'd loved her.

"Let's go, brother," Alexander said gruffly after a moment. "We have much to do, and… I'd like to be away from this place."

I nodded in agreement. Perhaps our tasks would take my mind away from all that we'd lost for a time.

As Lileen led us through the city, Alexander gaped, in awe of the Citadel. It was larger than he'd expected and more populous, easily equivalent to the Capitol in size. Most of the people we met were friendly, and many were deferential to Alexander. Those bearing the Mark could sense his power and knew he'd one day be capable of incredible things, despite his present uncertainty. As the day progressed, his mood lightened, and our tasks became less burdensome.

Our first stop was a tailor's shop. While they had garments that fit Alexander on hand, they didn't have anything sewn for my size. The woman who ran the shop took my measurements and apologized multiple times as she worked. She muttered on several occasions that there were few men in the Southlands as tall as I, but promised my items would be ready in two days' time.

Our next destination was a blacksmith, though I knew immediately upon arrival that he was not of the same caliber as those I'd worked with in the past. His craftsmanship was unparalleled; even Desmon

Gill couldn't hope to match his skill. I marveled at the weapons and armor on display, more enthralled by each item I passed.

The forges held a strong, cinnamon-like scent, and I assumed the smith was Marked. He took our measurements and informed us it would be several days before both sets of armor would be crafted.

There were several swords on display which caught my eye. They were finely crafted and perfectly balanced, with razor-sharp blades. I picked up several and tested them before selecting one for myself.

"If I'm not mistaken, you have considerable skill," the smith stated as I made the purchase. "There aren't many from the Southlands who could say the same. Where are you from?"

I glanced at Lileen, uncertain of how much I should tell the man, and she shrugged. It seemed it didn't matter what he learned of us.

"We came from the north," I replied. "It was unsafe for my brother."

He nodded in understanding. "No doubt." He looked beyond me, to where Alexander was testing a blade for himself. "My own Mark is a small thing and only assists me in running the forges, but even with my meager power, I can sense his. Typically, I can't." He paused to watch Alexander with his blade. "It seems he also has some skill with a sword—though it doesn't rival yours, does it?"

I laughed. "No, but I have a decade's more practice."

He frowned. "I would not have guessed you were ten years his elder. You look to be of the same age." He shrugged. "Not my business, I suppose."

Alexander strolled toward us then, his chosen sword in hand. "What were you discussing so intently?" he asked with a grin.

"Your brother here claims to be your elder by a decade," the smith replied. "I'm not sure I believe him."

Alexander laughed. "You ought to. He's a little more than ten years older. He just doesn't show his age as others do."

I gave him a look of consternation. I didn't want to have this discussion yet again. He laughed in response.

"Andrew, we're safe here. Besides, from what the tailor told us earlier, most of the city saw you fly in yesterday. You're the biggest news they've had in a long while."

The smith stared at Alexander, then at me, his eyes wide. "You're the dragon, then?"

I sighed, exasperated, and looked away. Alexander could take over the conversation since he seemed to relish in its telling. I was weary of repeating myself and disliked the attention.

"My surly brother is a skin-changer," he replied. "Don't mind him."

"You know," the smith said thoughtfully, "I could make you each the finest set of armor this land has seen in centuries if I could get my hands on some dragon scale."

I glowered at him, distrustful despite his previously friendly demeanor. "Standard armor is sufficient," I growled.

He blinked, taken aback. "I'm sorry. I meant no disrespect. While standard armor might keep you safe—you have your own natural defenses if the stories are true—it might not be enough for your brother. And truly, I didn't mean to offend. It was simply an offer."

I crossed my arms, disinclined to agree to whatever he had in mind. I didn't have to ask where the dragon scale would come from—my own hide—and I was wary of what might happen if I allowed even one man access to it. Would others hear of his work and come seeking further donations? How would losing scales affect my own health, my own protection? I didn't like the idea. We were both trained soldiers and could protect one another as needed.

Alexander sensed my mood and said, "I think the standard armor we requested will suffice. Thank you for your offer, but I believe Andrew needs time to think this over."

I left the blacksmith's and stood at the edge of the road while Lileen settled up with the man and Alexander continued their conversation. I wanted no part of his offer—no matter how innocent the request had been. I knew too little about my dragon half to fully understand what the consequences might be; I needed to speak with my father again.

Thinking it over as I waited for the others, I wondered if I'd overreacted. But if the stories I'd been told as a child were true, dragon scale had always been rare, even before the dragons departed. There had to be a good reason, and until I understood what it was, I would not agree to the smith's request.

When the others emerged from the forges, Alexander appeared apologetic. "Marcus, the smith, sends his apologies again, brother. I don't think he knew what he asked of you."

I sighed. "I'm not entirely sure myself." I turned to Lileen. "Can you take us to the Stone Grove when we are finished with our errands?"

"Of course. I sensed you might ask, given what just occurred." She smiled faintly, though her eyes betrayed her uncertainty. "Marcus is young. He was not alive when the dragons left and knows only legends. He didn't mean any harm, Andrew. He genuinely wants to help."

I shrugged uncomfortably. "I know. What I don't know is what his request will entail, and I don't know how it will affect me... I need advice."

"The provisions you require for your journey can be collected tomorrow," Lileen replied. "Since the tailor and the smith will both take some time to finish their tasks, I don't see any urgency in procuring the other items. I'll take you to the Stone Grove now."

We arrived in the decimated grove just after midday. Alexander was awe-struck at the presence of the petrified dragons but also by something more he sensed within the space. It seemed the ritual left an imprint behind that magi could sense even now, decades after the gateway had closed. Even untrained, Alexander was attuned to the enormity of what had taken place.

His eyes were wide as he surveyed the grove, turning to peer in every direction as he processed the scene. I could see the petrification, the blasted earth, the stone shells that trapped my father and his two associates. There was no odor in the Stone Grove, but perhaps I was only capable of sensing magic as it was performed and not the remnants of something that occurred years in the past.

While Alexander explored, I followed Lileen to Zayneldarion. As she'd done previously, Lileen initiated the conversation with him, then took my hand to form a connection. My hand tingled once more, but I ignored it. Lileen's magic didn't affect me as strongly as her mother's.

"Father, I need your advice."

"Lileen has informed me of this." Zayneldarion's tone was amused as it echoed through my skull. "It seems your companion must be related, Andrew. He has the look of your mother."

I smiled. "He's my half-brother."

"Ah, he's the one you spoke of. I can sense his Mark, and it seems he perceives something within the grove." He chuckled, a low rumble within my ears. "But we can speak more of your brother later. You came for another reason."

I nodded and told him of Marcus' request. Before I'd finished, he cut me off, his voice low and harsh with rage.

"He knows not what he asks of you! In my day, such a request would have left him in shackles, rotting in the ancient dungeons below the tower. A dragon's scales are not given freely. I hope you did not acquiesce."

I was stunned by the ferocity in his tone, and I shook my head. "No, I didn't. I wanted nothing to do with it, but then I began to wonder if I'd made a mistake. I don't know what it would require, nor what it would do to me. I… I want to help Alex, but I'm not certain this is the right way."

He was silent for a long moment. When he spoke again, his tone had calmed considerably. "A dragon's scales are not meant to be removed. They will regrow, but the space left behind remains vulnerable until new scale can form. In your case, it will also leave your human form wounded. Skin-changers rarely gave up their scales. It causes them greater pain than it does a full-blooded dragon and leaves them in a much weaker state." He paused as he gathered his thoughts. "The smith was correct when he said the armor would offer your brother unparalleled protection. Dragon scale is light-weight and stronger than steel, but it will come at great cost to you."

I turned my head, seeking Alexander. He stood near one of the other stone dragons, gazing up in reverence. I wanted Alexander to succeed in this maddening endeavor, but I knew that if I sacrificed my scales to help him, I might be unable to protect him from harm. I'd been named his guardian, and it was my duty to keep him safe. Better armor would help, but I would be less effective until I recovered from the ordeal. When I took an injury as a man, I healed rapidly, but I'd never been hurt in my dragon form. Was it worth the risk? I didn't know.

"It's clear you care for him." The voice was kind, understanding. I turned my attention back to my father. "The decision is yours. No one can force you to give up your scales." He paused, then said, "I would like to speak with him, Lileen."

"I'll tell him," I told her as I dropped my hand. My fingers continued to tingle for several seconds after we'd broken contact.

Alexander had moved on to the smallest of the three dragons and examined her closely. He glanced up in question at my approach.

"Alex, my father—Zayneldarion—would like to speak with you," I said.

Alexander blinked in surprise. "Why does he want to speak with me?"

I suspected that he wanted to evaluate Alexander's worth, his personality, perhaps his strength, but I didn't tell my brother this. "You'll have to ask him," I replied.

Alexander raised an eyebrow, as though he knew I'd omitted something, but he didn't press me further. "You look like him, you know," he said as we walked across the blasted earth at the center of the clearing. "When you're a dragon, I mean."

I nodded, unable to keep from smiling. "I know. Now, go."

Lileen held her free hand toward Alexander, and he took it as I had done earlier. His eyes went wide an instant later, and I knew that Zayneldarion had spoken to him. Alexander had been unprepared for the communication, whatever it had been. I watched his face for a time, amused as various expressions crossed his features while he spoke with my father. After a few moments, I turned away to study the grove more closely.

I walked toward the other dragons and wished I could speak with them as well. I was certain I could learn from each of them; perhaps Alexander could as well, since they'd been mages. They were all that remained of my kin, and I believed that no matter where life happened to take me, I would return time and again. The grove, as damaged as it was, provided me with a sense of belonging.

I sat down between the two other dragons and gazed across the clearing to where Alexander and Lileen stood with my father. I had come no closer to making a decision regarding the dragon scale, but I was no longer angry after speaking to my father. My natural reluctance had been justified, but it was at odds with my inclination to help Alexander. I didn't know what would yield the best outcome in the long term.

I sighed and leaned back to stretch my arms behind me. As I did so, my left hand brushed the stone claws of the larger dragon. I felt a tingling sensation akin to Lileen's and nearly pulled my hand away in surprise, but didn't when I heard him speak into my thoughts.

"You are Zayneldarion's son." His voice was deeper and richer than my father's, and its timber indicated he was significantly older.

I nodded and turned to face him. "How is this possible?"

He chuckled, amused. "I was the greatest of our people's mages. I have many abilities, but one is very similar to that woman's. I am Caelmarion Zorai."

I gazed up at his countenance; his features were broader, his snout shorter than my father's. There were a series of scars on his left flank, running in jagged lines from his shoulder toward his underbelly.

"I've heard your name," I replied. "My name is Andrew. From what I've learned, you also knew my mother."

He sighed heavily. "Yes, we met in Dresdin's Forge. She was quite taken with your father. I told him he was a fool. A dalliance with a human—and one from Novania, no less—was a great risk. He claimed he was in love. It was only after he revealed himself to her that he told me what he'd done. Fortunately, she reciprocated his feelings and didn't betray us to those who would hunt us like animals." He paused thoughtfully. "It was fortunate he acted as he did, reckless though it was, otherwise she would have been wholly unprepared when it came to raising you. Perhaps he wasn't as great a fool as I'd believed." He said the last in a kindly tone.

"She was angry with him, even after I was fully grown," I replied. "She refused to speak his name. What I learned about him was from a book. It mentioned you as well, and the other—" I glanced in the direction of the female dragon, "—and explained that you and my father had been in Dresdin's Forge. Based on that and the timing, I assumed one of you must have been my father, but it wasn't until yesterday that I learned he was."

"You knew him on sight, but it wasn't surprising. As with all skin-changers, your forms are nearly identical to those of your parents."

He paused, and I imagined he'd become thoughtful. The stone features frozen above my head didn't change. When he spoke again, his tone had become one of curiosity.

"The man with you today is clearly your half-brother. Even cursed as we are, we can sense his power. His Mark is unusual. Have you visited the Oracle?"

"Yes," I replied, resigned. I recalled our last conversation with mild unease.

"She's set him on a pilgrimage, no doubt. Or she will, if she hasn't already."

I nodded. "She has. We'll be leaving in a few days."

"You are going as well?" He was surprised. When I told him I'd been named Alexander's guardian, he said, "That is less surprising, given that you're related. What did she see in his Mark?"

I shook my head. "I don't know the details, only that his Mark has something to do with his physical strength. We were procuring arms and armor today." My tone had become bitter at the memory.

"Something happened, it seems."

I nodded. "It's why I've returned." I told him of Marcus' request and what my initial reaction had been before relating the conversation I'd shared with my father.

"Zayne is right. It is your choice. He didn't exaggerate when he said it would cost you very dearly if you agree to this madness—and madness it may be. It's why he asked to speak with your brother, is it not?"

"I believe so." I raked my free hand through my hair. "I promised our mother that I'd look after him. I'd betray her trust if I didn't do everything in my power to ensure he was safe, but this question of dragon scale... I don't know what to do. I can't protect him if I'm weakened, but in the long term, which option is best? Father said if I went through with it, I'd recover in time, but how long does the healing process take? I don't know enough to make an informed decision."

"No doubt you saw the scarring on my side," Caelmarion replied. "Those wounds were inflicted as we were leaving Novania for the last time. It was almost three months before we came here to perform the ritual. The scales were beginning to regrow by then, but it would have been another three or four months before the wounds were completely healed. As a skin-changer, you have our healing ability, but the wound would not only afflict your dragon form. You will be compromised for quite some time."

I sighed and closed my eyes, still undecided. "How many scales would need to be taken for that smith to craft his armor?"

"Perhaps a dozen." His reply was even and betrayed nothing of his thoughts. "Before you make your final decision, I suggest you speak with your father again. He may have new insights for you now that he has finished speaking with your brother."

"Andrew!" Alexander called from across the clearing.

"Thank you for your wisdom," I told Caelmarion before removing my hand.

The tingling in my palm continued after I stood up and made my way toward the others. Lileen's face was drawn; it was clear she was tired, though Alexander was energized.

"Andrew, he wants to speak with both of us," Alexander explained. "If we both take her hand, it should work."

I nodded, and as we both grasped Lileen's hand, I could hear my father's voice. "I cannot make this decision for you, Andrew, and I know you are uncertain. But I must tell you is this: Alexander is a good man, a worthy recipient of your gift if you choose to give it."

I beamed. I was thrilled my father had taken a liking to Alexander. He was not only my brother; he was my greatest friend and ally. In that moment, my decision was made.

"I...I don't know what to say," Alexander stuttered, stunned by his words. He glanced at me, eyes wide. "Andrew, I would never ask you to do this. After hearing what Zayneldarion had to say and what it would cost you... I can't ask this of you. It's too much."

I nodded. "I know."

He studied me for a moment as a frown creased his face. "You've already made up your mind, haven't you, brother?"

"Yes."

"If I may interject," Zayneldarion cut in, "I believe this decision is for the best. Alexander, you're a mage-warrior. Armor made of dragon scale would be of great benefit to you."

"No, I can't accept this," Alexander said with a vehement shake of his head. "Andrew, please, don't do this."

I held his gaze, determined to go through with it for his sake. In the long term, it was the best decision, and I'd uphold the promise I'd made to our mother years ago.

"I wouldn't do this for anyone else. If we're to aid Tom once your training is complete, you'll need it. This may be our only opportunity. And I want to. For you, brother."

Alexander looked down at his feet, overwhelmed. "Andrew…"

"I've made my decision, Alex." I watched him carefully for a moment, then said, "I'd like to speak with my father privately for a moment."

He nodded and released his grip on Lileen's hand. I waited until he'd walked toward the other dragons before speaking once more.

"I spoke to Caelmarion."

"I saw you with him." His voice was amused. "No doubt he gave you some valuable insight. When you returned to me, you seemed to know what you planned to do." He paused for a time, then said, "I believe you are correct. If you do this, you must do it now. Alexander told me what he went through at the hands of your other sibling, and it is abominable. He's fortunate you came to his aid."

"Colin is a damned tyrant," I growled. "I intend to stop him—after Alexander's training is complete."

"Then I believe you've made the right decision," he replied, his voice resigned. "Have the smith collect the scales from the same general location. It will ensure you only suffer one wound in your human form. I suggest he take them from the area between your wings. It's an unlikely target in combat while in your dragon form, and you can cover it easily as a human."

I nodded as I memorized his instructions. "Thank you."

"I have one final suggestion, Andrew. When the smith collects the scales, be sure he does it where you won't be overheard. The sound of a dragon in pain is not one people are likely to forget, and it can be terrifying for those who aren't prepared to hear it. And you *will* be in a tremendous amount of pain."

I frowned. "You speak from experience, don't you?"

"Yes." He paused, then said, "Your brother is fortunate to have you as his guardian. He will be the best-protected mage that has ever made the pilgrimage. While it pains me that you were forced into making this decision, I'm pleased you have. I'm proud to call you my son."

"Thank you," I said again, overwhelmed by his words.

"Go now, Andrew. Lileen grows weary. You will do well. Both of you."

# TWENTY-TWO

When we returned to the tower, the Oracle awaited us in the vast foyer. She was dressed in another flowing robe, this time in a pale shade of lavender. The color accentuated her strange eyes and complimented her pale features and snowy locks.

"Marcus visited the tower earlier," she said without prompting. "He told me of your discussion and wished to apologize for his ignorance."

"I've spoken with my father about his…suggestion," I replied. "I mean to help Alexander—and as you've pointed out, it's my duty as his guardian. I've decided to go through with it."

Alexander crossed his arms and refused to meet my eye as he continued to fume. "Is there nothing you can say to talk my brother out of this?" he demanded.

She shook her head. "It was his choice to make. Come." She turned and began the long ascent.

Alexander glowered, but followed in her wake. I hesitated a moment, then turned to Lileen. "Thank you for your help. I understand it's exhausting to use your power for long periods of time, but I'm grateful."

She managed a tired smile and waved one hand dismissively in the air. "I was merely doing my duty. Now go, before my mother grows impatient."

I took the stairs two at a time until I caught up with the Oracle and Alexander. It seemed she had not spoken since directing us to follow her, and Alexander continued to brood silently. When I rejoined them, he scowled in my general direction but said nothing. We traveled half way up the staircase before the Oracle spoke again.

"I think it's best if you have your scales removed here in the tower," she stated. "I will summon Marcus in the morning. I have an ancient tool in my quarters that was used to extract dragon scale, but it requires greater strength than I possess to wield it properly. The smith must perform the work." She paused in thought. "Are you certain of this, Andrew?"

I didn't hesitate. "Yes."

"Damn it, Andrew. Why?!" Alexander shouted, his temper reaching its breaking point.

I drew a breath, considered my words carefully, and turned to face him. "As the Oracle said yesterday, I'm a man of my word. I've made more than one vow to protect you. By doing this, I can always do so, even when we're miles apart."

He clenched his jaw as a range of emotions crossed his features in rapid succession. Frustration, pain, appreciation, self-doubt, grief… His eyes shone with unshed tears, which he rapidly blinked away. When he met my gaze, I knew he finally understood my reasoning. He nodded but said nothing more.

"Very well," the Oracle said after a moment. "We'll use the mosaic room below my quarters. It is the only room with sufficient space for the task. Marcus will extract the scales, and I will ask my assistants to ensure he does not attempt to keep any portion for himself. I don't believe him malicious, but greed is a powerful motivator, and dragon scale is a rare commodity. I will not allow your sacrifice to be wasted."

"Thank you," I stated, relieved.

If the process proved as grueling as my father insinuated, I'd be livid if Marcus used a single scale for anything but Alexander's armor. I'd personally see him punished if he deceived us.

"I will summon a mage gifted in the healing arts as well," she continued. "While I don't know if she can expedite the regrowth of your scales, she can tend the initial wounds. You must begin your journey as soon as possible. Your abilities will be needed—and sought after—in the days to come."

She stopped on the landing near the door to the room I'd been given. "A meal has been prepared for you. Please eat and rest well, Andrew. You'll need your strength in the morning."

I frowned at her dismissal, but entered the room. Belatedly, I realized she'd wished to speak with Alexander privately. It likely had something to do with the previous night's tryst, and I hoped for Alexander's sake that she didn't wish to repeat the experience. It was clear he felt betrayed.

I took an apple from the platter that had been left for me and moved toward the window. As I gazed into the twilight sky, I thought over the events of the next day, my father's words of advice, and Caelmarion's wisdom. I was no stranger to pain; I'd suffered battle wounds throughout the years, and though I healed rapidly, I was not immune to their discomfort. I was confident I could withstand this process and determined to see it through for Alexander's sake.

When I awoke the next morning, I rose swiftly and prepared for the day. I gazed out the window for some time as the Citadel's streets filled with people and came to life far below. I was brimming with nervous energy, eager to begin, yet ready for my next trial to be over and done.

When Alexander knocked on my door and I greeted him, I noted dark circles ringed his eyes, his clothing was rumpled, and his hair disheveled. His face was drawn and pale with worry, and he refused to meet my gaze.

"Andrew, we need to talk," he said as soon as I opened the door.

I moved aside to allow him entry and closed it behind him. He began to pace between the door and the window while I sat on the edge of the unmade bed.

"I spoke to the Oracle last night after you retired," he began. "She mentioned that legend again—the one about the two strangers from the north. I wasn't truly paying attention because it's only a story. It doesn't mean anything to us." He grimaced and looked down. "She said that she…conceived as she'd intended. I can't fathom how she knows after less than a day, but I believe she speaks the truth. And I will never be given the opportunity to see my child unless it bears her singular Mark. If my child becomes the next Oracle, I'll be granted occasional visits. If not, I'll never know them."

"Alex, I wish there was something I—"

He held up a hand and barked a bitter laugh. "You've done more than you should have for me, Andrew. What you plan to do today… When I spoke to Zayneldarion, he said this is the greatest gift you could ever hope to give. The dragons don't…" His voice cracked, and he looked away. "They don't willingly do this, Andrew. I'm not worthy."

"Is that what kept you awake all night?" I asked, amused. "You don't believe you're worthy?"

He stopped pacing to stare directly at me. He didn't have to speak; his answer was written clearly in his expression.

"Alex," I said, "I would never have agreed to this if I didn't think you were worth the effort. You're my brother, and we've always looked out for one another. I meant what I said last night—in this way, I can *always* be there to protect you. If the Oracle and her damned mysticism proves true, I believe you'll need every advantage."

"That's what I'm afraid of," he replied darkly. "Colin started this when he killed our father, and I'm beginning to believe that we are the only ones who can stop him." He looked up abruptly. "I want to send a message to Tom before we depart the Citadel."

"We should do that. It will be good to hear from him again."

Alexander rolled his eyes. "Here you are, prepared to go through hell today, and you're more concerned about Thomas?" He barked another laugh. "Andrew, why do you never consider taking care of yourself first?"

I shrugged. "I'll be fine in the end. It's you and Tom who need protection."

He shook his head, a mixture of amusement and frustration in his expression. "Ever the protector. 'Guardian' is an apt title for you, brother."

An hour later, Canna arrived to escort us to the mosaic room. She introduced us to a rotund woman named Belora, the healer who had been selected to treat my wounds. Canna assured us Belora's skill was unparalleled and that I'd be well cared for. She was perhaps half my height, but when she sized me up with hands on her ample hips, I felt as though I were on even ground with her. Her gaze was fierce and penetrating.

"Well met," she stated after the introductions. Her voice was lower than I'd expected, but friendly.

Marcus had also arrived ahead of us and stood across the room with the Oracle. As she spoke, he looked at his feet, thoroughly chastised. I suspected she'd scolded him a second time for his request and sensed he was genuinely apologetic.

An enormous tool, forged of a dark bluish metal, rested against the wall behind the Oracle. It was similar to a blacksmith's tongs but was far larger and curved in a different manner. I didn't have to ask what it would be used for, and I understood why the Oracle had indicated the smith must extract my scales. The strength required to maneuver and operate it was far greater than her slender frame could accommodate.

When the Oracle finished speaking to Marcus, she led him toward us. "Canna, I would like you to remain here to assist Belora. Though I'm certain Andrew will recover from this foolishness in time, I don't know the toll it will exact upon him."

Alexander and I exchanged a meaningful glance. I steeled myself as a sharp pang of anxiety shot through me. Was this the right decision?

"I want to stay with him," Alexander stated firmly. "I need to be here."

"I assumed you would say that. It's why you were summoned along with your brother." She turned to face me, and her violet eyes bored into mine. "I have explained to Marcus how the tool works." She gestured to the oversized tongs. "He understands what he must do. This process will be very unpleasant for both of you, Andrew, but you must remain still while he works. Do you have any advice for him before we begin?"

I nodded and recalled Zayneldarion's words from the previous day. "After I shift, you'll need to climb on my back. Take scales from between my wings. Try to remove adjacent ones. I've been told the healing process will be smoother if the scales come from the same location."

Marcus' eyes were wide with unspoken fear, his face pale with worry. He drew a breath, then said, "I understand."

"Caelmarion said you should need no more than a dozen," I continued. "If this process is as painful as I've been told, I'd appreciate it if you work quickly." I glanced at Alexander, then said in a steely tone, "I will do this for my brother, but do not ask me to go through this again. *Ever.*"

Marcus looked sheepishly at the Oracle. "I've been made well aware of my error in making the request. I'm truly sorry."

"Let us begin," the Oracle stated. She ushered Belora and Canna to one side of the room while Alexander and Marcus moved in the opposite direction. I removed my clothing and glanced around the room to ensure I had enough space to accommodate the transformation. Satisfied, I steeled myself and shifted.

Marcus' eyes widened in surprise, and he stood gaping for several moments. Alexander frowned at him, unable to conceal his irritation. Finally, he leaned toward Marcus and whispered something to the smith that caused him to redden. Marcus hefted the strange tool and strode toward me with purpose.

I lowered myself to the ground to allow him to climb on my back. He was not as agile as Alexander, and it took him several attempts before he found purchase and pulled himself into position. I could feel his weight as he carefully balanced himself just below the center of my spine.

He tapped twice, the location just below where I imagined the scales should be taken from. "Is this location suitable?" he asked.

"Higher," I ordered, and he adjusted his position. He tapped again. "That should suffice."

He placed the tool at the base of one of my scales, and I felt the cool metal as he closed it around the base. I clenched my teeth and braced myself in anticipation of the pain I knew would follow.

"I'm going to pull," he warned me. An instant later, a searing pain ripped through the entirety of my spine.

The magnitude of the agony took my breath away. Black stars erupted at the edges of my vision. He placed the tool again, working swiftly as I'd ordered, and pulled. The pain intensified, and I released a deafening roar. I couldn't stifle my reaction, though I'd tried. For the first time, I was uncertain if I could go through with this—if he must take ten more scales, I would find myself beyond the limit of my endurance. The dragons had done their best to prepare me for the ordeal, but their words were a shadow compared to the anguish I now experienced.

I dug my claws into the tiled floor and braced myself for the next pull, determined to finish this for Alexander's sake. When it came, I inadvertently writhed and collapsed forward while I roared a second time. Marcus grasped one of my spines in order to keep his balance as I struggled to remain steady. Something sticky and warm began to trickle along my right side, and I wondered if I was losing blood. I closed my eyes, steeling myself as best as I could.

By the time Marcus had extracted the tenth scale, I was hoarse, my entire body ached, and my muscles had begun to tremble. My grip on consciousness was waning, and there was a deafening ring in my ears. At some point, I'd bitten my tongue, and I tasted blood from the wounds my teeth had inflicted.

I couldn't go on any longer. My endurance was spent. I collapsed to the floor as my body succumbed to the pain.

Dimly, I was aware of Alexander. He rushed forward and shouted something I couldn't decipher at Marcus. His tone was furious, but I struggled to make sense of his words over the ringing in my ears. I looked at my brother, pleading with my eyes to make the smith stop. I was too exhausted for speech. Marcus placed the tool again, and I grimaced before he even began to pull the next scale. I'd never experienced pain of this magnitude, and I never hoped to again.

"*Enough!*"

The bellow had not come from Alexander, but Canna. The ringing subsided abruptly and I could hear her clearly.

"You can work with what you've taken, blacksmith. Leave him be!" She moved into my field of vision, and I was surprised to find she was openly weeping.

The tool released its grasp, and profound relief washed over me. I continued to lay on the tiled floor, lacking the energy to rise. Marcus slid clumsily down my side, the tool and my scales in his arms. I closed my eyes and clenched my teeth in an attempt to dull the pain that continued to wrack my body. I didn't want to move and feared doing so would only cause my anguish to double.

I sensed the others gather around me, but I paid them no heed. Someone climbed atop my back, and for one terrible moment, I believed Marcus had returned to finish the job. I opened one eye and noted the Oracle was escorting the smith toward the stairs. Two of her assistants stood awaiting him, prepared to oversee his work at the forge. He carried the scales he'd removed from my back, each the size of a platter, and most slick and glistening darkly with my blood. I closed my eyes once more, nauseated, and wondered idly who had climbed on my back.

Through the dull roar in my ears, I heard Alexander's voice. It was strained and full of concern. "I won't leave you, brother. We'll get through this."

I allowed the pain to overtake me and surrendered to the darkness of oblivion.

# TWENTY-THREE

When I awakened, early morning light was streaming through the many arches of the mosaic room. I blinked slowly, confused. How long had I been unconscious? I had no inkling of how much time had passed.

A short distance away, Belora perched on a cushioned stool while she watched me intently. As our eyes met, she stood and made her way toward me.

"Lie still," she instructed. "I need to look at your wound. And you shouldn't wake Alexander." She gestured to my left. I swiveled my head to find he'd fallen asleep nestled against my side.

She made her way to my right flank and deftly clambered up, more agilely than I'd expected. Her hands pressed against the scales of my back, just below the location where the others had been removed. At her touch, the wound began to throb dully, but the pain had decreased significantly from what I'd experienced during Marcus' extraction. I marveled at how rapidly I seemed to have healed.

"The wound is no longer seeping," she said. "This is good. I'm going to give you more healing magic, so try to remain still. It may cause you some discomfort, but I don't know for certain. You're the first dragon I've tended."

Her hands touched the wound directly. I inhaled sharply and tensed my muscles in response to the sudden, sharp pain. An instant later, a cooling sensation spread across the location, and a scent akin to that of herbal tea filled the air—green, yet floral. The aroma was comforting.

My reaction awakened Alexander, and he stumbled to his feet, rubbing the sleep from his eyes. His face was haggard, but the relief in his expression was unmistakable.

"Andrew, you're awake!" He laughed, giddy. "I was beginning to fear…" He trailed off with a shake of his head. "You're awake, which means you're healing."

"Of course, he's healing, you dolt," Belora replied gruffly but not unkindly. "I've been working tirelessly the past three days. Did you not believe my magic would have an effect?"

"Three daysss?" I asked, stunned. Had I truly been unconscious so long?

Alexander nodded. "I'm glad Canna stopped the smith when she did, else it would have been worse, or so Belora tells me." He sighed. "Andrew, hearing you go through that, seeing you in agony… I wanted to kill the ignorant little shit. He was torturing you."

"I can't do it again," I replied with a grimace. "I hope the armor will be worth it. I did it for you."

He closed his eyes, a pained expression on his face. "You shouldn't have done it at all, brother. The cost was too damned high. I thought… I thought when you collapsed that I'd lost you." He swallowed hard in an attempt to remain stoic, but tears began to spill down his cheeks nevertheless.

"And I told you he would be well in a few days, did I not?" Belora retorted. "You warrior-types never listen to healers, even though you ought to."

She continued to work, her hands moving to various locations around the wound while she pressed gently. The cooling sensation that came with her touch soothed the residual pain.

"Marcus should return with our armor this afternoon," Alexander said after a time. "Yours and…mine. The Oracle sent several of her assistants to accompany him when he left with the dragon scale. She kept her promise to you, though I wasn't certain we should trust her. What you did has left a lasting impression on all of us, Andrew. I hope I never have to witness it again." He shuddered.

Belora slid to the floor, finished with her ministrations. "You'll need to eat," she stated. "Canna acquired a good quantity of meat while you slept. You'll have your fill."

At the mention of food, my stomach rumbled loudly, causing Alexander to smirk. "I think he'll want breakfast sooner rather than later."

"I'll speak to Canna," she replied, business-like, and marched across the room to the staircase, leaving us alone.

Alexander strode toward me and threw his arms around my neck in a fierce hug. "You have no idea how relieved I am that you're awake and that you'll heal. I'd begun to wonder if we'd made a terrible mistake."

I managed a weary smile. "I had to try."

I wanted to stand, to stretch my wings and prove I was healing, but I was too weak to make the effort. I sighed and closed my eyes, exhausted though I'd only just awakened.

"Andrew?" he asked, concerned.

"I'm alright, brother," I replied without opening my eyes. "I'm tired. I feel like I've been on the battlefield for a week without relief. I'm weary beyond wordsss."

"I'll wake you when Canna brings your meal," he promised.

He may have said more, but I'd already fallen into a deep, dreamless sleep.


Canna had arrived with an array of platters piled high with roasted meat while I slept. My mouth began to water at the scent, and my stomach rumbled again. I stood shakily and grimaced as a searing pain ripped through my spine. I was determined to cross the room despite my weakness and discomfort.

"You be careful!" Belora shouted in warning. "If you undo all the work I've done, I'll have it in for you, dragon or not!"

I chuckled, amused by her outburst, and took a tentative step forward. As long as I moved slowly and deliberately, the pain was manageable. I crossed to the food and began to devour it hungrily. I realized belatedly I hadn't eaten in several days, and although I'd been unconscious, my body had been at work, trying to mend the hurt that had been inflicted. It was little wonder I was ravenous.

I wasn't sated until most of the meat was gone, and I felt much better with a full stomach. I thanked Canna, who shrugged dismissively.

"I'm merely doing my job, Lord Dragon," she said pointedly, then began to clear away the dishes.

Alexander was laughing as she departed. "Holy hell, Andrew, you ate enough for a small army. *By yourself?*"

I snapped my jaws in his direction, taunting him playfully. He laughed again and danced away.

"He needed to eat," Belora stated firmly, unimpressed by our antics. "It pleases me to see his appetite has returned and some measure of energy with it. It means he heals as he should." She moved to stand before me, hands on her hips. "I need you to lay still for a while. It's past time that I worked on your wound again."

While Belora tended my injury, the Oracle descended the spiral stair from her private quarters. She studied me for some time before she spoke, her violet eyes unreadable.

"It's good you're awake." She glanced at Alexander briefly, then said, "I hope you have both learned a valuable lesson. Dragon scale is not to be given lightly. It comes at great cost, as I'm certain your father warned you. And Alexander, you have a better guardian for your journey than even I had initially believed. Your brother is willing to do whatever is necessary to see you safe. This pleases me greatly."

Alexander ground his teeth together. Her words had been harmless, but he was clearly incensed.

"*Of course,* it pleases you!" he roared. "You got what you wanted without giving a damn about Andrew's safety. You *knew* what this would do to him, and yet you said nothing. You simply went along with his whole mad plan! If Canna had not stepped in when she did, this could have killed him!"

"Alexsss," I growled in warning, "I knew when I made up my mind. Do not blame her. Direct your anger toward me."

He spun to face me, his face scarlet with rage. "I was there, and I know what Zayneldarion said. It was frustratingly vague! You didn't know what this would do to you, but *she* did!"

I closed my eyes and turned my head away. He was right, but I believed his anger was misplaced. I didn't blame the Oracle; I'd made the decision on my own.

"You see?" Alexander continued relentlessly. "He didn't know what this decision would cost him, but you did! I am done with your damned manipulations! Once Andrew is healed, we will leave, and don't expect to see my face in your tower again."

He stalked away and headed toward the downward staircase. I let him go; he needed time to cool his temper.

I looked at the Oracle. She stood unmoving as Alexander stormed out of the room. Perhaps she was shocked by his explosive reaction, but her expression remained unreadable.

"I don't blame you," I said again. "He isss angry about your night together and looksss to blame you for thisss. He didn't mean what he sssaid."

She peered at me, then shook her head. "You are correct. He is still angry about the conception, but he truly believes I misled you. He will never forgive me for the wrongs he perceives I have done." She drew a breath and frowned. "It doesn't matter. You have ensured his safety, and that's the most important piece of this complicated puzzle. He will never forget what you've sacrificed for him, Andrew. Your actions were noble, if flawed."

I wanted to shrug but remained still. Belora continued to work her magic along my spine.

"I did what wasss besssst for him."

"I know," she replied. "It's why I accepted you as his guardian when you offered. You will protect him, even if it means keeping him safe from himself. He'll need your strength, but he'll also need your wisdom. He is young and temperamental but has great respect for you."

I wanted to tell her I believed Alexander would one day see the truth, but we were interrupted. One of the Oracle's assistants entered the room from below, followed by the tailor we'd met several days ago. A pair of cloaks were draped over her arm, and she carried a stack of folded garments in her hands. She stopped abruptly at the top of the stairs, eyes wide with shock as her eyes met mine. The Oracle waved her over with an encouraging smile.

I recalled Alexander's reaction the first time he'd seen me in dragon form. He'd said I was terrifying, and I grudgingly admitted there was truth to his words. My size alone would have been intimidating for most. Coupled with the teeth and claws I sported, I appeared dangerous even in my weakened state.

I sighed, weary, and lowered my head to the floor in what I hoped was a non-threatening position. I closed my eyes while Belora finished her ministrations. I was immeasurably fatigued.

The Oracle collected the clothing and spoke with the tailor regarding her business before the woman left, then Lileen was summoned to take our garments to the rooms we'd been given. I imagined Alexander would be in his, likely pacing as he fumed and muttered to himself.

I drifted to sleep again. I'd never been so tired, and I hoped my exhaustion would soon pass.

I was awakened a few hours later. Canna informed me that Marcus had returned with Alexander's armor and that both men were on their way upstairs. I blinked groggily and shook my head as though to clear it, but couldn't dislodge my lingering fatigue.

Alexander was somber when he arrived. Wordlessly, he crossed the tiled floor to stand at my side. He stretched out one hand to place it against my foreleg; I was uncertain if he was attempting to comfort me or if he was simply steadying himself. Regardless, I was glad he was there.

Marcus arrived several minutes later. Two of the Oracle's assistants accompanied him, and each carried various pieces of armor. Marcus held a set of finely-crafted steel plate mail, polished to a silvery sheen—my armor. The assistants carried Alexander's; it was glossy and black, crafted in a similar manner to my own, yet far more impressive upon inspection. I recognized the color and texture of Alexander's armor from looking at my own scales. I sighed, melancholy, and looked away.

No one spoke for an interminable amount of time. Finally, I heard footsteps move toward us from the center of the room and opened my eyes to find the Oracle had descended from her quarters to join us.

"Your skill is remarkable," she stated as she examined each set of armor in turn. "Few could have worked dragon scale so skillfully. You have a gift."

Marcus appeared profoundly uncomfortable at her praise and muttered something I could not hear. He stared at the floor, refusing to make eye contact.

The Oracle studied him for a moment, then nodded. "I see. Perhaps that is for the best."

"What did he say?" Alexander demanded fiercely.

Marcus swallowed, appeared to steel himself, then raised his gaze reluctantly to meet Alexander's. "I said I will never forge another piece of dragon scale armor again. This will be the only set I will ever craft, and I hope it will serve you well for many years."

Alexander dropped his hands to his sides and gaped, at a loss for words.

"I'm glad to hear it," I replied. "I can't go through that ordeal again, knowing the pain it bringsss."

"I can never do that again, either," Marcus replied. "Each time I removed a scale, it was torture for you, and I will never forget your anguished roars. It continues to haunt me, and will do so for the rest of my days." He looked down with a grimace. "I will never do it again. Not for you, nor any other."

"Good," the Oracle stated. "Dragon scale is a commodity that cannot be pursued. The dragons have left, and only Andrew remains. If Lileen had chosen a different smith, one with questionable moral character, this procedure could have placed Andrew's life in danger for many years to come. She chose you, and for that, I am grateful."

Marcus turned to address me. "Are you well?"

"Belora tellsss me I am," I replied.

"He is healing faster than I anticipated," Belora replied matter-of-factly. "It will take time before he is at full strength, but the scales have already begun to regrow."

"Caelmarion told me that it would take monthsss," I said, surprised by her words. "It mussst be your magic."

She frowned. "It *is* having an effect, I suppose. I wouldn't contradict the wisdom of a great mage like Caelmarion Zorai. He was the foremost healer amongst the dragon-kind."

"Months?" Marcus asked, incredulous. "You knew what this would require of you, and you went through with it anyway?"

I nodded. "My brother isss worth protecting."

He turned to stare at Alexander, wonder in his eyes. "I wish my own brother possessed a fraction of the nobility yours does. You are fortunate beyond measure."

Before he left, Marcus insisted that Alexander don the armor to ensure it fit properly. While they outfitted my brother, Belora climbed upon my back to apply more of her healing magic to the wound. I watched as Alexander transformed himself into an armored warrior; it fit him perfectly. Marcus beamed at Alexander's praise, though his expression remained troubled. Alexander turned to me, eyes wide with wonder and admiration.

"This is incredible," he breathed, moving his arms to test his mobility. "It's so light, I scarcely know it's there. Is it truly as strong as the stories say?" he asked over his shoulder to Marcus, who had a pained smile plastered on his face.

I snorted, and he looked up at me sharply. "You know very well what I endured in the Corodan trap," I said. "I came away unsssscathed. You would too, wearing that."

He grinned. "I'd forgotten. After everything that has happened, it seems a lifetime ago."

We passed the next six days in a similar fashion. Belora tended my wound every few hours and gradually, my strength returned while the fatigue slowly dissipated. Alexander spent hours simply sitting at my side. We talked about many things, but most often, our conversations were focused on the journey to come.

He was eager to be off—as was I—but we both knew I needed more time to recover. The Oracle made herself scarce and held audiences for those seeking her advice in her private chambers. While I still had many questions for her, I knew Alexander was happier when she remained out of sight.

When the day finally arrived that Belora asked me to shift, I was relieved beyond words. During the recovery process, I'd started to feel less awkward, but I still preferred to be human. I knew my upbringing and the rules of Novania were largely responsible, but the simple fact was I felt more like *myself* as a man. After spending ten days as a dragon, I was elated with the change.

Alexander made the trek downstairs to collect my clothing, and upon his return, I immediately shifted. There was no pain in my back as I'd anticipated, but I could feel the remnants of the wound there.

The skin was raw, and as Belora inspected the site, it was tender to the touch.

"I've done all I can to expedite your healing," she said as I dressed. "It will be some time before the wound is no longer tender, but your scales have begun to regrow, and your flesh is whole. So long as you do not acquire any further injuries to the site, you will be fully healed in perhaps another six weeks."

I thanked her for all she'd done. Without her aid, I would have been in significant amounts of pain, the wound raw and weeping, even now.

She turned to face Alexander, her hands on her hips. "I know you plan to leave the Citadel soon, but you must look after your brother. He has done much for you—it is time you do the same for him. Don't put yourself in a situation where he is forced to come to your aid unless you have no other option. I don't want the wound to reopen. It requires more time to heal—and I can't accompany you to oversee its progress. Swinging a sword may cause it to tear, and neither of you can afford that outcome. My advice is to stay out of danger for at least another two weeks, though four would be ideal."

Alexander nodded. "I think we can arrange that. From what I've been told, the first leg of the pilgrimage takes us through some wild lands, but there will be little danger until after we've reached our first destination."

Belora frowned, nonplussed by his cavalier attitude. "Don't take the journey lightly, Alexander. There will be many opportunities for danger to find you. Has she assigned you a guide?"

Alexander shook his head. "I don't know. I haven't spoken to her in some time."

"You'll need a guide before you depart," she stated. "I don't know the nature of your disagreement with her, but I advise you to move past it and seek her wisdom. You'll need it." She spun around to size me up a final time. "And you behave, Andrew. Don't do anything that will open up that wound again, or so help me, I'll find you and make you regret it!" Her words were gruff, but she said them with an affectionate tone.

I smiled. "I'll follow your orders, Belora. Don't worry."

"Good." Her expression softened. "I suppose this is goodbye, then. Take care of yourselves—and do as I've instructed."

# TWENTY-FOUR

Alexander and I returned to the Stone Grove with Lileen later that afternoon. I wanted to speak with my father one last time before our departure, and I encouraged Alexander to talk with Caelmarion. I believed he needed the elder mage's wisdom before we began our journey, and perhaps Caelmarion could succeed in forcing my brother to see reason where I had failed. He needed to speak with the Oracle but had remained steadfast in his belief that she would only betray him further. I believed he was making a mistake, but I didn't know what else to say that might change his mind.

"Your father has been anxious to learn how you fare," Lileen said as we crested the hill above the Stone Grove. "I visited him twice while you were recovering, but my words weren't assurance enough for him. He cares deeply."

I smiled, stunned by his reaction when we'd met only days ago. Once we'd entered the grove and Lileen established her connection, the depth of his concern became apparent.

"Andrew! I'm glad you have come. Are you well?"

I grinned. His concern was genuine, and I hadn't been expecting his eager response. "I'm well enough," I replied.

We spoke of Belora's aid in the healing process and discussed the armor Marcus had crafted for Alexander. Now that I'd recovered and had examined the set more closely, I was convinced it was a masterpiece of smithing. When Zayneldarion inquired about the smith's reaction to extracting the scales, I shared Marcus' promise and the smith's sincere apology.

Zayneldarion snorted derisively. "He didn't understand what he asked of you, and I'm glad he's seen the error of his request. Should he ever ask that of you again, I will find a way to free myself from this curse and tear him limb from limb myself. Humans have ever been arrogant and ignorant when it comes to dealings with other peoples— our kind in particular." He released a growl, then fell silent for a time. "Alexander is fortunate to have you as a brother and guardian. *He* is a good man, and I stand by my previous words. He was worthy of your gift. I would not have said the same for many others."

I glanced toward Alexander. He was across the grove, his hand pressed firmly against Caelmarion's foreleg, his eyes closed in concentration. I smiled at the sight and hoped he'd gain answers to some of his questions during their exchange.

"Alex is special," I replied. "I wouldn't have done this for my other half-brothers." I turned back to face the stone countenance of Zayneldarion. "You said you'd given up some of your own scales. Who was the recipient?"

He chuckled. "That was many years ago when I was much younger. There was a man who came to us, befriended us, and learned our ways. He was a skilled warrior and had been named guardian for his son's pilgrimage. He was growing old, however, and he pled with the Oracle to allow another to take on the role. He would not have survived the journey without additional support."

He paused, and I was uncertain if he would continue. I was about to ask him another question, but before I could speak, he said, "His name was Valyon. Caelmarion had great respect for the man, and at the time, I was merely his student—but I wanted to help Valyon. Caelmarion summoned a smith, and I gave up my scales. It was only after the armor had been crafted that Valyon learned what I'd done. He was grateful, but he refused to accept the gift. I don't know what happened to him, though we received word his son's pilgrimage ended in great tragedy. The armor was stored in the Caein clan vault, high in the mountain home we once ruled. It's likely still there."

"Holy hell. There was no one else to use it?" I asked, shocked it would be left to collect dust after the sacrifice it had taken to create.

"In the last days before we summoned the gateway, I spoke with the Oracle frequently," he replied slowly. "I was an emissary between our people and hers. She believed that one day, another man would come to me and that I would willingly gift him the armor that had been crafted for Valyon. At the time, I dismissed her vision as mere fancy. There would never be another worthy of my dragon scale, but I was mistaken. You are the same size, Andrew. I would be honored if you used the armor for your own."

I blinked; I didn't know how to respond. It was an incredible gift, but I wondered if my sacrifice for Alexander had truly been necessary. If there had been another set of armor, why had I been led to believe this was the best course of action to protect my brother? Could Marcus have modified Valyon's armor to fit Alexander? Why had he kept this information from me?

Frustrated, I said, "I don't understand."

"You're conflicted," he replied. "Perhaps I should have mentioned this sooner, but it would not have changed the outcome. Once dragon scale has been manipulated, it becomes too unwieldy to work any further. A smith must have great skill in order to work it successfully, for they have but one opportunity to mold it. The armor crafted for Valyon could not have been made to fit Alexander. Likewise, the armor that was made for Alexander cannot be modified to fit another. Do you understand, Andrew?"

I ran my free hand through my hair and nodded. "Yes."

"Good. I will give you the location of our family's vault. You will pass through our ancestral homelands during your journey and may retrieve it then. It is the only thing I have left to give you, and I hope it will serve you well." His tone was morose, filled with regret.

"Thank you," I replied, grateful. "I'll return when I can, but I don't know how long it will be."

"I know, Andrew. You and Alexander are destined for great things, and based on the recent events in Novania, your unique abilities will be required. I am cursed to remain here for eternity, it seems. Come back when you need advice. I will always welcome you. You are my only child, after all."

I nodded, unable to articulate a proper response. I'd only known him a short time, but already he'd accepted me, encouraged me, and fulfilled the role of mentor that I so desperately needed even as an adult. He acted the part of a father as well, if not better than Carlton had.

"When you return to the tower, tell the Oracle this: She was right. She will understand the meaning." He chuckled, but the sound was strained. "I am loath to see you go so soon after our first meeting. You will do well, Andrew. Bear the Caein name with pride."

Lileen and I waited for some time while Alexander finished his conversation with Caelmarion. When he finally dropped his hand, he was silent and contemplative. I wondered what they'd discussed but knew that given time, Alexander would tell me. I didn't press him as we made the journey back to the Citadel and the Oracle's tower.

As we entered the city, I asked Lileen if we might pay Bryson Feige another visit. I wanted to speak with Thomas one more time before we departed. Though she was clearly tired, she agreed, and led us to the message-writer's home. Bryson received us with a friendly smile, and when I asked him if he would send another message to Thomas, he heartily agreed.

Alexander and I decided we would not tell Thomas of what had transpired with the dragon scale and the armor, for it would cause him unnecessary concern. He had enough to contend with, given Colin's unpredictable temperament and his precarious position in Bridgewaters.

I penned the message, then Bryson began to work his magic. I left and returned to the yard with the hope I'd avoid another unseemly episode of sneezing. Night was beginning to fall, and the first pale stars glittered in the darkening sky above. There were only a handful of passers-by; I assumed most would be in their homes preparing for supper.

While I waited, I contemplated my father's last words with a smile. I welcomed his easy acceptance; after spending so much of my life in hiding, it was a wonderful change to finally be myself. I no longer needed to mask who and what I was.

After a few minutes, Alexander returned bearing a scrap of parchment lined with Thomas' neat handwriting. He handed it to me wordlessly, his expression troubled. The light had faded, and I could read his words easily enough, but for Alexander's sake, I returned to

Bryson's home, where the interior was alight with flickering candles. Lileen stood patiently near the door as I read the message.

*Andrew,*

*I thank you for contacting me again before your departure. I have often wondered where you might be and what you've been doing. I'm still with Duke Crossley, and am well enough.*

*Colin has summoned soldiers from every garrison to the Capitol. Our uncle believes he plans to march south in pursuit of you and Alex. I don't know if this is true, but it's worrisome.*

*I believe he may be planning a show of force simply to keep the nobility of the kingdom in a perpetual state of fear. The governors continue to refuse to act against him, and Claire is with child again, if the rumors from the Capitol are true.*

*I understand that it may be a long while before we can speak again. Take care of Alex, and take care of yourself. Contact me when you can.*

*Yours, Tom*

I turned to Bryson as I finished reading Thomas' message and thanked him for his services. While it was not good news Thomas had given in reply, it wasn't a turn for the worse either.

We took our leave of Bryson, then threaded our way through the torchlit streets to the white tower at the heart of the city. As we reached the tower, Alexander stopped for a moment in the foyer, a determined frown creasing his face. It took Lileen a few seconds to realize he was no longer following her, and when she turned, he looked down at his boots, his face flushed in embarrassment.

"Lileen, I… I need to speak with the Oracle," he said after an awkward silence.

I raised an eyebrow. Whatever Caelmarion had said to him had left an impression. To her credit, Lileen didn't pry and merely nodded.

"I'll be in my quarters," he said as she began to ascend the stairs.

Lileen hesitated, then shook her head. "No, I will take you to her now," she replied. "Both of you."

We followed Lileen in relative silence. While I knew why she'd agreed to take Alexander to the Oracle, I was uncertain why she believed I should be present as well. Lileen knew the Oracle's temperament better than we did, and I would trust her judgment. It was the least I could do after all she'd done for me.

As we ascended to the mosaic room, the Oracle was descending from her quarters above. She paused at the bottom of the spiral stair to await our approach with a puzzled expression. She studied us carefully as we crossed the tiled floor, but her eyes were sharp and did not waver from Alexander's. When we stopped before her, Alexander dropped his gaze to the floor with a troubled frown. He'd lost their silent battle of wills.

Without looking away from Alexander, who continued to stare at the floor between his boots, she said, "Lileen, please fetch our latest arrival. Erek can assist you with her location. While you are away, we will speak."

As Lileen departed, Alexander raised his eyes briefly to meet the Oracle's intense gaze. "I've been made aware of my error, and I have come to apologize," he said, his voice tight with anxiety. "I understand that by choosing me, you were attempting to bestow an honor—but in my defense, I wasn't aware of how things work in the Southlands—or amongst the magi. I simply wish it had been explained to me sooner."

The Oracle reached out and rested her palm along the side of Alexander's face while her expression softened. "That was my mistake, and for that, I'm sorry," she replied. "I've grown accustomed to would-be magi understanding our ways, and it was a failure on my part. It has been many years since we've hosted strangers." She sighed, the sound pained, and dropped her hand to her side. "I understand your desire to see the child and be a part of its life, Alexander, but this cannot be. The order the Oracles have established is tenuous at best. Long ago, we determined that the fathers must not interfere. It creates discord."

Alexander nodded. "I know. Caelmarion told me of Zaiden Venn."

She nodded in understanding. I watched their exchange with growing confusion; the name meant nothing to me. I'd ask Alexander what he referred to once we were alone. The story might prove irrelevant, but if I were to protect him, I needed to know all I could of the Southlands and its history.

Abruptly, the Oracle stood straighter as her eyes alighted on the staircase moments before Lileen emerged from below. Behind her was a woman with a weathered countenance, her cheeks ruddy from prolonged exposure to the sun, her tawny hair streaked with blond and bleached by the elements. She wore leather pants and a jerkin, sturdy boots, and carried a wide-brimmed hat in one hand. Her face was ageless, marking her a mage, and her dark eyes sparkled with excitement. She strode toward us and studied us with interest.

"Chela," the Oracle said, "It's good you've agreed to come. There is no finer guide in the Southlands."

Chela beamed and planted her hands on her hips. "I'm pleased you think so."

"Alexander is set to undertake the pilgrimage. Andrew," the Oracle said with a gesture toward me, "is his guardian. You will find they both have unique talents that will be of use along the way."

"Brothers, if I'm not mistaken," Chela replied. "And both warriors. Interesting."

"We're half-brothers," Alexander said, unimpressed by her assessment. "And yes. We've both trained in arms since we were children."

"The circumstances of their arrival is unusual," the Oracle replied cryptically. "There will be no better guardian for Alexander than his half-brother, and my readings of them have only reinforced my belief. They must undertake this journey together. Without one, the other will fail—and my visions indicate failure will doom the Southlands."

I blinked, at once both irritated and frustrated. "You said I must ensure Alexander finished his training. You forced me to promise that I would remain with him until the end of his journey—a promise I feel was coerced, using my loyalty as a form of manipulation. You did *not* tell us about this purported failure."

"You didn't understand enough of the situation when we last spoke of it," she replied dismissively. "You now know my words are true. You need one another—your fates are entwined."

I held my tongue, though I sorely wanted to protest further.

"Andrew, it's fine," Alexander whispered. "I believe she's right."

I crossed my arms, disinclined to agree, and frowned. Her mysticism and vague insinuations were tiresome, and my patience had worn thin.

"Chela will be your guide," the Oracle went on, ignoring my glare. "She has traveled through the lands south of the Mage's Gate, from one coast to the other, and from the gate itself far to the south, where the land meets the sea. There is no one better to lead you through the pilgrimage."

"My ability lies with tracking," Chela explained. "I can determine directions to anywhere once I've set my mind to it. I know the lands. I've been an explorer for decades. I can take care of myself in a fight if it comes to it, but my abilities don't aid me in combat." Her eyes raked across my form. "I hope you're as good in a fight as you appear to be. There will be times when we'll need strength and stamina to survive."

Alexander laughed. "Andrew will be fine. He's nearly invincible when he wants to be."

I snorted and rolled my eyes. "It will be a few weeks until I'm fully healed, or have you forgotten?"

"You need not worry about Andrew, Chela," the Oracle broke in. "He will be healed before your journey reaches the point of danger." She gazed at Chela for a long moment, then said, "He is the son of Zayneldarion Caien."

Chela's eyes widened slightly with mild surprise. "I see. I'd heard rumors about your unusual visitors, Oracle. So… This is them." She flashed a grin. "Well met, both of you—but especially you, Lord Dragon."

"I'm not—" I began, but the Oracle silenced any further protest with the wave of her hand.

"You must accept who you are, Andrew," she said firmly. "You may think you are 'merely' a skin-changer, but you are the only dragon-kind left in this world. You are as much dragon as you are man, and you are no longer in Novania. Embrace who you are."

I frowned uneasily, but a small part of me believed her words. I must leave the past behind and focus on Alexander's upcoming journey in order to secure our future. I could not allow my old fears to hold me back, given that I didn't know what dangers lay ahead. I nodded once, tersely, but I understood.

"Well then," Chela said after a moment's pause, "this will be quite the adventure. I've been told you procured all the necessary supplies for the journey, so there's little reason for further delay. We'll leave tomorrow with the dawn." She offered us a mischievous grin. "I look forward to seeing what you're capable of."

I spent the evening in solitude as I prepared for what lay ahead. Chela had outlined the general route she planned to take and had mentioned the key locations where Alexander must stop to complete his training as a mage. The endeavor would take several months and looked to be arduous, though I was certain we'd see it through.

As much as I disliked the half-truths the Oracle seemed fond of, I believed her on a fundamental level. We were stronger together, and I would not break the promises I'd made to Alexander. It seemed the defining thread in both our lives was that our stories were intertwined; first as the bearers of one another's secrets, and now as the facilitators of one another's fates.

I reflected on our journey thus far and recalled all that had happened since that day, not even two years past, when the king had drawn me aside to speak of his succession. I considered my decision to tell Claire the truth before she heard it from someone else, and recalled her cold reaction. In retrospect, I should have anticipated it, but I'd truly believed the feelings I held for her would be reciprocated. How wrong I'd been.

Her decision to leave me had wounded my pride, but I recovered. It led me to a battle with the Corodan, revealing my true nature to Alexander, and eventually, to the fortuitous evening with Vera. My heart ached with the memory of her lifeless body, lying face down in the vineyards she'd loved. She'd been one of a kind, taken from this world before her time by the madness of a tyrant.

A tyrant, my damned half-brother, the force behind our exile.

As my thoughts drifted to Colin, I felt a familiar, smoldering rage ignite within my core. One day, I'd make him pay for all he'd done. It wasn't only the loss of Vera, his mistreatment of Claire, or his planned execution of Alexander that he must answer for, but for the countless others who had been slain in his misguided quest to eradicate those he deemed enemies.

I knew I must set aside my anger; Alexander's pilgrimage came first. Once he was trained, however, Colin would be dealt with—and what a force he would have to reckon with if what the Oracle believed of Alexander proved true. I hoped when that day came, the people of the Southlands, those chased from their homes and ostracized for generations, would rise up to topple the latest threat from the north.

And when the time finally arrived, we would be leading the charge. I would hold onto my rage and unleash it upon my wayward half-brother. A dragon's rage was something few left in our world had ever encountered, and I was determined Colin would feel its devastation first-hand.

Colin would learn soon enough. I was merely biding my time.

*The Caein Legacy continues with Guardian.*

# THANK YOU FOR READING EXILE!

If you enjoyed reading this book, please consider leaving a review.
Information about new books and their release dates will be posted on my website (www.ajcalvin.net), as well as shared via my newsletter. If interested, you can subscribe by visiting my website and clicking on the "Newsletter" tab.

# ACKNOWLEDGMENTS

Foremost, I'd like to thank my husband. When I first began writing Exile, the process consumed me. I was writing almost constantly for the better part of seven weeks—when I wasn't at work—and didn't stop until the initial draft was complete. His patience and understanding during that time (and the subsequent revision and editing sessions that followed later) were incredible. I am deeply grateful for his support.

Next, I'd like to thank my brother. He was an unwitting inspiration for Alexander's character in many aspects. When I told him of this, he was genuinely thrilled. He was one of the first people who read Exile, and though the initial draft was incredibly rough, some of his feedback helped to shape the remainder of the series.

And what is a book without cover artwork? I've worked with Jamie Noble previously for my Relics of War series, as well as the revamp to the cover of Hunted, but I truly believe he outdid himself with The Caein Legacy. The covers are beautiful and captured my vision of the series perfectly.

Editing for this book was performed by the tireless and always patient Sheena Sampsel. She is always a pleasure to work with.

Lastly, I must thank my readers. I've stated this before, but I'll say it again: Without you, none of this journey is worth it. For everyone who has taken the time to read Exile or any of my other books, I am eternally grateful.

COMING IN NOVEMBER 2023:

GUARDIAN: BOOK TWO OF THE CAEIN LEGACY

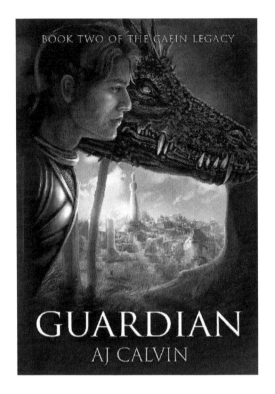

Alexander has been sent on a perilous journey through the Southlands, a pilgrimage all would-be magi must undertake in order to develop their abilities. His brother, Andrew, was named his guardian by the Oracle, a strange woman with the ability to see glimpses of the future. The brothers do not know the land or its dangers, but both understand the importance of the journey.

With the proper training, Alexander will become instrumental in opposing Colin's tyranny in their homeland of Novania. Colin is king; he has reinstated the Mark Inspections and seeks to execute anyone born with the Mark of the Magi, whether they are trained to use their abilities or not. That his brothers escaped his grasp once is a source of ire for Colin, and he plans to make war directly on the magi to the south who harbor the fugitives.

The natural dangers of the land may not stop Alexander from succeeding in his quest, but the royal assassins sent to pursue Andrew might prove to be their undoing. Andrew is sworn to protect his brother no matter the cost to himself... Even if he is the last of the dragon-kind.

# ABOUT THE AUTHOR

A.J. Calvin is a science fiction/fantasy novelist hailing from Loveland, Colorado. By day, she works as a microbiologist, but in her free time she writes. She lives with her husband, their cat, and a salt water aquarium.

When she is not working or writing, she enjoys scuba diving, hiking, and playing video games.

For more information on the author and news about her writing, please visit her website at www.ajcalvin.net.

Made in the USA
Columbia, SC
01 June 2023

17332791R00169